D0375646

OLD FRIENDS . . .
AND LOVERS

"Someone I loved used to tell me that, in the end, all we are is the sum of our memories. I think about that a lot," Carly said.

Profound words for an eighteen-year-old boy who had made love for the first time to the girl he'd vowed to love forever. "And do you think about where you were when I said that to you?" David asked.

"It would be a blessing to forget."

"I'll never stop loving you."

She turned her face away from him to stare out at the distance, unable to contain the pain of seeing him any longer. "Thank you," she whispered when she heard him turn to walk away.

———

Also by Georgia Bockoven

A Marriage of Convenience

Available from
HarperPaperbacks

Harper
Monogram

THE WAY IT SHOULD HAVE BEEN

GEORGIA BOCKOVEN

HarperPaperbacks
A Division of HarperCollinsPublishers

If you purchased this book without a cover, you should be aware that this book is stolen property. It was reported as "unsold and destroyed" to the publisher and neither the author nor the publisher has received any payment for this "stripped book."

This is a work of fiction. The characters, incidents, and dialogues are products of the author's imagination and are not to be construed as real. Any resemblance to actual events or persons, living or dead, is entirely coincidental.

HarperPaperbacks *A Division of* HarperCollins*Publishers*
10 East 53rd Street, New York, N.Y. 10022

Copyright © 1993 by Georgia Bockoven
All rights reserved. No part of this book may be used or reproduced in any manner whatsoever without written permission of the publisher, except in the case of brief quotations embodied in critical articles and reviews. For information address HarperCollins*Publishers,* 10 East 53rd Street, New York, N.Y. 10022.

Cover illustration by Jeff Cornell

First printing: March 1993

Printed in the United States of America

HarperPaperbacks, HarperMonogram, and colophon are trademarks of HarperCollins*Publishers*

10 9 8 7 6 5 4 3 2 1

Acknowledgments

A special thank you goes to Vince Kiley, M.D. who was invaluable in his assistance with the medical portions of this book. If any errors did slip through, they are mine.

I'd also like to thank Margaret Ormondroyd and Susan Thwaitis, companions on a slow boat to Hampton Court who became impromptu and enthusiastic sources of information about English life.

Finally, there's my tireless research assistant who tenaciously digs for the obscure and enlightening information that gives authenticity to my books. Thanks, John!

1

Sixteen years was a long time to hate someone. David Montgomery leaned against a dogwood tree and gazed at the large antebellum-style house across from him. He drew himself deeper into his cashmere overcoat in an attempt to ward off the late October cold. The soft fabric caressed the back of his neck, a gentle reminder of how far he'd come in the almost two decades since he'd called this inconsequential corner of the world home. Back then he'd faced the winters in coarse wool, faded blue jeans and long underwear from the JC Penney catalog. Now he thought nothing of paying what his father had earned in a month as a tractor mechanic for one shirt from his tailor on Savile Row.

Jesus, what idiot urge had brought him here? What could he have been thinking? What had he hoped to gain? He straightened and took a step to leave.

Peace of mind, an insistent inner voice answered, stopping him, rooting him with its teasing promise— to be rid of her once and for all, to bury her in his past, someone no more important than anything or anyone who'd come into his life during the eighteen years he'd lived in Baxter, Ohio.

Conflicting emotions had assailed him since he'd received word of his father's accident. The woman on the other end of the line had insisted his father couldn't last the night. David caught the first plane for Florida. Arriving twelve hours after the call, he'd expected to find his father gone already, with nothing left for him to do but make the funeral arrangements, but he hadn't taken into consideration what a tough old bird his father was. It took Jim Montgomery two weeks before he finally let go of the difficult life he'd lived. Fourteen days of sitting at his father's bedside had given David far too much time to think, to remember.

It wasn't as if Carly still haunted him every hour of every day. After he'd settled in England and his career had taken off, there had been weeks, even months, when he hadn't thought about her at all. Then, invariably, something would come along that triggered a memory—a song, a picture in a magazine —and thoughts of her would consume him.

The sound of a car drew his attention. He glanced down the narrow, tree-lined road and saw a maroon station wagon approaching. There was a woman behind the wheel; on the passenger side a small dog had its nose pressed to the front window. David saw a flash of dark auburn hair before the car turned into the driveway of the house he'd been watching—her house. His eyes lighted in quick triumph. How wonderfully fitting—the woman who as a young girl had vowed she was going to set the New York art world on its ear not only still lived in the same small town where she'd always lived, but she also drove the ultimate, flagrant symbol of suburbia. But then, he reasoned with a stab of bitterness, she undoubtedly needed a car like that to ferry around the three kids she'd had with good old Ethan.

David shuddered at his thoughts. What made him still care? She was nothing to him. He'd done everything he'd ever dreamed. More. And she'd done nothing, gone nowhere.

So why was he the one standing out in the cold?

Carly Hargrove shifted the cocker spaniel she was carrying to her left hip and unlocked the kitchen door. When she was inside, she gently put the old dog on the floor by his food. "I'll get your blanket out of the dryer, Muffin," she said, running her hand over his head, then pausing to scratch his ear.

As soon as she'd arranged the dog's bed, she went to the hall closet to hang up her coat. The long car ride she'd taken after dropping the kids off at school had managed to eat up a few hours, but it had done nothing to ease her restlessness.

She set her purse on the closet shelf, yanked off her knit hat and ran her fingers through her hair, fluffing it back to its normal unruly volume. She really ought to do something to calm some of the frizz, if for no other reason than to please Ethan. He hadn't actually said anything about her appearance, but he was quick to point out how attractive other women looked in sleek hairstyles.

At times her heart ached for the man she'd married, her pain wrapped in a ribbon of guilt. Mostly she just went on, letting one day merge into the next without conscious thought, reveling in the joy her children brought her, careful not to think about what her life would be like when they were grown and she and Ethan were alone.

And it had worked.

At least it had until three days ago when she'd run into Horace Manly at the PTA meeting and had been blindsided by the news that David was accompanying his father's casket back to Baxter to arrange for a memorial service.

Carly drew in a deep breath and purposefully

closed the closet door. Fear of the unknown had begun to insinuate itself into everything she did and thought and she was being dragged down by it. She started up the stairs to make the beds, seeking comfort in the familiar and mindless action.

Sixteen years was a long time, especially in the life of someone like David Montgomery. When he thought about her, it was undoubtedly with a sigh of relief that she hadn't weighed him down when he'd reached for his star.

If he even remembered her.

She tossed king-sized pillows onto the chair beside the bed and smoothed the comforter. Did she really hope that he'd forgotten her?

Dear sweet Jesus, the lives of everyone she loved depended on that very thing.

With mechanical movements, Carly finished tidying the master bedroom and moved on to her daughter's room. Bending to pick up Andrea's nightgown, she heard the front doorbell.

She jerked upright. It was probably only the mailman, she told herself, angry at how easily she could be shaken.

She started toward the stairs.

The instant her foot hit the landing and she saw the shadowed form of a man through the beveled glass of the front door, she knew. She considered slipping back upstairs but then thought how much more dangerous it would be to have David come back when Ethan or one of the kids were home. If she had to see him at all, it was better that she do it alone.

For days she had tried to imagine what it would be like to see him again. In her mind they'd already had a dozen conversations. He'd been the focus of her thinking when she drove the kids to school, when she stopped for groceries, and when she was lying beside Ethan at night listening to his breathing.

She opened the door wide, refusing to use it as a

shield. She wasn't prepared for the man who stood in front of her. There was no semblance of the boy Carly had known—the mouth that had once been so quick to smile was now hard and tight; the wonder and mischief that had shone from his eyes were gone, replaced with a chilling blue anger.

"Hello, David," she said. "It's been a long time," she added, an overwhelming sorrow settling through her.

"Yes, it has," he answered slowly, openly studying her.

"I'm sorry about your father. When he moved away, I missed seeing him." More than anything she'd missed the tie, however tenuous, he'd given her to David. "I heard you were coming and I . . ."

A corner of his mouth raised in a mocking smile. "And you were wondering if I'd stop by to catch up on old times," he finished for her.

"I admit it crossed my mind once or twice."

"Did you think I could come back to my old home town and not look in on you and Ethan? Come on, Carly. Ethan was my best friend. You were . . ." He shrugged. "I seem to have forgotten just what you were to me, Carly."

She folded her arms across her chest. "Time will do that."

"You seem to be doing all right for yourself."

A too-bright smile preceeded her cheerful, "I've been lucky."

"I doubt luck had anything to do with it."

An awkward silence followed. "What do you want, David?"

"I don't know," he admitted.

"You must have some idea or you wouldn't have come."

"Is that how you see things now? Every question has a simple answer?"

"I'm sorry," she offered helplessly, knowing it

wasn't what he wanted or needed but unable to stop herself. "I never meant to hurt—"

"Jesus Christ, Carly, after all the time we put in together don't you think I deserve a little more than that? Both then and now?"

She held her hands out in a pleading gesture. "That was sixteen years ago. If you came here hoping to find me wallowing in self-pity because I married Ethan and missed out on the opportunity to be the wife of a famous writer, you wasted your time, David. I may not cross oceans on the Concorde or spend my winters on a Greek island, but I'm happy. Can you say as much?"

David smiled wryly and rubbed his hand across his chin. "How is it you know so much about me?"

"Let it go, David," she begged him.

"I wish to hell I could," he admitted with a sigh. He stared at her for what seemed an interminable time as if searching for something more to say. Finally, wordlessly, he turned to leave.

Carly watched him walk away. Instead of setting him free all those years ago, she realized, she'd imprisoned him in the same tangled web of lies that she'd spun around herself. She'd made a hundred promises to David and then sent him a letter that broke every one. Now she had a chance to set things right.

"David?" she called, ignoring the terrible risk she was taking to settle her debt. He stopped and looked back at her over his shoulder. The wind caught his hair, brushing it across his forehead, giving her a glimpse of the twenty-two-year-old boy she'd once loved and believed as necessary to her existence as the air she breathed.

"Yes?"

"Don't go," she said, forcing the words past the lump of fear in her throat. For the first time in years she would do something unplanned and uncalculated. Something for herself.

"What's the point, Carly?" He retraced his steps.

She hesitated. "Why did you come, David?"

With an abrupt, angry movement, he grabbed her, his fingers digging into her arms. "To rid myself of you," he said as if the admission were being dragged from him. "I don't want to think about you anymore." He brought his face menacingly close to hers. "I don't want to remember what it felt like to love you. I don't want to care that you could throw away everything we had." With a look of disgust, he released her and took a step backward. "God—I swore I wouldn't let this happen."

"There's so much you don't know," she said. And so much she couldn't explain. "I was young and scared, and I really believed I was doing what was best for everyone."

"Are you telling me you regret marrying Ethan?"

"I don't let myself think about things like that."

"What were you afraid of, Carly? Me? Did you think I would become violent or go off the deep end if you told me you'd been sleeping with Ethan while I was in New York and that you were pregnant with his child? Or did you think I'd tell you to get lost, so you figured you'd grab Ethan while you could?" He swept the hair off his forehead with his left hand, his wedding ring gleaming in the morning sun.

Carly stiffened her spine, bringing herself up to her full five feet six inches. "I can't give you the answers you want, David, but if you give us a chance, we can be friends." He started to say something and she put her hand up to stop him. "Friends are infinitely easier to forget than lovers." When he didn't immediately answer, she went on. "Isn't that why you said you came here today, to find a way to forget me?"

"It's a little hard to think of you as a friend after all the years of hating you."

He could have hit her and it would have hurt less. "Come inside. I'll fix some coffee and we can talk." She stepped out of the doorway. "Or do you drink tea now?" Somewhere in the back of her mind a warning sounded. Gathering details of the life he had now would only add color to the canvas of her memories.

"I'll have coffee," he said, stepping inside the foyer. "Americans don't know how to make a proper cup of tea." A self-conscious grin played at the corner of his mouth. "I didn't mean that the way it sounded, it's simply a fact."

She'd always dreamed of going to England, or France, or China, longing to see for herself how other people lived. "Do you like living in London?" It was a dumb question. If he didn't like where he was living, why would he be there?

"Yes."

"How long—"

"Seven years."

"I read somewhere that your wife is English." She knew precisely where she'd read about Victoria Montgomery, in an upscale magazine called *European Life*. The article had been about the movers and shakers of London society and had included a photograph and several paragraphs on the bestselling author David Montgomery and his stunning wife, the former Victoria Digby, daughter of Lord and Lady Something-or-other.

"Is this what you had in mind, Carly, a cup of coffee and some idle chitchat? If it is, I'm not interested."

She sighed. "This isn't going to work if you don't bend a little, David."

After several seconds he took off his coat and handed it to her. "My agent tells me there are times I can be a real stiff-necked son of a bitch," he said in lieu of an apology.

Carly held the coat on her arm while she reached for a hanger. The coat was soft and obviously expensive and, for an unguarded moment, she thought about slipping her arms into the sleeves and letting David's lingering warmth envelop her. When she was in high school, she'd lived in David's varsity jacket and could still remember the incredible feeling of intimacy that had come over her when she'd be sitting in the middle of class and her own body heat would release a trace of his after-shave.

Forcefully shoving the memory to the back of her mind, she hung his coat next to hers and closed the closet door. "We don't have much time," she said. "I never know when one of the kids will decide to come home for lunch."

"That wouldn't bother me."

"They can't see you here," she answered, a little too quickly.

His eyes narrowed. "What are you afraid of, Carly?"

For once she could hide behind the truth. "I'm not afraid of anything. It's simply that when Ethan found out you were coming back, he asked me not to see you. I'd just as soon he didn't know you were here."

"That doesn't make sense," David said slowly, more to himself than to her. "He won. Why would he . . ." His head snapped up. "Well, I'll be damned. Could it be you don't like lying in the bed you made for yourself?"

"You always did use words as weapons, David."

But never against her. At least not until today. "It's an occupational hazard."

Carly pointed toward the back of the house and said, "Why don't we have our coffee in the kitchen? The sun is wonderful there this time of day."

David nodded and motioned for her to lead the

way. As they passed through the living room, he quickly scanned the pictures hanging there. Unless she'd stopped painting watercolors and her style had changed dramatically, and for the worse, none of the paintings were Carly's.

She turned to say something and caught him looking at a picture of a girl standing next to a tree. "Ethan collects turn-of-the-century artists," she explained.

He gave her a questioning look. "Since when?" The Ethan he remembered had taste that ran to Elvis on velvet.

"He started a few years after we were married."

"I don't see anything of yours in here."

"I got tired of looking at them."

Something wasn't right. And then it hit him. "You're not painting anymore, are you?"

The question made her uncomfortable. "I grew bored after a while. It's difficult to maintain enthusiasm for something that's third-rate."

What was it about artists and critics? Of the hundreds of glowing reviews that had been written about his books, it was the half-dozen bad ones he remembered word for word. "And just who was the genius who told you your work was third-rate?"

She turned her back to him and continued into the kitchen. "Me," she said, reaching into a cupboard for the coffee.

"I know what passes for art these days. I've seen too many paintings—hell, I own too many of them. I remember your work, Carly. You were never third-rate."

"It's past history," she said. "I hardly remember what it felt like to hold a brush in my hand." With a forced brightness, she added, "At least one of us made it."

Battling a streak of vindictiveness, he considered telling her how close he'd come to not "making" it, how after receiving her letter he'd dropped out of school and lived on the road, spending the next two years hitchhiking his way through South America and then hopping a freighter to Europe. The ship was ancient and painfully slow and only the cook spoke enough English to put more than a halting sentence together. Boredom had prompted him to borrow paper and start writing again—a cliché-ridden spy novel about Nazis who'd hidden in Argentina after World War II. The hours he spent working on the manuscript were the best he'd had since leaving school. After two years of trying everything from tequila to whores, he'd stumbled on the one way to escape her memory, if only for a few hours.

He crossed the kitchen and leaned his hip against the tile counter. She was thinner, almost fragile looking, a word he would never have used to describe her back then. From the time they were first allowed to cross the streets by themselves, she'd refused to be left behind in anything he and Ethan did, whether it was cross-country skiing or climbing trees. He liked that she'd finally let her hair grow and that she wore it loose; what he didn't like was that he could still remember the sweetness of its smell, and how it felt against his bare chest after they'd made love.

"I've read all of your books," she said, again turning the subject from herself to him. "They're wonderful." Softly, she added, "I'm so proud of you, David. You've done everything you wanted." She paused. "Everything you ever dreamed."

"Ironic, isn't it? I had the dream because of you and then succeeded in spite of you."

She flinched but never lost a beat, going on as if the jab had been a loving stroke. "Remember how you used to say your books would never hit the best-seller lists because really good books never did?"

There was no place to hide from her. She knew all

his secrets, every pompous thought he'd had back then. "Well, at least I was right about that."

She whipped around to face him. "You can't be serious. Your books are as literate as they are exciting. Especially the last four. I couldn't put them down when I was reading them and then I couldn't get them out of my mind after I finished."

A sickening thought occurred to him. It was like old times, each of them bolstering and defending the other. Only it wasn't old times; it was now and it was warped. Still, he couldn't stop himself from saying, "And your paintings were wonderful."

"Even if I had the desire, I wouldn't have the energy or time. This house, three kids, a husband, and a dog are about as much as I can handle." As if on cue, the dog stood, made a circle and lay back down in its basket.

"I can't believe what I'm hearing."

She stopped filling the coffee pot long enough to give him a sardonic smile. "Surprised?"

"Not at all. I knew you would have kids some-day—" A caustic laugh punctuated his remark. "Of course at the time I thought they would be mine." Defensively, to cover his exposed feelings, he added, "What does surprise me is that you would use them as an excuse for giving up painting."

She glared at him. "You always did try to put words in my mouth."

"What really happened, Carly?"

Now she was angry. "What are you trying to do to me, David? What do you hope to accomplish by pointing out how successful you are and what a failure you think I am?"

"When we were growing up"—he struggled for the words to express what until then had only been feelings—"our ambitions were so caught up together that at times I lost track of where yours ended and mine began. I've imagined you a lot of ways since then, but never once did I imagine you not painting."

She went back to making the coffee. "Can we talk about something else?"

"What did you have in mind?"

"Tell me about England." A deep hunger to know what she'd missed seeing for herself, came through in her voice.

"On the surface, it's a lot like we used to think it would be—the double-decker buses, the tea shops, the museums."

"And below the surface?" she asked eagerly.

He knew what she wanted, to live the experience through his eyes the way she had when he'd gone to New York without her. "What took me by surprise was the sense of history—the feeling of mortality, and the utter insignificance that I felt the first time I stood in the middle of Westminster Abbey. I went on a day when there was a blizzard outside and I almost had the place to myself."

He searched for the words that would make what he'd seen come alive for her. "It was incredible, Carly. There I was standing in the Poets Corner, sur-rounded by memorials to Chaucer and Jonson and Browning." He chuckled. "Talk about a humbling ex-perience. I went home and threw out everything I'd written since moving to England."

"Has it changed—your feelings, I mean? Have you gotten used to living there?"

"You mean, have I lost my sense of wonder?"

"Yes."

He thought back to how he'd felt the first time he'd seen Trafalgar Square and the River Thames and how he felt when he passed them now. "I guess I have," he said with regret.

"I suppose it was bound to happen." She reached into the cupboard and took down two mugs.

He didn't say anything then. The silence grew until it became awkward and she looked up at him. Her eyes were dark brown pools of sadness and fear that contradicted the seemingly casual turn in their conversation.

"Why did you turn your back on me, Carly?" he asked, unable to stop himself. "And why Ethan? What did he give you that I didn't? Was it because I wanted to postpone our getting married again?"

Carly looked away, sheltering herself from the hurt she saw on his face. Now, even knowing how much it meant to David to hear what she would tell him, she found herself stumbling over the words. "I was lonely. Ethan was here when I needed him. He loved me. I fell in love with him. I never meant for it to happen—it just did." Allowing herself a crumb of truth, she added, "I know it doesn't mean much for me to tell you this now, but not one day has gone by that I haven't regretted the way I hurt you."

He walked over to the window and stared outside, taking in but paying no attention to the shimmering red and gold leaves still clinging to trees no longer willing to nurture them. "I threw away all of your letters but that last one. Every once in a while when I was feeling particularly lonely or lost, I would reread what you had written and it would shore me up with enough anger to see me through until the next time. But then that stopped working after a while when the memories of how it really was between us started to creep in and thread their way through what you'd written. Once I even went so far as to make airline reservations to come over and confront you and demand that you tell me the truth."

Carly folded her arms across her chest and hugged herself. "What stopped you?"

"I met Victoria."

"Your wife."

"It took five months for that to happen." He'd been her rebellion, she his entrance into a world that would otherwise have been closed to him. Her parents had been less than enthusiastic at the prospect of having a Yank for a son-in-law, especially one who made his living writing books. Theirs was a symbiotic relationship, unhampered by a romantic notion of love, fueled by a mutually satisfying sex life.

"But you're here now—"

He kept his back to her. "The choice was taken out of my hands. My father's last request was that he be buried next to my mother."

"That explains why you came to Baxter, not why you came to see me."

"The few hours my father was lucid enough to talk, he wanted to spend remembering. When he fell asleep and I was alone again, it was my own ghosts that came out to haunt me. I guess you could call my coming here today an exorcism."

His pain had become hers and, added to her own, the weight became almost unbearable. "What can I say to convince you? What words do you need to hear?"

"I don't know," he admitted, again facing her. He held out his hands in a helpless gesture. "I thought I knew you so well, Carly. No, damn it, I *did* know you. We spent—"

She couldn't take any more. "Stop it, David. You're only making this harder."

"What I'm asking for isn't that complicated, Carly —just tell me the truth. When you do, I promise you'll never see me again."

"You changed when you moved to New York. Every time I visited you it felt like the wall between us was getting higher and harder to climb until finally I couldn't get over it at all. You stopped writing as often and when a letter did come, it was always filled with your problems, your disappointments, your failures. There was never anything about me or what I was going through." She was counting on his forgetting the love that had also been in the letters, the hope and the loneliness. "Every time we set a date to get married, you broke it. You even forgot I was coming to visit you that last time and didn't come back to your apartment until I had to leave for the train. I just couldn't take it anymore." It was all true but the last part. Her love for him, her determination to see them through the hard times, had never faltered.

"I didn't *forget* you were coming," he insisted, resurrecting an old argument. "You never told me. For God's sake, Carly, you must have seen how surprised I was when you showed up the weekend of your father's funeral. If I couldn't get the time off to come home for the services, what in God's name made you think I could get it off to be with you if you came to the city to see me? It didn't make sense then and it doesn't make sense now."

"I shouldn't have brought it up."

"Was what we had back then really that bad?" he asked.

"Why can't—" The rest died on Carly's lips as she froze at the sound of the front door opening.

"Mom?" a voice called out.

Panic gripped Carly.

"Are you upstairs, Mom?"

"What is it, Carly?" David asked, responding to her almost palpable fear.

"It's Andrea—she can't see you here." Carly's gaze flew to the doorway. It was too late.

2

18 GEORGIA BOCKOVEN

Andrea was brought up short by the look of dismay on Carly's face. Then she saw that there was a strange man in the kitchen with them. The man seemed on edge and upset. He had his hands shoved into the pockets of his pants and a wary look on his face.

"What's going on?" Andrea demanded, her mother's alarm infecting her.

Carly was the one constant in Andrea's life. At times her mother's predictability reached the point of boredom. She was always home when Andrea called, always ready to pick her and her brothers up from school to take them to whatever lessons they had that day or to drive them to the mall on a Saturday. She was the peacemaker of the family, willing to go to any lengths to end an argument or keep one from beginning.

"Nothing," Carly answered. "You startled me, that's all." She came toward Andrea, taking her into her arms for a quick hug and kiss. "What are you doing home this time of day? How did you get here? Are you sick?"

"I forgot the permission slip for the field trip and

today's the deadline," she said, looking past her mother to the stranger. "I tried calling to have you bring it to me, but you didn't answer the phone so I talked Victor into giving me a ride." She sent an accusatory glance in Carly's direction. "Where were you?"

"I had some things I had to do." Carly went to the refrigerator, pulled the folded permission slip from under a magnet on the door and handed it to Andrea.

Andrea's ponytail fell over her shoulder when she leaned in close and took the paper from her mother. "Who's he?" she whispered.

Carly hesitated a fraction too long before answering, triggering a tingling sensation at the back of Andrea's neck. She was getting the same kind of feeling she did whenever she walked into a room and the conversation between her mother and father stopped. Even though they always denied it, Andrea knew that they'd been talking about her. Her father hardly ever talked to her directly anymore. Instead he used her mother to tell her things—like when he thought her clothes were too tight or she wasn't doing things around the house the way he wanted them done.

Several awkward seconds passed in silence before Carly turned to David. "David, I'd like you to meet my daughter, Andrea." She turned back to Andrea. "Andrea, this is David Montgomery."

Hearing his name, a dozen bits and pieces of information came together and she was able to relax. "I know who you are," she said, brightening. "You're the writer who used to live here. Mrs. Rogers talked about you in English the other day. She said you were in her class a long time ago."

Mrs. Rogers had said a lot more, even calling Andrea over after the bell and, with a silly grin, asking to be remembered to Mr. Montgomery when he visited her parents. Andrea must have looked as confused as she felt because when she didn't answer right away, Mrs. Rogers started mumbling an apology, saying how she'd just assumed Mr. Montgomery would be seeing Andrea's mom and dad considering how close the three of them had once been. Until then, Andrea hadn't even known her mother and father knew anybody famous.

David grinned and ran his hand across his chin. "Does she still whip her glasses on every time she needs to actually see something?"

Andrea nodded, as much in agreement as in pleasure over having established a connection with him. She'd never talked to anyone even remotely famous before, unless she counted that time she'd seen Michael J. Fox in a restaurant in Canton and asked him for his autograph. "Did she wear those three-inch spike heels back in your time?"

Chuckling, David added, "And she always had her hair dyed the most awful-looking blond color."

"Only it's shorter now," Carly joined in as she gave Andrea a gentle, insistent nudge toward the door. Pointedly, she said, "Enough visiting—you can't afford to miss biology again."

"Are you going to be here for dinner?" Andrea asked David, sidestepping her mother's efforts. She could hardly wait to tell Susan and Judy she had a real live celebrity in her house. Tom Cruise or Kevin Costner would have been a lot better, but David Montgomery wasn't bad.

Instead of answering directly, David gave Carly a questioning look. Flustered, she stammered, "Mr. Montgomery is only going to be here a couple of days, and there are a lot of people he wants to see."

"He has to eat somewhere, doesn't he?" Andrea insisted, sending her mother a pleading look. She was unwilling to let go of what would probably be her one chance in life to hold something over Janice Wilburn whose first cousin was in a rock band that had opened for Guns and Roses when they were on tour. "You could ask him to dinner."

Carly shook her head. "I don't think—"

"I'd love to," David answered.

"*Fan*-tastic. I can't wait to tell everyone." She gave Carly a kiss on her cheek and headed for the door. "Gotta go. I promised Victor I'd make it fast."

Carly waited until she was sure Andrea was gone before she turned to David, her hands curled into tight fists at her sides. "Why did you do that? I told you Ethan asked me not to see you."

"And do you always do everything he says?" he asked. "Even when it isn't what you want?"

"This is his house. He has a right to—"

"*His* house?"

She ignored the dig and went on. "You can't come here tonight."

"How are you going to explain my absence to Andrea?"

"I'll tell her you forgot you'd promised to have dinner with someone else."

"She might buy that, but Ethan never will. If I don't show up tonight, he's going to think we're trying to hide something."

The important thing had been to keep Ethan from finding out David had been there at all. Now, she had about as much chance of pulling that off as she did convincing him to lay off drinking for the evening.

The thought terrified her. With David there, Ethan was sure to drink more than his usual cocktail before dinner, wine with dinner, and Courvoisier after. She'd heard the argument a hundred times—alcohol was a minor and innocent way of coping with the problems he faced every day at work, something she could never understand, living the stress-free life of a housewife. Besides which, her paranoia about drinking had nothing to do with him. It was her father's alcoholism that had prejudiced her. So what if there was that rare occasion—once or twice a year—when he said or did something he might later regret because he'd had a few too many? It didn't happen that often and besides, he made up for it in other ways. Had he ever forgotten a birthday or an anniversary? Wasn't he there for every one of the boys' basketball games? And hadn't he been in the stands for close to half of Andrea's swim meets, even though she rarely won and the boys played on championship teams? It was a constant puzzle to him how she could accuse him of loving his daughter less than his sons.

Enough. She mentally shook herself. If there was hell to pay later, she'd pay it. She went to the closet to get David's coat. Handing it to him, she said, "We eat at seven."

"Seven it is." He met her gaze with a determined look. "I'm sorry if that makes you uncomfortable, but I came here for something and I've waited too long to leave without it."

She shook her head sadly. "You're not the David Montgomery I used to know."

He took the time to put on his coat before answering her. "Who are you trying to convince—me or you?"

Fear crawled up her spine. If she was that transparent to him, he was even more dangerous than she'd first thought.

3

Carly reached for the oven door to check on dinner. Behind her, she heard a soft clink as Ethan added another ice cube to his drink. It was only his second, he'd been quick to point out when she'd given him a questioning look earlier. She hadn't bothered mentioning how full the glasses had been, knowing it would only lead to an argument.

From the moment Ethan had arrived home that night and she'd told him that David was coming to dinner, the tension had been unbearable between them, making it impossible to communicate on any but the most fundamental level. Even her choice of pot roast for the meal had brought comment. Ethan had been quick to point out that her seeming lack of imagination could only mean she'd spent the entire afternoon thinking about what to cook.

Experience had taught her that when he was like this nothing she could say or do would change or modify his feeling. In the morning she would begin the repair work. It was little enough considering what he had done for her in the past. Still, there were times when she grew weary of applying bandages to wounds that never healed.

From the time Ethan and David had been in preschool together, Ethan had perceived himself to be in David's shadow, losing every foot race by a pump of the arm, every spelling bee by a word, and the girl they both loved by a heartbeat. For a few short months after she and Ethan were married, he'd allowed himself to believe he'd finally won, but the victory—like the battles—was mostly in his mind. Still, she'd never stopped trying to give him what he needed even when she realized his hunger was insatiable.

He could not make love to her without remembering David had made love to her first. He could not look at the daughter he'd raised as his own without seeing David's blue eyes and light brown hair. Carly could not say "I love you" without seeing "But only second-best" in his eyes.

He lived for his sons, glorying in their athletic prowess and their unquestioned lineage. And Eric and Shawn worshiped Ethan, even to the point of canceling plans with their friends in order to spend time with him.

To an outsider they would seem the perfect family and, on the surface, they were. So what if on closer inspection it became clear that all was not as it seemed?

The cupboard door slammed behind Carly, startling her as she was checking the roast in the oven. "Damn it," she said, flicking her hand to cool it.

"Burn yourself?" Ethan asked with concern as he came up behind her.

She touched her tongue to the side of her finger. "For the second time today."

"You must be nervous." He swirled the amber liquid around his glass. "Or excited."

"Probably a little of both," she admitted, refusing to be baited. "I can't imagine what the three of us are going to find to talk about for an entire evening. We have nothing in common with David anymore." As soon as the words were out, she realized the opening she had given him. She said a silent prayer he wouldn't take it. She should have known better.

"Oh, I can think of something. But I'm sure he didn't come here to discuss that—not after all this time."

Impulsively, she slipped her arms around his waist and looked up at him. "I love you, Ethan."

The smile he gave her did nothing to modify the torment in his eyes. "I know you do, Carly, in your own fashion."

"It's the only way I know how."

He placed a kiss on the top of her head. "Would that it were enough," he said. "Think what glorious lives we would lead."

She leaned her cheek against his chest. At thirty-eight, he was as lean and muscular as he'd been in college and, although his dark brown hair had begun to recede the way his own father's had at that age, only those who'd known him all his life could notice the change. His eyes were warm and expressive, the barometer of his feelings. There were times he looked at her with such love and hunger, it broke her heart that she could not give him what he wanted. "Maybe tonight you'll be able to see for yourself that what we have is everything I want."

"God, wouldn't that be ironic?" he said, his arms closing tightly around her, drawing her to him in a hungry embrace. His voice a soft whisper, he added, "And wonderful."

Eric came into the kitchen, ignored them, and headed for the refrigerator. He stood in front of the open door for several seconds and then hunkered down to get a better look at the contents. "Hey, when's that guy supposed to get here? I'm starving."

Carly was reluctant to give up the first genuine intimacy she and Ethan had had since they'd learned

David was coming to town. She waited until she felt his arms loosen before she stepped away and glanced at the clock. "The 'guy's' name is David Montgomery." Her heart gave a funny flutter in her chest when she saw what time it was. "And he should be here any minute now."

Standing and stretching, Eric came up to her and let an arm fall across her shoulders. At thirteen, he was already a good three inches taller than she was. His wild spurt of growth that past year was all the encouragement Ethan had needed to start talking about a basketball scholarship to UCLA. "Shawn said this David Montgomery guy was your boyfriend in high school."

She flinched. "Who told him that?"

"Dad."

Carly sent Ethan a disappointed look. He'd had no right to involve the boys in their problem. "We dated in high school, but most of the time it was your father and me and David who did things together."

When Eric was out of earshot, Ethan smiled and said, "Nice save."

"Why did you tell him that?" she snapped.

"Why not? If it's all past history, what possible difference could it make?" He took a deep swallow of his drink. "Besides, I thought they might get a kick out of knowing their mother once dated a famous writer. Too bad he never dedicated a book to you. Now that really would have been something to brag about." He paused, and then as if the idea had just occurred to him, said, "Maybe I'll suggest that to him. After all, in a way, he owes his career to you."

She sighed, filled with frustration that she hadn't reached him after all. "Don't you ever get tired of wearing that same old hair shirt?"

Long seconds passed before he answered. "God knows I would take it off if I could," he said, with such naked honesty her heart felt as if it were breaking along with his. "But it's become so much a part of me, I no longer know where it ends and I begin."

She reached for his hand. "Let me help you get rid of it. Tell me how. I'll do anything."

Before he could answer, the doorbell rang.

"Mom, he's here," Eric shouted.

"Then let him in," she answered, cursing David's timing.

Ethan stepped away from her. "You'd better answer that yourself. We don't want to seem rude."

"Why don't I tell him we can't make it tonight?" she asked on impulse.

"Why would you want to do that?" he answered, slipping back into his shell. "Like you said, it's only three old friends getting together—and it's only for one night."

The smell of roses wafted up to David as he stood outside the Hargrove house and waited for someone to answer the door. The choice of flowers had been easy. Carly's practical side would cringe over the expense of something so short-lived, but she would intuitively understand his reasoning—they would be out of her life almost as quickly as he would.

The bottle of 1984 Chateau Montelena Cabernet Sauvignon he'd settled on for Ethan had been a harder decision. His first inclination had been to bring something French and very expensive. The impulse toward ostentation gave way to subtlety even before he'd gone to the local liquor store and discovered that he was lucky to end up with the excellent, if relatively inexpensive wine he had.

A tall, lanky young man, a clone of Ethan at that age, opened the door and gave David a toothy grin. He held out his hand. "Hi, I'm Shawn."

David stuffed the bottle of wine under his arm and shook Shawn's hand. "David Montgomery."

"I recognized you from the picture on the back of your books." He stepped out of the doorway and motioned for David to enter. "My mom and dad are in the kitchen. I'll get them for you."

David moved into the foyer, closing the door behind himself. A movement at the top of the stairs caught his attention. Andrea leaned over the railing and smiled in greeting. The cocker spaniel he'd seen that afternoon sat at her feet. "I told Mrs. Rogers you said hi. She wanted me to ask you if you had time to stop by and visit one of her classes."

Time was all he had until Victoria arrived. The memorial service had been easier to set up than he'd anticipated and he'd already paid his obligatory visits to the few relatives of his mother's who still lived in the area. "Tell her I'll give her a call." Out of the corner of his eye he saw Ethan and Carly approaching. Steeling himself against the impact of seeing Ethan again, he took a deep breath and turned in their direction.

David had come prepared to see the smug look of triumph he had pictured on Ethan's face for the past sixteen years. The resentment, the hesitation, the fear he saw instead left him confused and at a loss for words.

"You're right on time," Carly said in a feeble attempt to lighten the awkwardness of the moment.

David couldn't break eye contact with Ethan. It was as if they were locked in some bizarre mental battle.

Carly tried again. Grabbing another young man by the elbow and shoving him toward David, she said, "Have you met Eric? He's our youngest."

It was impossible for David to ignore the boy's outstretched hand. This son bore some resemblance to Carly, but still clearly carried Ethan's stamp. "Pleased to meet you, Eric."

"Dad says you used to—"

Carly drew in a quick breath that stopped Eric in midsentence. He turned his attention to her.

"—play basketball," he finished with a grin and a playful wink.

"Only on the summer league. Your father was the basketball player in high school," David told him, deciding to act as if he hadn't witnessed the interchange. "I wrestled."

A nervous smile played at Carly's mouth. "Would you like me to take your coat?"

David handed Eric the flowers and wine before he slipped off his coat and handed it to Carly. Unwilling to let the silence between Ethan and him become any more obvious, he said, "How's your father, Ethan? Still running the factory with an iron hand?"

"I've managed to pry the hand loose," Ethan said, taking the wine from Eric and holding it up to read the label. "As a matter of fact, the hand isn't even within grasping distance any more. He and my mother moved to Palm Springs last year to be near my sister."

David wondered if the attention to the wine was for effect or simply curiosity. "It's a label I discovered in California a couple of years ago and found interesting."

Ethan shot him a challenging look. "I find it a little pretentious myself. But then I rarely buy domestic wine."

David almost laughed out loud. It was as if they were competing to see which of them could be the biggest ass. "It's good to see you too, Ethan," he said, purposely lowering and softening his voice. He hadn't come here to do battle, just to engage in a light skirmish.

Ethan nodded slightly, acknowledging David's effort. "I was sorry to hear about your father. At least he got a few good years in the sun. Not many men who work as hard as he did get even that much."

"Thank you," David said. Ethan had been closer to David's father when they were growing up than he had been to his own. As far as David knew, the only grown man who'd ever taken Ethan fishing and the only one who'd ever put his arms around him had been David's own father.

"Can I fix you a drink?"

"Club soda with a twist if you have it."

Ethan studied him, an eyebrow raised in question. "I don't remember you having a drinking problem. Something new?"

Warning bells went off in David's head. There was a lot more going on here than he had bargained for. Ethan was acting as if the victor hadn't received the spoils. Jesus, what more did he want? "Nothing so complicated. I have some work to do when I get back to the motel tonight that requires a clear head."

"Speaking of dinner," Carly interjected, "it's almost ready. I hope you're hungry."

She was so obviously nervous. David almost felt sorry for her. "Whatever it is, it smells wonderful."

Carly took the roses from Eric and handed them to Andrea. "Would you please put these in water for me?" To David she said, "It's just pot roast. I didn't have time to go shopping."

"You know it's always been my favorite." He had no idea where that had come from. When he'd been a kid, pot roast was something you ate in order to get sandwiches the next day.

"No, I didn't know," she said.

Ethan let out a derisive chuckle. "Why don't I believe that? Pardon me while I get that club soda for you."

When he'd left the room and the kids were out of earshot, Carly moved closer to David. "Why did you do that?"

"What?"

"Tell him pot roast was your favorite food."

"How do you know it isn't?"

"Because you like pork roast and lamb chops and beef Wellington."

"How is it that you remember so much about me?" he asked.

"David, please don't do this. Ethan is—" She stopped when she saw him returning.

Taking the expensive cut-crystal glass from Ethan, David suddenly wished he'd never come. Discovering Carly's and Ethan's lives were not the bliss he had imagined brought him none of the satisfaction he would have anticipated. He raised his glass to them. "I hope you don't mind if we make it an early evening," he said, paving the road to retreat. "I have a lot of things to do tomorrow."

"Not at all," Ethan said, turning to Carly. "Why don't you see if you can't hurry things along a little?"

Throughout dinner Andrea, Shawn, and Eric provided enough conversation to cover the fact that hardly any was instigated by the adults. Andrea plied David with questions about being a writer while the boys filled him in on the status of the local basketball teams.

Carly and Andrea were in the process of clearing the table when Andrea innocently asked, "How old were you when you left Baxter, David?"

"Eighteen. I moved to New York the week I graduated from high school."

"Weren't you scared being all alone in a place like that? I've read awful things about how dangerous—"

Shawn groaned and rolled his eyes. "That's just like a girl."

David smiled. "I was a little intimidated at first," he admitted. "But being there was something I'd dreamed about for such a long time, I was too excited to let anything slow me down."

"I want to go to New York someday," Andrea said.

Eric handed her the silverware he'd gathered. "Since when?"

She made a face at her brother. "Since I heard Mom talking to Grandma about it."

"How come you didn't come back to Baxter before now?" Shawn asked.

David looked up in time to see Carly and Ethan exchange looks, hers stricken, his angry. "There wasn't any reason to come back."

The scowl on Ethan's face deepened as he leaned heavily back in his chair.

"But didn't you miss all your friends?" Andrea prodded.

Before he had a chance to answer, Carly interjected, "I think the three of you have asked David enough questions for one night."

Ethan crossed his arms. "It's an intriguing question, don't you think, David?" His words were rounded instead of crisp, each of them bumping into the other in an alcohol slur.

David glanced at the bottle of wine. It was nearly empty while the original glass Ethan had poured for Carly was untouched.

"Andrea's turned into a real beauty, wouldn't you say?" Ethan went on. "Looks a lot like her mom. Except her hair. Don't know how it turned out the way it did—so straight and light colored. You should have seen her when she was a baby, the peach fuzz on her head was so blond, it was nearly white."

Oblivious to the undercurrent that gave importance to the conversation, Eric blithely changed the subject. "Hey, Mr. Montgomery, why don't you come to the basketball game with us tomorrow? We're playing Westbend."

"I don't think—"

"It's going to be a blowout," Shawn added. "We

beat them by twenty-six points at the Northeast Tournament last month."

"Please come," Andrea added enthusiastically, reaching over his shoulder to retrieve the salt and pepper shaker.

Ethan poured the last of the wine into his glass. "She's on the cheerleading squad." He tossed the drink down. "They're just window dressing, of course, but they're damned good."

David looked up in time to see a hurt expression flash across Andrea's face.

"I get there early so I could save you a midcourt seat," she said, choosing to ignore her father's remark.

The last thing he wanted to do was go to a high school basketball game. "That sounds like fun," he told her in spite of himself.

Ethan tipped his empty glass to David. "Somehow I thought you'd come if she was the one to ask."

4

David excused himself from two women he'd known in high school who were in the process of telling him why his last book hadn't been as good as the others and went over to say good-bye to Andrea. "It was a great game," he said. "I'm glad you asked me."

The cheerleader standing next to Andrea offered a shy smile, which he returned with an acknowledging nod. Again focusing his full attention on Andrea, he told her, "If the cheerleaders had been as good in my time as you are now, I wouldn't have minded coming to these things half as much."

A blush of pleasure colored her cheeks. "We practice almost every day."

"Next summer we're going to compete in the state championship," the girl standing next to Andrea told him.

"That's kind of unfair to the other squads, isn't it?"

Andrea shook her head and made a clicking sound with her tongue. "Are all writers like you?"

"How's that?"

"Always coming up with just the right thing to say?"

Andrea was her mother's daughter in more than looks. She would hold her own in the world, even in the bullshit world of Los Angeles where she'd confided to him she wanted to study acting before she took on New York. A lump formed in David's throat. She was the fresh, bursting-with-promise young woman Carly had been at fifteen, the clean canvas, the pristine page. God, what he wouldn't give to have just one of those days back, to remember what it felt like when anything was possible, to know with an adolescent certainty that he'd have the world by the tail the day his name hit the top of *The New York Times* bestseller list, to believe his and Carly's love a constant so pure it could survive without nurturing.

"I think what you're telling me is that I'm full of crap," he answered.

She laughed. "You really do have a way with words. I'm going to have to break down and read one of your books someday."

The other cheerleader let out a gasp. "You mean you've never read one? Oh, Andrea, you've just got to—they're fantastic. Especially the one about the woman spy. When she fell in love with the Russian guy and then got orders to kill him, I thought I'd die."

She'd chosen his least favorite book. *Echoed Footsteps* had been his one attempt at a story that was more focused on people than plot and he'd never felt he quite pulled it off. Even his editor had expressed disappointment, telling him his readership wouldn't stay with him through too many more experiments like that one.

"Thank you," he said. "I'm glad you liked it."

"Are you coming back to the house for dessert?" Andrea asked, stooping to pick up her pom-poms.

"Mom always bakes something to celebrate when we win."

"And if you lose?"

She laughed. "Then whatever she's made is supposed to make us feel better."

"I'd like to, but I have a manuscript that needs going over back at the motel," he said.

"Nonsense," Ethan said expansively, coming up to them. "You don't want to miss one of Carly's after-game desserts. They're an old family tradition."

The word came out "tra-dick-shun" on a breath reeking of alcohol. David took a wary step backward, sensing that Ethan was in a confrontational mood. He'd wondered about the frequent trips to the bathroom until he'd caught sight of the silver flask in Ethan's coat pocket.

Ethan threw a playful punch at David's shoulder. "Can't skip out of a family tradition. After all, everybody always said we were just like brothers. They're still saying it. I'll bet a dozen people have come up to me tonight to tell me how good it is to see the two of us together again." He feigned another punch. "Don't you remember how we used to share everything?" Receiving no response, he gave David a leering smile. "What was mine was yours and what was yours—"

David took hold of Ethan's arm and propelled him toward the door leaving Andrea behind. "What the fuck are you trying to prove?"

Ethan jerked his arm free. "Listen to the innocent act. You missed your calling, David. You should have been an actor."

"You're drunk."

"And you're a gold-plated piece of shit. You might have the rest of the world fooled with that big-time writer garbage you hand out, but you don't fool me. I've been—"

David looked up to see Andrea was following

them. "For Christ's sake, Ethan, keep your voice down."

"What's the matter? 'Fraid somebody might hear what a hightailing bastard their home-town hero really is?" He taunted. "'Fraid they might learn how he ran out on—"

Andrea took her father's arm. "*Stop it*," she demanded. "Everyone is looking at you."

"What the fuck do I care?" he told her, prying her fingers from his coat.

"Shawn and Eric can see you," she said.

They were the magic words. Ethan stopped struggling. He made a show of straightening his coat, and for a second, David thought it was over. Then Ethan glanced at him, his eyes filled with loathing, and David saw how wrong he had been.

"You're not getting away with it anymore," Ethan said, his voice low and menacing. "We can settle this at my house tonight or at your dad's memorial service in front of God and the whole goddamned town. Take your pick."

Andrea gasped. "Daddy, why are you fighting with Mr. Montgomery?"

David looked past Ethan and saw Carly approaching. Intuitively, he knew that if he was still around when she reached them, Ethan would begin his tirade all over again. He glanced at Andrea. She looked as if she were praying for the floor to open up and swallow her.

"I'll be there," he told Ethan, then turned and left, ignoring the questioning look Carly sent him as they passed.

Needing time alone to think about the confrontation with Ethan, David aimed his rental car for the nearest town exit, not caring where he was going, only that he get away for a while. Ten minutes later, he recognized an achingly familiar landmark and pulled off the main road onto a narrow country lane. Memories assailed him as he steered the Taurus around axle-breaking potholes and through weeds as tall as the windows.

He rounded the final curve, stopped the car, and flicked the headlights on high. Half a lifetime faded as he stared at the ghostly apparition. Lender's Mill was precisely the way he remembered it, not larger or smaller or, amazingly, any more decrepit. When he'd dropped out of college and started his wanderings, he had held on to the memory of this place like a talisman, putting himself to sleep at night by going over every inch of the century-old building. He'd heard of prisoners of war doing similar things to maintain their sanity.

Seeing the mill again brought memories so pure, so powerful, and so touchingly innocent, they over-whelmed him.

He and Ethan had been nine the summer they dis-covered the mill, Carly an insistent, tag-along seven. In the beginning they'd used it as their fort, spending afternoons and summers fighting off Indian attacks to make the frontier safe for settlers. Carly was the scout, sent on all the reconnaissance and supply mis-sions. He and Ethan had convinced her it was be-cause she was the smallest and the logical one to sneak through the enemy lines, but in reality it was because her mother baked cookies and theirs didn't.

The mill was also where Ethan had gone when he was twelve and decided to run away from home. They'd all wound up in trouble for that one. When he and Carly made their blood vows to Ethan that they would tell no one where he had gone, they'd had no idea how far it would lead.

Carly's father was the town sheriff and a first-class hard ass when it came to dealing with kids. He'd hauled the two of them down to the station and grilled them for over an hour before giving in and putting a missing-child bulletin on the wire. After he ordered his deputy to organize a search-and-rescue team to comb the woods surrounding the town, he took Carly aside and told her she wouldn't be able to sit down for a week if he discovered she knew something she wasn't telling.

When they found Ethan's hiding place at the mill, not only did Carly's father make good on his promise, he confined her to the house for the rest of the summer. Ethan was put to work cleaning the offices and bathrooms at his father's factory. David couldn't remember the punishment that had been leveled at him. Whatever it was, it was forgotten a few days later when the doctor informed his mother that she had cancer and likely wouldn't see another Christmas.

She'd seen four more, none of them good.

The mill was also where he and Carly had made love the first time. The abrupt transition from friend to lover had taken them both by surprise. Although they'd often tried, neither was ever able to pinpoint exactly when their feelings changed. The closest David could come was the day he saw Carly at the movie arguing with Billy Webster about copping a feel and realized he no longer wanted to teach Carly how to defend herself, he wanted to be the one doing the defending.

Ethan bitterly resented the change in their relationship, insisting that Carly was just looking for a ticket out of Baxter and that David just wanted someone convenient to stick it to while he was still in town. The three of them eventually became friends again, but it was never the same.

In hindsight, David understood the real reason Ethan had been upset wasn't the disruption of the friendships, it was that he'd fallen in love with Carly himself.

David opened the car door and started to get out. He had one foot on the ground before the futility of what he was doing hit him. What possible good could come of seeing the room where he and Carly had fumbled in their virginity, where they had lain in each others arms and talked of the time he would be a writer and she a painter, of the studios they would build in their house, hers full of light, his with a fireplace, of the walks they would take along the Thames, the Seine and the Volga, of the children they would have when they were old and settled?

With renewed purpose, he turned the car around and headed back to town. He would listen to what Ethan had to say and then, when his father's memorial service was over, he would be on his way out of town, leaving Baxter and all that it represented behind him forever.

Carly reached up to pull her hair free from under the collar of the cardigan she'd just put on. The set-back thermostat had shut off the heater fifteen minutes ago and the house was already starting to get cold. Ethan had insisted she stay up with him, saying that David had promised to stop by and it would be impolite of her not to be there to greet him. She'd agreed, unwilling to take the chance that it was alcohol and not Ethan doing the talking. She cringed to think what could happen if David and Ethan were ever left alone.

"There he is," Ethan said triumphantly as a car pulled into the driveway and its headlights swept across the front window. At the sound of footsteps on the walkway, he drained his drink, got up from the recliner, went to the front door, and opened it with a flourish before David could knock.

"So glad you could make it," Ethan said, indicating with a broad sweep of his arm that David should come inside.

David hesitated. Ethan had obviously continued to drink after he left the game. "Why don't you tell me what this is about before I come in? I'm tired, and if it can wait, I'd just as soon make it another time."

Ethan's face flushed in instant anger. "Another time?" he roared. "You want more time when you've already had sixteen fucking years?"

Before he could say more, Carly stepped between them. She put her hands on either side of Ethan's face and forced him to look at her. "Don't do this."

He pushed her away. She stumbled backward and hit a wooden plant stand, knocking it over. The glass vase shattered, spilling water and roses across the marble tile floor.

A piece of broken glass crunched beneath her foot as she came at him again. At the last minute she turned her attention to David. "Get out of here," she said. "And don't come back."

The pleading look in her eyes belied the harshness of her words. He was drawn and repelled by what he saw, perversely wanting to protect her and feeling satisfaction at her unhappiness.

Again, Ethan pushed her out of the way. He loomed threateningly over David. "Where've you been all these years? What'd you think you could do, plant your seed and leave good old Ethan to take care of it forever?"

David's heart slammed against his ribs. He stared at Carly. "What is he talking about?"

"Nothing," she insisted. "He's just rambling. It's what he does when he's drunk." She reached for the door, but Ethan refused to move out of the way.

"What's the matter?" he goaded David. "Didn't like what you saw? Not pretty enough for you? Or were you hoping she'd get Carly's hair instead of yours? You always did like that wild look." He made a grab for David, but missed.

"If you think I'm gonna let you just walk out of here and dump your responsibilities on me all over again, you got another think coming," he went on. "I'm tired of carrying the load for you. That girl of yours has it in her head I'm gonna send her away to some big fancy college when it's everything I can do to set aside enough money for the boys."

A sob caught in Carly's throat. "Ethan, listen to yourself. You don't mean what you're saying. If you don't stop, you'll never be able to forgive yourself."

His head jerked back as if she'd hit him. He stood perfectly still for several seconds, then let out a groan and covered his face with his hands.

Carly focused her attention on David. "Please leave," she implored. *"Now."*

David's mind searched wildly for an explanation for what was happening. As much as he might wish it were so, there was no way he could be Andrea's father. He and Carly had only seen each other once in the five months before she married Ethan—the fateful weekend she'd arrived without telling him she was coming—and then it had only been long enough to accompany her to the train. "I don't know what hair you've got up your ass, Ethan, but I've got better things to do than stand here and listen to you work it out."

"What the hell is the matter with you?" Ethan said, so softly and with such defeat in his voice that it was difficult to hear him. "I'd give ten years of my life if it would make Andrea really mine, and you don't want anything to do with her."

There it was, impossible to ignore or rationalize any longer; Ethan truly believed David was Andrea's father. David was too stunned to answer immediately. He looked at Carly for guidance. Unshed tears shimmered in her eyes. He saw sorrow, fear, and desperation, but most profound was the plea for his silence.

Ethan waited, plainly expecting an answer. David ran his hand across the back of his neck, stalling for time. A powerful voice demanded that he tell Ethan the truth, get out of there as fast as he could, and never look back. Only one thing stood in his way.

Carly.

She was why he was here and why there was only one answer he could give Ethan. Feeling the loss even before the action, he tore his gaze from Carly to look at Ethan. "It's late and you're drunk. There's no way in hell I'm going to talk to you about this tonight."

It was neither an admission nor a denial. It was a way to buy a little time. He chanced looking at Carly again before turning to leave. There were shiny trails down her cheeks where the tears had finally broken free.

The image was burned into his mind, haunting him on the drive back to his motel. It was the last thing he saw when, five hours later, he fell into a troubled sleep.

5

The invasive sound of the telephone woke David the next morning. It was Carly.

"I have to see you," she said.

"No shit," he answered, swinging his legs over the side of the bed and sitting up. He glanced at the clock. It was six-forty-five.

"In an hour?"

"Where?"

"The mill."

Seeing her at the mill would only deepen the emotional mire they were already in. "Don't you think that's one sleeping dog we should let lie?"

"I tried to keep you out of this, but you wouldn't listen."

He ran his hand through his hair. "There has to be someplace else we could go."

"Not where we wouldn't be taking a chance on someone seeing us."

"All right," he finally, reluctantly agreed.

"I'm sorry," she said softly. "I wouldn't ask if there were any other way."

Despite himself, David felt the old compulsion to

do whatever it took to make her world right again. "Who *is* the father, Carly?"

There was a long pause. "I'll tell you what I can when I see you."

It wasn't what he'd wanted to hear, but then nothing had been since he'd arrived in Baxter. He hung up the phone and headed for the shower.

David skipped breakfast in order to arrive at the mill first, wanting the small territorial advantage it would give. This way, she would be coming to him.

On the drive out he'd determined that, no matter how compelling her reason for asking him to meet her that morning, no matter how intriguing her excuse for giving the impression he was Andrea's father, he was going to bring whatever fragments remained of their relationship to an end. When he left Carly that morning, his past would be behind him once and for all. Her problems, whatever they were, didn't involve him and he sure as hell wanted no part of them.

Thank God Victoria had decided to wait to join him. The only American soap opera that had ever interested her was "Dynasty;" the intrigues of the people in a small town in Ohio would seem hopelessly melodramatic and middle class.

But then, if she had been with him from the beginning, he wouldn't have become involved in the intricacies and intrigue of Carly's life in the first place.

Ever since Ethan had dropped his little bomb the night before, David had toyed with the idea that Carly had betrayed them both. But he couldn't make himself believe it. He knew her—at least he'd known her—too well to believe she would ever sleep around. But if not that, then what? A one-night stand at a wild party? Retribution for the weekend he'd missed being with her in New York?

Andrea had to have been conceived within a week or two of the time Carly had come to New York. No wonder Ethan had assumed the baby was his.

The mystery was why Carly had let him.

So much for the sudden grand passion she'd tried to convince him had taken place between her and Ethan.

He looked up at the sound of a car easing its way through the brush. The sun reflected off the front window, making it impossible for him to see inside Carly's station wagon. He strained to catch a glimpse of her, realized what he was doing, and felt a sinking feeling in the pit of his stomach. A sudden and sure knowledge assailed him: No matter how the morning ended, he would not walk away unscathed.

Carly chanced looking away from the weed-choked road to search for David. She'd seen his car as soon as she'd come around the final curve, but he wasn't with it.

She'd lain awake all night, counting the soft ticks of the grandfather clock at the foot of the stairs, waiting for morning while trying to decide what she should do. No matter how she approached a solution, David played the key role. Without his cooperation, everything she'd done to protect Andrea would have been in vain. She had no right to ask him for help. He had every right to refuse.

She would do whatever it took to make sure that didn't happen.

Bringing her car to a stop beside David's, she turned off the motor and unbuckled her seat belt. As she stepped out into the frigid morning air, she caught sight of him standing beside one of the paddles of the discarded water wheel. He was dressed in faded jeans and a leather bomber jacket and, for the first time since he'd come home, looked as if he could have once belonged in a town like Baxter. His hands were stuffed in his back pockets and he was staring at her, an unfathomable expression on his face.

The speech she'd rehearsed all morning escaped her. It wouldn't be words that convinced him. He would either help her because he had once loved her or he would walk away for the same reason.

She stood her ground beside the open car door, saying a silent prayer that he would make the first move.

After an excruciatingly long time, he took his hands out of his pockets and started toward her. "You always were better at this than I was," he said, stopping several feet away.

"Only because you knew it was more important to me."

He ran his hand across his chin in a touchingly familiar gesture. "This is your show," he said.

She swallowed. "You must have a hundred questions."

"I did, but you already answered them with a hundred lies. I'd just as soon not hear them again, so why don't you go ahead and tell me what's on your mind?"

For as long as she'd known him, whenever David felt himself emotionally threatened, he shielded himself with a cloak of toughness, using offense for defense, striking out at whatever or whomever was near. The last months of his mother's life, he and his father had hardly spoken to each other. When she died, he'd refused to be a pallbearer. He'd sat dry-eyed through the church service and had taken off immediately afterwards, skipping the graveside services. When it was the middle of the night and he still hadn't come home, his father had called Carly. She'd found David at the cemetery, lying on the ground beside his mother's freshly closed grave, his arm flung across the mound of flowers, deep, heartbreaking sobs wracking his body.

Not knowing how else to reach him now, she said, "I'm sorry."

The shell cracked, but only a little. "Yeah, me too."

A wind blew a tangle of hair across her face, giving her temporary shelter from his intense gaze. She reached up and tucked the strand behind her ear. She couldn't hide from him any longer. "Sometimes I let myself think about decisions I made back then and the consequences." It was hard to put words to thoughts and feelings that she'd spent so many years repressing. "Once in a while I even allow myself to wonder how different all of our lives would be if I'd been a little older and a lot wiser." She gave him a sad smile. "I don't do that very often."

David looked past her, his eyes focusing on something in the distance. "Why did you let Ethan believe I was Andrea's father?" he asked, abandoning his resolve to let her take the lead.

"All the way out here I wondered which question you would ask first."

"So that you could practice the answers?"

She closed the car door and walked over to the broad tree stump they had once painted with lopsided white and black circles to use as a target the year Ethan got a BB gun for his birthday. Not bothering to brush the leaves aside, she sat down. "I never told Ethan you were Andrea's father. He drew his own conclusions."

"Which you conveniently chose not to correct."

She'd decided the only way she could convince him to help her was to tell him as much of the truth as she possibly could. Still, the thought terrified her. Andrea's world had been constructed out of a fragile deck of cards, held in place with the insubstantial glue of secrets and lies. Telling David what he had to know would give him power she'd steadfastly refused to give anyone else.

"I was raped," she said, plunging gracelessly into what had to be said.

David stood motionless. His immediate reaction was to reject what she'd said, not, to his humiliation, because it was too horrible to contemplate, but because it seemed so very convenient. Before he could say anything in response, the cynical man he'd become gave way to the trusting boy he'd been. A rage welled up in him as the years disappeared and he was thrust back to the period of his life he'd relived a hundred times in his mind. "Who—"

"That's the one thing I won't tell you," she said evenly. "If you can't accept that condition, there's no use going on."

"You let him get away with it?" he asked, incredulous. "Your father let—"

"If you recall, my father was dead."

The pieces of information hit him like successive blows from a sledgehammer. "Jesus, I forgot."

"There was a lot going on in both of our lives back then."

"What about your mother?" It was a stupid question, one he immediately regretted asking. Carly's mother had stood in her husband's shadow throughout their entire marriage. She would have been as helpless after his death as a hummingbird with a broken wing.

"She had her own problems."

"Who *did* you tell?"

"No one."

Having no other vent for his frustration, she became his target. "You just went on like it had never happened? How could you let the son of a bitch get away with what he did to you?"

"I didn't want anyone to know."

"Not even me?" he asked, an unreasoning hurt at being excluded coming over him.

"I was going to tell you. It was the reason I came to see you that weekend. But you were so caught up in whether or not you were going to make the rent that month, and the story you'd had rejected by *The New Yorker*, and the test you'd taken the day before and . . ." She didn't finish.

"And the political science paper I had to turn in the next day," he said, the argument they'd had that Sunday afternoon playing in his mind with agonizing clarity. He'd been worn out from working two back-to-back shifts and so damned wrapped up in his own problems that he'd had little energy left over for her. Beyond putting his arms around her and letting her cry on his shoulder, he'd done nothing to help her through her father's death.

He felt compelled to stay and listen to her, if for no other reason than to do penance for not having figured out for himself why she'd done what she had. And he felt like running, knowing if he stayed, he would never stop looking at his life as it was now and thinking of the way it should have been.

"Two months later, I learned I was pregnant. . . ." She put a scarlet leaf in her hand and closed her fingers around it. When the whole had become a dozen parts, she slowly opened her hand and let the wind take the pieces. They all disappeared save one, which stubbornly clung to her palm.

"I didn't tell anyone. At first I was too ashamed, later when I discovered I was pregnant, I didn't want anyone trying to tell me what I should do. Besides, talking about it wasn't going to make what had happened go away."

"I found the name of doctor in Kentucky who did abortions, and I made an appointment. The morning I was getting ready to leave, Ethan came over and found me crying. He kept at me until I told him where I was going and what I was planning to do."

She brushed the last fragment of leaf from her hand then hugged herself and began to rock slowly back and forth. "Ethan was incredible," she said, her voice taking on a softness it had lacked before. "He was exactly what I needed at the time—someone who didn't ask questions or make judgments or try to reason with me."

"Someone who had time for you."

"Yes," she admitted.

"What happened?" David asked, fighting a surge of jealousy.

"I was on the table with my legs up in stirrups." She shrugged. "But you know what they say, once a Catholic, always a Catholic. I couldn't go through with it."

Even after all this time, it hurt that she hadn't tried harder to get through to him. He should have been the one she confided in, not Ethan. "I understand why you left New York without saying anything, but how could you have given up on me so easily? Why didn't you give me another chance when you found out you were pregnant?"

At last she looked up at him. "What would you have done?"

"You know what I would have done."

"Precisely. And the more I thought about it, the more determined I became not to let you. I don't expect you to understand this, at times it's even hard for me to remember why I felt so desperate and alone back then, but when I decided to have the baby, I truly believed the life I had planned for myself was over. All I could see in my future was a struggle to find enough money to take care of myself and a baby. Art school became a cruel joke."

The wind caught a pile of leaves and scattered them across the clearing. "I decided I would do anything to make sure your dream didn't die along with mine," she said. "And that's exactly what I did." For an unguarded moment, there was a look on her face that gave him a glimpse of the terrible price she'd paid for her sacrifice.

"On the way home, I told Ethan that I'd decided to go away to have the baby. I made him promise he wouldn't tell anyone where or why I'd gone—most especially you."

David felt sick to his stomach. Ethan had been in love with Carly for years, but she'd been too blind to see it. He must have been beside himself to find he was finally at the right place at the right time. "And he came up with the perfect solution," he said.

"At first I refused. I told him it didn't matter how much sense marrying him made, it wasn't fair. He said he knew how I felt about you, but that it didn't matter." Her voice became so soft he had to strain to hear her. "Then he told me he didn't care whose baby I was carrying, that my child would be his child and that he would raise it with all the love he had stored inside to give me." The deciding factor had been when she'd realized marrying Ethan was the one sure way to keep David from abandoning his own future.

"From what I've seen, he's fallen a little short on his promise," he said, surprising even himself with how angry he sounded. A bizarre, protective instinct had surfaced in David. It was almost as if Ethan's assumption that David was Andrea's father had given him the proprietary right to behave as if it were true.

"Don't judge him by what you saw at the house. Ethan loves Andrea, but most of the time he's too afraid of her to let it show. He's been hurt so much by me, and Andrea is so much like me, that he instinctively protects himself."

As if to lessen his vulnerability, Ethan had insisted they have another child as soon as possible after Andrea was born. Shawn arrived fourteen months later; Eric eleven months after that. When, less than a year later, Ethan started pushing for yet another child, she realized that he was trying to tie her to him with children. He'd convinced himself that as long as she knew he would never relinquish custody of their children, she would never leave.

Already exhausted with taking care of the three she had, Carly had renewed her efforts to bolster Ethan's confidence in other ways. There were brief shining moments when she'd almost succeeded, but then Ethan would remember how she had once lit up when she looked at David or the secret smiles the two of them had once shared or how everyone else became an outsider when she and David were together. Ethan couldn't get over the feeling that he was still standing on the outside. What he failed to realize was that she was standing out there too and that it was a compelling, significant thing for them to have in common.

David shook his head sadly. "I can't stop thinking how different all of our lives would be if you had just come to me first."

"There was a time when that kind of thinking almost drove me crazy. Especially when the older I got, the harder it became for me to understand why I'd done what I had. But then the older Andrea got, the more I saw and understood the girl I'd been back then. None of us is ever as intense or as selfish or as self-sacrificing as we are when we're young. Through all the tears I shed over losing you, I never felt more noble."

"Hypothetically speaking, of course—if you had it to do all over again?"

"Oh, David, that's such an unfair question. If I chose you, I would lose Shawn and Eric."

He went to her, hunkered down, and took her hand in his. In a day of lightning-bolt revelations, he'd just been struck by another. For all these years, he'd believed it was the lover he'd so desperately missed in Carly, now he knew it had been the friend. "I'm sorry I wasn't here for you when you needed me."

She curled her fingers around his. "I need you now."

"What do you want me to do?"

"Go on letting Ethan think you're Andrea's father."

"That doesn't make sense. Not the way Ethan feels about me."

"It's the only way to keep him from trying to find out who Andrea's real father is."

"Is? You mean he's still around?"

"I'm not going to play semantics with you."

"Goddamn it, Carly," he said, fighting to keep his anger in check. "You've had sixteen years to make some kind of peace with what happened. I've had less than ten minutes."

"I know it's asking a lot, and if there were any other way, I wouldn't involve you." When he didn't answer right away, she rushed on. "Is it Victoria? Are you worried about what she'll think?"

"Victoria doesn't care what I did before I met her." He could have added that she didn't care all that much what he did with his life since, either, but the intricacies of his marriage weren't something he wanted to share with Carly.

"If you think about it, the only thing that's changed is your knowing."

He'd come there that day to put an end to what they'd once had. What she was asking would tie them together, if only mentally, for the rest of their lives. It was on the tip of his tongue to say no, but the word wouldn't come out. "All right."

She squeezed his hand. "Are you sure you know what you're doing?"

Her reaction was so like the Carly he remembered, he couldn't help but smile. "I know that asking me was the last thing in the world you wanted to do."

"I can't have Ethan trying to find out who Andrea's real father is."

"Would that really be so bad?"

"Too many people would be hurt."

"I can't believe you still want to protect him, not after all this time."

"Not *him*, Andrea. The truth would destroy her."

"You may be underestimating your daughter. She didn't strike me as fragile as you seem to think she is."

She stared at their intertwined hands. "You're going to have to trust me on this one, David."

"Meaning I couldn't and shouldn't have trusted you before?"

"It's imperative you understand how important this is," she said, ignoring his jab.

"I believe you."

She pulled her hand from his. "Goddamn it, David. Don't give me lip service on this. It's too important."

When she made a move to get up, he grabbed her arms and held her. "You don't get it, do you?"

"This isn't a game," she said, anger in her voice.

"The reason I'm willing to go along with what you want and tell Ethan that Andrea is mine is that I would give everything I have if it were true."

She caught her breath. "Why would you say something like that?"

"Because it's the truth," he said simply. "God knows I've tried to stop loving you, but nothing I do seems to work. If Andrea really were my daughter, I would have a piece of you no one could take away from me."

She didn't want to hear this. Whatever stability and comfort she'd found with Ethan would be lost knowing David still loved her. "You're living in the past. I'm not the girl you once knew."

"Oh? How are you different? Have you stopped crying in sad movies? Do you hate bread pudding now? Maybe you've stopped snoring?"

"Those are all superficial—"

"All right—do you still reach a climax faster when you're on top and in control?"

She jerked back as if he'd hit her. "You bastard. You have no right."

"What? To remember? When it's all I have?"

Her anger was as transitory as snow in August. "So much has happened, how can you still love me?"

He reached up to touch the side of her face. "I guess it's because I never stopped loving you, not even when I was hating you. Every woman I've known I compared to you. I married Victoria because she was nothing like you."

"This is wrong. We shouldn't be doing this." She closed her eyes against the rush of longing that swept through her. "It's not why I came here today."

"Do you ever think about me?"

Carly slowly leaned forward and pressed her cheek to his shoulder. He put his arms around her. "There are times I miss you so much I can hardly— never mind. You were more than my best friend and my lover. Somehow, when we were growing up, I think you actually became a part of me. When I lost you, it was like losing a part of myself."

He closed his eyes. "The day I received a copy of my first book, all I could think about was showing it to you."

"I wish I could have been there."

"What would you have done?" he asked, pressing the side of his face into her hair, breathing in the just-washed fragrance.

She smiled. "I would have done something pre-posterous, like filling the bathtub with Dom Perignon and making you sit there with me while you read every golden word aloud. Then later we would have toasted your success with wine in Lalique goblets and thrown them in the fireplace.

They were engaged in a dangerous dance. David could feel all that he had worked so hard to become slipping away from him. "And then?"

Carly stiffened and tried to pull away from him. It was as if the realization of what they were doing had hit them both at the same moment. "We've got to stop this. It isn't fair to Ethan or Victoria."

"Or us," he said, reluctantly letting her go.

She nervously combed her hands through her wind-tossed hair. "When you see Ethan, tell him that you didn't want Andrea sixteen years ago, and that you don't want her now. It's important to convince him that being her father means nothing to you."

"My God, that's what's been eating him? He's been waiting all this time for me to show up to take his daughter away?" David felt a sudden, over-whelming sadness for his old friend. The bond that tied him and Carly together had broadened to include Ethan.

"And there was no way I could reassure him by telling him the truth."

"What makes you think he's going to believe me?"

"There's a way to improve the odds." She hesi-tated, as if considering whether or not to go on. "Of-fer to pay her way through school." Before he could reply, she held her hand up to stop him. "I know what you're going to say, but then you probably know what I'm about to say, too. In the unlikely chance that Ethan agrees to let you send money, I'll find a way to pay you back."

He brushed her offer aside, zeroing in on what mattered the most to him. "You intend to stay with Ethan even after the kids are grown?"

"I'll stay with Ethan as long as he wants me."

He got up and brushed the leaves from his jeans. He had to get away from her before he did something stupid, like trying to convince her to abandon her family and come to England with him. "I'll go to the plant to talk to Ethan this afternoon. Do you want me to call you afterwards?"

She shook her head. "Ethan will tell me about it when he gets home."

"Are you coming to the memorial service?"

"Considering all that's happened, I don't think that's a very good idea."

"Then this is it?" How could he just walk away?

She brought her legs up to her chest and wrapped her arms around them. "Someone I loved used to tell me that, in the end, all we are is the sum of our memories. I think about that a lot."

Profound words for an eighteen-year-old boy who had made love for the first time to the girl he'd vowed to love forever. "And do you think about where you were when I said that to you?"

"It would be a blessing to forget."

"I'll never stop loving you."

She turned her face away from him to stare out at the distance, unable to contain the pain of seeing him any longer. "Thank you," she whispered when she heard him turn to walk away.

It was almost two o'clock in the afternoon when David got in his car and drove out of the parking lot at Hargrove Furniture Company. The sky had been clear and blue when he'd gone in to see Ethan; now, it was gray and overcast. Soon the rains would come to steal the crispness of autumn, then the snow, to shroud the nakedness of the forests.

He would see neither of those things happen in this place ever again. It was a classic case of not wanting something until it was taken away.

On his way out to see Ethan he'd searched for even a niggling sense of guilt that he hadn't taken Victoria into consideration before telling Carly he would go along with her plan. That in itself was bad enough, but worse was knowing he would never confide in his wife. Given a choice, it was the way she preferred things done.

At least now the deed was completed and he could leave with the knowledge that he'd been able to do something to repay Carly in small part for what she'd done for him. Too bad her sacrifice hadn't meant more to him in the end. But then how was she to have known that his success would seem hollow without her there to share it with him?

Thank God Ethan had had the good sense to regret what he'd said and done the night before, and not for David's sake, but Andrea's. Ethan obviously loved her—at least as much as he could let himself. Perhaps knowing David wouldn't be a threat anymore, perceived or actual, would help Ethan's relationship with the child he'd raised as his own. It was something to hope for.

Not until Ethan had refused his offer, had David realized how much he'd wanted to pay for Andrea's schooling. It would have been a tenuous contact with Carly, but at this point, he was willing to settle for anything. Ethan's adamant rejection of the idea had destroyed even that possibility.

David pulled up to a stoplight on the outskirts of town. While he waited for the light to change, the headache he'd been trying to ignore all day began an insistent pounding in his left temple. He glanced around for a store where he could get some aspirin and spotted Turner's Market on the opposite corner.

Walking across the front of the store, intently staring down each aisle in search of the drug section, he was startled and then irritated to hear someone calling his name. Engaging in small talk with someone from his past was about as appealing as the free sample of Polish sausage a woman had tried to press on him in the meat aisle.

"David?" a female voice repeated.

Unable to ignore or escape the woman headed toward him, David slipped on his professional smile and forced himself to look up. The smile disappeared when he saw who it was.

"Mrs. Strong," he said, mentally shaking his head at the irony of running into Carly's mother just when he'd convinced himself he'd cut the last tie. She was a preview of what Carly would most likely be at that age—her back unbent by the hard life she'd lived, her dark brown eyes quick and filled with intelligence, and her once fiery hair turning a golden blond.

"It's Mrs. Friedlander now, but I'd really prefer you called me Barbara."

"You married Wally Friedlander?" he asked, the surprise evident in his voice.

"I know it must seem strange," she said. "I hated being the sheriff's wife when Frank had the job and here I am married to the man who took his place."

"I always meant to call you to tell you how sorry I was about Frank's accident. It must have been hell for—"

"That's all in the past now," she said, abruptly stopping him. Her voice softened when she went on. "Actually, the reason I wanted to talk to you was to tell you how sorry I was to hear about your father. He was such a good man. I can't tell you how much I missed running into him around town after he moved. But then, isn't that the way it always goes?"

"I think he missed living here, too." As hard as it was to admit, David had reluctantly reached the conclusion that moving his father hadn't been the magnanimous gesture he'd convinced himself it was at the time. Believing his father the last thread that tied him to Baxter, it had only seemed reasonable that severing it would free him.

"Mabel said it was his heart but that you were able to spend some time with him before he went."

"Two weeks."

"That can be a blessing . . . or not."

"In this case it was." To steer the conversation in a different direction, David asked, "I'm looking for aspirin. Could you tell me where they are?"

"I'll show you." She parked her cart and motioned for him to follow.

David marveled at how comfortable Barbara obviously felt being with him. There was none of the anger or chagrin he would have expected her to feel depending on the reason Carly had told her about the breakup.

At the end of the second aisle, Barbara stopped, took a box off the shelf, and handed it to him. "This is the brand I use."

He nodded in thanks and made a move to leave before she could ask him something he really didn't want to answer. "I wish I had more time to visit, but I have a dozen things that need doing this afternoon."

"Have you seen Carly?"

He could pretend he hadn't heard her and just keep going. She would understand. She'd always understood him when he didn't want to talk about things that hurt him, like when his mother had died. "Yes," he admitted.

"When?"

"Two days ago."

Barbara frowned. "She didn't tell me."

"I'm not surprised. The visit didn't go all that well."

"Ethan?"

Sensors awakened in David's mind. Barbara knew a whole lot more about what had happened back then than Carly had led him to believe. She wasn't just pumping him for information, she was afraid of the answers he might give. "I guess it all boils down to Thomas Wolfe being right, you really can't go home again."

A sadness flickered across her eyes. "You never should have left."

6

David's breath created billowy clouds of fog that blocked his vision as he tried and failed to insert his room key into its paint-encrusted lock. He cursed the streetlight on the corner that threw more shadow than illumination, bent lower and tried again. The Taj Mahal Motel was a strong dose of reality, placing him in his past as effectively as the jog he'd just taken by his old house. The motel was more than a continent apart from the Ritz; he couldn't remember the last time he'd stayed anywhere that didn't have either a health club on the premises or access to one.

Haunted by the look of sorrow in Carly's eyes, the agony in Ethan's and his own sense of loss, David had sought release in exhaustion. He'd put on the sweats he'd picked up at a local sporting goods store earlier that afternoon and taken off, determined to run until the only thing on his mind was the pain in his legs.

It was a good plan; too bad it hadn't worked. He'd stayed out an hour and a half until his lungs felt on fire from the cold air, and all he could think about was how Carly had looked when he'd told her he still loved her.

The phone rang. For a brief, irrational moment, he allowed himself to imagine it was Carly.

He made another stab at the lock; this time, the key slid in smoothly. The telephone was on its fourth jarring ring when he picked up the receiver. "Yes?"

"David? You sound out of breath. What in the world have you been doing?"

Victoria. His knees gave out and he sank to the edge of the bed. "Jogging," he answered, guilt washing over him at his keen disappointment. For weeks he'd been adrift on the sea of his past, first with his father and then with Carly. Still, he wasn't ready to be snatched back to the safety of shore. He glanced at the clock on the nightstand and added five hours. "Why are you calling me in the middle of the night? Is something wrong?"

"Precisely what I was going to ask you," she said, a note of reproach in her voice. "I've been trying to reach you for two days to see how you've been getting on and to give you my flight number. You did tell me you were going to pick me up yourself, didn't you?"

Actually she'd insisted he meet her plane, unwilling to trust that there were limousine services in a place as provincial-sounding as Cleveland, Ohio. "Hold on while I get something to write with." He tossed the receiver on the bed, took a sheet of paper out of the drawer, then dug through his coat pocket for a pen.

When he reached for the phone again, the paper slipped out of his hand and fell to the floor. He bent to pick it up and noticed a large brown coffee stain on the rust-colored carpet. From there his gaze swept the rest of the room. He shuddered to think how Victoria was going to react when she saw where she would be staying. Frowning, he put the receiver up to his ear. "You know, Victoria, I've been thinking that your coming here was probably not such a good idea after all. If you're worried that it might seem strange to everyone at home that you didn't come to the memorial service, you can just tell them that I was the one who insisted you stay home."

She let out a heavy sigh. "David, don't be a bore about this. You know I would have been with you at the hospital if I could, but it's been impossible for me to get away until now."

Her reaction startled him. He'd had no idea she'd even thought about joining him in Florida, and it had certainly never occurred to him to ask. Funerals were eminently more suited to Victoria than bedside vigils. "I only meant that it seems a little idiotic to fly all the way over here for a half-hour memorial service and then just turn around and fly back."

"Oh, but I'm not."

David's shoulders sagged. She'd obviously made arrangements for them to do something that would delay his return to England. Under normal circumstances he would keep his mouth shut and go along with whatever she'd planned. It was a tacit agreement of theirs. As long as he wasn't holed up with a manuscript, he'd go along with any social regime she set up for them.

This time it was different. It wasn't just that he wanted the peace of mind he found by immersing himself in his work, he needed it. "Meaning?" he asked.

"It's going to be a splendid surprise."

He sat down on the bed again and wearily ran his hand through his hair. "You know I don't like surprises."

Her voice lowered and softened. "I'm afraid you've a short memory at times, darling. I seem to recall one or two you didn't mind at all."

Victoria was the ultimate male fantasy—a lady in the parlor, a whore in bed. "How wonderfully uncomplicated you are," he said.

Several seconds passed before she answered. "I'm going to give you the benefit of the doubt and assume that's your typical roundabout way of telling me you've missed me as much as I've missed you."

"Of course it is," he said automatically, and then realized it was the truth. He did miss her. Victoria had provided the calm water after the hurricane in his life called Carly. The years, the life, he'd lived with her were predictable and utterly inconsequential —the perfect environment for a man who wanted to write bestselling novels. Carly had been right about one thing: he could not have devoted the time and energy it took for him to turn out a thousand pages of manuscript every year if he had married her. With Carly, he would not have insisted on the months of isolation where he put his own needs foremost. There would have been her career to consider . . . and the children they would surely have had together.

"Must you save all your clever words for your books?" she chided gently.

"I'm sorry," he told her. "It's been a long day."

"Rather a long month, I should say."

He was drawn to the warmth in her voice. "Coming back here has been a lot harder than I'd imagined it would be." There was a deep need in him to talk about what he was feeling, if only on the superficial level they used with each other.

"Well, it will all be over soon," she said with a crisp finality.

With consummate skill, she'd firmly closed the door on any further intimate revelations. Emotions were messy and unproductive, certainly not something anyone of good breeding brought up in polite conversation.

"Yes," David said, "just two more days and then I've got to get back to work."

"Oh, darling, please don't tell me you're going to insist upon coming home straight away," she said.

The rigid structure of the world Victoria lived in was one of the things that had drawn David to her. Knowing that, as an outsider, he would never truly be accepted, had given him an implicit permission not to go beyond the superficial in his relationships. He could exist in his own sphere while the lives of others swirled around him. Thanks to Victoria's position, there wasn't a party worth being invited to that he didn't attend, or a door that didn't open when he knocked. With the exception of rare, isolated moments when a sense of something missing would steal over him, his life was exactly as he wanted it.

"I don't really have any other choice, Victoria. I'm a month behind on the book already."

"Another week or two shouldn't matter. You'll catch up. You always do."

He could fight her and he'd win, but he wasn't sure it was worth the effort or the guilt he'd feel. Besides, going home wasn't the answer. This time his retreat from reality would not be so easy. "A week then," he said, meeting her halfway. "I can't afford any more."

"I should hardly be recovered from the trip by then."

Weary of their trivial exchange, he wanted to shout, *Then stay where you are*, but that bit of self-indulgence would only prolong their conversation. "I didn't say you had to accompany me home."

"That's thoughtful of you, but I expect once you've seen what I have in mind for us, you'll be staying, too."

He pulled the cap off the Mont Blanc pen his agent had sent along with the first million-dollar contract she'd negotiated for him to sign. "Why don't you give me—"

There was a quick, soft knocking on the door.

David turned toward the sound. "Hold on a minute," he said into the phone. "I've got—" He stopped. Did he really want to explain a late-night caller to Victoria?

"David?"

"I'm here," he said quickly. "I've, uh, I've got a cramp in my leg. Give me your flight number and we'll finish this conversation when you get here."

He wrote the information down, said a hasty good-bye, and headed for the door. As he put his hand on the knob, the thought crossed his mind that it made more sense for Ethan to be standing outside than Carly.

But it was neither.

"Andrea—what in God's name are you doing here?"

She took a small step backward as if she might turn and leave without saying anything. Several seconds passed before she swallowed convulsively and said, "I need to talk to you."

David looked past her, down the walkway, and out into the parking lot.

"I'm alone."

Cold air swirled around him, making his sweats cling like a frigid second skin. "Does your mother know you're here?"

She shook her head. "Please, can I come in?"

"I don't think that's such a good idea, Andrea. It's late and . . ." He left the thought dangling. Was it her reputation he was worried about or his own discomfort over seeing his supposed "daughter" actually standing in front of him? She was plainly upset about something and in need of someone to talk to. "Of course you can come in," he said at last. "Could I get you a Coke? There's a machine by the office."

"No, thank you."

Where the room had seemed small before, Andrea's presence made it feel like a closet. He motioned to the sole chair. "Do you want to sit down?"

Instead of taking the chair, she perched on the corner of the bed, her spine rigid, her feet planted squarely on the floor. She had an abandoned, out-of-place look about her, like a flamingo sitting in a snowdrift.

"What can I do for you?" David asked, forcing his tone to sound receptive, encouraging.

Andrea lifted her gaze from her folded hands and looked at him, as if taking his measure and finding him wanting. "I'm not sure."

"Well, why did you come here tonight?"

"To talk to you."

"About?" he prompted.

"I wanted to find out what kind of person you are."

David frowned in puzzlement; *that* hadn't even been in the running. "For any reason in particular?"

"I know about you," she said, a flush coloring her cheeks.

David tensed. "You know what about me?" he asked evenly.

Her gaze bore into him. "I was awake last night when you came to the house."

It was stupid to continue to dance around the truth but easier than confronting it. "How much did you hear?"

"Everything." She used the word like a weapon.

"Could you be more specific?"

"I know you're my real father." Glaring at him, she added, "Is that specific enough?"

He went to the chair and sat down heavily. It took a major effort to appear calm when every time his heart beat it felt as if it were about to leap from his chest.

"Have you talked to your mother about this?"

She shook her head.

Jesus, how could the three of them have been so blind as not to have planned for this possibility?

What in the hell was he supposed to do now? "Have you talked to anyone about it?"

Again, she shook her head.

Stalling for time, he got up and started to pace the narrow aisle between the chair and the door. "I really think your mother should be here. She should be the one answering your questions."

"Why? So she can tell me more lies? I've already had fifteen years' worth. I don't need any more."

"She can explain things to you."

"I didn't come here for explanations," Andrea said, a catch in her voice. "I want to know what my father is like. That's not such a big thing, is it?"

At that moment, he would have drained the ocean with a teacup if she'd asked. He sat back down in the chair. Tomorrow was soon enough to deal with the Pandora's box that had been opened. Tonight, he would do what he could to ease the questioning soul of an innocent young girl whose world had just slipped off its axis. "What would you like to know about me?"

She hesitated, as if caught off-guard by his capitulation and unsure where to begin. "When is your birthday?" she finally asked.

No other question could have told him more completely how convinced she was that what she'd overheard last night was the truth. In her place, he'd have asked for dates and details, some kind of proof that he was really her father. "Three days before Christmas."

She thought about that for a minute. "My girl friend, Faith, was born on Christmas Eve. I always thought it was kind of a bum deal to have a birthday in December."

Their conversation had taken on a surreal quality. Where were the accusations, the bitterness, the hostility that should have been aimed toward him? "If I could pick another day," he told her, "and it had to be a holiday, I'd pick the Fourth of July."

A small smile appeared and was gone. "Me too. I love fireworks." She unzipped her jacket but made no move to take it off. "Did you always want to be a writer?" It was as if she were plucking her questions out of a grab bag.

"Not always. Until the sixth grade, I wanted to be a fireman."

"My mom used to paint," she said, leapfrogging in yet another direction. "But she must not have been very good at it. All of her stuff is hidden away in closets around the house."

So that was how Andrea was dealing with her pain. She'd found a target in Carly, the one person she was confident would not strike back. He was an unknown quantity, someone she had to court favor with in order to get him to like her. Ethan was the outsider, a father but not her father anymore, or so she believed. "I remember," he said.

"I guess it's not so strange that I want to be an actor after all—what with you a writer and Mom a wannabe artist."

"I'm sure it's your mother you take after. Her talent is innate. The little I have comes from struggle and tenacity."

She gave him a long, hard look. "Why do you do that?"

"What?"

"Put yourself down. Whenever anyone says anything nice about your writing or one of your books, you act like they don't know what they're talking about."

Could she really have seen that in him or was it something she'd overheard? "I guess it's more comfortable for me to deal with criticism than praise," he said, something he'd never admitted to anyone else.

"It's the way you say thank you, like you're not really listening to what someone is saying."

"That's quite an observation."

As if afraid she'd gone too far, she added, "It's not like you're being rude or anything. I don't think most people would even notice."

Since he could give her so little else, he gave her this. "I'll try harder from now on," he said.

Several long, agonizing seconds passed before she spoke again. "I looked London up in the encyclopedia today—it's as big as New York. I can't imagine living someplace where there's seven million other people living right next to you."

"You get used to it. After my time in New York, London was easy. If you're open to it, the kind of intensity you find living in a big city is almost addictive. But I don't stay in London all the time. I have a house in the country, too."

"A lot of my friends' parents have cabins, but I've never known anyone with more than one real house before. I suppose the one in the country is really big?"

"Yes."

"What about your house in London? Is it big, too?"

"It's comfortable."

She hesitated, as if reluctant to ask her next question. "Did you . . ." She stopped to clear her throat. "Did you love my mother?"

He'd expected her to ask something along that order. Still it hit like a blow to his midsection. "Yes," he answered simply. To tell Andrea how much he had loved Carly would only add to her confusion.

"Then why—" She caught herself. "Never mind," she said. "It's not important."

He was out of his element. He had no idea what to say or do to ease her pain. Telling her that he wasn't her father would destroy any faith and trust she had left in the people she loved. Ethan could not be taken away from her without giving her someone to take his place. She needed to believe the man responsible for her birth was good and loving and kind, despite the fact that he had abandoned her and her mother.

"I'm sorry," was all he could think to say.

"I've known there was something wrong for a long time now," she said, abruptly dropping her defenses. "My dad doesn't like me."

"That's not true," David said, hoping his words sounded more convincing to her than they did to him. "I happen to know that he loves you very much. We had a long talk about you this afternoon and the reason he seems to hold back at times is he's been afraid that I would come back some day and take you from him."

"Really?"

"Really."

"What made him think you would do that?"

"Because he knows how a father feels about his children."

"Is that how you feel about me?"

He'd fallen into a trap of his own making. "I'm sure that's the way I would have felt if I'd known you existed," he said, reluctant to add to the lies already told. "If you haven't talked to anyone about this, then you probably don't know that I found out about you the same time you found out about me."

"We look a lot alike," she said.

In reality, except for the color of her hair and the shade of blue of her eyes, Andrea was the spitting image of her mother. Ethan was so caught up in believing what he wanted to believe, he'd blinded himself to any other possibility. Or maybe it was knowing the truth that kept David from seeing what Ethan saw. "Actually, I think you look more like your mother than—"

"Do you like me?" she rushed on, making no effort to hide her need for his approval.

He could crush her with a word. "I like you very much," he said.

Her head dipped in an almost imperceptible nod, as if she were privately confirming something she'd already decided. "Then it's okay if I come to live with you?"

7

Carly slid the tray back into the dishwasher, closed the door, and wiped her hands on a dish towel. Seeking a way to escape the doubts and questions that had haunted her about what had happened that day, she'd spent the past hour cleaning counters that were spotless, a stove that had been wiped down after dinner, and a floor Andrea had swept only hours ago. Everyone else had gone to bed early, Ethan less than ten minutes after the kids. When she'd made a move to follow, he'd pointedly told her that he was going to bed to sleep, not talk. He was plainly relieved when she chose to stay downstairs.

The only thing she'd been able to get out of Ethan about his meeting with David was a cryptic, "We've worked things out." When she'd pushed, he'd begged off, saying he needed time to think things through before he talked to her about it.

Twice, she'd had her hand on the phone to call David but had come to her senses before completing the call. In time, Ethan would tell her what she wanted to know. It was going to be hard enough to put their lives back in order again when David left.

Making contact with him again, no matter how valid the reason, would only make the process harder.

She had a sudden, overwhelming urge to be with Andrea, to sit beside her in the moonlit room, to look at her the way she had when Andrea was a baby, to be filled once again with wonder that something so beautiful could be the result of something so violent and ugly. Even more vital was the need to reassure herself that Andrea had been left unharmed by the turmoil that had just occurred in their lives.

On her way to her daughter's room, Carly paused at her own bedroom door to listen for Ethan's rhythmic breathing. The fact that he was asleep reassured her.

She was in Andrea's room and actually sitting on the corner of the bed before she realized it wasn't her daughter under the blankets, but several pillows artfully arranged to make it look like someone sleeping. Carly realized she should have known something was wrong the minute she came in the room and saw that Muffin was not curled up at Andrea's feet. Still, her mind balked at the evidence of her daughter's calculated deception. Sneaking out in the middle of the night was as alien to Andrea's personality as wearing cosmetics that had been tested on animals.

Where in the hell was she?

Carly moved one of the pillows out of the way so that she could see the glowing numbers on the clock radio. It was almost midnight.

How long should she wait before she called someone? Who should she call? Wally? If nothing else, he could phone the station and have the officers on patrol keep an eye out for Andrea. But the telephone was on her mother's side of the bed and there was no way to get to Wally without going through her. Carly wasn't ready to deal with anyone else's fears.

She went to the window and pulled the curtain aside. A deserted road greeted her. A soft rain was visible in the glare of the streetlight. The fear that had taken root in her grew like a living, breathing entity, feeding on her inability to make a decision. Carly had started to turn from the window when the headlights from a car turning the corner caught her attention. Her hand closed around the sheer lace curtain as she murmured, "Please God, let it be her."

A half minute later, the car turned into the driveway. Two doors opened. Andrea got out and came around to the driver's side where a man waited for her.

David.

Carly's relief was buffeted in a sea of confusion as she hurried downstairs to meet them. She flung the door open and took a step toward Andrea but was brought up short by the look on her daughter's face.

"I see you already found out I was gone," Andrea said, carefully avoiding contact as she moved into the house past her mother.

"I wanted to call," David told Carly, stepping up to the landing. "But I was afraid you'd be in bed."

Carly glared at him. "What's going on?" she said, her jaw rigid with anger. David was to have been out of their lives by now.

"I think we'd better go inside to talk about this."

She turned to Andrea. "Are you all right?"

"Yeah. Sure. Why wouldn't I be? What could possibly be bothering good old reliable Andrea?"

David took a step closer. "Could we please go inside?"

"I'll take over now," Carly told him.

"I want him here," Andrea said.

"What possible reason—"

"Because what I have to say to you involves him."

"I don't see how David could be involved in anything—"

"I *know*, Mom."

Carly stiffened. "You know what?"

"She overheard us last night," David supplied.

Carly looked into Andrea's eyes for confirmation. "Oh, my God," she said. "I'm so sorry," was the only other thing she could think to say. Over and over again she spoke the words, and then, "You shouldn't have found out that way."

"You're fuckin'-A right about that one, Mom. You should have told me about this a long time ago."

"Don't talk to me like that," Carly said automatically, more fear than anger in her voice.

David quickly stepped inside. He was angry when he took Andrea by the arm and turned her to face him. "Are you trying to wake up the whole neighborhood or just everyone in this house?"

"What difference does it make?" she asked, looking past him to fix her mother with a venomous stare. "They're all going to find out about it sooner or later."

"I don't know about your mother, but I prefer later," he said. He steered her down the hall to the family room. There would be time enough tomorrow to break the news to the rest of the family. Tonight, especially after Andrea fired her second salvo, Carly would have plenty to handle on her own.

Andrea sat on the sofa. Carly went over to sit down beside her. She reached for her daughter's hand, tightening her grip and holding on when Andrea tried to pull away. "I wish I knew what to say to you."

"You don't have to say anything," she said with a dismissive shrug. "David explained it all to me."

"What did he tell you?" Carly asked, her resentment growing. If it was necessary for Andrea to find out that Ethan wasn't her father, it was Carly's job to do the explaining. How else could she be sure Andrea understood she wasn't some shameful secret Carly had tried to hide away?

Andrea glanced over to David as if seeking his approval. He nodded his encouragement. "He told me how much you loved each other and that when you learned you were pregnant with me, you didn't tell him because you were afraid he would quit school to take care of us."

Carly cringed as the words she had spoken that morning echoed in her ears. She desperately wished David had taken the role Ethan had assigned to him and told Andrea that he'd walked out of their lives to pursue his career. The truth, or at least the slightly altered version David had agreed to go along with, was far too romantic and compelling to an impressionable fifteen-year-old. "What else did he tell you?"

She hesitated. "That Daddy loves me."

Carly grabbed hold of the thought. "He's loved you from the first moment he felt you kicking inside my stomach. A moment's passion doesn't make a man a father, Andrea. It's the years of caring and being there for a child that matter."

"Daddy has never felt the same way about me that he does about Eric and Shawn. He talks to them—he lectures me." Andrea pulled her hand free and hugged herself.

"You're wrong, Andrea." Her words were met with a deafening silence. "It's just that no father feels about a daughter the way he feels about a son."

"Mom, it's more than that, and you know it. You can tell he likes them better than me every time he looks at one of them. He never gets that crinkly smile in his eyes when he's around me."

"What can I say to convince you that you're wrong?"

"Nothing."

Needing the reassurance of physical contact, Carly reached out and ran her hand over Andrea's hair. "So much has happened in the last couple of days. You'll feel differently when David is gone and our lives are back to normal."

Andrea pushed Carly's hand away. "You don't understand anything about how I feel. If you did, you could never say something like that. My life will never be the same again."

Carly felt as though she were trying to crawl out of a hole dug in the sand. "It just seems that way now. Once you've had time to get used to the idea, you'll feel differently." She was doing this all wrong, saying all the wrong things. Andrea had every right to be angry, to question, to believe her life was forever changed.

"Do Eric and Shawn know?" Andrea asked.

"Of course not."

"Does Grandma Barbara?"

Carly hesitated a fraction of a second too long.

"How could you tell her and not me?" Andrea demanded.

"No one had to tell her. She figured it out for herself."

"How?"

David stepped in. "Your grandmother knew how much your mother and I loved each other."

Andrea thought a minute. "How come she could figure out what really happened and you couldn't?" she said to David.

"I was too caught up in feeling sorry for myself to see much of anything else," he said with brutal honesty.

"Who else knows?" Andrea asked, turning her attention back to Carly.

"Grandpa Wally."

A low moan escaped Andrea. "Who else?"

"No one," Carly said.

"I feel like a joke—like you've all been laughing at me behind my back."

"Stop that," Carly said with as much sternness as

she could muster. "I'm not going to let you make this worse than it is."

"You weren't ever going to tell me, were you?" Andrea asked, as if the idea had just occurred to her. "Not even when I was old enough to move out."

"No."

"Why?"

"Because too many people would be hurt and it would all be for nothing. You already have a father who loves you and wants you and would do anything to make you happy."

"I have a right to know what my real father is like."

"Damn it, Andrea, Ethan *is* your real father. He's the one who—"

"But he doesn't look like me, David does."

"That's a genetic fluke," Carly snapped, her frustration getting in the way of caution. Sick to her stomach at the mistake she'd almost made, she quickly added, "You could just as easily have wound up looking like me."

David got up from the chair where he'd been sitting. "Andrea, I think you should go to bed. It's been a long day. You and your mom are tired and there's nothing you have to say that won't keep until tomorrow."

Carly's gaze moved from Andrea to David. Something was going on between them that made the hair on the back of her neck stand on end.

Andrea lifted her head to look at David. "I can't wait until tomorrow," she said, a silent plea in her voice.

"It would be better if you did," he told her.

"Please?"

He shrugged and then sat back down. "All right."

Andrea turned back to Carly. "I want to live with my real father from now on."

Carly was too stunned to answer immediately.

"You can't be serious," she finally managed to say, a hundred disconnected thoughts racing through her mind trying to form a cohesive whole.

"Why not? Just because you didn't have the guts to go after something you really wanted doesn't mean I don't." As if suddenly realizing she was not going to get what she wanted the way she was going, she continued in a more reasonable tone. "I've thought about this a lot and living with David is something I really want to do."

"Well, I won't let you. It's out of the question." Carly could feel the walls of her hole in the sand collapsing on her.

"I have a right to know my real father," Andrea insisted.

Carly did not look at David, afraid she would use him as a target and alienate Andrea even more. "What does David have to say about this?"

"He told me I had to talk to you."

"And now you have, and the answer is no," Carly said. Why in the hell hadn't he just told her that he wouldn't take her with him, that she didn't fit into his life? The whole thing would have ended there. Andrea wasn't the type to force herself on anyone, not even the man she believed was her father. "I want you to go to bed, and let me talk to David alone."

"Why can't you see how important this is to me?" Andrea asked, tears welling in her eyes.

"It's a whim," Carly said. "You've had a terrible shock and you aren't thinking rationally."

"I'm sick of hearing things like that. You think you know me so well, but you don't. I'm not your little girl anymore, Mother. I'm my own person. I belong to me, not you. I have a right to make my own decisions."

"I'm sorry, that was a stupid thing to say," Carly told her. "But no one, I don't care how old they are, would be thinking clearly after going through what you just have. Give yourself some time—that's all I'm asking."

"I'm not going to change my mind."

Carly pressed the heels of her hands to her temples. "Could we please discuss this in the morning?"

Andrea got up and started toward the door. When she was beside David, she paused for several seconds as if deciding what to do. Finally, impulsively, she threw her arms around him. "Talk her into letting me go," she begged.

David awkwardly returned Andrea's embrace. Over her shoulder, he met Carly's frightened stare. "Your mother loves you very much," he said. "Why don't you let it go for tonight? We could all use some time to think."

She looked up at him. "You're not going to change your mind about letting me come, are you?"

How in the hell was he supposed to answer? "I wouldn't do that to you."

"Okay, I'll go. But nothing is going to change my mind either."

When Andrea was safely upstairs, Carly turned on David. "Is this your way of getting back at me?"

David was caught off-balance by the attack. With obvious effort, he reigned in his own frustration. "Andrea came to me," he said.

"And from the looks of it you did nothing to dissuade her."

"What did you want me to do, for God's sake, throw her out? Remember, thanks to you, she believes I'm her father."

"You could have told her how impossible it would be for you to take her with you."

"I tried. Listen, I don't like this any more than you do. Probably less. Now would you stop acting as if I'm the enemy and start working on a way to get us out of this?"

Seeking a physical vent for her frustration, Carly picked a pillow off the couch and threw it across the room. It bounced off the wall and landed at David's feet. "Damn it, you should have called me the minute she got there."

"She asked me not to." He stooped to pick up the pillow.

"And you listened?" She knew she was being unfair, but she couldn't stop.

"I did what I thought you would want me to do," he said.

Carly covered her face with her hands. "God in heaven, what am I going to do?"

"Have you considered telling her the truth?"

She lowered her hands to her sides. "I can't. I wasn't being melodramatic this morning when I told you the truth would destroy her."

"How can you be so sure? She's stronger than you think she is."

"No one is that strong."

David turned the pillow over and over in his hands before he tossed it back on the couch. He let out a sigh of resignation. "Maybe if you told Andrea she could come to England for a visit next summer it would satisfy her. That's months away. She'll forget all about me by then."

"What if she didn't?"

"Then I'd deal with it."

"How?"

"Why are you pushing me on this?"

"Because I need to know whether or not I can count on you if she doesn't forget about you."

His eyes widened in anger. "You know goddamn well you can count on me. I'm the same man I was sixteen years ago. If you'd put some trust in me then, none of this would be happening now."

"Please, David."

"What choice do I have, Carly? You've put me in a position—"

"If I could have handled it any other way, I would have." He combed his fingers through his hair, then stopped to rub the back of his neck. "Jesus, she really thinks I'm her father. That doesn't leave me a lot of room to maneuver. What kind of father would just pack up and refuse to be a part of his daughter's life when she's begging to come with him?"

"I don't know what to say to you."

He shook his head in disbelief. "It's been an interesting week. I lost my father and gained a daughter."

"What will Victoria say when she finds out?"

"Not much."

"Why not?"

"If Andrea ever does come to England, Victoria will simply find something else to do while she's there. We lead separate lives most of the time anyway."

"I don't care how busy Victoria keeps herself, teenage girls can be pretty hard to ignore. Andrea loves to—" Carly jerked backward, as if she'd been struck. "Listen to me. I can't believe I'm saying these things to you. It's like I'm getting ready to send her to summer camp."

"Are you sorry I came back?"

"Oh, David, that's the second stupid question you've asked me today. Of course I'm sorry. How could I not be?"

"I'm not."

"Because you've gained something."

"I have to admit, I'd given up on ever becoming a father."

"I wasn't talking about Andrea."

The coolness in her voice caught him off guard. "Then what—"

"The peace of mind you said you wanted."

"Why are you angry?"

"Andrea's mine, David. If she does go to England to see you next summer, it will be for a visit, nothing else. Don't ever forget that."

"She's not yours alone anymore, Carly," Ethan said, from the doorway.

Carly started at his voice. "What are you—"

"Andrea came to see me when you sent her upstairs," he said, cutting her off. "She was crying. I could hardly make out what she was saying when she tried to tell me what was going on down here." He moved into the room, passing David without looking at him.

David tilted his head back and stared up at the ceiling. "Ethan, don't get the wrong—"

"Shut up, David," Ethan said. "You'll get your chance in a minute. Right now, this is between me and Carly."

"Where's Andrea?" Carly asked.

"Upstairs waiting for me. I told her I would be back as soon as I'd convinced you to let her go to England to live with David."

Tears of rage and betrayal filled her eyes. "You *bastard*."

Ethan answered, "We have no right to keep her from David any longer."

"No right?" David interjected. "It seems to me anyone who spends fifteen years raising a child has any right they choose."

"We can't use the time we've had with her as a weapon," Ethan said. He pointedly ignored David and focused on Carly. "It's every child's birthright to know their real father. Would you deny Andrea?"

Carly tried to see in his eyes whether he was reacting out of pain or responding to logic. She had been counting on him to fight for Andrea, not provide the means for her to leave. She put her hand to her chest. How many times could her heart break? Choking back a sob, she said, "She already knows her real father."

"We have to let her go. She'll hate us if we don't."

David put his hand out to grab Ethan's arm but pulled back before he'd made contact. "I'm going to leave you two alone," he said. "Call me when you've come to your senses."

Ethan looked at David. "If you let anything happen to her, I'll come after you myself," he said with a show of concern that didn't quite ring true.

"Damn you, Ethan," Carly said. "If you think I'm going to sit back and let this happen, you're crazy."

"If we don't let her go now, the minute she's old enough, she's going to leave anyway." Ethan crossed the room and put his arm around Carly. "It's only human nature, darling," he said with a show of compassion. "We always want what we can't have. If we make her wait until she's eighteen to be with David, we'll never get her back. Do you really want to take that chance?"

David shoved his hand in his pocket and took out his keys. "This is insane. Rational people don't turn their kids over to strangers."

Ethan sent David a triumphant look he was careful to hide from Carly. "But then you're not a stranger, are you, David? You're Andrea's *real* father."

David had no words to answer him.

8

The next morning Carly dropped Eric and Shawn off at school and headed for her mother's. She had made several attempts to talk to Andrea that morning, even taking her breakfast up to her on a tray so that they could be alone. As soon as Andrea discovered Carly had not changed her mind about letting her go to England, Carly might as well have been talking to the dog. The rest of their morning together passed in strained silence. Shawn and Eric had made several attempts to smooth the waters while sidestepping any inquiry into why those waters were troubled.

Barbara opened the door before Carly had a chance to ring the bell. "I saw you drive up," she said, taking her daughter in her arms, crushing her against her pink satin robe. She held her for long seconds before adding, "I hope what you've come here to tell me isn't as bad as the look on your face."

"It's worse, Mom."

Barbara put her arm through Carly's and led her inside. "Have you had breakfast?"

"I don't think I could keep anything down," she said. "Is Wally home?"

"He left about a half hour ago, but I can have him back here in a couple of minutes if you need him."

Carly sat down on the raised hearth and held her hands out toward the fire. "No, don't," she said. "He'll find out what's going on soon enough."

"I don't think I like the sound of that."

"I'm sorry." She clasped her hands and shoved them between her knees. "I've tried to think of an easy way to tell you this, but there isn't any."

"Then just spit it out."

Still Carly hesitated. It was as if saying the words aloud imbued them with even more power and validity. "Andrea thinks David is her father. She wants to go to England to live with him."

As if her legs would no longer support her, Barbara dropped into the chair beside the fireplace. "I saw David at Turner's Market yesterday. I had a feeling something was going on, but I had no idea it was anything like—"

"David didn't mention seeing you," Carly said.

"How in God's name did Andrea find out that Ethan wasn't her father?"

"He had too much to drink the night before last and decided to confront David. Andrea overheard them." It seemed obscene that something so life altering could take only two short sentences to tell.

"How could we have grown so complacent, so careless?" Barbara said. "We should have made plans to get you and Ethan out of town the minute we heard David was coming back."

"Hindsight isn't going to help. I have to deal with what I've got." She stood, took off her jacket, and tossed it in a chair. "This wouldn't have happened last year. Nothing could have convinced Andrea to leave then." She turned back to the fireplace and stared at the leaping flames. "She's changed. It's as if I don't know her anymore. We used to be so close."

"Part of growing up is finding out who you are.

You can't do that tied to your mother's apron strings."

"Was I like this?"

Barbara got up and put her arm around Carly's waist. "There were times when I wondered if we would ever speak a civil word to each other again."

"I don't remember . . ."

"Time has a way of doing that to us. What we were going through was natural and right for you—it was only painful for me."

"How are Andrea and I ever going to find each other again if we're four thousand miles apart?" She turned into her mother's embrace, holding her close, as if somehow her mother's strength could be absorbed through contact.

"I remember reading somewhere that it's every child's fantasy that they were adopted. It must seem terribly exciting to Andrea to be suddenly presented with a father like David Montgomery."

"She thinks she's finally discovered the reason she marches to a different drummer. I tried to talk to her this morning, but she won't have anything to do with me. In her mind, I'm the one who betrayed her. Ethan and David are innocent bystanders."

"She's just found out she isn't who she thought she was," Barbara said reasonably. "She has to blame someone. Who better than you? Besides, what girl who's been born and raised in a small town like Baxter wouldn't jump at the chance to have a father like David? He's rich and famous and lives in a castle in a magic land across the sea."

Compulsively, Barbara dug into the pocket of her robe for cigarettes she'd given up smoking two years ago. She reached up to cup her daughter's face and gave her a loving kiss. "It's no wonder you look the way you do."

Carly sat back down on the hearth. "Ethan thinks we should let her go."

"Wait a minute," Barbara said. "There's a piece missing here. I understand Ethan's part in this and I can even understand Andrea thinking it might be fun to have a celebrity father for a while, but how did you get David to agree to the subterfuge?"

"He's doing it as a favor to an old friend."

"Remember who you're talking to here. What's the real reason?"

Carly tilted her head back to look up at Barbara. "I told him the truth—or at least as much as I could."

Barbara shoved her hands into her empty pockets. "And he let it go at that? He didn't try to pump you to find out who Andrea's father really is?"

"When I said I wouldn't, that I couldn't, tell him, he let it go."

"He's still in love with you, isn't he?"

Carly shrank from her mother's gaze. "Why do you say that?"

"Because it's the only sane reason he would even consider laying claim to a child that isn't his."

There was no hiding from her. "God, I've made such a mess of things," she said. "I've put David in an impossible position. Everything depends on his going along with being Andrea's father and there isn't a reason in the world why he should."

Barbara gently stroked Carly's hair. "Stop that. You married Ethan in order to allow David to go on with his life. Even if he thinks you handled it all wrong, he can't fault your motives. If David didn't want to help you now, there's nothing on God's green earth that could make him."

"It isn't just David who's affected by this, it's his wife."

"Would you stop borrowing trouble?"

"What ever made me think Ethan would change?"

"Carly, pull yourself out of this. You did everything you could to make sure your baby would grow up in a loving family. There was no way you could have foreseen that Ethan would let David's ghost haunt you all these years."

"I've never been the wife Ethan deserved."

"Oh? And what kind of wife is that?"

Carly opened her hands in a helpless gesture. "Someone better than me."

"What you really mean is someone who loves him the way you loved David." She lowered herself on her haunches so that she could look into Carly's face. "Or should I say the way you still love him?"

Carly's eyes remained fixed on the crease in her slacks. "David was the best part of my life when I still believed in happy endings. I never would have married Ethan if I hadn't been pregnant with Andrea."

"If you hadn't been raped, you mean," Barbara said.

"It doesn't matter. What matters is that there's no way Ethan could compete."

"He knew what he was getting into when he married you. It didn't slow him down for a second. He was willing to take you any way he could get you."

"And that's supposed to make everything all right?"

"What is it with you and these guilt trips of yours? You've made a wonderful life for Ethan and the kids. They couldn't ask for more."

"Then why has my husband taken up drinking and my daughter wants to leave home to live with a man she's known less than a week?"

"Where do you fit in all this? You haven't said one thing about how you feel."

"I don't count."

"Where have I heard that one before?" Barbara said, disgust heavy in her voice. "The feminist movement really missed out on something when they didn't make that their battle cry."

Carly got up and added another log to the fire. She

used the poker to nestle the new wood into the embers, then watched to see if it would catch before closing the screen again. "I appreciate what you're trying to do, but it's not why I came here today. I need help, not my morale boosted."

"What do you want me to do?"

"Help me find a way to keep Andrea from leaving."

"You mean short of telling her David isn't her father."

"We both know why I can't do that."

"I need a little time to think about it."

Carly dropped the poker and threw her arms around her mother. "You've always been here when I needed you."

"Don't get your hopes up, sweetheart," she said. "Andrea's painted you into a tight corner. You're going to do whatever it takes to protect her, just like you always have—even if this time it means letting her go."

"How can I do that? Even if David were crazy about the idea, he has no idea what it takes to be the father of a teenage girl. His wife obviously doesn't want children of her own—what's she going to think when David presents her with a half-grown daughter who cries over rock lyrics and thinks denim is the height of fashion?" Carly could feel the tears she'd been fighting all morning burning her eyes. "What am I going to do with myself if she goes? It will break my heart if I lose her."

"Mine too," Barbara said softly.

9

David glanced at the dashboard clock on the Taurus. An hour and a half had passed without Victoria saying a word. They were only thirty minutes from Baxter and nothing had been resolved.

"We need to talk about this," he said.

"You had no right to tell that girl she could live with us without consulting me first."

"That *girl* happens to be my daughter." Jesus, what was he doing? Had he lost his mind? What was he going to do if Andrea really did come to live with them?

"Rubbish. This whole thing is a trifle too convenient for my taste." She smoothed the skirt of her Georges Rech suit in an elegant, offhand manner. "I have to tell you, David, I'm disappointed you haven't insisted on blood tests. How can you really know this child is yours?"

"I know her mother."

"What a provocative statement." She eyed him. "Would you care to interpret for me?"

"We were lovers at the time Andrea was conceived."

"And now we're supposed to believe that this

woman has waited all these years to tell you about it because—" She frowned. "I seem to have forgotten how it goes. No, wait, I have it. She wanted to be sure you were free to pursue your writing career."

David sighed wearily. "Sarcasm isn't going to get us anywhere."

"Forgive me. I've had little practice in this sort of thing. How is it I should be behaving?"

"All right," he conceded. "Maybe it's asking too much to expect you to be happy about this. I'm not so caught up in finding out I'm a father that I can't see that Andrea will probably cause some disruption in our lives, but can't you at least consider the possibility that a portion of the disruption will be positive." How could he be arguing so passionately for something that scared the hell out of him? He didn't have the first clue what it took to be the father of a fifteen-year-old.

"I don't understand how you could be so cruel. Don't you realize that having this girl in our home will be a constant reminder to me? Every time I look at her I'll see the children I lost."

David flinched. He'd never completely been able to convince himself Victoria hadn't been secretly relieved when she'd gone through two miscarriages early in their marriage. The "heartache" she suffered was the reason she gave for never trying again. "Maybe I was hoping you would see the possibilities in having her live with us."

"There you go with that conveniently selective memory of yours again. We discussed adoption, David. I haven't changed my mind. I'm quite content with things as they are. I work hard to cultivate our friends and maintain our lifestyle."

"That's hardly something I'm going to forget."

"Then how could you—"

"What in the hell did you expect me to do?" He needed a vent for his anger and frustration at being boxed in the way he had, but there was nothing, no one. Carly was beside herself with fear and Ethan wasn't worth the effort.

Victoria drew herself up into a rigid position. "Either talk to me in a civil manner, or not at all."

"I wish you had listened to me and stayed home," he said, losing his battle to control his temper.

"How convenient that would have been. What would you have done then, shown up with child in hand and presented her to me a fait accompli?

"This argument is pointless. If Andrea is going to come home with us, there are a hundred things that have to be done before we can take her out of the country."

"What do you mean 'if'?" Victoria said, jumping on the unintentional qualification. "I was under the impression her coming to live with us was already settled. Does this mean there's hope for a reprieve?"

"The only thing that's been settled is that she can come, not how or when. For all I know, she changed her mind after I left this morning. Isn't that a woman's prerogative?"

Anger radiated from her. "The choice is entirely hers? I have no say in the matter?"

"Would you at least try to understand my position? How can I tell my own daughter I have no room for her in my life?" It was more than a little disconcerting to realize how easily he'd already begun to immerse himself in the lie.

Victoria grew quiet again. Several miles had ticked off on the odometer before she turned to David. "It will be difficult to enroll her in a decent school this late in the year, but not impossible. I'm sure Anne and Richard would help if we asked."

David had known Victoria too long to be sucked in by her seeming change in attitude. "Doesn't their daughter go to school in Switzerland?" he asked conversationally.

"Yes, Aiglon. They wouldn't dream of sending her anyplace else. Think how exciting it would be for Andrea to learn to ski in the Alps. How many of her friends would be given such an opportunity? Of course, there's always Le Rosey. They would teach her to ski there, too, and I understand they're very receptive to foreign children."

David pulled off the main highway onto the road that led to Baxter. He had to hand it to her. She'd had sense enough to suggest only the best—schools that would expose Andrea to the children of kings and diplomats and the privileged of the world while providing her with credentials to help her gain entrance into the top colleges in Europe and the States. "Sorry, Victoria, but it won't work. We're not shipping Andrea off to some boarding school on the continent. It's going to be hard enough on her to leave the only home she's ever known. She sure as hell doesn't need the additional emotional burden of being dumped in a boarding school."

Victoria turned away from him to stare at the passing countryside. "Just what did you have in mind to do with her then?"

A sudden, protective feeling came over him. "There are plenty of good public schools in London." Even after living in England more than twelve years, it still gave him pause to say public schools when, in reality, they were not "public" at all, but private.

"She'll never be able to keep up in any of the really good ones. If you insist that she stay in England, she'd be better off somewhere like Millfield or my old school, Wycombe Abbey, where they can keep a close eye on her."

"How typical," he said. "You haven't even met Andrea and already you've formed an opinion. How the hell do you know what she can and can't handle?"

"I'm simply being realistic," she answered in a

placating tone, as if finally aware of the dangerous territory she'd entered. "She may be bright, but no one could expect a child raised in some provincial little town in the States to be able to compete with children who've gone to school in London their entire lives."

As much as David hated to admit it, she had a point. "We'll hire a tutor if necessary."

"For the sake of argument, let's say she is bright enough that with the help of a tutor she'll be able to keep up with her classmates. Has it even once occurred to you how difficult it will be for her to fit in socially?"

He refused to let her throw him off track, no matter how persuasive her argument. "Children adapt more easily than adults. The change might be hard on her in the beginning, but she'll work it out. I'll make sure she isn't the only American in whatever school she goes to."

"I'm surprised at you, David. It isn't her nationality that will give her problems, it's her background. You generally aren't so eager to see someone unhappy, especially not someone you profess to care about. Whether you want to admit it or not, you know I'm right about this. I shouldn't be making this fuss otherwise."

He slowed the car as he entered the outskirts of town. "What I know is that Andrea wants to live with me and I'll do whatever it takes to give her what she wants."

"And your wife be damned."

"Give it a rest, Victoria."

"Wouldn't that rather defeat the purpose of a discussion?" Before he had a chance to say anything, she added, "I will not be held down or hampered by this child of yours. The minute she gets in my way, she goes or I do."

He made a left turn into the parking lot of the

motel. "Welcome to Baxter," he said, steeling himself for the next round of confrontation.

She looked out the window and then back at him. "Is this some kind of joke? You can't seriously expect me to stay in a place like this."

"I tried to tell you not to come."

"David, this isn't funny."

"No, but it is the best motel in Baxter."

All traces of anger were gone, replaced by a look of revulsion. "Why didn't you rent a house?"

"That's not the way things work around here."

"I can't stay here—I won't."

David reached for the door handle. "There is nowhere else."

"Don't get out," she told him.

He leaned his head back against the seat and closed his eyes. "I've been here a week and nothing's happened to me. Surely you could make it through one night."

"You did this on purpose."

His eyes flew open. "Good God, Victoria, would you listen to what you're saying? How in the hell could I have arranged something like this just to pull your chain?"

Tears came to her eyes. "You could have told me."

From somewhere in the memory of the good times they'd had together came a spark of compassion. He had no more right damning Victoria for the way she'd acted than he had damning a mole for destroying a garden. "Last night you said something about our going on a trip after the memorial service. Where was it?"

She dug a handkerchief out of her purse and dabbed the corners of her eyes. "Round Hill." When he didn't immediately pick up on her answer, she added, "You know, in Jamaica. I was at a charity function with the Howards and Paul happened to mention that they were going to have to cancel their trip. He asked about you and when I told him why you weren't there, he suggested we use their reservations."

"Why don't you go there now and wait for me?"

She refolded the handkerchief and put it back in her purse. "It was supposed to be this wonderful surprise—a second honeymoon. Linda said the cottage is—"

"I'll get there as soon as I can." If gathering the necessary papers to take Andrea out of the country turned out to be half as complicated as he anticipated, he would have more than enough time to hop over to Round Hill to be with Victoria for a few days.

"And you really wouldn't mind if I missed the memorial service for your father?"

He reached over and took her hand in his. "I would feel worse having you stay someplace that made you feel this uncomfortable."

"I'm sorry, David. I did want to be here for you."

"I know you did." He adjusted himself in the seat, started the car and pulled back onto the road. A school bus drove by as they slowed for a stop sign. The thought flashed through his mind that he should look for Andrea, but he let the idea go.

Andrea took her hand down from the window and laid it back on her lap. Because it was starting to get dark, she couldn't be sure whether David had seen her or not. She wouldn't have waved at all if she'd seen that he had someone in the car with him, but the woman hadn't been visible until they had driven past. At first, because of the height of the bus to the car, she'd thought it was her mom; then she'd seen the black hair and bright blue suit in the light from the street lamp and knew it must be David's wife. Seeing him with her gave Andrea a funny feeling in her stomach.

"Was that him?" Susan Gilroy asked in a conspiratorial whisper.

Susan was Andrea's best friend and the only person outside her family who knew Andrea was planning to go to England to live with David. Afraid Susan might try to talk her out of going, Andrea hadn't intended to tell her about it until just before she left. But the field trip to the Columbus art museum had been long and boring, and not only could Andrea think about nothing else, she couldn't concentrate on what Susan was saying. Finally she'd just told Susan what was going on. They'd talked about little else since. "Uh-huh," Andrea answered softly, thoughtfully.

"Who was that with him?"

"His wife, I guess."

"She's gorgeous."

"How can you tell?" Andrea asked, instantly annoyed. "You only saw her for two seconds." She didn't want David's wife to be beautiful. She wanted her to look like her Grandma Barbara or Susan's mother—a little on the plump side and with a smile that made you feel as if you were her best friend.

"How long does it take to see something like that?" Susan crossed her legs, looked at her stockings and groaned. "This is the third pair I've ruined this week."

Brian Webster leaned forward and laid his arm along the back of the seat, his hand touching Andrea's shoulder. "If I let you see my notes on the Oriental art, can I see yours on the sculptures?"

She turned to look at him. "Will you get them back to me before first period?" Knowing Ms. Phillips, she'd pop a quiz on them about their trip the minute they got in the classroom and Andrea was already struggling to maintain a B in the class.

"I'll do better than that. I'll bring them by your house tonight."

"Tomorrow's fine," she said dismissively.

"That's okay by me," he said, shifting back in his seat.

Brian's effort to cover the hurt expression that came to his face was not lost on Susan. "Why did you do that?" she asked under her breath. "You know he likes you."

"David might come over tonight. I don't want him to get the idea I've got a boyfriend I'll be leaving behind."

"What difference would that make?"

"He might think I'll get over there and get homesick and then just want to come back."

The bus turned a corner and headed toward the high school. "You're the bravest person I know," Susan said. "There's no way I would leave here, even if I found out I wasn't related to either one of my parents. This David Montgomery guy might be your real father, but you don't know the first thing about him. What if it turns out he's weird or something?"

Andrea began to gather her belongings. "My mother wouldn't have had an affair with him if he wasn't okay."

Susan shivered. "It's gross thinking about your mom sleeping with some other guy. Doesn't it bother you?"

It was easier to ignore the question than answer it. "Do you suppose your parents would let you fly over next summer and spend some time with me?"

"No way. They're saving for us to go to Disney World."

Everyone around Susan and Andrea stood and began jockeying for position in the aisle as the bus turned into the parking lot. Andrea wished Susan hadn't told her how brave she thought she was.

In order to be really brave you had to do something dangerous.

Or stupid.

The bus pulled to a stop beside a line of waiting cars. Andrea bent down to look out the window to see who was picking her up and spotted her grandmother's bright red '65 Mustang. In another couple of weeks the car would be put up on blocks in the garage to spend the winter out of the snow and road chemicals. Until then, it was the hottest thing being driven around town. There wasn't a kid anywhere in the county who got within a year of having his driver's license who hadn't tried to buy the car from her grandmother Barbara. But the car wasn't for sale —it was in safekeeping for Andrea when she turned eighteen.

As she stepped from the bus, Andrea caught sight of her grandmother. The welcoming smile, the knowing look in her eyes, and the outstretched arms were more than Andrea could bear. She put a hand over her mouth to hold back the sob working its way up her throat. When that didn't work, she bit her lip to keep from crying out.

Barbara came forward to put her arms around Andrea and led her to the car. "Have a good time?"

Her throat too constricted to allow speech, Andrea nodded.

"I always did enjoy art museums myself," Barbara said, opening the car door and waiting until Andrea was inside. When they were safely out of the parking lot, Barbara asked, "Your place or mine?"

Andrea wiped the tears from her cheeks with the backs of her hands. "Yours," she said softly.

10

David stepped out onto the balcony of the "cottage" Victoria had rented for them—or more appropriately, he supposed, subleased for them from the Howards. Anywhere else in the world the place would have been called a villa, but here everything was low-key. Even their pool, which spilled over the cliff into the ocean, had a natural, unobtrusive feel to it.

The disappearing sun had ignited the sky, setting the clouds on fire and turning the sea into a sheet of gold. He had to admit the setting was everything Victoria had claimed, and after the cold of Ohio, the warm tropical breeze had been a welcome change. The only thing missing was the peace of mind that should have come hand in hand with such beauty.

Before leaving Ohio, he'd done everything he could to facilitate the transfer of Andrea's guardianship, discovering that the busier he kept himself, the less time he had to think about the overwhelming responsibility he'd so blithely taken on. Now it was simply a matter of waiting for the papers to make it through the courts, for Carly to gather Andrea's medical and school records, and for her passport to arrive.

After a week and a half at Round Hill by herself, Victoria had found it difficult to exchange even the most banal of civilities with him when he'd called two days ago to tell her there had been yet another delay. Yesterday he'd had to acknowledge to himself that his presence in Baxter wasn't as urgently needed as he'd tried to convince himself it was and that he couldn't move things along any faster by standing around with his hands in his pockets waiting for something to happen. It was obvious that the prudent thing to do, if he ever hoped to close the gap between Andrea and Victoria, was spend some time in Jamaica.

Montego Bay wasn't the easiest place to reach from Cleveland. He'd arrived tired and out of sorts and it was all he could do to keep his mouth shut as they drove from the city to the peninsula to the accompaniment of Victoria's endless tirade about being abandoned at the lush resort.

As was her custom, the minute she'd finished venting her anger, she was on an even keel again, as if nothing untoward had happened. Her unwillingness to let disagreements carry over for days was one of the things he found most appealing about her. She could carry a grudge, but was disinclined to sustain an argument.

Not until he'd been forced to accept the impossibility of ever getting together with Carly again, had he realized the hope of doing so had somehow survived their meeting at the mill. Not even losing her daughter to him, could make her desert Ethan and her sons. He would have to be content knowing she still loved and trusted him enough to turn Andrea over to him.

The soft fall of footsteps drew his attention. Victoria came up behind him, slipped her arms around his waist and brought her hands up to splay them across his chest. The breeze picked up traces of her Panthere perfume, surrounding him with its exotic fragrance. She pressed her lips to the middle of his back. He could feel her heat through his shirt.

"I've missed you," she said between the kisses she rained on his shoulders. "Do you realize how long it's been since we made love?"

An intense, bizarre thought gripped him. Responding to Victoria's touch made him feel as though he were indulging in an infidelity. How could that be? For Christ's sake, she was his wife.

He was even more fucked up than he'd thought.

He had to stop thinking so much.

He forced himself to relax and was startled to discover just how tense he had been. "It's been too goddamned long," he finally said, turning to look at her. She was wearing the robe he'd given her for her birthday, a thin pink thing with lace and pearls at the neck and sleeves. Only she wasn't wearing the gown that went with it. The breeze caught the material and pressed it to her skin. Three dark points formed an erotic, beckoning triangle.

A fierce hunger consumed him. He caught her to him and covered her mouth with his own, as if he meant to devour her. She responded in like, raking her hands through his hair and pulling him closer. She pressed herself hard against him, fitting her curves into his planes.

"I thought I would go out of my mind waiting for you to get here," she said, standing on tiptoe to touch her tongue to his ear. "All of those gorgeous men on the beach and the women fawning over them." She pulled his head down for another kiss.

He fumbled with the closure on her robe; when it refused to yield, he grasped either side in his hands and ripped it open. Pearls scattered across the pavement. He bent his head to her breast.

"David, you just threw away three hundred pounds," she scolded with a quick intake of breath.

It didn't surprise him that she knew the price he'd paid for her gift. He lifted her into his arms. "And it was worth every one of them."

She smiled in satisfaction. "It's been a long time since you reminded me so clearly why I married you."

He carried her into the bedroom and laid her on the bed. After hastily stripping off his own clothes and tossing them on the floor, he joined her. She wrapped her hand around his penis, opened her legs, and guided him inside.

She was wet and warm and eager, lifting her hips to meet his thrusts, catching her breath and letting it out again in pleasured sighs. He closed his eyes and drifted into the red void of sensation.

Just as he felt himself climbing the final peak, he heard a voice whisper his name. An ache went through him as he felt more than saw Carly and remembered how it had been to lie with her. Without intending that it happen, the woman under him became Carly. Making love changed from a need for release to a hunger to give. He felt Carly's name on his lips and closed them tightly against the urge to call to her.

Caught in a trap of his own making, David could only go through the motions, listening to Victoria's breathing, waiting for the quick cry that would tell him she was near climax and then kissing and stroking her until she had settled or was ready to go again.

He would match her motions and mimic her sounds and then, as soon as they were finished, take her to the pool and make love to her again. She would never know his mind and heart had been hundreds of miles away. His secret would be safe.

But for how long?

11

Andrea transferred her carry-on bag from one hand to the other while she stood next to her mother in the airport terminal and waited for her father and brothers to park the car. She'd told them that she didn't want a big deal made out of her leaving, but they'd all come to see her off anyway—all except her grandfather Wally, who had a deputy sick and had had to stay in Baxter to cover for him.

When David had returned from his week in Jamaica and discovered none of the paperwork had been completed that was needed to take Andrea to live with him in England, he'd been forced to admit that the process couldn't be rushed, and had reluctantly left for home without her. He'd offered to fly over to accompany her back as soon as everything was ready, but Andrea had refused to let him, saying it was unnecessary. After all, she wasn't a little kid who was going to get lost changing planes.

It was a day of firsts—first time she'd flown, first time she'd been away from home, first time she couldn't think of anything to say to her mother. Carly kept trying to start a conversation, but it was things like, Are you sure you packed your boots, Do you want something to read on the plane, Isn't the fresh snow pretty on the bare tree branches, when it was obvious what she really wanted to ask was, Why are you leaving your family and friends to live with someone you hardly know, and, Isn't there some way I can talk you out of going?

Maybe her mom had run out of ways to ask the same questions. Or maybe she'd just gotten tired of Andrea telling her how much she hated living with people who lied to her and how much she was looking forward to being with her real father.

In Andrea's room at night, when the house was quiet and she could hear every tick of the clock downstairs, she would think about her decision to leave home to live with a man she hardly knew and a woman she didn't know at all. She'd get so scared her heart would beat as if it were going to come right out of her chest. Then she'd think about how hard everyone was making it for her to change her mind and it would hurt so much she'd force herself to get mad so she wouldn't cry.

It was almost as if her friends actually wanted her to go, the way they kept telling her how neat England was and how much fun she was going to have. Even though her dad always said something about her trip just being a visit and how she shouldn't feel bad if she didn't like it over there and wanted to come home, he seemed excited that she was going, not sad. Shawn and Eric avoided her and didn't say much of anything until one day she just asked them right out if they thought she should go. That was when she discovered they weren't upset about her leaving, they were mad at her because she was acting as though David were a better father than the one she already had.

It seemed as if everyone wanted her to go but her mom. Not once had she said it was all right for Andrea to leave. She'd even tried laying on a guilt trip, saying how much Andrea was hurting her father by turning her back on him and how upset Shawn and Eric were that she was leaving. But Andrea didn't believe that any more than she believed her mother had told all those lies to protect her. Her mom just didn't want everyone to know that she'd been sleeping around and got caught.

And what did that make her, Andrea wondered? A mistake? Someone who had to be swept under the rug and lied about? Did you call girls bastards or just boys?

She'd never forgive her mother—not in a million years.

"Andrea? Are you all right?" Carly said, breaking the silence between them.

"Of course," Andrea told her. "Why shouldn't I be?"

"You looked so lost."

"You always say stuff like that. Anybody else would have said I looked like I was daydreaming." After a while, she added, "I was just thinking."

Carly tried to put her arm around her daughter, but Andrea moved away. "About what?"

"How neat it's going to be to spend Christmas in England," she said, knowing it would hurt her mother. Strangely, she felt none of the anticipated satisfaction when she saw that she'd succeeded.

Carly glanced over her shoulder in the direction Barbara had gone to find a rest room. "Christmas dinner won't be the same without you."

"Of course not. With me gone, you'll have to clean up the kitchen all by yourself."

Carly let out a weary sigh. "You've gotten what you want, Andrea. Can't we call a truce?"

Andrea was instantly, wildly angry. How dare her mother say she'd gotten what she wanted? None of this was Andrea's doing. She wasn't the one who'd slept with one man, married another, and then lied to the entire world about who had fathered her baby.

"You'd like that, wouldn't you?" Andrea said so loudly a man passing close by paused to see if she'd been talking to him. She lowered her voice. "You've ruined my life and you expect me to—"

Carly grabbed Andrea's arm and pulled her out of the flow of traffic. "I've heard as much as I'm going to about how I ruined your life," she said. "I don't expect you to appreciate what I went through—what I gave up to keep you—but it's about time you realized I did have a choice. *I could have had an abortion.*"

Andrea felt the blood drain from her face. "Abortion wasn't legal back then."

"That doesn't mean it wasn't available," Carly said.

"Then why didn't you?"

"Because you were mine and I wasn't going to let anyone take you from me."

Before Andrea could answer, Barbara came up to them. "I saw Andrea's flight on the monitor," she said. "Don't you think we should get her checked in?"

Andrea maneuvered her arm out of her mother's grasp. "Dad isn't here yet," she said, glad for her grandmother's presence. She was confused and scared and wished with all her heart that she could wake up from the nightmare she'd been living.

"Here he comes," Barbara said.

Ethan stopped beside Carly, put his arm around her shoulder and gave her a comforting hug. "All ready?" he said to Andrea.

She nodded and looked at Shawn. "I left something for you on my bed."

"What is it?" he asked. They were the first words he'd spoken since leaving the house.

"You'll see," she told him, forcing a smile. She turned to Eric. "Since you'll be getting my room, I didn't leave you anything extra, but there's a present for you under the tree."

"I don't want your room," he said.

"Why not? It's a lot bigger than yours."

"I don't care."

"We're leaving it just the way it is," Carly said. "For when you come home again."

It was on the tip of her tongue to say she was never coming back, but the words wouldn't come out. Her grandmother Barbara had told her that when doors were closed too tightly, sometimes they were impossible to open again. What would she do—where would she go—if David decided he didn't like having his daughter around after all?

"It's time to go," Carly said, her voice flat.

Andrea dropped her carry-on bag and hugged everyone in turn. Everyone except her mother. Carly had received permission to accompany Andrea past the passenger-only point to make sure she got off all right. They went through the baggage X ray and then down a long corridor until they found Andrea's departure gate.

As if weary of the effort it took to try to talk to her daughter, Carly remained quiet while they waited for the passengers to start boarding.

Finally, Andrea's row number was called. Her heart felt as if it were in her throat. She looked at her mother and saw that there were tears in her eyes. "Say good-bye to Muffin for me," she said, unable to turn her back and leave without saying something.

"I will," Carly told her.

"Remind Shawn and Eric to write me. They'll forget if you don't."

"I'll make sure they send a letter at least once a week."

She took her ticket out of her purse just in case she needed it when she got on the plane. "And Daddy and Grandma and Grandpa, too."

"They won't need me to remind them," Carly said gently.

"Well, I guess I'd better be going."

Carly caught Andrea's sleeve. "I love you," she said.

Andrea twisted free. "If you really loved me, you would have found a way to keep me here."

12

It *was almost* noon when Ethan pulled into the driveway at home after dropping Barbara off at her house. "You're not going to make us go to school, are you?" Eric asked.

Ethan twisted around in the seat to look at him. "What'd you have in mind?"

"I was thinking we could take in a movie."

"Maybe you should try for something a little less conspicuous," Carly said. "I'd just as soon it didn't get back to your teachers that you were out fooling around when you should have been in school."

"We could drive over to Linndale," Shawn suggested. "I like their theater better anyway."

Ethan looked at Carly. "What do you think?"

"It would probably do the three of you good to get away. The house is going to seem pretty empty for a while."

"You're not coming?"

She shook her head. "I think I'd like some time alone, if you don't mind."

Ethan put his hand over hers where it lay on the seat between them. "She's going to be all right, Carly. David will take good care of her."

She tried to smile, but it was a wasted effort. "I'm just tired," she said. "It's been a long day and it's not even half over yet."

Shawn got out and opened Carly's door for her. "She shouldn't have gone," he said softly when Carly was standing beside him.

"No, she shouldn't," Carly said as softly. "But there was no talking her out of it."

"How could she stop loving us so fast?" he asked, dropping his chin to his chest and staring at the ground.

Carly put her arms around him. "She didn't stop loving us," she said, holding him tightly, wishing she could take his pain. "She stopped loving herself. We have to give her time. One of these days, she'll come back to us."

"When?"

He pressed his face in the curve of her shoulder. She felt a sob catch in his chest. "I wish I knew," she said.

Ethan came around the car. "How about some lunch before we take off?"

Reluctantly, Carly let go of Shawn. "There's some leftover turkey in the refrigerator. I'll make sandwiches." The night before, over Andrea's protests, Carly had fixed a full Christmas dinner.

When Ethan opened the front door Muffin was there to greet them. He dutifully made the rounds, sniffing each of them in turn and pausing long enough for a pat on the head. When he'd completed his ritual, he sat on the tile floor, his head cocked, staring at the closed door. After several seconds, he looked over to Carly, barked and looked back at the door. Carly bit her lip, using one pain to divert her from the other. "Come on, Muffin," she said and bent to pick the dog up in her arms. "Let's go in the kitchen and see if we can find you a snack—something sinful and distracting."

◆   ◆   ◆

Forty-five minutes later, Carly was standing at the front door again, only this time waving good-bye to Ethan and the boys as they took off for the movie in Linndale. She stood in the doorway for several minutes after they'd gone, hugging herself against the cold, staring off into the distance.

Could it really only have been seven weeks ago she'd opened this same door and found David standing there? It seemed half a lifetime.

She felt something rub up against her leg and looked to see Muffin standing beside her. The dog let out a short, yipping cry. Carly bent and gathered him in her arms. "Don't do this to me, Muffin," she said, pressing her face against his floppy ear. "You can't possibly miss Andrea already."

She went back inside, stopped to put the dog in his favorite chair, and noticed someone had turned on the Christmas tree lights. Without conscious thought, she walked across the room to unplug the cord. As she reached around the tree, she saw that there were several presents that had not been there the night before. Curious, she sat down and began to go through them.

She should have recognized Andrea's deft hand in the wrapping even before she looked at the tags. She picked up a small round package with Eric's name on it and ran her finger across the bow. Until this year, Andrea and Carly had done their Christmas shopping together. It was as much a tradition as the holly wreath on the front door.

The Christmases Carly gave her family were steeped in tradition, each of them her own creation. Her own childhood memories of the holiday were clouded by a stiff-necked father who went to too many parties and drank too much alcohol. Instead of reading *The Night before Christmas* to his daughter every year, Frank Strong had terrorized her with stories about a righteous Santa Claus who waited until bad little girls were asleep and then sneaked into their rooms to cut off their pony tails. He never told the stories when Barbara was around and it wasn't until years after he'd died that Carly had told her mother about them. Barbara had cried.

Carly put Eric's gift back and picked up another, slipped her finger under the tag and saw Shawn's name written in Andrea's sweeping stroke.

With infinite care, Carly put the package back under the tree. She gingerly lifted the tags on the remaining presents. Andrea had remembered everyone —even her Grandmother and Grandfather Hargrove —everyone, it seemed, but Carly.

Carly was more distressed than disappointed to have been left out. To try to hurt someone purposely was such aberrant behavior for Andrea it was almost inconceivable. She felt torn. A part of her took solace in her daughter finding a release for her own torment, the mother in her agonized at the injustice of being the target.

England would only be a month or two out of their lives, a refuge for Andrea where she could come to grips with her perceived betrayal, a period of calm for Carly where she could focus on Ethan and Eric and Shawn and try to restore a semblance of normality to their lives.

She laid the last package beside the others, got up, and headed for the kitchen and the lunch dishes that still awaited her. Glancing at the clock, she did some quick calculations. Four hours had passed since Andrea's plane took off. Assuming the flight from New York had left on time, Andrea was somewhere over the Atlantic. Two takeoffs and one landing—one landing to go before she was safely on the ground again.

Carly filled the sink with hot soapy water, seeking

comfort in physical activity. The job was mindless, but it brought its own feeling of satisfaction. When the last dish had been put away and the last counter wiped, there was that brief moment as she walked out of the room when she could look back and see that in this small way, she'd made a difference.

Today, she was in desperate need of something to feel good about, no matter how inconsequential or fleeting.

Carly wandered around the empty house, looking for something to do. Finally, unable to take the confinement, she grabbed her coat and went for a walk. Thinking her direction random, she was gone an hour before she realized she was heading for the mill. She stopped and stared down the seldom-used country road. The mill beckoned to her like a warm fireplace, offering comfort and security with its benign memories. The idea was tempting. She could escape in those memories, if only for a few hours.

But was escape what she wanted?

Or was it time for her to stop wallowing in her own sorrow and move on?

She turned and headed back to town. Nearing Cindy's Café, she glanced at her watch to see whether she could stop for a cup of coffee and still beat Ethan and the boys back home. To avoid questions about where she'd been and how she'd spent her day, she would have to be there when they arrived. She hesitated, and then checked for traffic and crossed the street.

She went inside, placed her order for coffee and a piece of apple pie, and then sat down in one of the booths. A song by Garth Brooks, sad and filled with longing, filled the air.

She tried to ignore the music. Instead, she focused her attention on the waitress. When the pink-uniformed woman went into the kitchen to get the pie, Carly's gaze drifted to the regulator clock over the cash register. Andrea had been gone five hours and twenty minutes. Not so long when compared to the time she spent in school every day.

Only she came home from school.

Carly's gaze drifted from the clock to the sign that pointed to the rest rooms. Below the sign was a pay telephone mounted on the wall. An eternity seemed to pass while she stared at the telephone.

Before she could dwell on the idea too long and change her mind, Carly got up, went to the phone, and dialed the number she had memorized weeks ago. At the last minute, she charged the call to her mother's number.

David answered on the third ring.

Carly turned her face to the wall, seeking even more shelter and privacy in the out-of-the-way alcove, regretting that she hadn't waited until she'd gotten home to make the call, all the while knowing she would have talked herself out of it if she had.

"David, it's Carly," she said.

"I had a feeling it might be you."

"She's on her way."

"I'll be heading for the airport in a couple of hours."

"I thought you should know that she's confused and hurt, and that she's looking for someone to blame for what's happened to her."

"From the things she's said to me, I think she's already found someone."

"She doesn't like me very much right now." The words were squeezed past the lump in her throat.

"I'm sorry," he said. "What can I do to help?"

Carly took a breath and held it for several seconds. "Send her back to me," she said, struggling to keep her voice even. "She's everything to me, David."

"I know that."

A motion caught Carly's attention. The waitress was signaling that her coffee and pie were at the booth waiting for her. Carly nodded. "Promise me you'll do whatever it takes to get her to come home to me."

"I promise," he said.

"Thank you." She started to hang up then remembered something else. "Did the packages arrive?" She'd sneaked the small Christmas presents into Andrea's suitcases, and mailed the larger ones almost three weeks ago.

"Yesterday," he told her.

"I sent away for a sweater she saw in an Eddie Bauer catalog," she said, questioning why she was telling him, even as she spoke the words. "It arrived just after I sent everything else. It should be there in a couple of days."

"I found some things to put under the tree for her, and Victoria added some of her own when she went shopping last week. There's no way we can make this the Christmas she's used to having, but we're doing what we can."

Carly fought a surge of jealousy that made it difficult to speak. "I've tried to call Victoria several times," she said. "I wanted to tell her how much I appreciate what she's doing, but she never seems to be home."

"This is a busy time for her," David answered without apology, his voice even and accepting. "There are a lot of parties and social obligations. It's the way things are over here during the season."

He might as well have slammed a door in her face. "Well, 'over here,' no matter how heavy our social obligations, we find the time to return phone calls."

"I'm not going to try to explain Victoria to you, Carly. It would take too long and you wouldn't understand."

There it was again, that underlying snobbery that

had surfaced in their conversations before. "You'd be surprised at the things I understand. I may not be—"

"I didn't mean that the way it sounded," he said, responding to her anger. "Just because Americans and British speak what approximates the same language doesn't mean they think alike."

"And the rich really are different," she said.

"Like it or not," he said. "They are."

Carly recoiled with frustration at being on the outside of a place she'd never wanted to enter. "I don't want my daughter exposed to that kind of life."

Several seconds passed before he answered. "You should have thought of that a month ago. I can't see where you have any choice, now."

"Damn you, David," she said, furious with him for pointing out the obvious.

"How like you to thank and damn me in the same conversation."

David still knew her almost as well as she knew herself. He'd always heard the fear in her voice when others thought they heard serenity. He felt her desperation when everyone else saw acceptance. "I want her back, David."

"I'll do whatever I can," he told her. "The minute I see a sign that she's ready, I'll put her on a plane."

"Would two thank-yous cancel out one damnation?"

He laughed softly. "God, how I've missed you, Carly."

The depth of emotion in his words caught her off guard. "I've missed you too, David," she said before she could stop herself.

"Merry Christmas," he said in lieu of good-bye, then broke the connection with a soft click.

"Merry Christmas," she answered to the soft hum of an empty line. She held on to the receiver several seconds longer, before sighing and putting it back on its hook. Her coffee was probably cold by now and the ice cream on her pie melted. Still, they were a reason to delay the lonely walk back home.

At the booth, she took one look at the pie and knew it was useless to try getting it down. She laid five dollars on the table, gave the waitress an apologetic smile, and left.

Large, quarter-size snowflakes were falling from a gray sky when Carly arrived home. The station wagon was in the driveway and someone had turned the Christmas lights on again. She stopped a moment to take it all in. To the casual observer, the scene would appear idyllic—a home, a family to envy.

Her feet made soft crunching sounds in the fresh snow as she moved up the walkway to the front door. She pulled her knit hat off, shook it, and scraped her boots on the mat. Unable to put off going inside any longer, she opened the door.

"I'm home," she called out.

Ethan answered from the family room. "Where've you been?"

"I went for a walk and lost track of time." She went to the closet and hung up her coat. "I hope I didn't worry you."

He came up behind her, moved her hair from her shoulder, and lightly kissed her neck. "I was an hour away from even being concerned."

She closed the door and eased out of his reach. "Where are the kids?"

"I sent them over to your mom's."

"Why?"

"I figured we could use some time alone." He ran his hand down her arm. "I've missed you."

She couldn't believe what she was hearing. How could Ethan possibly think she was ready to focus her attention on him when she'd just put Andrea on the plane that morning? Was he so blind he couldn't see the pain she was in? "I've missed you too, Ethan," she said, sidestepping a confrontation.

"I was hoping you'd say that."

"I've had a lot on my mind lately." She saw by the look in his eye that he hadn't picked up on the sarcasm in her voice.

He moved to put his arms around her. "That's all going to change now." His lips brushed her hair. "I don't want you to take this the wrong way, Carly, but I've come to the conclusion that once we all get over the shock of Andrea being gone, we're going to find—"

She stiffened and tried to pull away from him. "Be careful what you say, Ethan."

He refused to let her go, hanging on to her arms and forcing her to look at him. "Would you just let me finish?"

"I don't want to hear anything bad about Andrea."

"No, you never do."

"For Christ's sake, *she's gone.* Isn't that enough? Do we still have to fight about her?"

"That's what I was going to say. Don't you see? Without Andrea here, we have a chance to turn our marriage into what it should be. She's been a wedge between us from the very beginning. I'm not saying it was her fault," he quickly added. "She was as much a victim in this as we were."

Carly blinked. He'd conveniently forgotten that without Andrea, there never would have been an Ethan and Carly. "Victim?" Carly said.

"Of circumstance."

She couldn't argue with him. Andrea might have been a wedge between them, but in the beginning at least, she'd also been the glue. Until Shawn and Eric. Ethan had been so clever, and so right about binding her to him with children. "And now that she's out of the way you think we'll be much happier? Is that it?"

"Be honest, Carly. Andrea is what's kept us from being as close as we could be. She's been a constant, daily reminder of David and the fact that your relationship with him was never brought to a satisfactory conclusion."

"And you think that's changed?"

"Hasn't it? It's obvious he doesn't love you anymore. And now that I've seen the two of you together, I can finally let myself believe you no longer have feelings for him." He took her arms and put them on his shoulders then slipped his own around her waist. "We're free, Carly. We can start living the way we should have been living all along—if I just hadn't been so goddamned blind to what you were trying to tell me."

A hysterical bubble of laughter worked its way up her throat. He really believed what he was saying. The entire time David had been in Baxter, Carly had lived in fear that Ethan would pick up on the feelings that were passing between her and David. Some of the unguarded looks David had given her were more intimate than anything that had ever happened between her and Ethan. How could he have missed seeing them?

Her impulse was to leave, to find a quiet place where she could sort through the events of the past month and a half. With time and distance the unthinkable would become familiar and then, finally, tolerable. When that happened, she would be able to function as a wife and mother again, playing her role with the same expertise she had before, being everything to everyone while she patiently waited for her daughter to forgive her and come home. But instead, she laid her cheek against his shoulder, feeling more alone than she had the night they were married. They had lived together sixteen years and were strangers.

"I love you, Carly," Ethan said, tilting her chin up and kissing her.

"I know you do, Ethan." In time she would be able to say the words back to him again, but not now, not yet. First she had to find a way to forgive him for not loving Andrea enough to want her to stay.

He grabbed the bottom of her sweater and pulled it over her head. His mouth moved over the swell of her breasts in hot, hungry kisses. "I want you," he murmured. "Don't put me off, Carly. Not again."

Tears burned the back of her closed eyes. "Not here," she said. "Upstairs."

He let out a groan as he covered her mouth with his own and thrust his tongue past her teeth. He kissed her chin and then her throat. "It's going to be better than it's ever been," he told her, his voice ragged.

With no words to answer him, she silently took his hand and led him to the stairs. She would get through this, she told herself as they entered the bedroom.

With the skill that had come from years of practice, Ethan stripped her, laid her on the bed, performed what had become the almost ritualistic movements meant to arouse her, separated her legs, and thrust himself inside.

Carly cried out at precisely the right moment and seconds later it was finished. Several seconds after that, Ethan rolled off of her. When his breathing had calmed, he kissed her on the temple and said, "This was only the beginning. It's just going to get better and better from here on out."

"When are the boys coming home?" she asked.

Misinterpreting her meaning, he turned to her and smiled. "Not for hours yet."

She caught her breath at his look of unadulterated happiness. Against her will she was reminded of the joyful young man Ethan had once been—before he'd married her and taken her troubles as his own. She didn't want to feel sorry for him, she wanted to hold on to her anger. But the harder she tried, the more elusive it became.

How could she hate him for loving her?

How could she not?

13

Juggling fear, anxiety, and a case of homesickness that had hit the minute clouds covered her last glimpse of Ohio, Andrea stepped from the plane at Heathrow Airport. She walked through an enclosed ramp and entered a huge hall with moving walkways. Confused and all but overwhelmed by the rush of people around her, she stepped out of the mainstream of traffic and tried to get her bearings. She'd forgotten the information David had given her over the phone about what she would have to do to get from the plane to where he would be waiting for her.

While Andrea moved through long serpentine lines of people, she tried to overhear what kinds of questions were being asked by the officials, but she was too far away. What if they wanted to know about her mother and David? How would she answer them?

After retrieving her luggage and going through customs, she rejoined the ever-flowing stream of passengers and headed up the ramp, turned a corner, and ran into a wall of people. They glanced at her, found her wanting, and looked away.

She slowed her pace to sweep the crowd, searching the eager, smiling faces for one that looked familiar.

David wasn't there.

Her heart slammed against her ribs. Could he have forgotten she was coming today? Had he changed his mind and decided he didn't want her living with him after all?

David saw the stricken look on Andrea's face and renewed his efforts to get to her, roughly shouldering a portly man out of his way and stepping in front of a woman with her arms outstretched to welcome a man who'd arrived seconds before Andrea.

"Andrea," he called, trying to draw her attention.

She turned at the sound of her name. "David?"

"Over here." He raised his hand.

Relief flooded her face. She started toward him. "I forgot where you said you'd meet me."

The thought crossed his mind that he should hug her, but he was unsure how she might feel at the familiarity. Instead he offered her a smile he hoped expressed his pleasure in seeing her and reached for her suitcases. "I'd hoped to get a spot where you'd see me right away, but there was an accident on the M4 that held us up and I didn't get here as soon as I'd planned."

Andrea looked around expectantly "Did Victoria come with you?"

She'd tried to make the question sound casual, but David could see how anxious she was about finally meeting the woman she would be living with. "The 'we' I was referring to was my driver," he said, making his way through the crowd. He glanced at his watch. "It's nearly eleven. I'm sure Victoria has been in bed for hours by now." The explanation felt lacking. "Christmas is a particularly busy time of the year for her," he went on. "With all her social and charitable obligations, she has to catch up on her sleep whenever she can." He should have stopped while he was ahead. Not only had he put Victoria's soirées ahead of meeting Andrea, he'd put her need for sleep there, too. "I'm lucky if I see her at the breakfast table," he concluded, making one last attempt.

"Oh," Andrea said.

There was a myriad of meanings in the single word and the way Andrea had said it. He turned and gave her a conspiratorial wink. "You'll be pleased to know she's set tomorrow morning aside just for us."

Andrea offered him a tentative smile. "I'm looking forward to meeting her."

David almost laughed aloud at the contrast between her words and the look on her face. Andrea was clearly no more eager to meet Victoria than Victoria was to meet her. He stopped to let a woman with a stroller pass in front of him. "She's nothing like your mother, but once the two of you get to know each other, I'm sure you'll do fine."

"She doesn't want me here, does she?" Andrea said, following him outside into the freezing night air.

David hadn't been gone from the States so long that he was taken aback by Andrea's American bluntness. What surprised him was her acumen. "What makes you say that?" he asked.

"It's just a feeling I get."

"She needs a little time to get used to the idea of having you around." *As do I*, he could have added. He moved toward the car. As soon as the chauffeur spotted David coming, he got out to greet them. "Andrea, this is Harold Duncan, the best driver in London, and a man who will soon to be as indispensable to you as he is to me." In a spontaneous gesture that surprised David as much as it surprised Andrea, David slipped his arm around her shoulders. He would have to remember to go with his instincts from then on and let propriety be damned. "Harold, this is my beautiful, almost grown daughter, Andrea."

"I'm most pleased to meet you," Harold said, with a slight bow.

"I'm pleased to meet you, too," she said, extending her hand, but careful not to move so much she dislodged David's arm in the process. "Especially since I'm not old enough to drive myself yet."

He smiled indulgently. "I think you'll find me useful a bit past the day you've got your license. Even for the stout-hearted, London traffic can take some getting used to."

David laughed. "I've been here thirteen years and I'm still not used to it."

Harold picked up Andrea's bags and put them in the trunk. When he was finished, he came around the side and opened the door for her and David. "When you think you're ready to give it a go, we'll take you outside the city for your lessons."

Andrea looked to David for confirmation. "If you aren't afraid of some snow and ice, you could start next week," he said. "We'll be spending Christmas at Hawthorne. There are back roads on the property where you and Harold can slip and slide to your heart's content."

She climbed inside and scooted over for David to sit next to her. "I hope you have another car—something a little smaller than this?"

He hesitated at telling her the "other cars" were a Porsche and a Mercedes. "I think we could probably find something."

Andrea looked around the interior. "What is this thing, anyway?"

He chuckled. "It's called a Bentley. Not much to look at, I admit, but it'll grow on you once you get used to it."

"The only thing I ever had grow on me was a wart."

This time it was Harold who chuckled. Refraining from commenting on her remark, he said, "Home, sir?"

"Unless Andrea would like to stop for something to eat."

"Gosh, no. It seemed like they never stopped feeding us on the plane. I must have had ten Cokes."

"Then home it is."

They were on the M4 and Andrea had been quietly staring out the window for several miles when David decided to begin laying the groundwork for her eventual return home. "I talked to your mother earlier today."

Andrea didn't move. "Why?"

"She called to tell me how angry you were when you left."

"I was mad at her, not you."

David let several seconds pass before he went on. "It seems to me you've directed your anger at the wrong person."

She turned to look at him. A frown drew her softly arched eyebrows together. "Meaning I should be mad at you? How could I? You didn't even know I existed."

"I should have figured out what happened— maybe not at first, I wasn't thinking too well back then. But a lot of years have gone by since your mother and I last saw each other."

"All that means is that you didn't know her as well as you thought you did."

This time it was David's turn to look out the window. "How much has she told you about me, about the years we were together?"

"Hardly anything."

He took a deep breath. Should he tell her everything, or only what she needed to know to heal herself and return home? "Carly and I have known each other since we were little kids. She and Ethan were my best friends the entire time we were growing up. But it was Carly who knew me the best, better than anyone ever has—or will. If I hadn't been so caught up in my own problems when I was in New York, she never would have been able to—" He stumbled on the words, wondering if he would ever come to terms with the what-ifs and if-onlys that had been plaguing him lately. "Let's just say she would never have married Ethan."

"Are you telling me she didn't love my dad when she married him?"

He'd gone too far to back down now. "She loved him as a friend. She would have done anything for him—and he would have done anything for her."

Andrea cast a nervous glance at Harold. "You mean like him marrying her because she got herself pregnant," she said softly.

"Andrea, no one gets *herself* pregnant," he said with a touch of impatience. "It takes two."

"She should have been more careful."

It was on the tip of his tongue to say, "Accidents happen" when he realized how callous it would sound. No one wanted to think of herself as an accident. The only thing worse would be to know she was the result of rape. "If she had taken better precautions, you wouldn't be here now. Frankly, even taking into consideration my feelings about missing out on my daughter's life up until now"—the lie just kept getting easier and easier—"the heartache your mother has gone through, and the pain you're in right now, I can't say I'm sorry this has turned out the way it has."

"She should have told you the minute she found out she was pregnant. You had a right to know."

He'd lost count of the number of times the same

thought had gone through his mind in the past two months, only in a slightly altered form.

David struggled to find a way to help Andrea understand what he was still trying to work out for himself. "What would you do if someone told you that your brother, Eric, was going to break his leg in such a way he would never be able to play basketball again, but that you could keep it from happening if you were willing to have the broken leg for him?"

"That's not a fair question."

"Why not?"

"Eric loves basketball more than anything."

"Exactly," he said, pleased that she had caught on so quickly. "Your mother knew that was how I felt about writing."

"You can't compare the two. Lots of writers are married and have children."

She had him there. "At one time or another, all of us are put in positions where we end up making the wrong choices for the right reasons. What your mother did wasn't easy for her, Andrea. Her decision to push me away wasn't made lightly." He couldn't convince her without telling her things that would cause more pain. "Carly loved me every bit as much as I loved her—probably more. I don't think I've ever done anything so selfless. She sacrificed a great deal for me."

"You're making her sound like some kind of saint."

"And you're not buying it," he said, keenly disappointed to discover he hadn't gotten through to her after all.

"She didn't have to marry my dad. There were other things she could have done."

"Like what?" he asked, beginning to lose his patience.

"She could have put me up for adoption."

"Do you think your life would have been better if she had?" he asked.

Her lip quivered as she answered. "I don't know."

"Did you ever hear that old saying, don't judge someone until you've walked a mile in their shoes?"

She shook her head and pressed her shoulder deeper into the corner.

"Other than Carly herself, you and I were the most affected by her decision to marry Ethan. Unless there were some way we could actually go back and *be* her, unless we could feel what she was feeling, we have no right to sit in judgment on her, especially not sixteen years after the fact." He reached across the seat and gently touched her arm. "Think about it, Andrea. She was only five years older than you are right now when all of this happened. She was in an impossible position. There was no clear-cut answer, no way to keep someone from being hurt. So she did what she'd been doing all her life—she took care of the people she loved in the best way she knew how."

Somewhere in the telling, he'd lost track of whose pain he was trying to lessen, his own or Andrea's. An easy silence grew between them. As they entered central London, the only sound in the car was the steady click of the windshield wipers as they brushed away the lightly falling snow.

"My dad doesn't want me to come back," Andrea said, breaking the silence.

He tilted his head back and looked up at the ceiling. "What gave you that idea?" he asked evenly, not wanting her to hear how upset he was. It didn't matter whether there was any basis for feeling the way she did. In something so close to the heart, the imagined was as hurtful as the real.

"He told me so."

She'd spoken so softly, the words were so devastating, he tried to convince himself she hadn't said what he thought he'd heard. "What did you say?"

"When he came to my room to get me up this morning, he said he was sorry how everything had worked out." She stopped to take a deep breath, as if fortifying herself for what would come next. "Then he told me he'd spent a lot of time thinking about me going to England to live with you, and that he'd decided it was the best thing for all of us—I would be happier here and the four of them could become a real family."

A rage surged through David, stealing his vision, his reasoning. He sat perfectly still, knowing if he moved or said anything before he regained control, he would frighten Andrea with his anger.

After several long seconds, he managed to say, "Does your mother know about this?"

"I don't think so." She hesitated. "No, I'm sure. She would have said something."

"I don't know what to say to you."

"That's okay. I was just afraid I would get here and find out that you'd decided you didn't want me, either."

Ethan had put him in an impossible position. How in the hell was he supposed to do as Carly had asked and encourage Andrea to return home as soon as possible without making her feel as if he was trying to get rid of her? He leaned over and pressed a kiss to the top of her head. "And here I was afraid you'd decide not come at all."

She looked up at him. "Really?"

Everything between them was based on a lie. It was time for some honesty. "I don't kid myself that you're here because you have this burning desire to get to know me. You were looking for a way to hurt your mother and it got out of hand. With all the time it took to get the necessary papers for you to come here, I really believed the two of you would find a way to work things out."

"You must think I'm a real bitch."

"What I think is that you're your mother's daughter. I never knew anyone more stubborn." He chuckled. "Until I met you, that is."

"And still you let me come," she said, as much to herself as to him.

"How else was I going to get to know you?"

She thought about that for a minute. "Then I can stay for a while?"

"You can stay as long as you want," he told her, feeling a twinge of guilt for not following through on his promise to Carly, but trying in some small way to make up for Ethan's callousness.

Andrea grew quiet and thoughtful again. After several more blocks, she said, "Maybe after a while, my dad will miss me and want me to come home."

David had never hated Ethan more than he did at that moment.

14

Andrea opened the door to the bedroom David had given her the night before and stepped into the hallway. She'd drifted in and out of sleep when she'd first gone to bed, but had become wide awake at three o'clock and had stayed that way since. Had she not been afraid of running into Victoria, she would have gotten up and wandered around the house.

She'd never seen a house like this one, not even in magazines. The few rooms she and David had walked through when they arrived last night were filled to overflowing with old furniture. There were heavy curtains at the windows and gaudy oriental rugs on the floors. It was like walking through an antique store—not quite as crowded, but close. When he'd taken her to her room, David had promised a full guided tour of the rest of the house in the morning. Andrea had her fingers crossed that the rooms she'd seen were for show and that the rest of the house would be a little more modern, like within the last century.

She'd noticed some Christmas things sitting around the rooms she'd seen, but nothing compared to the way her mother decorated for the holidays.

Here, the focus was the tree in the living room. It stood in front of an enormous window, and was pretty enough, but in a department-store kind of way, with just enough ornaments and gold bows to let you know it wasn't really some overgrown house plant.

All of the presents were wrapped alike—gold foil paper and green velvet bows—except for a small group set out of the way behind a chair. Andrea guessed right away that they were from her mother. Short of actually pointing them out to her, David had done everything he could to make sure she'd seen them.

As soon as he'd helped her put her suitcases in the room where she'd be staying, David had insisted she call home to let everyone know she'd arrived safely. She had tried to talk him into letting her wait until morning, but he'd refused, saying her mom would spend the night worrying if she didn't get a call.

Shawn had answered the phone on the second ring. "Hey, it's about time," he'd scolded.

"It's a long way from the airport to David's house," she told him, hoping he'd let it go at that.

"So, how is it there?"

"I haven't had a chance to see anything yet. It was dark when the plane landed."

"What's *she* like?"

She lowered her voice. "I haven't seen her yet, either."

"We went to the show today."

"What'd you see?"

"*Die Hard*. I thought it was stupid. Dad and Eric loved it."

His effort to sound normal, as if she were spending the night at a friend's house instead of having moved thousands of miles away, let her know he wasn't mad at her anymore. Or at least not as mad as he had been that morning. "What did Mom think?"

"She didn't go." He paused. "Hold on. I'll get her for you. She just went out to get some more wood for the fire."

"Don't bother," she said quickly. And then, "Just tell her I'm okay and I'll call again in a couple of days."

"She's going to kill me if I don't get her, Andrea. She's been driving everybody crazy waiting for you to call. Eric about got his head bit off for not telling her he'd been using the phone in your room."

"I've got to go. David is waiting for me."

She'd said good-bye and hung up before he could say anything else. Now, she was sorry she hadn't at least said hello to her mother—not because it might have hurt her feelings, but because David was sure to ask what Carly had to say and Andrea didn't want to admit she hadn't talked to her.

She took a couple of steps down the hallway, stopped, and looked around. Nothing seemed familiar. The picture facing her was of a dog and a little girl in a long dress. She was sure it wasn't the one she'd seen last night. She turned around and peered at the painting at the opposite end of the hall. This one was of a squatty dog with a ball in its mouth. It didn't seem familiar, either. Her gaze swept the paintings lining both walls. They were all of dogs, every kind imaginable.

She was staring at one particularly ugly example when she heard footsteps coming toward her. As if caught in the act of doing something she shouldn't, Andrea stared at the ornate ceiling and stuffed her hands in the pockets of her jeans.

A tall, thin woman with shoulder-length black hair came around the corner. She was dressed in a dark gray suit, white blouse, and black heels and looked a lot like the way Andrea had imagined someone rich and royal might look.

The woman pulled up short and gave Andrea a

look of disapproval. The look was quickly modified with a tight smile. "Did I startle you?"

"I was just looking at the pictures."

"The one in front of you is a Benson."

Andrea frowned. "I thought it was a bulldog."

"The painter's name is Benson," Victoria said with an air of indulgence.

"Oh," was all Andrea could think to say. She couldn't remember ever having felt quite so stupid. "My mother used to paint. Only she did watercolors."

There was a pause and another smile, only this one was small and private. "That explains David's interest in the medium." She came forward, her hand extended. "I'm sure you've already figured out who I am for yourself, but that's no excuse for bad manners. Victoria Montgomery—your father's wife."

Andrea placed her hand in Victoria's. "Andrea Hargrove," she said.

"I'm pleased to see that you're up. I wanted to go over your wardrobe with you. There are three parties here in London that you will be expected to attend with your father and myself before you leave with him next week for Christmas at Hawthorne. When I talked to him this morning, he said that he'd neglected to mention them to you, and that chances were you had not packed anything appropriate."

She breezed past Andrea and into the bedroom. Andrea followed, saying a silent prayer of thanks that she'd had the foresight to make her bed as soon as she'd gotten up. Before Andrea could say anything, Victoria opened the cupboard where David had told her she could put her clothes. It was empty. "I haven't unpacked yet," Andrea said. "I was going to do it after breakfast."

A look of impatience was followed by, "Then why don't you just show me a few of the things you brought with you and I'll decide what you might need to fill in?"

Andrea opened her suitcase, took out several dresses, her best wool slacks, and the emerald green cashmere sweater her grandmother Barbara had given her for her birthday.

Victoria sighed. "They're all lovely," she said dismissively. "But don't you have anything suitable for special occasions?"

"We don't dress up much in Baxter." Andrea nearly groaned aloud. She sounded like some backwoods farm girl. She might as well stick her toe in the carpet and add an "aw shucks."

"Well, I can see we have our work cut out for us," Victoria said crisply, either not picking up on what Andrea considered a country bumpkin statement or showing no surprise because it was exactly what she'd expected. "I'll set up appointments for you to get what you need this afternoon—as soon as you and David are finished visiting the school he's chosen for you and you've gotten that business out of the way. We don't have much time, so try to select things that can be altered with a minimum of fuss." She turned and headed for the door. "I'll make up a list of what you'll need, where to go and who to see and give it to Harold before I leave this morning." Almost as an afterthought she added, "I suppose you might as well be fitted for your school uniforms while you're out and about. No sense putting it off."

Andrea started after her. "Won't you be going with me?"

"Whatever for?"

"To make sure I buy the right things," she said, torn between fear of being turned loose on her own and fear of having to be in Victoria's company all day.

"The clerks you'll be seeing will take care of that."

Not knowing what else to say or do, Andrea followed Victoria downstairs. David was waiting in the dining room. He got up when he spotted them.

"How did you sleep?" he asked, coming around the table to give each of them a kiss on the cheek.

As if summoned by a secret signal, a woman in a black-and-white uniform appeared, carrying a tray. She gave Andrea and David a plate of scrambled eggs and sausage and Victoria a half grapefruit.

"Tea?" he said.

Andrea shook her head. She hated her eggs scrambled. "Is there any coffee?"

David pushed back his chair and started to get up. "I forgot to ask you what you eat for breakfast, and when Mrs. Rankin asked, I told her just to fix double whatever she was making for me." He started toward the kitchen. "You'll have to fill her in on your eating habits later today."

Victoria returned her cup to its saucer with a loud clink. "David, would you please stay at the table. I'm sure Andrea can do without coffee this one morning."

"It will only take a second," he said, disappearing into the kitchen.

Victoria turned to Andrea. "Your father seems intent on indulging you," she said with a sigh.

Andrea swallowed. What was she supposed to say to something like that? "I'm sorry. I didn't mean to interrupt his breakfast."

"Of course you didn't. That's not what I meant at all." Finally there was a genuine smile. "I'm afraid we'll have to give David a bit of leeway the next few weeks, at least until he's convinced you aren't going to hop on the next plane home and abandon him." She stared at her grapefruit for several seconds before going on. "I'm sure it won't come as any great surprise if I tell you that, in the beginning, I was against your coming to live with us. But then I saw how happy the prospect of your being here made David and I was forced to rethink my position."

Now Andrea really didn't know what to say.

"With a minimum of effort on both of our parts," Victoria went on, "we should be able to stay nicely out of each other's way."

If Andrea had been hoping for more, Victoria plainly had not. It was obvious she believed she'd gone further than called for in making her husband's daughter welcome. "I'll try," Andrea told her.

"I'm pleased to hear it," she said with a slight nod.

David came back into the room. "The coffee will be here in a minute," he said and smiled.

Andrea returned his smile, picked up her fork, and took a bite of sausage.

It was awful.

15

Carly gathered the last of the stray pieces of wrapping paper and ribbon left over from the morning of opening Christmas presents and stuffed them into a trash bag. Her hands were trembling from a mixture of fatigue, frustration, sorrow, and repressed anger. She had to make several attempts to get the twister wrapped around the top of the bag.

Ethan had been outside with Shawn and Eric for the past hour and a half, all of them trying out their new cross-country skis. Eric had made a halfhearted attempt to get her to join them, but she'd begged off, saying if she didn't get the turkey in the oven, they wouldn't be eating until midnight. He hadn't pushed, just given her a quick kiss and a quiet, "It wasn't the same without Andrea, huh?" before he headed out the door.

For days the muscles in her throat had ached from the effort to hold back tears. She'd been so sure Andrea wouldn't be able to stay away for Christmas. When she'd gotten out of bed that morning, and it had seemed as if her grief would choke her, she'd stepped into the shower and finally let go of some of the pent-up heartache. The rest of the morning had been spent with a stuffed-up nose and a raging headache.

Since the day they'd all seen Andrea off at the airport, Barbara had shadowed Carly, popping up with small surprises at unexpected times of the day, calling first thing in the morning and insisting Carly accompany her shopping, sending Wally by in the patrol car to check on her in the afternoon.

Barbara and Wally were more than shoulders to lean on, they were the only ones Carly could really talk to about Andrea. At home, it didn't matter whether it was Carly or the boys who mentioned Andrea's name, the effect was the same. Ethan would immediately get up and leave the room, a look of sadness about him that gave Carly pause. It didn't take long for Shawn and Eric to catch on that they were not to talk about their sister when their father was around.

Instead of Shawn and Eric coming to Carly with their questions and feelings of abandonment, it was as if Andrea's leaving had left a gap they were each trying to fill in isolation. Eventually, anger became their weapon against sorrow. Carly could see little else to do but wait them out. Shawn and Eric were loving and forgiving people. They only needed for their pain to ease a little to rediscover the ties that bound them to their sister.

Ethan was another matter. He would not allow himself to miss Andrea until he saw that her leaving was not the path to the marital bliss he envisioned.

The doorbell rang, startling Carly and yanking her back to the present. She ran her hand through her hair and tucked a strand behind her ear as she headed for the door. Wanda Starling, her next-door neighbor, greeted her with a beaming grin.

"Merry Christmas," Carly said, shivering at the cold blast of air. She moved out of the doorway. "Come in before you freeze to death out there."

"I can't stay," Wanda said, stamping the snow from her boots before stepping inside. "I just wanted to give you this." She handed Carly a homemade fruitcake wrapped in cellophane and topped with a sprig of evergreen. "And this," she said, reaching inside her coat and withdrawing a large, plump envelope. "The courier service delivered it to our house by mistake yesterday and Ed signed for it without even looking to see who it belonged to. You'd think we get this kind of thing all the time. Anyway, wouldn't you know, he forgot to tell me about it until this morning. I hope it's nothing important."

Carly's heart skipped a beat as she set the fruitcake on the hall table and took the envelope. The return address said London. "Thank you," she said.

"From Andrea?"

Carly nodded.

"Well, isn't that nice. I'll bet Christmas morning just wasn't the same without her. Too bad she couldn't have waited until the holidays were over before taking off to live with her new father, but then that's so typical of this generation. They don't know what it's like to wait for anything. Instant gratification, that's what it's all about."

Carly was frantic to open the letter. Other than the phone call when Andrea had arrived two weeks ago, it was the first communication they'd had from her. Carly had sent two letters, long, rambling missives filled with bits of gossip and news of home. She'd started each of them on a Sunday, written something every day, and then mailed them on the following Saturday. "Would you like a cup of coffee?" Carly asked, silently praying Wanda would decline.

"Thanks, but I've still got a couple of pies to make."

"I appreciate you taking the time to run this over." And then, as an afterthought, "The boys will be especially happy to see the fruitcake. I didn't get much baking done this year."

"That's not surprising, what with all you've had on your mind." She stepped outside and turned for one last thought. "If you ever need someone to talk to, Carly, I'm just next door."

"I'll remember," she said.

"Merry Christmas."

"To you, too," Carly said, for the first time that day believing it was possible.

As she closed the door, she was torn between waiting for Ethan and the boys to come inside or reading it right away, while she could do so in privacy. It didn't take long to decide. She ran her finger along the flap on her way into the family room.

Inside was a letter along with a flat, soft package wrapped in Christmas paper and tied with a silver ribbon. Carly ignored the present and studied Andrea's handwriting on the letter. She took note of the uncanceled stamps and looked again on the outside of the courier package. David had made out the bill of lading. Plainly Andrea had intended to send the letter surface mail and David had been the one who arranged for it to arrive sooner.

Being careful not to destroy the perfectly good stamps, Carly opened the envelope and unfolded the two sheets of crisp parchment stationery.

Dear Mom and Dad and Shawn and Eric,

It seemed like the plane ride over would last forever but I finally got here and I haven't stopped doing things since. I've only been here nine days and already I've gone to three parties, seen the Tower of London, Big Ben, and Harrods department store. (We don't shop there— Victoria thinks there are too many tourists—but it was fun to see anyway. It's HUGE!) David told me there would be lots of royal people at the parties, but I didn't see any of them. Or if I did, I didn't notice.

Oh, by the way, Mom, you can stop worrying about Victoria. She's being really nice to me. The first day I was here, she bought me all new clothes. She was worried I wouldn't fit in if I wasn't dressed like everyone else. Which meant no jeans and sweaters, but really expensive stuff, like leather skirts and matching jackets and silk blouses and a really neat coat called a Barbour Thornproof to wear when we're in the country. I also had to get a whole bunch of uniforms for the school I'll be going to—including, if you can believe this, a really dumb-looking straw hat.

Shawn and Eric, you wouldn't believe what the school is like. It's at least a thousand years old and it's all girls—I suppose you'd like that, but I'm not so sure I will. David said he looked at a bunch of schools, but liked this one the best because it has the most American kids and it wouldn't be so hard for me to get to know everyone.

School is really different here. Everyone takes a big test when they're sixteen, and if you don't want to keep on going, you don't have to. (Victoria said that's what Princess Di did, so it's not like you're considered a dropout or anything.) If you do go on, you only take three subjects (David says I should try to take a language, too, if I think I can handle it) and then you graduate at eighteen. College is only three years over here unless you decide to do something that takes longer, like being a doctor. I like that.

Carly felt as if a cold hand had been laid against her spine. The letter was light and breezy and completely out of sync with the turmoil that was really going on in Andrea's life. And why had David gone to such lengths to find just the right school for Andrea when the whole idea was to get her to come home as quickly as possible?

Tomorrow is David's birthday. Victoria is having a big party for him with lots of famous people. As soon as it's over, we're going to Hawthorne—me and David, that is. Victoria is spending Christmas in London this year because she has to do something with her parents on Christmas Eve. David said he wants to take me to Hawthorne (for some strange reason, people here give their houses names) because it's prettier there and he doesn't think I'd have as good a time if we stayed here. We won't be spending the day alone, though. He's arranged for us to have dinner with some really good friends of his. We'll take all the presents to the country with us so there will be something to open on Christmas morning. You should see how many have my name on them. (Did you find the ones I left under the tree for you?)

I won't get to practice driving this trip because Harold has to stay in London to take Victoria around and to be with his family, but David promised that if Harold doesn't come next time, he'll teach me how to drive the Mercedes himself.

A log fell forward in the fireplace behind Carly. She got up to push it back and to check that no sparks had escaped through the screen. The activity provided enough break to let Andrea's words hit with their full impact.

What in God's name were Shawn and Eric going to think when they read their sister's letter? New clothes, parties, a country home, learning to drive in a Mercedes? Carly couldn't decide how much of what Andrea was reporting was calculated, and how much ingenuous.

Either way, it was hard to keep her anger in check.

Dad, you wouldn't believe what the streets are like over here. As much as you hate driving in a city like Cleveland, you'd go crazy trying to find your way around London. The streets change names right in the middle, and not just once or twice, but lots of times. Even when I learn to drive, David said he won't let me have a car in London. He's going to teach me how to use the Underground to get back and forth to school when Harold can't take me in the Bentley.

I've got to go now. David is taking me to see *Les Miserables*. Since I want to be an actor someday, he thinks it's a good idea for me to see some really good plays and musicals, and since all of the best ones are coming from here now, I'll get a chance to see them before they get to the States.

Give Muffin a big hug and tell her I miss her,
Andrea

Carly closed her eyes against the outrage that gripped her. All of Andrea's love and affection sent to the dog, and none for her family. She refolded the letter and stuffed it in the pocket of her slacks, no longer wondering whether or not Andrea was still striking out. Not for a minute did Carly question that everything Andrea wrote was true; the doubt entered over the breezy enjoyment.

She decided not to show the letter to Ethan right away. He wouldn't read between the lines and see the lonely, frightened girl behind the bravado. Instead, he would joyfully point out how obviously happy and well-adjusted Andrea was in her new home already and how wise they had been to let her go.

Shawn and Eric would be jealous and hurt and not understand either emotion. Carly could hardly expect them to take this latest hit and keep smiling when she was having trouble getting through it herself.

She got up to throw the courier envelope into the fire when the package that had been inside fell to the floor. She bent to pick it up and saw that there was a small tag attached to the bow. Her name was written inside the tag in tiny block letters too small for her to be able to tell who had written it.

Carly released the tape and spread the paper. A brilliantly colored silk scarf slipped out of her hand and landed at her feet. She froze when she saw the designer name written in the corner. Hermès.

David.

The present was his doing, not Andrea's. The weight of disappointment bore down on Carly, stealing her brief moment of happiness. It all made sense now. Andrea would never have asked David for the money to buy anything so expensive and she sure as hell didn't have enough to buy it on her own. Andrea hadn't bought the present, nor had she been the one who'd arranged for a courier service to make sure her letter arrived in time for Christmas. It had all been David's doing.

Carly snatched the scarf off the floor and stuffed it inside the envelope along with the wrapping paper and ribbon that had been around it.

Damn him for interfering.

Damn him for caring.

But most of all, damn him for letting her believe, even for a minute, that Andrea hadn't forgotten her after all.

Unable to sit still any longer, Carly got up and went to the window. Her warm breath on the cool surface soon isolated her again. The deepest pain came from knowing Andrea hadn't missed her nearly as much as Carly had believed she would. If she had, she would never have been able to stay away this long, and especially not through the holidays.

Could David be the answer? Why was he being so wonderful to Andrea when he'd promised he would do everything he could to see that she returned home?

The voice of reason surfaced in her emotional storm and put a stop to her panicked railing. She forced herself to take a calming breath. If she was to have any hope of getting through the next few months, she had to deal with what was ahead of her, not waste time and energy on wild speculation.

She heard the sound of the back door opening and realized the time for self-indulgent breast-beating was over. She had a lot of Christmas to get through yet. There would be time enough for leisurely contemplation tomorrow.

"Mom?" Eric called out.

"I'm in here," she answered, tucking the envelope and scarf into the bookshelf, behind a leather-bound set of the complete works of Shakespeare, where she was confident they would never be found.

He came into the room seconds later, unwrapping the muffler Andrea had given him from around his neck. "The turkey smells great."

"It still has a couple of hours to go."

He sat down on the sofa next to her. "What've you been doing?"

"Some odds and ends, picking up. How come you came inside? Bored with your new skis already?" She smoothed the hair back from his forehead and then, feeling a compelling need for physical contact, let her arm slip over his shoulder.

"Dad and Shawn decided to ski over to the pond

to see what's going on over there. I didn't want to go."

"I'm glad. I like having you around." She gave him a squeeze. "How about a cup of hot chocolate?"

He tilted his head to touch hers. "No, thanks."

"Not even if I put marshmallows in it?"

He didn't answer. Instead, several seconds later, he asked, "Did Andrea call?"

Now Carly understood the real reason Eric had come inside. "No," she said. She might have told him, "not yet," but after reading Andrea's letter, she didn't want to get his hopes up. It was better to face disappointment now than wait the rest of the day for something that wasn't going to happen.

"Nothing says we can't call her," he suggested.

In his innocence, Eric had cut through the protocol that bound Carly. "I think that's a grand idea," she said. "I've never been very good at waiting myself." She stood and held out her hand to help him up. "I'll get the number and you can make the call."

"Shouldn't we wait for Dad and Shawn?"

"If they want to talk to her when they get back, we'll just call her again."

He grinned. "Thanks, Mom."

She gave him a quick hug. "No, Eric," she said softly. "Thank you."

16

Andrea stared with disgust at the bright pink spot the punch she'd been drinking had left on the skirt of her white silk dress. If David hadn't been so worried about her having a real Christmas dinner, she would have tried to talk him out of coming tonight. The day had turned out even harder than she'd imagined, and she had imagined it would be pretty awful. She'd been looking at her watch all night and thinking what time it was back home and what everybody was doing.

She'd almost cried when she opened her packages and saw that her mom had gotten her the Eddie Bauer sweater she'd been saving to buy for herself. Andrea couldn't remember telling Carly about the sweater. It was a good thing she'd broken down and sent her mother the scarf, or she'd have felt like a bigger jerk than she already did.

She'd thought her mom would call when she got the package. Christmas Eve Andrea had made a show of listening to the carols being sung on the radio by the King's College Chapel at Cambridge while in reality she was listening for the telephone. She'd waited again on Christmas day, right up until they'd had to leave for dinner. David must have guessed what she was thinking because she hadn't even said anything when he told her that courier services messed up sometimes, too.

Wondering where he was now, she glanced around the enormous living room and found him deep in conversation with the gray-haired man who had greeted them at the door when they'd arrived. When David had said they were having Christmas dinner with a few friends, she'd thought he meant a casual get-together with a couple of his neighbors. She should have been suspicious when he'd come downstairs in a tuxedo—something she'd only seen at proms and weddings before coming to England.

The last time she'd bothered counting, there were over thirty people standing around waiting for dinner. She couldn't imagine a table big enough to seat everybody or a turkey big enough to feed all of them.

Deciding the spot on her dress would be less noticeable if she were sitting down, she sidled over to a big, ugly chair with carved arms and sank into the overstuffed cushion. A boy David had introduced her to earlier, Murdock Armstrong, sat opposite her listening to a woman in a green dress.

As soon as they realized she was there, they turned to include her in their conversation.

"You're David's daughter, aren't you?" the woman asked.

"Yes," Andrea answered.

"From America, is it?"

"Yes."

"Sorry, but I can't seem to recall which state you said you were from," Murdock said.

"Ohio," she told him.

The woman frowned thoughtfully. "I don't believe I know Ohio."

Andrea wasn't surprised. No one she'd met since coming to England had the foggiest idea how the states were arranged between New York and California. "It's across Lake Erie from Canada." She waited to see if the added information was enough to spark recognition. When it became clear it wasn't, she added, "A couple of hundred miles southwest of Toronto."

"Ahh," the woman said.

They all smiled politely while Andrea tried to think of something else to say. Finally, she focused on Murdock. "Do you go to school around here?"

"Eton," he said.

"Is that close?" she prodded, thinking he would be flattered at her interest. Instead, what she got was a barely concealed look of disdain.

"Eton is across the river from Windsor," came a voice from behind her. The young man attached to the voice stepped around Andrea's chair and perched on the arm of the sofa next to Murdock. "Murdock forgets not everyone is as caught up in name dropping as he is." He extended his hand, "I'm Jeffery Armstrong, this oaf's brother."

Andrea placed her hand in his, and returned his smile. He had the most remarkable eyes, and she had to remind herself not to stare. They were light blue in the middle, surrounded by a deeper, almost navy blue. The color was a startling contrast to his black hair and bronze skin. "Andrea Hargrove."

He brightened. "David Montgomery's daughter— I should have known."

She nodded.

"I've been hearing about you for days now. It's nice to be able to put a face to the name finally."

"You've been hearing about me?" She could just imagine what was being said—poor David, saddled with a daughter he didn't even know he had. And poor, poor Victoria. She'd certainly never signed on for something like this when she married David.

"All wonderful, I can assure you."

Murdock stood up and smoothed the wrinkles from his pants. "If you'll excuse me, I think I'd like a bit more of the eggnog." He gave a slight bow. "Is there anything I can get anyone?"

"No, thank you," Andrea said. With her luck, she'd have a cream-colored spot to go along with the pink.

"I'll just go along with you," the woman said, gracefully excusing herself.

When they were gone, Jeffery returned his attention to Andrea. He smiled. "Looks like it's just you and me," he said. "Hope you don't mind."

She was attracted by his smile but captivated by the twinkle in his eye. "Not at all," she said, making an effort to sound casual. "As a matter of fact, if *you* wouldn't mind, you could answer a few questions for me."

"Fire away."

"What is Eton?"

He put his hand over his heart and feigned a horrified look. "It's customary to bow your head and lower your voice when you say the word aloud." Leaning closer, he whispered, "It's a school for the sons of very rich, very influential, very well-connected men. There are, of course, a sprinkling of high achievers from the state schools, and then there are the King's Scholars, but for the most part, we're very careful about keeping out the riffraff."

" 'We're?' " Andrea questioned.

"I'm afraid that I, too, am one of those impossibly spoiled young men." He broke the rigid line of his tuxedo when he pulled back the jacket to stuff his hands into his pants pockets. "Next question?"

Andrea leaned back in the chair and crossed her legs, forgetting all about the pink spot on her skirt. "How come every one else here looks like they've never seen the sun and you look like you've spent the past month on the beach?"

"And here I thought no one had noticed."

"I'm sorry. I didn't mean—" David had warned her that it was considered impolite to ask personal questions.

He chuckled. "Don't apologize, Andrea. I'm not the least offended. In fact, I've been dying to tell someone all about the fantastic week I spent skiing in Verbier," he leaned closer, "but everybody I know is too bloody polite to ask."

She shook her head. "Everything is so different over here. Back home, if somebody went on a trip, it would be rude not to ask them about it."

David propped his shoulder against the door frame of the study and surreptitiously watched Andrea. He was pleased to see that she and Jeffery Armstrong had finally connected. Jeffery was a terrific kid, unusually mature and sensitive for a seventeen-year-old, the perfect friend for Andrea while she was in England.

David still hadn't been able to figure out whether Andrea was a master at disguising her feelings or if she just hadn't reached the point of homesickness yet where swallowing her pride was secondary to seeing her family again.

She was a remarkable young woman, bright and curious, eager to see everything. Even though he was months behind on his book and had no business acting the tour guide, he'd found an almost addictive pleasure in discovering London again through her eyes. He would miss her when she was gone.

As if she'd somehow picked up on his thoughts, Andrea turned her head and looked directly at him. She flashed a quick smile and then went back to her conversation with Jeffery.

David was stunned at the memories and emotions her action unleashed. For a heartbeat, it hadn't been

Andrea he'd seen in the youthful, upturned face, but Carly.

He stood upright, squared his shoulders, and looked for someone to talk to, something to distract him.

Nothing had changed. Nothing would. To believe anything else was self-destructive.

Andrea was unusually quiet on their way home that night. Finally, just as they were pulling onto the road that led to the house, she said, "Do you suppose Mom didn't get her scarf?"

"Why do you ask?"

She hesitated. "Because she didn't call. Maybe she thought I forgot her after all."

"And you're afraid you might have hurt her feelings?" David asked carefully, not sure how far he could push without having Andrea slam the door between them.

"She probably saw there wasn't anything for her under the tree as soon as she got home from the airport. She notices things like that."

"Is that why you did it?" he asked, holding his breath as he waited for her answer.

"I was really mad when I left."

"I think it was more that you were really hurt. With everything that happened, that's understandable."

"Do you think Mom understands?"

"I've never known anyone more willing to make allowances for the people they love than your mother. Carly doesn't have it in her to hold a grudge. Especially not against you."

"She hardly ever gets mad, even when she has lots of reasons to."

"Like what kinds of reasons?" David asked, suppressing the guilt he felt for prying, for wanting to hear about the intimate details of Carly's life he had no right to know.

She went on as if she hadn't heard the question. "I should have sent the package sooner."

"Maybe she called while we were away."

Andrea turned to look at him. "Do you have an answering machine?"

He shook his head. "Not up here."

She grew quiet again, not saying anything until they had pulled up to the front of the house. "If it's okay with you, I think I'll go right to bed. I'm really tired."

When they were inside and he'd hung both of their coats up in the closet, he held his arms open to give her a hug. "I want to thank you for making this the best Christmas I've had in years," he said against her lilac-scented hair. And then realizing how much it would mean to her, he added, "I'm sorry I wasn't there for your first fifteen."

She tilted her head back to look at him. "You would have been if you'd known."

"Nothing could have kept me away," he said softly. Having Andrea with him these past weeks had given him insight into how much he had missed—both with Carly and by not having children of his own.

"Good night, David," she said, standing on tiptoe to give him a quick kiss on the cheek. She let go of him and headed for the stairs.

He waited until she was halfway up before he called out to her. "Andrea?"

She stopped to look at him. "Yes?"

"Say hello to your mother for me."

After several seconds, she asked, "How did you know?"

"It's what Carly would have done in your place."

She hesitated, as if unsure whether she should say what she was thinking. "Do you ever wish she had gone to you instead of my dad when she found out she was pregnant?"

She might as well have doubled up her fist and hit him. "I try not to think about things like that," he lied.

It seemed to satisfy her. "I'll see you in the morning," she told him and started back up the stairs.

David waited until he heard her bedroom door close before he went into the study and poured himself a glass of scotch.

17

The spicy smell of persimmon cookies hit Carly the instant she opened the door of Barbara's house. Shrugging out of her coat, she called, "Didn't you tell me less than two hours ago that you were going on a diet?"

"They're for Andrea. The last ones I sent got waylaid somewhere and she ended up with hockey pucks." Barbara came out of the kitchen, wiping her hands on a towel. "To what do I owe the honor of this visit?"

Carly laughed. "You mean, what am I doing back here so soon?"

Barbara whipped around to stare at her daughter. "I do believe that's the first time I've heard you laugh in months. Is it this beautiful March weather we've been having or do you know something you're not telling me?"

Carly was fairly bursting with the need to share her excitement. "When I got home, there was a letter from Andrea waiting for me."

"And?"

"I've been trying not to read too much into it, but it sounds like she's close to throwing in the towel."

Barbara's enthusiasm dimmed a little. "Nothing specific though?"

"I know, I've done this before and ended up disappointed. But I honestly think this time is different. She wrote more about home than she has since she left. Another thing—I forgot to tell you that I saw her friend Susan Gilroy the other day and she acted as if it were a foregone conclusion that Andrea would be home before summer. It seems reasonable that she's basing that feeling on Andrea's letters to her, wouldn't you think?"

"Yes, you would." Barbara let out a frustrated sigh. "I still think there's something going on with Andrea that we don't know about. We were so sure she wouldn't last a month over there." The timer sounded in the kitchen. Barbara headed that way, talking over her shoulder to Carly as she went. "How could we have been so wrong about something like that?"

Barbara was only echoing the thought that had haunted Carly the entire time Andrea had been gone. She followed her mother into the kitchen. "The only reason I can think of is that David has made it so comfortable for her, she feels torn between him and us. Knowing Andrea, she's probably caught up in worrying about hurting his feelings, too. Remember, she really believes he's her father. Did I tell you he bought her diamond earrings for Christmas?"

"If you did, I forgot." Slipping a mitt on her hand, Barbara removed the cookie sheet from the oven and put another filled with dough in its place. "I thought he promised you he would do everything he could to make her want to come home."

Carly took a cookie from the cooling rack. It was still warm. She broke it in half and saw that it was loaded with raisins and walnuts. This was the way persimmon cookies ought to be but never were when she baked them because Ethan was sensitive to walnuts and hated raisins.

God, she was getting petty.

"I wondered about that myself at first, but then I started thinking about the kind of person David is and there's no way he could do anything that would make Andrea feel she wasn't welcome. It isn't in his makeup to treat anyone that way, especially not a trusting young girl who thinks he's her father."

"I don't know another man who would do what he's done for you and Andrea. David's either operating under his own private agenda, or he should be put up for sainthood."

Carly grew quiet. "There are times you can have a pretty selective memory, Mother. Think about what Wally did for you and your daughter," she said.

Barbara cast a sidelong glance at Carly. "All right, so there's more than one cut from the same cloth."

"Wally stuck his neck out a hell of a lot farther than David could ever think of doing."

"Can we talk about something else?"

There were times Carly ached to talk to her mother about what had happened to the three of them all those years ago. There were questions that needed answers, fears that needed to be put to rest, and absolutions that needed granting. "How about the party we'll have when Andrea comes home?"

"Let's not forget to involve Shawn and Eric," Barbara went on, as if the emotional detour had never happened. "We don't want them to feel left out."

Carly smiled. "No fatted calf for the returning Prodigal Daughter?"

"I can't tell you how good it feels to see a smile on your face again."

"It feels good to me, too."

The telephone rang. "Would you get that?" Barbara asked, wiping her hands on a towel.

Carly waited through another ring to swallow the

last of her cookie. "Hello," she said, her voice upbeat, reflecting her mood.

"Thank God," Ethan said. "I've been looking everywhere for you."

A warning chill shot up her spine. "Why? What's wrong?"

"The hospital in Linndale called me over two hours ago. They tried you first, but you weren't home."

How like him to give guilt before information. "The hospital?" she repeated. "In Linndale?"

"Shawn's been in an accident."

Her stomach convulsed. "What kind of accident?"

"What is it?" Barbara asked, coming around the kitchen island.

"Motorcycle," Ethan said.

This couldn't be happening. There had to be some mistake. She couldn't lose another child, not this way. Dear God, please let Ethan be wrong. "Damn it, Ethan, stop playing games and tell me if he's all right."

"If who's all right?" Barbara insisted.

"I don't know," Ethan said, his voice cracking. "He's still in surgery."

Carly raked her hand through her hair as she turned to mouth the name Shawn to her mother. "Why did they have to take him to surgery?" she said, struggling to find something to hang on to.

"I'm not sure."

The sounds of his hyperventilation increased and she knew she was wasting her time trying to get any more information out of him. "I'll be there as soon as I can, but first, let me talk to one of the nurses."

Barbara left the room.

"You can't," Ethan said. "They're all too busy to come to the phone."

Only knowing it would do her no good kept her

from shouting her frustration at him. "Does Eric know?" she asked.

"He's here with me now."

"You had time to find him, but not me?" She pressed her palm hard against her forehead. "Never mind, don't answer that. Just try not to let Eric see how scared you are."

"That's easy for you to say."

"I'll be there as soon as I can," she repeated, still unable to hang up the phone. It was as if the connection to Ethan had become her only connection to Shawn. "If he comes out of surgery before I can get there, tell him I love him."

"The doctor said it would be a couple of hours at least. We'll wait for you in the hallway by the operating rooms," he said, and hung up, cutting the contact for her.

Barbara came back in the room, Carly's and her coats in hand. As she was putting hers on, she went to the oven, turned it off and then took the half-baked cookies out and put them on the counter. "I called Wally on the radio. He'll be here in five minutes."

"I can't wait that long," Carly said, threading her arms into the sleeves of her jacket.

"Wally can get us there faster in the squad car."

Carly hugged herself and let out a soft moan. "I can't just stand around here and wait. I'll go crazy if I don't do something."

"Finish packing the cookies for Andrea."

"*Andrea.* I should call her."

"And tell her what? You don't know anything yourself yet." Barbara put her arms around Carly. "It's going to be all right. Just remember Ethan isn't at his best under these circumstances. You can't take what he has to say as gospel."

Carly couldn't move. "I'm so scared, Mom. I don't know what I'd do if anything happened to Shawn."

"Would you please put that overactive imagination of yours back in the creative side of your brain where it belongs? Shawn's going to be as good as new before you know it."

She reached up to wipe a tear from Carly's cheek. "There, I think I hear Wally driving up now."

Forty-five minutes later, they walked into the surgical waiting area at Linndale Hospital.

"Thank God, you finally got here," Ethan said, his relief mixed with accusation.

"How is he?" Carly asked. "Have you heard anything?"

Eric got up and threw his arms around Carly. "A nurse came by about five minutes ago and said everything was going the way it should," he said.

Carly looked at Ethan for conformation. "Did she say anything else?"

"Just that the doctor would be out to talk to us as soon as she was finished."

"How did Shawn get hit by a motorcycle?" she asked.

"He didn't get hit," Eric answered before Ethan had a chance. "He fell off."

Carly's mind couldn't take in what he was telling her. He might as well have been talking in a foreign language. "That doesn't make sense. What would Shawn be doing on a motorcycle?"

"It seems the oldest Bradford boy got one for Christmas," Ethan said. "When he went off with a friend this afternoon, Joey Bradford talked Shawn and Eric into taking the bike out for a little spin." He cast a meaningful look at Carly. "They went there looking for you because you weren't home when they got out of school."

"Joey's brother is only a sophomore," Carly said, refusing to rise to Ethan's bait. "What in God's name is he doing with a motorcycle?"

Eric buried his face in Carly's jacket. "His uncle gave it to him 'cause he got a new one," he said, his voice muffled but loud enough to hear.

She could feel him catch his breath as if he were trying to hold back tears. "You rode it, too?" she asked him.

He shook his head without lifting his face from her coat. "I was supposed to go next."

The image of Eric sitting on a motorcycle made her lightheaded with fear. She placed her hands on the sides of his face and gently forced him to look at her. "Thank heaven you didn't. Now I want you to tell me how badly Shawn is hurt." It infuriated her that he had to be the one to answer her questions about Shawn's condition when it would have taken so little for Ethan to do so.

"He was crying and he couldn't move, because every time he tried, it made him hurt worse." Eric winced at the memory. "He wasn't going very fast, Mom. The only reason he got so messed up was because the motorcycle landed on top of him when he hit the curb."

"He was awake and talking to you the whole time before the ambulance came?"

"Uh-huh. He kept saying you were going to kill him when you found out."

The band snapped from around Carly's chest and she could breathe again. She gave Eric a grateful, reassuring hug. "It must have been awful for both of you."

"What are you going to do to Shawn when he gets better?"

"I need to stop being so scared before I can think about that."

"What about me?"

"After about ten more hugs like this one I'll give that some thought, too."

Barbara stepped forward. "I think you and Ethan

should have some time alone. Why don't Eric and I go to the cafeteria and get us all something to drink?''

Carly turned her attention to her mother. "Where's Wally?''

"He went to Admitting to see if he could find out how the Linndale police plan to handle this."

How like Wally to take care of the potentially messy little details so quietly and unobtrusively. Releasing Eric and guiding him toward Barbara, Carly said, "Bring me back a cup of tea, would you?" She turned to Ethan. "Do you want something?"

He answered without looking at either of them. "Nothing for me."

"We won't be gone long," Barbara told her, slipping her arm through Eric's and heading down the hall.

When they had rounded the corner, Ethan said, "You never used to drink tea."

She blinked. "What?"

"Up until three months ago I don't think I ever saw you drink anything but coffee. It just seems kind of strange that you've changed, that's all."

She was too dumbfounded to answer immediately. When she did, she didn't try to shield him. "Your paranoia has reached new heights, Ethan. You even managed to take me by surprise this time." On a roll, she made no attempt to hold back. "You've known all along that Shawn was going to be all right and yet you let me spend the past hour in hell."

"I didn't—"

"Don't try to defend yourself." She was seething. It would take a long time to forgive him this one. "Don't make excuses. As a matter of fact, I don't even want you to talk to me."

"What's with you, Carly? I've done everything I could to make you happy these past few months. I give and give and you take and take and where does it get me?"

"For Christ's sake, could you stop thinking about yourself for just one day? This is hardly the time or place to get into what you think is wrong with our marriage."

"With you there's never a time or place. How long do you think I can go on putting in ninety percent to your ten?"

"I won't talk to you about this now."

"When, then?"

"Ethan, stop it."

"I want to know when you think you might find a little time for me, Carly? Is that so much to ask?"

He wasn't going to let it go. "All right. We can talk about this as much as you want when we get home."

"The minute we walk in the door or after you've unloaded the dishwasher and fed the dog? What's it going to take for me to get through to you that this is important to me? Damn it to hell, I want to know when."

"Tonight, after Eric is in bed. Is that specific enough?" She saw Wally approaching out of the corner of her eye. He had his red-and-gray plaid jacket draped over his arm and the hint of a grin on his angular face. With two quick strides he was beside them.

"What did you find out?" she asked, folding her hands in her lap to keep him from seeing how badly they were shaking.

"I talked to the Linndale sheriff. He told me as far as he was concerned the ball was in my court and I could play it any way I wanted."

"What does that mean?"

"Neither one of the kids will be charged with anything. I am going to talk to the Bradfords, however, and see if there isn't someplace else they can keep that thing until both of their boys get a few years on them."

She went to him, stood on tiptoe and gave him a kiss. "You're always here for me when I need you."

He put his arms around her and held her tight. "My pleasure, missy."

They stood holding each other for several minutes while Carly drew quiet strength from the man she passionately wished had been her real father.

"Where've your mom and Eric got off to?" Wally asked when she finally lifted her head from his shoulder.

She stepped back and glanced down the hall. "The cafeteria. They should be back in a few minutes."

Wally took off his jacket and laid it on the chair. "How ya holdin' up, Ethan?" he asked, as if just noticing him.

"I'll be all right."

"It's a scary thing to have something like this happen to one of your kids."

Ethan gave him a look that said, "How the hell would you know?"

Carly could have kicked him. She had her mouth open to tell Ethan to go outside and walk around until he'd worked off some of his anxiety when she noticed his gaze was fixed on something down the hall. She turned and saw Barbara and Eric in the company of a woman dressed in surgical scrubs all headed their way, and smiling.

"He's okay, Mom," Eric shouted, breaking ranks and running toward her.

Carly caught her breath in a quick cry of relief. She looked at the doctor for confirmation. The tall, slender woman nodded.

"He's one lucky young man," she said, coming to a halt in front of Carly. She held out her hand. "Evelyn Webster. You're the mother?"

"Yes—Carly Hargrove." After · shaking hands, Carly introduced Ethan and Wally.

"I should start out by telling you that thanks to the

helmet he was wearing, he's going to be fine," Dr. Webster said. "The breaks were clean and relatively easy to set—"

"Breaks?" Carly repeated. "Plural?"

The doctor reached up and pulled off her surgical cap, then ran her fingers through her short, dark blond hair. "There was a compound fracture of the right humerus and a hairline crack in the right tibia."

"He broke his arm *and* his leg?"

"No one told you about the results of the X rays and what we were going to do in surgery?"

Carly spoke quickly, her compulsion to present a perfect family picture to the outside world taking over. "We haven't had a chance to talk. I only got here a few minutes ago."

The look the doctor gave Carly told her the good doctor wasn't buying her explanation. The openness and warmth turned crisply professional. "Is Shawn left or right handed?"

"Left," Eric answered.

"That will help some. I'm going to keep him here for several days, and even though he's been fitted with a walking cast, he's still going to need a lot of help moving around when he gets home, especially for the first couple of weeks. Is there someone who'll be available?"

"My wife will be taking care of him," Ethan said.

The doctor looked to Carly for confirmation. Carly nodded. "I'll want to meet with you before I release him."

Finally, it was Carly's turn to speak. "When do you think that will be?"

"Four or five days. It depends on how his arm does." She made a move to leave.

"Can I see him?" Carly asked.

"He should be in his room in another hour or so. You can check with his floor nurse." She added a nod of finality and headed back down the hallway.

When she was sure the doctor was out of earshot, Carly turned on Ethan. "You knew all this and you didn't tell me?" Her rage left a bitter taste on the back of her tongue.

"Keep your voice down," Ethan said, taking her arm and steering her away from the others. "You of all people should realize how upset I get when something like this happens. The nurses in Emergency stuck the release papers in front of me and told me to sign them at the same time they were telling me what they were going to do to Shawn. I was having trouble remembering my own name, let alone all the medical jargon they were throwing my way."

She wrenched her arm free. "Broken bones are pretty hard to forget."

"What is the matter with you? You're acting like this is my fault when you're—"

"Don't say it, Ethan. Don't even think it."

Whether it was the fury in her eye or the tone in her voice, something made him back off. "Look, we're both tired and upset. Why don't we get out of here for a while and find someplace to eat? We have an hour before they bring Shawn to his room."

If pressed only a little, she could have come up with a hundred things she would have preferred doing, none of them involving him.

When she didn't immediately answer, he went on, "Eric is upset enough by everything that's happened. The last thing he needs is to see us fighting."

"I should call Andrea."

He checked his watch. "It's after ten there. She's probably already in bed. Besides, if you wait until tomorrow, Shawn will be able to talk to her, too, and she'll believe you when you tell her he's okay."

She knew he was right, but she hated giving in. She went over to where Barbara and Wally were waiting with Eric. "Ethan has suggested we go out somewhere for dinner instead of waiting around here."

"I think that's a terrific idea," Barbara said. "You're going to have to keep your strength up for what you've got ahead of you."

"I know a good place close by," Wally added.

Ethan clapped his hands in triumph before rubbing them together. "Then it's decided."

Carly shuddered when he helped her on with her coat, adjusted her collar, and let his hand linger lovingly at her neck. She realized with a start that something had changed between them; she wasn't yet sure what it was, only that from the feel of it, it was permanent.

They were outside, on their way to Ethan's car, when he put his arm across her shoulders and brought her close. "I can't help but feel that you think I owe you an apology," he whispered.

When, after several seconds, she didn't respond, he went on, "Aren't you going to say anything?"

If he were to say the right words, in the right way, she would not be able to stop herself from forgiving him—there were too many years of precedents. "I'm waiting to hear what you think you've done wrong."

He nuzzled his face against her hair, making a soft sighing sound. "I knew you'd come around," he said.

She pulled away from him. "What's that supposed to mean?"

He gave her a stunned look. "That you realize I've done nothing wrong and there isn't any reason for me to apologize."

She started to answer him and then stopped. Without the need to play to Ethan's ego, she could concentrate on Shawn and getting him home. "Thank you, Ethan," she said, not at all surprised that he had completely misunderstood her.

He smiled, then pulled her to him for a kiss. "You're welcome."

18

The sounds of breakfast trays being delivered to patients brought Carly out of a drifting sleep. She opened her eyes and focused on Shawn. He was staring at her. "Good morning," she said, sitting up in the chair and stretching.

"Where's Dad?" he asked.

She got up and went to the bed to touch his forehead and then place a kiss where her hand had been. "He and Eric went home last night, but he'll be back as soon as he gets Eric off to school. How do you feel?"

"Crummy."

She gave him a commiserating smile. "I'm not surprised."

"Are you mad?"

Plainly he'd been doing some thinking while he waited for her to wake up. The night before he'd still been under the effects of the anesthesia and unable to finish a sentence without falling asleep. "A little. But I'll get over it."

"What about Dad?"

"You'll have to ask him."

"Is Eric okay?"

She brushed the hair back from his forehead, taking incredible pleasure in the simple gesture. For the past months she'd been so caught up in Andrea, she'd been temporarily blinded to the daily riches Shawn and Eric brought into her life. "He was pretty upset for a while, but as soon as he found out you were going to be all right, he calmed down."

"I'll bet he was scared."

"That's one bet you'd win."

"You were probably pretty scared, too."

She thought about all she had gone through the day before and an unexpected grin formed. "I was terrified until I got here and found out for myself that you were going to be all right."

He reached up to grab the bar hanging down from a hook in the ceiling and caught his breath against the pain the motion caused. "I had no idea it would be so heavy."

"What?"

"Joey's motorcycle. It must weigh a ton."

"Grandpa Wally stopped by there on his way home last night. He said it looked like when you hit the curb the bike just went out from under you."

"All I know is that I was sitting on the thing one minute and it was sitting on me the next."

"It must have really hurt."

"Not at first. I think I was too scared to feel anything. But I knew my arm was broken as soon as I tried to move it. I thought my leg was just stuck."

"Well, it looks like you're finally going to get that computer you've been wanting."

He brightened. "No kidding?"

"It's the only way you're going to be able to keep up with your schoolwork."

"Gosh, maybe I should have done this when school started."

She chuckled. "And missed out on basketball season? Fat chance."

"How long am I going to have to be like this?"

"They won't give us a time frame until they see how your arm is healing." She hesitated, unsure how much to tell him. In the end, she settled for the truth, wishing the decision had been as easy with Andrea. "Apparently some compound fractures can get pretty complicated."

"What about my leg?"

"Six weeks and it will be like new."

He thought a minute. "I'll bet if you told Andrea about my arm, she'd come home to see me."

Carly smiled. "I think she would, too. But I'm not going to tell her."

The conspiratorial gleam left his eyes. "How come?"

"Because you are."

This time it was his turn to smile. "Can we call her now?"

Carly gave his hand a squeeze, caught up in his enthusiasm. "She wouldn't be home from school yet."

"Mom?"

Carly looked back to Shawn. "Yes?"

"I'm sorry."

"Oh, honey, I'm sorry, too. If I'd been home, you wouldn't have gone looking for me and none of this would have happened."

He stared at her long and hard. "Did Dad tell you to say that?"

"What do you mean?"

"It just sounds like something he would say, that's all."

She busied herself opening the cellophane package that held a napkin and silverware. "When did you get so smart?" she asked softly.

"I see lots of things you think I don't."

She really didn't want to get into this discussion

with him. He was a child. It was his right to be sheltered from the sins of his parents.

A soft knock on the door drew their attention before she could respond. Ethan poked his head in and smiled. "How's my kid?"

Shawn's return smile was slow to form. "I'm doin' great," he said.

Ethan came in the room. "Well, you're going to be doing even better when you hear what I've got to tell you."

"Andrea's coming home," Shawn said excitedly.

Ethan's jaw dropped. It was obvious he had completely misjudged what it would take to please Shawn. "Guess again. No, don't," he quickly added. "I want to tell you myself. I talked Arnold Livingston into selling me tickets for three of the Piston games."

"But he only has two tickets."

"So where's the problem?"

"What about Mom and Eric?"

Ethan shrugged in frustration. "I was thinking it would be fun for just you and me to do something."

"I didn't want them to feel left out," Shawn said.

"You don't have to worry about that. Eric won't mind, not if we bring him something afterwards. And you know your mom—she prefers staying home to going somewhere with me."

Anger shot through Carly. "That's not true."

Ethan gave her a withering look. "Then why was it you broke your promise about last night?"

"Last night?" she asked.

"We were supposed to set some time aside to talk, to get things back on track between us."

She glanced at Shawn, who was staring at his father. "Could we talk about this later?" she said to Ethan.

"Now where have I heard that one before?"

She had her mouth open to answer when it hit her what he was doing. Shawn, even more than Andrea, was compulsive in his need to defend the underdog, and Ethan was playing to that need by maneuvering her into the role of heavy. To defend herself by saying she'd felt Shawn needed her more would only put him in the middle. "I'm sure it was last night when I told you I was too tired to drive all the way home and that I wanted to stay here instead."

Not waiting for his answer, Carly again focused her attention on Shawn. "I don't know about you, but I don't think your breakfast looks all that appetizing hot. I have a feeling if we let it get any colder, Muffin wouldn't even eat it."

Shawn grinned, plainly relieved to have his parents' confrontation over. "There's nothing Muffin wouldn't eat."

Carly tucked the napkin under his chin. "What would you like to try first?"

His eyes became big questioning circles. "I can't eat lying down."

"Wanna bet? Now open wide."

Reluctantly, Shawn let her put a forkful of egg into his mouth. He spent a second chewing, then made a face. "Yuk," he said when he'd swallowed.

Ethan came up to the bed. "How about if I pick you up an Egg McMuffin?"

Shawn looked at Carly. "Can he?"

She returned the fork to the tray. "I don't see why not."

"I'll be back in twenty minutes," Ethan said. He put his hand under Carly's chin and kissed her. "What would you like?"

She was sorely tempted to tell him exactly what it would take to please her. Instead, she said, "Nothing. I'll just pick at this. There's no sense letting it go to waste."

"You could always take it home to Muffin," Shawn said, the mischievous twinkle back in his eye.

When Ethan had gone, Carly and Shawn slipped

into a comfortable silence. For a while, she thought he'd gone back to sleep, but then he opened his eyes and spoke.

"What time do you think it would be all right to call Andrea?"

"You really miss her, don't you?"

"Yeah, but don't tell her."

"Why not?"

"She'd never let me forget it."

"Well, I'll let you in on a little secret—she really misses you, too."

"Then how come she's still over there?"

"Because of me," Carly admitted.

"How long is she going to be mad at you for not telling her about David?"

"I think she's gotten over that."

"So, what's bothering her now?"

"She doesn't know what to say to me."

"You've gotta be kidding. Andrea's always got her mouth going. She's—" He stopped. "Oh, I know what you mean. She doesn't know how to tell you she's sorry for being such a jerk about everything."

Carly gently tweaked Shawn's nose. "I love you."

He took her hand in his and gave it a squeeze. "Yeah, me too."

"What's that supposed to mean?" she teased. "That you love you, too?"

"You know what it means."

"Yes—I do," she said, feeling good inside. "But do you suppose you could actually put the words together in their proper order for your sister?"

He looked horrified. "You expect me to tell Andrea that I love her?"

"Don't you?"

"Yeah, but I'm not going to tell her."

Carly hesitated. "Would it be all right if I said it for you?"

He eyed her. "I guess so. Just don't get sloppy about it."

"Would I do something like that?"

He groaned.

She knew he would make a show of hating it if she just bent over and gave him a kiss, but she didn't care. This one was for her.

Instead, he kissed her back.

19

David leaned back in his chair and stared at the computer screen. He'd run into problems with books before, including a couple of bouts of writer's block, but this was different. His concentration wasn't what it should be. Ideas and possible solutions to plot problems would come to him and then disappear before he could get out a notepad to write them down.

Granted his life had taken some rather unexpected and disruptive turns of late, but nothing he hadn't handled. Besides, if he used Andrea for an excuse now, what was he going to use when she left in two days and his protagonist was still stuck with an attaché case, three kids, and two hundred pages to come up with an answer to his problems?

David propped his feet on the desk and ran his hands through his hair. Andrea's leaving was preying more heavily on his mind than he wanted to admit. They had carefully kept up the fantasy that she was only going home for a visit and that she'd be back in a week, but David was finding it harder and harder to lie to himself about it. There was too much to hold her when she got there. It had taken every bit of his persuasive powers to keep her from hopping the first plane headed west when she found out about Shawn's accident. Finally she'd agreed it made sense to finish the final four days of school before Easter break and give Shawn time to get home from the hospital.

Once she stepped back in her old life, nothing would be able to pry her loose again. He'd be lucky to see her for a couple of weeks in the summer.

But then hadn't that been the whole idea? Just because Andrea had already stayed far longer than he and Carly had expected wasn't sufficient reason for him to allow himself to think she might stay forever.

From the day she'd arrived, their time together had been set up to be finite.

At least that was how it was supposed to have been. Who could have known she would stay so long or that he would derive such pleasure from her company?

He countered the sense of loss he was already feeling by telling himself that when she was gone, he'd be able to get his life together again. The book would flow; his publisher would be happy; Victoria would be happy. All would be right with the world.

He'd never been much good at self-delusion; now was no exception.

David looked up when he felt, more than heard, someone enter the room. Prepared to go on the attack at the intrusion, he buried his anger when he saw it was Andrea.

As soon as it had become obvious her stay was going to be longer than a couple of weeks, David had explained his working methods, stressing that when the door to his office was closed, he was not to be disturbed under any but the most pressing circumstances. What he hadn't taken into consideration was a teenager's interpretation of pressing.

"I'm sorry to bother you, David," she said, hesitantly stepping into the room and closing the door.

"If you're at an important part, I can come back later."

"It's okay," he said, swiveling his chair to face her.

She came across the room and sat down in the maroon leather chair opposite his own. The enormous wing chair seemed as if it would swallow her and she shifted forward so that she was sitting on the edge. She was still dressed in her school uniform and looked young and innocent and fragile.

"I just wanted to tell you that I won't be needing the ticket home, after all," she told him, her hands folded primly in her lap.

Since six o'clock that morning David had been living in another world, one of his own making where, for the most part, he had control. Now the real world came crashing back. He leaned forward, his elbows on his knees, his chin resting on his fists. "You've changed your mind again?"

"Sort of," she said.

"Want to talk about it?" He put aside any possibility of getting back to the book that afternoon.

"My dad called about an hour ago."

David looked at the clock on the mantle. It was a lot later than he'd thought. He'd worked straight through both tea and dinner without so much as a stomach rumble. "Did he say something that made you change your mind?"

She started to answer and then stopped. "I don't know how to answer that."

In the four months that she'd been living with him, he'd learned there were times when she wanted him to dig for answers and others when she wanted him to supply them for her. The indications were that this was the former. "Then why don't you just tell me what the two of you talked about?"

"Mostly it was about Shawn and how hard it is for him to get around and how much work it is for my mom to take care of him."

Although Carly would have to be pressed to admit it, David had recognized her deft touch in using Shawn's condition to nudge an already receptive Andrea into coming home. He couldn't blame her; under the circumstances, he would have done the same thing. "You already knew that."

Again she hesitated. "But I forgot how much more work she'd have if I came home."

"Bullshit." He couldn't believe he was doing this. By all rights he should be celebrating, not pushing her into changing her mind yet again. "You're no work to have around."

"Just having another person to cook for and to think about can be a burden sometimes, especially if someone in the family is sick."

"Shawn isn't sick," he said. "He's temporarily incapacitated." Anger welled in David. The words weren't Andrea's, they were Ethan's. The son of a bitch was not only shutting her out, he was making sure she took full responsibility for the decision. Carly would be devastated when she learned Andrea wasn't coming. And who would be standing by with a shoulder to cry on? Good old Ethan.

"If you're worried about me getting in your way during Easter break, Jeffery said I could go skiing in Verbier with his family."

"Good God, whatever gave you that idea?"

She looked down at her hands. "I know how much trouble you're having with your book."

He never discussed the details of how a book was going with anyone. "How could you know that?"

"You hardly talk at breakfast, and when you do, it's like you're saying things you memorized especially for times like that. Victoria told me you get that way on every book and that I shouldn't worry about it. But it seems to me that if you were happy about the way things were going, you'd at least smile once in a while."

His immediate reaction was to defend himself, to give her one of the stock answers he used during interviews about a writer's need to immerse himself in his work. It was all true, but she deserved more. "You're right, the book isn't going well, but it has nothing to do with you."

"You're just saying that because you don't want me to feel bad. But I know that if I weren't here, you'd be at Hawthorne. Victoria says you always go there to write."

"What else does Victoria say?"

She flushed in embarrassment as if she'd actually been caught talking about him behind his back. "That you get moody when you're working and really mad if she plans anything that you have to do with her."

He couldn't deny either. "Then you should realize that your being here hasn't changed a thing."

"I'm not sure what you mean. Are you trying to tell me you want me to stay here with you during Easter week and not go to Switzerland with the Armstrongs?"

He thought a minute. Then, before he could reconsider, he said, "What it means is that the two of us are going to spend our Easter together—in Baxter."

She caught her breath. "But my dad—"

Screw your dad, he wanted to shout. "Ethan never intended for you to stay home—" His throat felt as if it were going to close on him and he stopped a second. "What I mean is that he wasn't telling you to stay with me Easter week. He simply wanted to be sure you didn't get your feelings hurt when you came home and Carly wasn't able to spend as much time with you as she'd like. Ethan is going to be just as excited to see you step off that plane as everyone else."

A slow smile spread across her face. "Do you really think so?"

"I've known him a lot longer than you have and I

think I can read him a little better when it comes to something like this."

She waited a long time before saying anything else, and then it was as if the words were being dragged from her. "If you're going to go home with me, you should probably know that my dad doesn't like you very much."

It was all David could do to keep from laughing out loud. "That's all right. Considering the circumstances, I can't say I blame him."

"I don't understand."

His answer came from the heart, not the mind. "I would give anything to have the years he's had with you. He knows that and he doesn't want to share you any more than I do."

She studied him. "Is that why you're going with me, to make sure I come back here?"

She'd caught him off guard. There was no way he could deny the accusation without making her feel she wasn't wanted by either of the men who claimed to be her father. "Would that bother you?" he asked.

"I guess not."

Realizing the untenable position he'd put her in, he added, "I don't want to put any pressure on you, Andrea. If we get to Baxter and you decide that's where you want to stay, it will be all right with me."

"I could still come back for visits, couldn't I?"

"As often and for as long as you want."

She stood. "I guess I should call and say I'm coming after all."

She was halfway to the door when David thought of something else. "Andrea?"

"Yes?"

"Did Ethan phone you from his office?"

"Uh-huh. Why?"

If he'd needed confirmation that the call had been made without Carly's knowledge or permission, he'd just gotten it. "It just occurred to me you might want to wait until he got home from work so you could check on Shawn at the same time." He hesitated and then went on as if the idea had just struck him. "Better yet, why don't you just leave the message with your mom? That way, you can get to bed at a decent hour tonight."

She smiled indulgently. "I don't have school tomorrow—today is Friday."

He couldn't come up with another reason for her to call now without making it obvious he didn't want her to talk to Ethan.

"But that's a good idea," she said. "Jeffery's taking me to the Hard Rock Café for a hamburger tonight and if I call now, I won't have to worry about when I get home."

It took a second for the details of what she'd said to settle in. "You want to run that by me one more time?"

Andrea laughed. "I was wondering how long it would take for you to jump on that one."

"Midnight, no later."

She rolled her eyes and headed out the door. "Yes, David."

When she was gone, he forced himself to shift her out of his conscious thoughts and get back to the computer. An hour later he realized he was no further along than he'd been when she'd come into the room, and he decided to call it a night.

David reached up to flip the computer screen off, promising himself he'd get an earlier start in the morning and work later into the night.

But then he'd promised himself the same thing the day before and the day before that. Another day or two like the ones he'd just put in and he would run out of hours he could bargain away.

He reached the doorway and stopped for one last look before turning out the light. His gaze settled on the English Gothic desk he'd found in an antique shop in Kensington only months after he'd arrived in England. It had taken up half the living room in the flat he'd rented and had stripped every last pound from his savings account, but owning it had made him feel like a real writer. Somehow, when he'd worked there, he'd known he would succeed.

Then he'd had a used typewriter—now it was a computer; yet the clutter that invariably surrounded him when he was working was the same.

His gaze shifted to the bookshelves that lined three of the walls. Made of oak and hundreds of years old, they held the model ships he'd been collecting for the past ten years, each of them purchased in celebration of a book being published. The first had been a prisoner-of-war model, made out of soup bones by a French prisoner during the Napoleonic War. After that he'd concentrated on admiralty models dating from the seventeenth century. Together they represented more money than his father had earned in a lifetime.

The books that filled the rest of the shelves were an eclectic assortment, ranging from a Charles Dickens first edition to the copies of his own books that Victoria had had printed on acid-free paper, edged in gold, and bound in dark red leather. She'd given him the obscenely expensive gift for Christmas the previous year with a note telling him what little favors she expected in return. He'd been neither surprised nor disappointed. Victoria was Victoria; to expect anything else was not only foolish, it was self-defeating.

There were times he wondered if he was keeping up his end of their relationship, but then the thought would pass. She didn't want or expect much from him, just a marriage that appeared solid and loving to the outside world.

The saddest part was not that his was a loveless marriage, but how little he cared.

20

The closer she got to home, the faster Andrea's heart raced. She was glad David had talked her into letting him rent a car rather than having someone come to the airport and pick them up. This way she could get used to the idea of being home again without anyone watching her do it.

She gazed at the passing countryside that was struggling to move into spring. It felt strange that she'd missed an entire winter when, until that year, she'd never been gone from this place more than a week. She kept looking for changes even knowing it was silly to do so. She'd only been gone four months, not four years. Still, she didn't like thinking the snow had come and nearly gone without her seeing it or that she hadn't knocked the icicles off the porch, or competed with her mother to see who could spot the first flock of migrating geese.

And now here she was less than five minutes from the house she'd lived in since she was five years old and she was scared to death of what she would find when she got there. What if all the changes she'd been looking for on the way there had actually taken place inside her own home? She realized her thoughts were being reflected on her face when, out of the corner of her eye, she saw David looking at her, his eyes narrowed in concern.

"Nervous?" he asked.

"No." She met his gaze. "Yes," she admitted sheepishly.

"I don't blame you. I would be, too."

"Is this how you felt when you came back?"

"Last fall or when I went away to school?"

"Last fall."

He took a deep breath and let it out slowly. "I had a lot of other things on my mind back then."

She had a habit of forgetting she wasn't the reason he'd returned to Baxter. "Your dad?"

"That and seeing your mother again."

She brushed the bangs from her forehead then gathered her hair and twisted it into a single curl that she draped over her shoulder. "It seems like that happened such a long time ago."

"This has been a rough six months for you."

"I just thought of something. Your father would have been my grandfather."

He smiled. "You're right."

"In a sad kind of way, he's the one responsible for us getting together."

"He wouldn't have minded," he said, thinking about the number of times his father had made pointed comments about wanting grandchildren. "What would have bothered him, though, is knowing he missed out on the opportunity to spoil his granddaughter."

She settled more comfortably into the seat, bringing one leg up and tucking it under the other. "Tell me about him."

David's voice changed, becoming soft and thoughtful. "He was a quiet man who liked to read and loved to fish. When I was in high school and he finally accepted that I was serious about becoming a writer, he told me not to listen to anyone who said I should learn a trade to get me through the hard times. He said that if I had another way to get by or something to fall back on, I'd never make it through the rejection that every writer faced at one time or another."

"Was he right?"

David smiled. "It's one of those things you can never know for sure. I've met people who have been writing for half their lives and had nothing but rejection and yet they continue to go at it with an amazing enthusiasm. But I don't think I was cut from that cloth. I need the feedback, the give-and-take that comes from having a book published and out there on the stands." He chuckled. "Having the money coming in isn't bad, either."

Andrea had never known another adult who talked to her the way David did, like a friend instead of this impressionable sponge that was supposed to absorb wonderful and profound thoughts and ideas. He shared who he was with her, and he never judged or lectured or criticized when she shared back. "What was Grandma like?"

"My memories of her aren't as strong." He hesitated. "No, that's not right—it isn't that I don't remember her as well, it's that everything about her is clouded by the last four years she was alive—that was how long it took her to die." He hesitated again, as if struggling with dormant, painful memories. "There are times when I'm sure I can remember her laughing and horsing around with me and my father, but then I can't put those memories in context with anything else. It's like the spots you see dancing in your eyes when you close them against a bright summer day. When you're watching them, you'd swear they were real, that you could touch them if you could only figure out how, but then you open your eyes and they're gone."

Andrea leaned her head back against the seat. "I like to listen to you."

He smiled. "What you like is me keeping your mind on something besides what's waiting for you at the end of this ride." He made a left turn. They had less than a quarter mile to go.

"Nay, kind sir," she said with a sweep of her hand. "You do yourself an injustice."

He laughed. "So a little bit of England has rubbed off on you after all."

She was taken aback by the statement and took some time to think about it before answering him. "More than a little," she said. She could have told him that she was convinced the four months she'd been in England had made her a different person, had changed who she was forever, but things like that always came out sounding stupid.

"I'm glad. For me, showing you London was like seeing it for the first time all over again. You made me realize how much I'd begun to take the place for granted."

"Do you think you'll ever come back to the States to live?" She'd tried to make the question sound casual, but could tell by his reaction she hadn't succeeded.

"Can you imagine Victoria living anywhere but England?"

"You could have a house here like Hawthorne. It wouldn't take much longer to fly over here than it does for you to drive up there."

He didn't answer her. Instead, he pulled the car off the road and onto the driveway. "We're here."

Andrea's heart did a funny little skipping beat when she looked at her house.

This wasn't one of the dreams she had used to put herself to sleep at night. She was really home.

"It looks the same," she said.

"What did you expect?" David asked gently.

She sat very still, not reaching for the door handle or making any move to get out. "I don't know. Maybe it's because I've changed so much, I expected everything else had changed, too."

"I think once you get settled, you're going to find you like the sameness. There's something to be said for familiarity." He opened his door. "Come on—we didn't come all this way to sit in the car."

Still she didn't move. "I'm scared," she finally said.

"Of what?"

"I don't know."

He twisted around to face her. "Ethan isn't here."

She shot him a questioning look. "How do you know?"

"I called Carly from the airport before we left when you went to pick up the candy for Eric. She said Ethan had to go to Columbus on business today."

The butterflies left her stomach and she offered David a grateful smile. "You're always doing things like that for me."

"Like what?"

"Making my life easier. I know how hard you looked to find a school that I would like and that you didn't go to Hawthorne to write your book so that you could be in London with me."

David had his mouth open to tell her that the pleasure had been his, but then realized she would never buy into his pretense that it was a simple thank-you. "I just wanted your mother to know what time we'd be arriving so she didn't start looking for us too soon."

After several more seconds and a deep, calming breath, she got out of the car and came around to the driver's side where David was waiting for her. "How do I look?"

"Like a million dollars."

"Only dollars?" she said with a show of indignation. "Why not pounds?"

He grinned. "You're a cheeky little bundle."

She put her arm through his and made a move toward the house. "I can hardly wait to show Shawn the model ship you got him."

David held back. "This is your show," he said. "I'll be up with the luggage in a couple of minutes."

"But I want you—" She stopped at the sound of the front door opening. They both turned to look as Carly stepped out on the porch.

She was wearing a green sweater and slacks and had her hair plaited into a long braid that hung across her shoulder. A sharp pain cut through David's chest, stealing his breath. For a heartbeat he allowed himself to imagine what it would be like if he were the one Carly was waiting to welcome, how he would put his arms around her and, between the long, lingering kisses he would give her, tell her how lonely he'd been without her.

His heart beat again and he shoved the image into the corner of his mind he reserved for plot ideas and other impossible fantasies.

"Hi, Mom," Andrea said.

"Hi, yourself." Carly came down the walkway, her arms outstretched. She caught Andrea to her in a joyous hug. After several seconds, she leaned back to see her daughter better. "You look wonderful," she said, tears of happiness making her eyes glisten in the crisp afternoon sunlight.

David fought a stab of jealousy when he saw how tightly Andrea had returned Carly's embrace. The last spark of hope that she would return to England with him died a quick, painful death.

"Where's Shawn?" Andrea asked.

"Inside waiting for you." Carly brought her close again and held her as if she never intended to let her go. "God, I've missed you."

"I've missed you, too, Mom," Andrea said, finally letting go of her, but not moving away.

The smile that spread across Carly's face rivaled the sun. "I'm not the only one. As soon as the word got out you were coming home, the phone started ringing and it hasn't stopped since."

Andrea looked embarrassed but immensely pleased. "Who's been calling?"

"Susan and Janice and Patty and Brian—I could go on all morning. The list is endless." She took Andrea's hand and started walking toward the house.

"Brian called?" Andrea asked, obviously pleased.

"Twice," Carly said.

David watched them until they got to the porch, then went back to the car and took Andrea's suitcases out of the trunk. He was fuming. Carly must have been rehearsing what to say all morning. The phone calls had been a particularly brilliant touch, tailor-made to delight Andrea and make her feel wanted.

He slammed the trunk lid harder than necessary, seeking physical release for his frustration. Reminding himself he had no right to be feeling the way he did, didn't ease the knot in his stomach. He jammed his hands on his hips, tilted his head back to look up at the cloudless sky and took several deep breaths.

"Aren't you coming in?" Carly asked.

At the sound of her voice, David turned so quickly he upset the bag of last-minute souvenirs Andrea had picked up in Harrods duty-free shop at the airport. "I thought you might like some time alone."

"Shawn has taken over. They're so wrapped up in each other, they didn't even see me leave." Carly hugged herself against the cool air. "She looks fantastic, David."

A flash of irrational anger shot through him.

"What did you expect—black leather and punk hair?"

"Why are you mad at me?"

He bent to pick up the Harrods bag. "I'm not."

"Then what's wrong?"

"What did you expect, Carly? How the hell am I supposed to act? You turned Andrea over to me to take care of and then return, as if she were a car on loan. Now you expect me to disappear from her life —and yours—and pretend none of this ever happened."

"Nothing has changed, David. I never promised you—"

"That's right. You never promised me a damn thing. But then you never warned me about what it would feel like when Andrea left, either."

"She was only supposed to be with you for two weeks." She picked up Andrea's carry-on bag and fit the strap over her shoulder. "How long will you be staying?"

"Long enough to see that she's settled, and then I've got to get back to the airport."

"But I thought—"

His mouth curled into an acerbic smile. "Don't tell me you went to all the trouble of fixing up the extra room for me?"

"I made reservations for you at the motel."

"How thoughtful. But to what point? So that I would be available to tell Andrea what a good thing she's got going for her here should she begin to have second thoughts about coming back?" He moved closer, purposely invading her personal space. "I'm through playing your games, Carly. If Andrea decides she wants to come back to England to live with me, I'm not going to do anything to dissuade her."

She took a small step backwards. "You have no right to—"

"Think about it, Carly. Thanks to you, I have every right where Andrea's concerned, and the papers to prove it."

Carly searched his face as if looking for something to guide her, a direction to go in dealing with him. "But she isn't your daughter," she said, her voice a frightened whisper, plainly confused by his outburst.

"Are you going to tell her that?" he asked evenly.

"You know I'm not." Alarm replaced the confusion in her eyes. "Why this sudden paternal interest in a child you only met six months ago?"

He shrugged expressively. "I just figured that as long as I had the name, I might as well play the game."

She slowly lowered the carry-on she was holding. The fear had disappeared, leaving indignation. "Let me get this straight—you're actually considering pressing your supposed rights as Andrea's father over my very real rights as her mother?"

"All I'm saying is that she has a home with me if that's what she wants."

"What are you trying to prove?"

"Not a goddamned thing."

"When you agreed to help me, you said you understood that she was mine, David. Nothing's changed."

"The hell it hasn't. Thanks to you, there are hundreds of people on two continents who believe I'm Andrea's father. Your manipulations have put me in a position where I either act like a parent or get tagged an uncaring bastard."

"So that's it," she said, the words dripping with venom. "You don't really care about Andrea. You're just afraid of what everyone might think. Or could it be that you've decided it might be nice to add a father-of-the-year award to all your other trophies?"

"Believe what you want." David stopped himself from saying more when he heard the sound of the front door opening. He looked up to see Andrea holding an overjoyed Muffin in one arm and waving at them with the other.

"What's keeping you two?" she called out. "Shawn wants you to sign his casts, David, and I want to show Mom what I bought for her in that shop in Soho."

"We'll finish this later," Carly said under her breath.

"As far as I'm concerned," David told her, "I've said everything I wanted to say. Unless, of course, you change your mind and decide to tell Andrea I'm not her father after all."

He went back to the car and gathered the remaining bags. When he looked up again, he carefully kept his expression neutral. "Now why don't we do as *our* daughter has suggested and go inside?"

"You're not going to win this one, David," Carly said, closely following him.

In his gut he knew she was right. What were his four months compared to the almost sixteen years she'd had with Andrea? And where in the hell had this sudden compulsion to keep Andrea with him come from? And then he understood. He was reacting to the reality of losing her. Until then he had been able to cling to the small hope that Andrea would not stay. Even caught up in his own confusion and self-doubt, he couldn't keep from taunting her, "Want to bet?"

"Don't put up anything you can't afford to lose," she snapped back at him.

A spark of hope ignited in David. There had been a distinct note of anxiety in Carly's bravado. Could it be she didn't know she'd already won? Or was there something else going on he knew nothing about that could throw the balance his way? "The only thing I have that I can't afford to lose is Andrea," he told her, knowing the statement was as good as issuing a challenge, but unable to stop himself.

Somewhere, sometime, in the past twelve hours, the game plan had changed. Now, all he had to do was figure out what he was going to do about it.

21

Carly entered Andrea's room, trying not to wake her if somehow she had managed to fall asleep already after the day's excitement. Having Andrea home again was every bit as satisfying as Carly had anticipated it would be. The empty feeling was gone, replaced with a deep contentment. Not even David's peculiar behavior had put a damper on the celebration.

Andrea rolled over and Muffin let out a soft grumble of protest at being disturbed. "Mom?"

"Go back to sleep. I was just checking on you."

"I'm awake." She doubled her pillow to prop herself up.

"Is something wrong?"

"It's just jet lag."

The words sounded strange—too grown up and sophisticated to be coming from her daughter. Carly had never experienced jet lag and probably never would. It was disconcerting to think Andrea had. "How long does it take to get over something like that?"

"I was in England a whole week before I slept eight hours straight."

Carly nudged Muffin over and sat down on the edge of the bed. "My guess is that there were one or two things besides the time difference that were contributing to your sleeplessness."

Andrea pulled herself up to a sitting position and leaned against the headboard. "I understand about David now," she said when she was settled.

The hair on the back of Carly's neck stood on end. "What do you understand about David?"

"Why you loved him enough to do what you did."

"That was a long time ago."

"What was he like when he was my age?"

Carly didn't want to remember and she sure as hell didn't want to share those years with Andrea. "I think David should be the one to tell you about himself."

Instead of pushing, Andrea came at her desire to talk about her father from another direction. "David likes me."

Carly put her hand over Andrea's. "That's not surprising. You're a pretty special person."

"No, I mean he really likes me. He never said anything, but I don't think he wanted me to come back here, not even for a visit. And I know that's the reason he decided to go to New York rather than stay in Baxter. He's afraid I'm not going to go back with him."

Carly was grateful Andrea had broken the ice. She'd been wondering how she was going to bring the subject up without it seeming as if she were prying. "That doesn't surprise me, either. David knows that this is your home—your real home. Your family and all of your friends are here. It's only natural that you would want to be with them." She couldn't let it go at that. She had to lay the groundwork for Andrea to be able to turn her back on David as well as England. "I'm sure that part of the reason he doesn't want to let you go is that he enjoys having people around him and there just isn't anybody better to have around than you."

"You're wrong about him liking people to be around him. He doesn't—at least not most of the time." She turned her hand over and wrapped her fingers around Carly's. "I think he's lonely."

"How could that be?" Carly said, choosing her words carefully. Being needed was an incredible lure to a girl Andrea's age. The last thing she wanted was to put Andrea in a position where she felt she had to defend or protect David. "He has a life most other people can only dream of having."

"That doesn't mean it's the life he wants."

"But if it wasn't, he would do something to change it," Carly said, trying to sound reasonable and neutral at the same time.

"He can't."

Reason would not work with Andrea. She had it in her head that David was some tragic, isolated figure who needed rescuing by his long-lost daughter. Carly felt like taking her by the shoulders and giving her a good shake. "David has been able to take care of himself emotionally the entire time I've known him."

"How do you know what he's been like since you dumped him? You didn't see him for sixteen years."

"I didn't 'dump' him, I let him go. There's a big difference."

"To you maybe, but not to him."

"Did he talk to you about this?"

"Not on purpose. We'd be in the middle of something else and little things would come out. I just put the pieces together."

"Well, you put them together wrong."

"I don't know why you try to make everything so complicated. David still loves you—as much now as he did then. Maybe more."

Anger shot through Carly. David should never

have told Andrea how he felt. She was too impressionable. "He had no right to tell you that."

Andrea leaned her head back. "So I'm right."

Only then did Carly realize how cleverly Andrea had maneuvered the conversation. To try to backtrack or deny the obvious would not only be useless, it would be destructive. "You never forget your first love, no matter what happens to the relationship."

"Does that mean you still love him, too?"

"In a sentimental way."

Andrea looked at her mother speculatively. "Where does that put Dad?"

Carly's answer depended on which man Andrea was talking about and she was reluctant to give David any more of a leg up than he already had.

As if she'd been able to read Carly's thoughts, Andrea added, "I don't call David Dad. We talked about it and he said he thought it would be better if I called Ethan Dad, because of you and Shawn and Eric."

"It puts Ethan right where he should be," Carly answered, not wanting to hear positive things about David. "My life is wrapped up in him—all the things I have or am, including my loyalties and aspirations, are tied to him."

"What about your love?" Andrea prodded.

Plainly she was not going to let go of her romantic fantasy about David. Carly could either lie to her or confuse her even more by telling her the truth. She settled for something in between. "I've never felt about Ethan the way I used to feel about David," she admitted. "But that doesn't mean I don't love him as much—just differently. Think about how you love—"

"If you're going to tell me to compare the way I feel about you and Grandma and Dad and David, don't. You can't love anyone else the way you're supposed to love the man you marry."

"Something tells me we're dancing around what's really on your mind," Carly said. "Why don't you tell me what that is? Maybe if we come at it straight on, we can work it out."

Andrea didn't say anything for a long time. When she did, she made several false starts before she finally gathered the courage to come out with it. "I was wondering why you and David couldn't get together again."

Carly's heart went out to her daughter. "Oh, sweetheart, that's a lovely dream, and I can understand why it would appeal to you, but it's never going to happen."

"Why not?"

"I'm happy with the life I have now. Besides, even if I wanted to get back together with David, how could I justify hurting so many other people?"

"Victoria doesn't love David, Mom. I don't think she ever did."

"I was talking about Shawn and Eric."

"Why do I have to be the one who chooses?"

"And the one who hurts?" Carly said, finally understanding what Andrea was trying to tell her.

"David doesn't want me to stay here."

"Did he say that?"

"He didn't have to. I could see it on his face."

"I didn't want you to go, either. But you did, and I had to learn to live with your decision."

"And you think the same thing will happen to David, and that eventually he'll get over missing me?"

"I'm sure of it."

"He never got over you."

"I'm not so sure you're right about that. But even if you are, the way he felt about me was different than the way he feels about you. I was the woman he wanted to marry." She almost choked trying to get the rest out. "You're his daughter." Without that one deception, none of this would be happening.

"You don't want to talk about this anymore, do you?"

"I can think of happier, more productive ways for us to be passing the time."

"Such as?"

"Figuring out how you're going to return all those phone calls from your friends." Noticing Andrea's lack of enthusiasm, Carly said, "You don't seem as excited tonight about seeing everyone as you did this afternoon."

"No one in my own family seems to care about what's happened to me while I've been gone. How can I expect my friends to be any different? All anyone here wants to talk about is what they've been doing and all the great things I missed when I was away." She plucked at a loose thread on the quilt. "I feel like I'm on the outside and the only way I can get back in is to forget everything I saw and did when I was in England."

Realizing she'd been as guilty as the rest, Carly apologized. "I'm sorry. Maybe we're all just a little bit jealous."

Andrea made a face. "Even Grandma and Grandpa? I don't think so."

"Give me another chance. I'll do better. I promise."

But Andrea wasn't going to let go that easily. "I know you can't be responsible for how everybody else feels, but could you at least tell me why you haven't asked one question about the people I met or the places I saw? In my letters I told you how nice Victoria has been to me, and I know I told you how much I like Jeffery Armstrong, but when I tried to tell you about them at dinner, you started talking about getting Grandma's Mustang ready for the summer."

Carly got up and went over to the window. She folded her arms across her chest and stared blindly out at the moonlit lawn. She still had her back to

Andrea when she said, "I suppose the main reason I've been putting you off is that I didn't want to hear you tell me how much you liked England. When you left, I thought you would miss us so much you would be back home in a week. But the weeks turned into months, and I got more and more scared you were never coming back."

"I couldn't leave school. We were getting ready for exams."

"You left school here."

"That's different."

Carly turned to look at Andrea, but the deep shadows hid her face and whatever expression was there. "How is it different?"

"You could have asked me a long time ago and you'd already know."

"I'm asking now."

"The school I'm going to in London isn't like the school here. It costs a lot of money and the kids are way ahead of where I was when I transferred. At first, I didn't think I'd ever catch up, but the tutor David hired helped a lot."

"I don't think it's a matter of the school you've been going to being better just because it's over there." Even as she spoke the words, Carly knew she was using the wrong approach, but she couldn't stop herself. "Private schools—no matter where they're located—do a better job because they have more time to spend on their students. If that's the kind of education you want, we can look into something over here for you."

"But then I wouldn't be living at home anyway."

Carly jammed her hands in her pockets. "Why don't you tell me about Jeffery Armstrong?"

"What do you want to know?"

"You can start out by telling me what he looks like."

"He's a couple of inches taller than I am and built

a lot like David." Her voice took on an animation it had lacked before. "He has black hair and the most incredible blue eyes. When I first met him, he had this great tan because he'd just gotten back from skiing, but now he's just as pale as all the other guys over there. His dad is a barrister—that's like a lawyer over here—and he's in the House of Lords because he's an earl."

"Does Jeffery go to school with you?"

Andrea sighed. "I told you about that in the letter I sent after Christmas."

"I'm sorry. I forgot."

"That's okay. You probably thought Jeffery was just some boy I met at a party."

"But he's more than that, isn't he?"

"I've never met anyone like him, Mom. He acts like he's no better than anyone else, but David told me that Jeffery is one of the top students at Eton and he's one of the best soccer players the school has ever had. He's in Pop, too—that's like a really big-deal fraternity over there. There's only twenty boys, all seniors, and they kind of rule the other kids. You have to be asked to join. When he graduates from Eton, he's going to Christ Church College at Oxford, which is only about the best school there is anywhere."

"He sounds almost too good to be true," Carly said.

Andrea laughed. "That's what I thought, too, when David told me about him."

"All those accomplishments must keep him busy." Carly couldn't believe how stilted she sounded. It was as she were talking to a stranger she'd met at a cocktail party. "How do the two of you ever find time to see each other?"

"He's a sixth former—that's like a senior over here —so once in a while he gets to come home on weekends. Instead of going to the country, he's been taking the train into London and staying with his dad so we can go out."

With each new revelation, the crack in Carly's confidence grew bigger. "I had no idea you were so involved with Jeffery."

"He's my best friend."

Carly almost said, "You mean, in England," but stopped herself before the potentially divisive words could be spoken. "He must have been upset when you told him you were leaving," she said in a shameless attempt to find out how much and what Andrea had said to Jeffery about her plans.

"Everything happened so fast, I didn't have a chance to tell him anything. He was supposed to get last weekend off, but couldn't." She adjusted the pillow at her back.

"I envy you all you've seen," Carly said softly, admitting something she'd only just then realized.

"You probably think David took me all those places so I would stay with him," Andrea said, a defensive note in her voice. "But what I didn't tell you is that we never went anywhere or did anything that he didn't say something about how much you missed me and that someday I was going to have to show you everything he was showing me."

Carly didn't want Andrea to tell her good things about David. It was easier to think of him as an enemy to be guarded against. "He was right about my missing you."

Long seconds passed without either of them saying anything. Finally, Andrea broke the silence. "It's hard being in the middle," she said, a catch in her voice. "I love you both."

"But this is your home," Carly said. "This is where you grew up. It's where you belong."

"Does that mean if you and Dad were to move someplace else I wouldn't have a home anymore?"

Carly flinched. Andrea was getting too old and too

clever to have such sloppy reasoning used on her. "Of course it doesn't. The house, the place, doesn't matter. It's the people who count, and it just so happens your people are in Baxter, Ohio."

"David isn't. Or don't you think he counts?"

"Of course he—"

"There you are," said Ethan, stepping into the doorway. He crossed the room and put a proprietary hand on the back of Carly's neck. "I've been looking all over for you. Don't you think it's time you were in bed?"

It was everything Carly could do to stand still while his hand moved across her shoulder and down her arm. "You go on without me. Andrea and I have a lot of catching up to do."

"Bad idea," he said. "How are you going to be able to take care of Shawn tomorrow if you don't get the sleep you need tonight?"

"Andrea will help me."

As if he'd just realized she was in the room with them, Ethan glanced over to the bed. "Is that any way to treat a guest?"

Carly battled a wave of anger that made her want to double up her fist and hit him. She frantically sought something she could say or do that would lessen the impact of his thoughtlessness. "You know guest status only lasts twenty-four hours around here. Then it's back on the chain gang." She had to get him out of there before he did any more damage. "But I am a little tired. It always surprises me how really special days can take as much energy as the bad ones."

Ethan started for the door and then, almost as an afterthought, went over to the bed where he bent and placed a quick kiss on the top of Andrea's head. "Nice to have you with us, Andrea, even if it's only for a little while."

"I'll be right behind you, Ethan," Carly said, guiding him out of the room. "Why don't you check on Shawn?"

"Two minutes," he told her, making an attempt at a teasing voice. "That's all you've got before I come back after you."

When he was gone, Carly sat down on the bed again and drew Andrea into her arms. To say something about Ethan's behavior would give it too much importance, and it would force them to talk about something Carly still didn't know how to handle.

Thank God, Carly didn't have to come up with an answer that night. Andrea was home now. There would be plenty of time to work things out between them. "I'm so glad you're back," Carly said. "This house finally seems like a home again."

"I love you, Mom," Andrea said after several seconds had passed.

At that moment, Carly would have given ten years of her life to be able to put words together the way David could. But how did you tell someone they were the air you breathed, the music you hummed, the beauty that blinded you to ugliness? In the end, all she could think to say was, "I love you, too, sweetheart."

22

Andrea stood at the kitchen doorway and watched her mother. Carly was sitting at the table, holding a mug of coffee between her hands, slowly moving the cup back and forth across her forehead as if fighting a headache. She seemed more alone than just being in the room by herself should have made her look.

It hurt Andrea to see her mother so sad, especially knowing that she was probably the reason. Their past week together had been both wonderful and awful at the same time. They had talked every night, once almost through the night, much to her dad's irritation. And it hadn't been all fun and easy things, like Andrea filling her mother in on what kind of clothes English women were wearing that year or Carly telling how Grandpa Wally accidently sat on the surprise Valentine cake Grandma Barbara had made for him. Andrea had asked pointed questions about Carly's decision not to tell David that she was pregnant. She'd also wanted to know why Carly had married Ethan when she didn't love him. And she'd wanted to know about Carly's painting, too, why she'd given it up and if she ever intended to start again.

Andrea continued to watch her mother as Carly lowered her cup to the table and reached up to rub her temples with the tips of her fingers. As she silently stood there, an uncomfortable feeling came over her. It suddenly seemed as if she were spying on her mother, as much as observing. She announced her presence by knocking lightly on the door frame.

"Good morning," Carly said, turning to look at Andrea.

Andrea smiled and came into the kitchen. "Did I tell you that I actually got to touch the Rosetta Stone?" she said, searching for something that would lift her mother's spirits.

"No, you didn't," Carly said with a show of enthusiasm that didn't quite succeed. "What was it like?"

"Big and black with tiny white writing. It was sitting out in the open on the main floor of the museum and when David pointed it out, I figured it had to be a reproduction. But he told me it wasn't. I looked all over the place for a sign that said Do Not Touch, but there wasn't any."

"I didn't know you'd even heard of the Rosetta Stone."

"My tutor told me about it."

Carly pushed back her chair and stood up. "What would you like for breakfast?"

"Nothing—I'm not hungry."

"How about a cup of cocoa?"

Andrea shook her head. "I guess I've gotten spoiled by the chocolate they have in England. Now the stuff we have here tastes funny to me."

Carly went to the sink, dumped her old coffee out and poured herself another cup. "How long have you been awake?"

"About an hour, give or take."

"But you didn't want to come down until you

heard your father leave." It was a statement, not a question.

Andrea pulled out a chair and sat down at the table. "I have to talk to you," she said, her tone serious.

"Why do I get the feeling I'm not going to like this?"

"Probably because you already know what I'm going to say."

"You're going back, aren't you?"

The look on her mother's face made Andrea flinch and turn away. "I'm sorry, Mama," was all she could say, knowing it wasn't enough, but that nothing she could do would take away the hurt.

Carly let out a pent-up sigh. "Is there anything that could get you to change your mind?"

Andrea chanced a look. "I have to finish what I started." Even from across the room, she could see tears welling in her mother's eyes. "Just because I'm going back doesn't mean I love David more than I love you."

"I know," Carly said in a whisper, as if afraid to trust her voice.

"And it doesn't mean I won't be back."

"In my heart I knew the day would come when I'd have to let you go, but I never dreamed it would be this soon. I'm not ready, Andrea. If we lose these years, we'll never get them back." She laid the length of her finger along the bottom of her eye to catch the tears before they had a chance to spill.

"If I don't spend them with David, we'll never have any at all."

"Goddamn it. I wish he'd never come back."

Andrea had promised herself she wouldn't cry, it would only make things harder for both of them. "Please tell me it's okay for me to go."

"When will you come home again?"

"This summer? After school is out?" Whether her

return would be permanent or for another visit hung heavily between them.

"It's going to be lonely around here without you."

"You could come with me," Andrea said softly. "David wouldn't care."

"I have a feeling Ethan might."

"He could come, too—and Shawn and Eric."

"Maybe someday," Carly said. "Perhaps when David isn't such a painful reminder of something Ethan has spent half his life trying to forget."

"Is that why he doesn't want me to live here anymore? Because I remind him of David?"

Carly looked stunned. "Where in God's name did you get that idea?"

How could she explain a feeling? "He didn't want me to come home for Easter."

"He told you that?"

Andrea felt squeamish, as if she were tattling on Ethan. She moved her shoulders in a casual shrug, trying to diminish the impact of her words. "He said you already had too much to do taking care of Shawn, and that I should wait a while before I came home to visit."

"I didn't know you'd talked to him," Carly said, her voice artificially calm.

"He called a couple of days after you and Shawn phoned me from the hospital and I told you I was coming home." She tried to remember the reason he'd given her. "I think he said it was because you asked him to give me a report on Shawn."

She studied Andrea. "Even though you thought Ethan didn't want you here, you came anyway. Why?"

"David convinced me that I was wrong about him, that he really did love me and wanted me to come home." She noticed several grains of salt that had been spilled on the table and methodically began to gather them with the tip of her finger. "But that wasn't why I changed my mind. David told me how much it would hurt you if I didn't come." She looked up and smiled. "And I missed you, too."

Carly put her hand to her mouth as if trying to hold back a sob. "What am I going to do without you?"

"Can't you come to see me and leave Dad here?"

"Maybe someday," she said, repeating the evasive answer.

"I hate it when you say that. What it means is, there's no way in hell."

"I can't promise you anything now."

"I'm not asking you to promise you'll come, just that you'll think about it."

Carly let out a disparaging laugh. "Oh, you can count on that."

Andrea stood up. "I should call David now. He told me if I changed my mind about staying, he would come and get me so that we could fly home—" She saw the look on her mother's face and felt like biting her tongue. "So we could fly back to London together," she finished lamely.

"It's all right," Carly said, taking Andrea into her arms. "I wouldn't want you to live anyplace you couldn't think of as home. I just don't want you to ever forget you have a home here, too."

Andrea hugged her mother tightly. "David was right—you are the best mom in the world."

"When will he come for you?"

"I don't know—probably tomorrow. I have to be back to school on Monday."

"Tell him I want to talk to him when he gets here." She tilted her head back to look Andrea in the eye. "Alone."

"There might not be enough time."

Carly brushed the bangs from Andrea's forehead. "If he wants me to let you go with him," she said softly, "he'll find the time."

23

"*Aren't you taking* a hell of a chance being seen with me like this?" David asked, turning left onto the road that led to Lender's Mill. "After all, we wouldn't want to mislead anyone into thinking we still actually cared about each other."

"Sarcasm has never been your strong suit, David," Carly said. "You hit the jugular better when you're being direct."

"Is this why you wanted time alone? So we could trade insults out of Andrea's earshot?"

"We have some things that need to be settled."

"I hope you don't intend to waste my time and yours by going over the same old crap you've been throwing at me the past six months. If so, tell me now and save us both the effort." He checked the rearview mirror before turning onto a narrow dirt road.

Carly didn't answer him.

David drove the final mile to the mill without trying to draw more information out of her. When Andrea had called the day before, she'd been strangely uncommunicative, saying little beyond that she had decided to return to England to finish school and that her mother wanted to talk to him when he came to pick her up. He still had no idea what had happened to make her change her mind or how the family had responded to her decision.

He parked on the shady side of the mill and waited for Carly to make the first move. She stayed in the car for several more seconds, then opened the door, got out, and started walking toward the creek. David took a deep breath and followed.

When she reached the creek, she took off her jacket, laid it on the new grass, then sat down and gazed at the swiftly moving water. "You won," she said, at last breaking the long silence.

David wasn't sure he'd heard her correctly. Carly had never given up this easily. He couldn't believe she was doing so now. "What's the punch line?"

She ignored his pointed comment and went on as if he'd said nothing. "She loves you, David."

It was as if she'd stuck a knife in the defensive shield he'd built around himself. "It's because she thinks I'm her father."

"That may be what drew her to you, but it's not what's made her stay. Somehow, you managed to say all the things a fifteen-year-old wants and needs to hear. You're rich and famous and, in her eyes, Super Dad to boot. How could she keep from falling in love with you?"

He sat down, being careful not to crowd her, but near enough for the breeze to taunt him with the smell of her perfume. "She was sad and confused when she came to me. All I did was listen."

"Having someone hang on my every word would be a heady experience for me. I can only imagine what it must feel like when you're fifteen-years-old."

"I honestly tried, Carly. Everything I did was aimed at making her feel good about herself so that she would want to go home again."

"She told me."

He plucked a blade of grass and stuck it in his mouth. "But you didn't believe her?"

"You can stop being so defensive. I didn't ask you here to fight with you about what you did or didn't do."

"Then why did you ask me?"

"For my own peace of mind, I have to know what kind of person you've become." She turned to look at him. "How have you changed, David? What has living a privileged life done to you?"

"What you really want to know is what kind of influence I'm going to have on Andrea and whether or not it's something you're going to have to overcome when you get her back."

She shook her head sadly. "You have so much anger. How does it come out when it isn't directed at me?"

Her eyes were filled with such pain, he couldn't look at her any longer. "You want a guarantee that I'll be the perfect parent, but I can't give it to you. What do I know about being a father? It's crazy. The whole time she was with me, I kept telling myself how great it was going to be when she was gone and I could finally get my life back in order again. And then when I woke up one morning and she was actually getting ready to leave, I realized how much I liked having her around, and how much I was going to miss her when she was gone. I didn't know what to do."

"You learn to get by one day at a time," she said softly.

"What's happening to me, Carly? I feel about Andrea the way I imagine a real father would feel about his daughter. I'm ready to call the police if she and Jeffery are ten minutes late coming home from a date. And I find myself taking pride in her accomplishments even when I've had nothing to do with them."

"Is it possible you've become so attached to her because of me?" she said.

The way she asked the question told him they had finally gotten to the real reason she'd wanted to see him. "In the beginning. What other explanation would fit?"

"But not now?"

"I'm sure there's still some of you wrapped up in how I feel about Andrea, but mostly it's Andrea herself." He hesitated. "That doesn't mean I don't see you in everything she does, and that there aren't times I let myself wallow in useless memories."

Carly dropped her gaze and asked in an even, clear voice, "Is it possible you want her because you can't have me?"

David felt as if she'd hit him. "My God, is that what this is all about?" She knew him better than anyone ever had or would; it made him sick that the thought had even occurred to her. "Do you honestly believe I could be capable of something that perverted?"

"I don't know. That's why I'm asking."

He got to his feet, walked toward the mill, stopped, and came back. "You can sit there and listen to me tell you that in every way but biological Andrea has become my daughter and still ask a question like that?" His anger threatened to choke him. "What kind of a warped bastard do you think I am?"

Before answering, she looked up and fixed him with a cool stare. "It's not as if it has never happened before."

"Now I really don't understand you. If you've felt this way all along, how could you let her come with me in the first place?"

"You didn't love her then." She shifted her gaze away from him. "And I never believed she would stay."

He hunkered down in front of her, took her chin in

his hand and forced her to look at him. "It isn't the daughter that keeps me awake nights," he said, not caring how uncomfortable the truth would make her, "it's the mother. I've made love to you a hundred times in the past six months—Andrea was never there."

"Do you want to make love to me now?" Carly asked without emotion.

David dropped his hand. Five minutes ago he would have made a bargain with the devil to hear those words from her. "Why the big turnaround, Carly? What happened to the life-long debt you owe Ethan?"

"Things change."

"That's bullshit." He stood and backed away from her. "You think if you make the big sacrifice and give yourself to me, I'll stay away from Andrea." Her silence was all the confirmation he needed. "What in the hell happened to you that left you so fucked up you can't even trust me anymore?"

"I was raped. Remember?"

"But not by me," he snapped. His shoulders sagged in defeat. "What can I do—what do you need, to reassure you it won't happen to Andrea?"

She didn't answer right away. Finally, with great effort, she said, "I don't know."

He reached for her hand and pulled her to her feet. "You never were very good at dealing with the unknown. Why don't you come with us and stay for a couple of weeks? That way you can see for yourself what her life is like with me."

"I can't."

"Why not?"

"I have to take care of Shawn."

"Then come as soon as he's out of his casts."

"By then Andrea will be ready to return home."

He started to correct her, to tell her that she knew as well as he did that Andrea was never coming back to Baxter to live, but then he saw the small spark of hope in her eyes and couldn't be the one to extinguish it. "If you change your mind . . ." He left it open-ended.

"We should be getting back. Knowing Andrea, she'll still be in the middle of packing."

"Who was it, Carly? Who raped you?"

"Why do you want to know, David? So you can find him and beat him up?"

"I don't understand how you can be so brutalized by it one minute and flippant the next."

She touched his arm in an affectionate, wistful gesture. "I've had sixteen years, you've only had six months."

"Didn't you ever want to see him punished for what he did to you?"

"I had more important things to think about." She shrugged. "I don't know, maybe keeping Andrea had something to do with how I feel now. I might hate the man who raped me and damn him for the way he changed my life, but with Andrea the result, how can I wish it had never happened?"

"If only you had come to me."

"Don't do that, David."

He picked up her jacket and handed it to her. "Remember, you've had sixteen years to think about that, too."

"Say I had come to you and the scenario I'd imagined played out the way I figured it would. We might have ended up hating each other for the missed opportunities. Think about what you've accomplished, David, the millions of people you've reached with your books. And best of all, we're friends again."

"I'd give it all up if—"

"You can't. And even if you were free, Shawn and Eric would still tie me to Ethan. Too many people have been hurt because of me—I won't include them."

"Do you really think Ethan is going to put up with us being friends again?"

"He's willing to tolerate just about anything to have Andrea gone."

"I wasn't sure you knew what he's been doing to try to manipulate her into staying away."

"I didn't at first, but then Andrea said a couple of things that were in marked contrast to Ethan's version of conversations between the two of them. It wasn't too hard to put the pieces together after that." She put her arm through David's and started back toward the car. "I was furious when I found out, but it didn't last. I should have known what was going on from the beginning. Ethan sees himself in a desperate fight to hold on to the only thing he's ever wanted."

"And all's fair—"

"Can you be my friend?" she asked.

He matched his stride to hers so that they moved together in an easy rhythm. Only knowing that she was aware of what she was asking gave him the freedom to say, "If you're asking me to give up hope, the answer is no."

"And if it's really far more simple than that?"

"Then, yes, I can be your friend."

They were almost to the car when Carly abruptly stopped. She tossed a challenging look up at him. "Race you to the car," she said, taking off before he could respond.

He sprinted after her. For several wonderful seconds, they really were just friends again—glorious, uncomplicated best friends.

They were in the car and halfway to Carly's house when David remembered something he'd wanted to talk to her about. "After everything that's been said this afternoon, I'm a little reluctant to bring this up, but I need to know how you feel about birth control."

"In what context?" Carly asked.

David smiled at the stunned look on her face. "Andrea and Jeffery are getting a lot closer than I like. She's going to be sixteen in a couple of months. If you recall, that's how old you were when we—"

"You don't have to remind me," she said. "I'll talk to her as soon as we get back to the house."

"I don't understand how you can be so calm about this."

"I would have preferred having the discussion during her wedding shower, but it's nice not to have to do it long distance." She looked at him and smiled knowingly. "What did you have in mind to do about it, lock her up at night?"

"Actually, I was looking into a chastity belt of some sort. The museums at home are filled with them. Barring that, I'm open to advice."

"The only thing I can tell you is to try to remember what you were like at Andrea's age and do whatever would have worked on you."

"Was that meant to reassure me or scare the hell out of me?"

Carly laughed. It was a wonderful, joyous sound. "A little bit of both."

David tried to keep himself from imprinting in his mind the way she looked and sounded at that moment. But even as he was doing so, he knew that it was useless.

A million other memories were at the ready.

There was no escaping her.

There never would be.

24

Carly poured herself a cup of coffee and followed Barbara into the family room. "I was so mad at Ethan I got up and walked out before he was finished with his little speech," she said.

"You still haven't told me what he said before you left," Barbara said, sitting in her favorite overstuffed chair and propping her feet up on a stool.

"It isn't worth repeating, just a bunch of garbage about why we can't possibly go to England again this year."

"I must admit, there does seem to be a pattern of sorts where this trip is concerned." She brought her cup to her mouth, blew the steam away, and took a sip. "This will be the third summer he's managed to skinny out of going. I figured it out. We've only seen Andrea ten weeks in three and a half years."

"I promised Andrea this wouldn't happen again. What am I going to tell her?"

"How about the truth? I doubt it will come as much of a surprise."

"I can't do that."

"Why not?"

"Because it would hurt her too much."

"I'm beginning to wonder if your willingness to put up with Ethan's manipulations are for Andrea's benefit or your own."

"Where in God's name did that come from?" Carly snapped.

"You've convinced yourself it's Andrea you're protecting, but in reality, it's Ethan. You've let him get away with absolutely reprehensible behavior for the past two years. No," she said, warming to the subject, "it's more than 'let,' you've actually facilitated his conduct."

Carly put her cup on the table, held her hands up in a gesture of surrender, and started toward the door. "I don't need any more grief today."

"So what are you going to tell Andrea?" Barbara asked, stopping Carly as effectively as if she'd clamped a hand around her arm.

Carly stood with her fists on her hips and stared at the wall. "I don't know," she said, expelling a weary sigh.

"She's going to be crushed. All she ever writes about anymore is what the five of you are going to do this summer. She's packed two months of activity into the seven days Ethan promised her last summer."

Carly turned to look at her mother. "Is all of this leading up to something or are you just adding another layer of guilt?"

"I don't deserve that."

Carly ran her hand across her forehead. "You're right. I'm sorry."

"I haven't told you anything you don't already know. You just don't like hearing it said out loud."

"I need answers, Mom, not confirmation of my problems." She retrieved her coffee and sat down on the couch.

After several seconds, Barbara asked, "Why does Ethan have to go on this trip with you?"

"He's part of the family," Carly answered.

"You know as well as I do they'll be throwing snowballs in hell before Ethan steps on a plane that's heading east. Give Andrea a couple more years and she'll stop asking—if it takes her that long."

"According to Ethan, there's been another crisis at the plant—you can stop me when this begins to sound all too familiar—and it would be 'fiscally irresponsible' for us to spend money on ourselves when it could mean livelihood of all those employees."

"Use your private stash."

"I don't have one."

Barbara shook her head in disgust. "I told you when you got married that every woman needs to have some money tucked away for emergencies."

"Nice in theory, but a little hard to pull off when you're married to a man who collects receipts the way some people collect baseball cards."

"My God, how can you stand to have your every move monitored? You should have put your foot down in the beginning."

"Until now I just didn't give a damn. Next question?"

"You can borrow the money from me," Barbara said, a mischievous smile forming.

"Do you have any idea how much it costs to send three people to England for seven days in the middle of summer?"

"I don't care," Barbara said. "It would be nice to see some real return on all those cursed coupons I've clipped over the years. I haven't made a fortune at it, but you can have everything I've got."

Carly brought her cup up to her lips, but didn't take a drink. Instead, she absently tapped the rim against her bottom teeth and waited for the idea floating in her mind to settle and take form. "Ethan would make all of our lives unbearable if I took money from you. I need to find a way to protect the boys," she said, expressing out loud her coalescing thoughts. "One of the things he laid on me this morning was that the basketball camp the boys have been begging to attend just happens to fall on the week we were supposed to be gone."

"Isn't it interesting that there's money enough for that?" Barbara asked, plainly not expecting an answer.

"Rather than taking a loan from you, what if you gave me an early birthday present?"

Barbara sat up straight in her chair. "You mean like a ticket to England?"

"Ethan doesn't believe you have it in you to do anything devious, so there's no way he'd come back on you. Of course, Andrea would be disappointed we couldn't all—"

"But she would be thrilled that at least one of you didn't let her down." Barbara smiled. "Oh, Carly, that's a wonderful idea."

"I don't fool myself he's going to let me go without a fight. As a matter of fact, I expect my life will be rather uncomfortable for the next couple of months." A grin formed. "Are you absolutely sure you can afford to give me the money?"

"I managed to put that much away once, there's nothing saying I can't do it again. Besides, you won't come close to using it all."

Carly drew her feet up and tucked them under her. "I know how my going off alone is going to look to Ethan. In his mind Andrea has become a package deal with David."

"Good. Maybe it will get him to change his mind about going himself."

"He'd rather put up a good front and imagine the worst."

Barbara started to say something, hesitated, and then asked, "Is there any reason he should be worried?"

A bubble of longing burst in Carly. "If anything was going to happen between David and me, it would have happened the year he brought Andrea home for Easter."

"As much as I want you to be happy, it can't be at the expense of Shawn and Eric. They're the innocents in this."

Carly eyed her mother. "Are you afraid I'm going to get over there and not want to come back?"

"The thought crossed my mind," she admitted.

"Did you forget about Victoria? She and David may have an unconventional marriage, but that doesn't mean she wouldn't do battle to keep it intact." Carly unfolded her legs, rocked forward, and stood. "I might as well get it over with. If it were done when 'tis done, then 'twere well it were done quickly."

"Practicing?" Barbara asked, standing and following Carly to the door.

"For Ethan?"

"For England."

A surge of excitement shot through Carly. It wasn't a dream anymore. She was really going to England.

Two months later, Carly was maneuvering her luggage carrier around yet another hallway in Heathrow airport, when she looked up and saw Andrea smiling at her.

"Mom!" Andrea called and rushed forward. "You're really here. I can hardly believe it."

"Me, too," Carly said, releasing the carrier to give Andrea a hug. "It seems like forever. How are you?" She let go of Andrea long enough to gaze into her face. "You look wonderful—and so grown up. My God, when did that happen?"

"Yesterday."

"You couldn't have waited one more week?"

Andrea's leaned back to gaze at Carly. Her eyes sparkled with joy and merriment. "It happened while I was asleep."

A melancholy threatened Carly's happiness. "I'm sorry I wasn't here."

"Well you're here now and that's all that matters." The look she gave her mother said she refused to let anything spoil the moment. "When Eric wrote that Dad was having financial problems, I thought for sure none of you would be coming. I was trying to figure out a way to tell David I'd be leaving again this summer when I got your letter."

A man with several suitcases in tow gave a discreet cough behind them. Andrea let go of Carly so that they could move out of the way. "You should have seen me when I got your letter," she continued without missing a beat. "David said he didn't know it was possible for anybody to smile for three days straight."

"We have Grandma to thank for my being here." Carly couldn't take her eyes off Andrea. The charming young girl with chubby cheeks and mischievous looks had stepped away from childhood and turned into a breathtakingly beautiful and sophisticated woman. How could the nine months since they'd seen each other have made such a difference?

"I know. I tried to talk her into coming with you, but she said she wanted to give us some time alone. The best I could do was to get her to promise she'd fly over next year and that she'd bring you and Grandpa with her."

Carly suddenly realized they had become an island in an ever-swelling stream of people. She reached for the luggage carrier with one hand, took Andrea's arm with the other, and stepped into the flow of traffic.

"How was the flight?" Andrea asked.

"Wonderful."

"Were you able to get any sleep?"

Carly shook her head. "I was too excited." She grinned. "It's so good to see you. And to be here. I thought I'd go crazy waiting for this day to arrive."

"Me, too."

"I want to see everything. That way, I'll have a picture in my mind and I'll be able to see the places you write about from now on."

Andrea laughed. "We've only got two weeks, Mom. We may not make it everywhere." She hesitated. "I didn't want to dump this on you the minute you got off the plane, but I guess now's as good a time as any. I could only get one week off from school."

Carly didn't want Andrea to hear the disappointment in her voice, so she waited until she could hide her feeling before she answered. "That's okay, honey. I don't mind saving some things for next time." The look on Andrea's face told Carly her often-wounded daughter didn't believe there would ever be a next time. "Besides," she went on, "who says I can't do some exploring on my own? You can point me in the right direction before you leave for school and I'll give you a full report when I get back."

"You won't have to do that. David said he would take you wherever you wanted to go."

"I thought David was going to be at Hawthorne working while I was here," she said cautiously, not wanting to let Andrea see how uncomfortable she was with the idea of having David around.

"When he found out I couldn't get the time off school, he volunteered to stay in the city."

"What about Victoria?" Carly asked. "I don't imagine she was too thrilled with David's offer."

"She's in Vienna working on some Mozart exhibit her women's group is putting together for the two-hundred-year anniversary of his death. It's only been one hundred and ninety-nine so far, which gives them a whole year, but the bunch of them are running around like it's happening next month."

"When will she be back?"

"Not for a month, maybe more, depending on how much time she spends shopping in Paris when she's finished in Vienna."

"Did she know I was coming before she left?"

Andrea shot a questioning look at her mother. "Of course she did. Why do you ask?"

"The arrangements seem a little unconventional," she said. Under her breath she added, "To say the least."

"David's not worried about you being here while Victoria's gone. Why should you be?"

When they reached a line of waiting cars, Harold moved ahead of them, unloaded Carly's luggage on the sidewalk, then opened the door of a black Bentley for Carly and Andrea. While he was putting the luggage in the trunk, Carly took advantage of the moment of privacy. "You and David both know that Ethan would have a fit if he found out David was staying with us while I was here."

"Good grief, Mom. It's a great big house with lots and lots of rooms. The maid is there all day and I'll be there every night." She studied her mother. "Are you sure it's Ethan you're afraid of?"

Carly busied herself adjusting her skirt. "Meaning?"

The trunk lid slammed shut. "Never mind," Andrea said. "Why are we talking about something so dumb anyway when we could be talking about Grandma or Grandpa or Shawn or Eric. . . ." She batted her eyelashes several times for effect. "Or even Jeffery."

This time it was Carly's turn to laugh. "I'd love to hear about Jeffery."

Andrea reached for her purse. "It just so happens,

I've brought along a few dozen recent photographs of the gentleman in question."

Harold opened the driver's side door and peered into the backseat. "I'm pleased the nap you took on the way here has set you to rights again," he said to Andrea.

Carly frowned. It was ten o'clock in the morning. Andrea couldn't have been out of bed more than a couple of hours. On impulse, she reached across the seat and touched her hand to Andrea's forehead. She felt slightly warm, but that could easily have been from excitement. "Do you feel all right?"

Andrea removed her mother's hand with a show of impatience. "I feel fine," she said. "I stayed up late last night studying for a test."

"Why didn't you tell me you had a test today? I could have taken a cab."

"Because it isn't today—it's tomorrow. I just wanted to get the studying out of the way so we could be together."

Carly backed off. She sure as hell hadn't flown all that way to get into an argument with Andrea. "By the way, before I forget, I want you to dig out a couple of old sweatshirts for me to take home when I leave. I figure the only way I'm ever going to get Muffin to let go of the one she's got is if I give her another."

"She's still sleeping on the other one?" Andrea asked, plainly pleased she had not been forgotten by her childhood companion. "It must be a rag by now."

"She'll let Eric take her for a walk now, but not without coaxing. Shawn thinks she's so senile, she can't remember anyone but you. I told him it was selective memory. Muffin was your shadow when she was still spry enough to do fun things."

"David wanted to get me another dog, but I wouldn't let him."

"Why not?" Carly asked, already knowing the answer.

"It wouldn't be fair to Muffin."

Deciding it was time to change the subject, Carly said, "I believe you had some pictures you were going to show me."

A look of relief washed over Andrea's face, as if she'd been given an anxiously awaited reprieve. "I really am glad you're here," she said. "I've missed you so much."

Carly lost track of time on the drive in from the airport. As eager as she was to get her first look at London, she found it impossible to take her eyes from her daughter.

Two weeks wasn't enough time. She was an idiot not to have pushed for more. Twenty-one days couldn't have made Ethan any angrier. Why had she settled for fourteen?

She had to give him credit. Even when she'd first approached him, he'd had sense enough not to involve Shawn and Eric in their arguments. He'd saved the majority of his hostility for the times the two of them were alone, only exposing the boys to his long periods of silence. But then he'd used that method to control Carly their entire marriage. As far as Shawn and Eric knew, Ethan was as excited about Carly seeing Andrea as they were.

Or so she'd thought until two days ago when she was in the middle of packing. Shawn came into the room and sat on the bed to watch her. It took ten minutes for him to build up his nerve and then the question slipped out so innocently, Carly wasn't sure she'd heard him correctly.

"Are you going to stay over there forever?" he'd asked.

Instead of answering him right away, Carly had

finished wrapping tissue around her blue purse and closed the suitcase. His question and the fear behind it demanded more than a quick denial and reassurance. "Why don't we go for a walk?"

While she'd found and expressed the words it would take to convince him she would return, they wandered through the woods seeing who could find and identify the most birds. Afterwards, reluctant to end their time together, they'd gone over to Cindy's for apple pie and ice cream.

In the hours they were together, Shawn gently renewed his claim on his mother, making sure she knew Andrea wasn't her only child in need. Not until she'd come into his room that evening to kiss him good night was she convinced she'd managed to put his fears to rest.

"We're here," Andrea announced, leaning forward in her seat to look out the window.

Carly tried to follow Andrea's gaze, but it was impossible. Finally, when Harold turned off the main road, it became obvious that she was referring to the Georgian house with the narrow circular driveway.

"It's beautiful," Carly said, staring. For the past two and a half years, she'd tried to imagine how and where Andrea lived. For some reason, she'd always pictured her in a place that leaned toward Victorian gingerbread. Georgian was formal and rigid and precise, not like Andrea at all. How had she fit in so effortlessly?

As she was looking at the house, Carly spotted a figure standing behind one of the tall windows. Her throat tightened.

"Look, there's David," Andrea said, pointing to the window Carly was watching.

"Why didn't he come to the airport with you?" Carly asked, putting voice to the question that had been with her since learning David was waiting for them.

"He said this was our time and he didn't want to interfere."

The car stopped. When Carly looked up again, David was gone. She resisted the impulse to search for him.

25

"Andrea wanted me to tell you she'd be down in a couple of minutes," David said, coming into the living room.

Carly gave him a quick smile of thanks and reached for the cup of tea the maid had brought in earlier. "You have a lovely home, David," she said formally, having decided to keep distance between them with words as well as space.

"Actually, it belongs to Victoria. Her father gave it to her as a wedding present."

When she and Ethan were married, Carly had thought receiving a place setting of her china a generous gift. "How nice."

"It was for me. It's amazing how trappings influence people."

"Success breeds success?"

He came farther into the room. "Something like that."

"I'm sorry Victoria couldn't be here."

"Why's that?"

The teacup rattled against its saucer as she put them back on the table. "I was looking forward to meeting her."

"Now, why do I find that hard to believe?"

"I have no idea. I wanted to thank her in person for being so good to Andrea," Carly snapped, realizing she'd taken his bait.

David sat in the chair opposite her. "Finally, an honest reaction. I was wondering how long it would take."

"What did you expect?" she asked, lowering her voice to keep Andrea from overhearing them. "You've put me in an impossible position. Either I lie to Ethan when I get home about Victoria being here, or I spend the next ten years trying to convince him nothing happened between the two of us."

"I don't see the problem," David said. "You're quite good at both lying and convincing."

"Why are you doing this?"

He leaned back in the chair, stuck his legs out in front of him and crossed them at the ankles. "Because I'd rather fight with you than listen to that god-awful polite chatter you've been mouthing since you got here."

"That's what I have to look forward to for the next two weeks?"

"You won't last the day. Once you realize I'm not going to stop riding you until you loosen up, I figure that peace-at-any-cost streak of yours will kick in. After that, we can get on with enjoying Andrea for what will probably be the first and last time the three of us will ever have a chance to be alone together for more than a day or two." He drew his legs back up and leaned forward. "We've been given a once-in-a-life-time opportunity, Carly, let's not waste it worrying what Ethan or Victoria or anyone else might or might not think."

"The time we have together can't be any more than an isolated moment," she said, relenting.

He stared at her long and hard, his eyes filled with

an undisguised hunger. "We can talk about that later."

"No, we can't," Carly insisted. "I came here to—"

"I'm ready," Andrea announced, stepping into the room. When neither of them responded, she made a face. "Obviously I've interrupted something. Should I leave and come back later?"

"David and I were just talking about how much you've grown up in the past year," Carly said in a rush. "And how sorry I am to have missed being with you to see the changes."

Andrea put her hands on her hips and looked from David to Carly and then back again. "What's your version, David?"

He chuckled. "I think I'll stick with Carly's."

"I'll let it go this time," Andrea said with mock sternness, "but you're both going to have to work on the subtleties." She turned to Carly. "Now, what's on the agenda? Where would you like to go first?"

Carly shrugged helplessly. "How do I choose?"

"You don't," David said, standing. "You let us choose for you."

As Carly watched him, it hit her that David was one of those rare people who improved with age. He was even better looking at forty than he had been at twenty. Physically, he was within five pounds of what he'd weighed when he was on the wrestling team in high school. And although his eyes no longer projected the innocence of a young man who believed he could conquer the world, in the loss of naïveté, his face had taken on an enigmatic quality, as if he had witnessed great sorrow and not just come away wounded, but wiser. He was the kind of man women wanted to nurture and then take to their beds.

"Do I get veto power?" Carly asked, purposely keeping her voice light.

"Absolutely not," David told her.

"I know," Andrea said, turning to David. "Let's take her to the Tate. No, better yet, let's go to Bond Street and wander through the galleries there. You can take her to the Tate one of the days I'm in school."

Carly's eyes narrowed speculatively at the scripted sound of the dialogue. "Since when are you interested in art?" she asked Andrea.

"Jeffery paints," she said with a sheepish grin.

"Oh, I see." Carly was surprised at how disappointed she felt.

"Well, how does Bond Street sound to you?" David asked Carly.

"I haven't spent a day wandering through galleries since—" Realizing what she was about to say, Carly stopped. The situation between David and her was volatile enough without her bringing up New York and the weekends she'd spent there with him. "Anyway, it's been a long time. I think a day rummaging through art galleries sounds like great idea."

Carly chanced a look at David; his eyes reflected the same memories that had assailed her. She tried to dismiss them with a casual smile, but her lips refused to move.

When the three of them arrived home that evening, Carly no longer feared that two weeks was not enough time to spend with Andrea—she knew it wasn't. Not only had Andrea and David tolerated her enthusiasm over the paintings and watercolors at the galleries, they had shared it, insisting on going through the back rooms to search out the work of obscure artists, delighting when they found one that stood out from the others.

In the years since Carly had indulged her love of art, she had purposely closed her mind to the excitement it had afforded her. That wouldn't be possible anymore. It had only taken a few hours for the long-dormant hunger to be reawakened.

She would probably still be in the galleries if Andrea hadn't pled starvation and decided they should go to Claridge's for tea. In a day already filled with magic for Carly, Claridge's became the rainbow, the long-stemmed cherry on top of the ice cream sundae, the sequined party dress. Even as she was drinking the tea and eating the pastries, she told herself the food couldn't be as good as it seemed. Sustenance hadn't been as satisfying or sensual since the picnics David used to bring her when she went into the countryside to paint.

They were walking down Shepard Street when Andrea suggested they take a cab for home rather than walk the relatively short distance. Carly had started to protest that she wasn't ready to end the evening, but before she could say anything, she noticed how tired Andrea looked. Knowing that Andrea would stay up all night if asked, Carly feigned a yawn of her own and said a hot bath and bed sounded good to her, too.

The bath turned out to be yet another luxury in a day already filled with excesses. There was lilac-scented soap in a Wedgewood bowl and a towel big enough to wrap around her twice. After a self-indulgent half hour, she'd gone back to her room and read several chapters of the mystery she'd picked up at the airport, then dozed for an hour and come wide awake again at ten-thirty.

Another two hours of tossing and turning went by before she accepted that she was not going to go to sleep again. She turned on the light, picked up her book, and started to read. Her eyes tracked the lines on the page but her mind didn't register the words. Instead, she thought about the day she'd spent with Andrea and David and how dangerously good it made her feel.

It seemed the harder she tried to concentrate on the book, the more her mind wandered. Frustrated, she gave up, put on her robe, and started for the kitchen for something to drink.

She didn't see David sitting in the moonlit living room until it was too late to keep him from seeing her. Instinct demanded that she get out of there as quickly as possible. A longing she didn't stop to analyze demanded that she stay.

"I heard you stirring and wondered whether or not you'd come down," he said.

"You've been sitting here all night?" she asked, reaching up to pull her robe closer but then stuffing her hands in her pockets when she realized how defensive the gesture would seem.

"Just the last hour or so. I couldn't sleep, either."

"What's your excuse?" she asked, shifting her weight from one foot to the other.

"Do you really need to ask?" he said, the words as unguarded as his voice.

The moonlight coming in through the tall, mullioned windows bathed the room in a soft white light. "This isn't what I expected jet lag to feel like," she said, sidestepping the intimacy of his question.

He didn't comment and she rushed to fill the silence. "You live a privileged life."

After a moment, he crossed the room to stand beside her. "I would be the first to admit my circumstances are comfortable, but it wasn't until Andrea came here that I became privileged."

Coming from anyone else, the words would have been too flamboyant to ring sincere. "You're good with her," Carly said, letting her defenses momentarily drop.

"She saved me from myself, Carly. I was just existing before Andrea came to live with me." As if unable to keep himself from touching her any longer, he reached out and straightened the collar on her robe. His hand brushed her cheek and then dropped back to his side. "She gave me back the joy I felt when you and I were together."

Her gaze fell to the hastily tied knot in the belt holding his robe closed. It struck her that all it would take was a gentle tug and the knot would give. "In the beginning, I hated having to share her with you," she said. "But after a while, when I saw how she'd come to love you and how good you were for her, I allowed myself to take vicarious pleasure in your relationship. The calls you made to tell me about some small wonderful thing Andrea had done or accomplished became the only intimate moments in my life."

David touched her cheek again, only this time with confidence that she wouldn't turn away. "We could have had it all," he said.

With a whispered sigh, she surrendered, weary of fighting a battle she wanted to lose. She turned her face into his hand and touched the palm with her lips.

With a soft moan, he took her in his arms and held her close. She laid her head against his chest. She could hear his heart beating through his robe. "You've turned my life inside out, David," she said. "I don't know which way is up anymore."

"I once asked you if you were sorry I came back."

She closed her eyes against the memory. "And I told you I was."

"Do you still feel the same way?"

"After seeing what you've done for Andrea, how could I be?"

"Forget Andrea. I want to know how you feel."

"If I tell you what you want to hear, you'll think I've changed my mind about us."

"Haven't you?"

"We have no future."

He stood back, cupped her chin in his hand, and

forced her to look at him. "Maybe not. But we have now, Carly."

She turned her head, extricating herself from his grasp. "Good God, David, this is Victoria's house—you're her husband. I couldn't do that to—"

"All of a sudden it's Victoria who's standing in the way? What's going on, Carly?" When she moved to walk away, he grabbed her arms and held her. "At the mill it was Ethan and the enormous debt you owed him."

"Ethan has worked very hard since then to absolve me of that debt," she admitted.

His hands closed tighter around her arms. "Are you thinking about leaving him?"

"I couldn't do that to Shawn and Eric."

He released her. "No, of course not."

"After seeing what Andrea's gone through the past two and a half years, you of all people should understand how important a stable home life is to a child." She waited for him to say something. When he didn't, she went on, "I can't buy my own happiness by hurting someone else."

"What would you say if I told you the sole reason Victoria left was so that we could be alone together?"

"But Andrea said she had a meeting in—"

"She had to come up with some reason. The Mozart thing was as good as any."

Carly shook her head in disbelief. "Are you trying to tell me she not only doesn't care if you're unfaithful, she facilitates it?"

"She does more than that—she encourages me to take lovers. That way, it clears the road for her own infidelities, if and when the opportunity should present itself."

"I realize it's none of my business, but how often have you—" She couldn't finish. "Never mind. I don't want to know."

"Never," he said, telling her anyway. "Unless you

count the number of times I've made love to you in my mind."

"I wish you wouldn't tell me things like that."

He studied her. "You do the same thing, don't you?"

"I don't know what you're talking about."

"I'd venture to say pretending I'm the one making love to you is just about the only way you can stand to have Ethan touch you anymore, especially after you found out the way he tried to manipulate Andrea into staying with me, and how difficult he made it for her to come home again."

"Manipulation is a way of life for Ethan. It's the only way he knows how to operate. He never would have confronted you about Andrea if he hadn't been drunk."

"How can you stand to live with someone like that?"

Her temper flared. "What gives you the right to throw stones?"

His eyebrows rose in surprise at her sudden anger. "Touché," he said softly.

She hugged herself against the sudden cold. "Ethan is the man he is because of me. There are times I almost drive myself crazy wondering how different he would be if he'd married someone else. I feel so goddamned guilty."

"You've got to be kidding."

"He's knows I don't love him—hell, I don't even like him anymore. It gets harder and harder to pretend. No wonder he does such stupid, desperate things to keep his world from falling apart. Wouldn't you?"

"I'd like to think I would love you enough to put your happiness above my own."

She gave him a piercing look. "Are you sure you're not just saying that because it's what you want him to do?"

"Don't paint me with the same brush, Carly. never tried to manipulate you."

"This is insane," she said. "Why are we bloodying ourselves in a fight we both know is already lost? There's nothing we can do or say here tonight that will change anything. You're never going to leave Victoria and I'm never going to leave Ethan."

"Even if I let myself believe our futures were that cut and dried, we still have now. Why are you so intent on throwing even this away?"

"Two weeks, David. That's all. Think how long it took to get over losing each other last time. Do you really want to go through that again?"

"That's like asking a starving man to turn away the first course because he can't have the whole meal."

"I can't make love to you, David."

He grabbed her shoulders. "Why not?"

She placed the flat of her hand against his chest, needing to touch him physically even as she pushed him away mentally. Tears burned her eyes. "Because I would never be able to make love to Ethan again without feeling I was prostituting myself."

He threw his head back in frustration. "Is that what you call coupling with Ethan? Making love?" he demanded. "When was the last time you initiated anything with him? When was the last time you felt anything?" When she moved to withdraw her hand, he brought her closer. "How long has it been since you sent the kids over to Barbara's to have an evening alone? Better yet, how many nights a week do you stay up late hoping he'll be asleep when you come to bed?"

She could feel the warmth of his breath on her face. For long seconds they stood perfectly still, suspended between desire and rectitude. And then Carly's defenses gave way to the force of nineteen years of denial and she swayed toward him. Their lips touched. David groaned and covered her mouth with a fierce devouring hunger.

"I want you more this moment than I've ever wanted anything in my life," he told her.

In answer she put her arms around his neck, stood on tiptoe, opened her mouth, and kissed him again. All restraint disappeared; she gave herself to him freely. She would deal with whatever consequences loving David might bring when she was home and alone again.

David ran his hands down the length of her back, stopping to cup her buttocks. He lifted her and brought her against him. She caught her breath in anticipation. Her breasts throbbed with the need to be touched.

As if innately understanding that need, he parted her robe and lowered his mouth to caress the satin-covered nipples with his tongue. She cried out against the ache building inside her.

He bent and picked her up in his arms. "I love you, Carly," he said, a catch in his voice.

"And I love you, David," she answered. She was a young girl again, filled with sweet promise and consumed by love. She closed her eyes and saw the green meadow behind the mill. She breathed deeply and smelled the tall grass swaying in the breeze. The sun beat down on them and made them warm and safe.

Later in her room she lay cradled tightly in his arms. "Don't be sorry, Carly," he said, his mouth touching her temple. "And don't be sad. Two weeks is more than we had any right to expect."

"I love you, David." She reveled in the freedom to tell him.

He lifted up on an elbow and looked down at her. "I want to look at you when you say that."

She traced a line along his jaw with her fingertip. "I love you."

"For nineteen years I've tried to imagine what it would feel like to hear those words from you again."

She smiled. "And?"

"It's how I imagine a man marooned on a desert island would feel watching a ship drop anchor in the harbor."

She ran her hand across the smooth expanse of his chest. "How are we going to hide this from Andrea? She's too observant not to notice the change in us."

"Would it be so bad if she found out?"

"I don't want to put her in the position of keeping secrets from Shawn and Eric, or worse yet, having to lie to them."

"If you stay in bed tomorrow until she's left for school, we can tell her we spent the day working out our differences."

"She would like that."

"There's something she'd like even better."

Carly put her hand over his mouth. "Don't spoil what we have, David."

He lay back down beside her and then pulled her into his arms. "I can't let it go. I feel like I've been given another chance and if I can only find the right words, I can make it right between us again.

She closed her eyes against the hope she heard in his voice. "There are some things that can't be fixed with words no matter how beautiful or compelling."

"You're wrong, Carly," he said. When she didn't answer him, he went on. "You have to be."

26

David balanced a breakfast tray with one hand and tapped lightly on Carly's bedroom door with the other. Not expecting a reply, he turned the antique brass knob and quietly went inside. He moved across the room, his footsteps muffled by the thick Chinese carpet. As he neared her, he saw that she was still sound asleep.

He wasn't surprised. Recalling the night they had just spent together, a feeling of love and contentment swept through him. Their lovemaking had been frantic one minute, controlled and tender the next, as if they were trying to make up for the years they'd missed and storing against the future at the same time. He had told her he loved her a hundred times and each time had seemed as new and wonderful as the first.

He carefully put the tray on the dresser and sat on the edge of the bed to watch her as she slept.

Carly had never been beautiful in the classic sense. Her nose was a little too long, her forehead a little too high. Her lips were too full and too quick to smile to give her an air of mystery, her eyes too honest and revealing for coquettishness. Still, with all her supposed flaws, she was the standard by which he judged all other women.

A tightness gripped his chest, constricting his breathing. He'd lied about being able to get on with his life when she was gone. And that asinine metaphor about a starving man not denying himself the first course of a meal because he couldn't have the rest should have gone one step further—that man would live the rest of his life unsated, forever doomed to know and remember what he had missed. A part of him would die when she left, the part that believed anything was possible if you wanted it badly enough.

As if sensing his presence, Carly rolled to her back, stretched, and let out a soft groan. Seconds later, she opened her eyes. "Good morning," she said, and smiled. "You wouldn't believe how deliciously sore I am."

He bent to kiss her. "Would you rather sleep in this morning?"

"What are my options?"

He kissed the top of her breast, then nudged the satin gown lower with his chin. "Mrs. Rankin and Harold won't be back for another forty-five minutes."

"Mmmmmm, that's not nearly enough time for us to finish what you're starting."

"My God, Carly," he said with a pleased laugh. "You're insatiable."

"Nineteen years is a long time." She ran her hand down the front of his shirt. "And we only have—"

He pressed his fingers to her lips. "We agreed we wouldn't do that."

"I'm sorry." She sat up and touched her lips to the end of his nose. "You were about to list my options."

"Before Andrea left this morning, she suggested we take the boat to Hampton Court."

"Ah yes, the magnificent castle built by Thomas Wolsey and ceded to the envious Henry VIII."

"You've been doing your homework."

She laughed. "I've learned more about England in the past two months than I did the whole time I was in school."

"Andrea will be pleased."

"Do you have any idea where she plans to take me next week?"

David tucked a strand of hair behind Carly's ear, taking profound pleasure in the small intimacy. "I'll let that be her surprise."

"Sounds intriguing." After several seconds, she added, "If I were to hazard a guess, I'd say whatever she has in mind has something to do with a young man named Jeffery Armstrong."

"You'll get nothing from me, woman. I've been sworn to secrecy."

"And I suppose you're the type who's impervious to bribes," she said with an exaggerated sigh.

"What kind of bribe did you have in mind?"

"Oh, the standard kind—me, naked, kinky, available any time night or day—that sort of thing."

Even as he laughed there were tears stinging his eyes. "I love you, Carly," he said, feeling the weight of what their lives could have been.

She seemed to understand what he was feeling, because instead of answering with an "I love you, too," she touched the side of his face and smiled sadly.

He brought her to him and kissed her, long and hard and deep. The banked embers became fire. They could have the rest of their lives and it wouldn't be enough time. He wanted to grow old with her, to see the silver gradually overtake the auburn in her hair, to look into her eyes and see his own memories reflected back to him, to hold hands with her as they watched their grandchildren graduate from college.

With effort, he gentled his kiss and then released

her. "If we want to get to Hampton Court in time to see anything, we'd better get going."

"Oh, no you don't," she said, her voice husky with the passion he'd aroused.

He smiled his pleasure as he reached up to unbutton his shirt. "What do you suggest we tell Andrea about getting such a late start?"

"We can always say we got stuck on a slow boat." She grabbed the hem of her nightgown and pulled it over her head.

David stopped and stared, purposely letting his gaze sweep from the top of her head to the pink polish on her toes. "I wish I could take you to an island where you never had to wear any clothes."

"Okay," she said, raising up to her knees and pressing her breasts against his bare chest. "When do we leave?"

He threaded his hands through her hair and looked deeply into her eyes. "Be careful."

She groaned. "Do you want to talk or make love?"

He moved his hands to her bare waist. "Talk," he said.

"Liar," she said, moving against him.

His answer was a laugh of pleasure.

A stream of water fell from the canvas awning on the ancient riverboat as it maneuvered around a curve in the Thames. The stream had dwindled to a trickle when a gust of wind picked it up and carried it the three feet to where Carly was sitting. She looked at David, who was sitting next to her on the wooden plank seat. "I thought May was supposed to be the ideal month to visit England," she said, tucking her hands into her coat sleeves.

He put his arm around her and drew her into his side. "The sun will come out tomorrow."

Despite herself, she laughed. "If you burst into song, I swear I'll dump you overboard."

"Would you like me to get you another cup of tea?"

"I'd rather freeze than chance having to use that bathroom again. I swear the graffiti dates back to the Middle Ages."

He gave her a quick kiss. "Hang in there. We'll be pulling up to the dock any minute now."

"Ha, that's what you said four hours ago."

"Has it been that long? Time really passes when you're having—"

She poked him in the side. "Don't say it."

The humor left his eyes. "It's true, you know. I promised myself I would hold on to every minute we have together until it seemed like two."

"Worrying about my leaving the whole time I'm here isn't going to make it less lonely when I'm gone."

He held her closer and gently rested his chin on the top of her head. "You're the best thing that ever happened to me."

"You can still say that after all I've put you through?"

If he wasn't careful, he'd drag her down in his emotional hole with him. At least he had Andrea. Carly had two boys who loved her, but who would never understand what their mother had given up for them. "I'll still be saying it when I'm sitting in a rocking chair at a nursing home and some fine-looking nurse is feeding me stewed prunes and wiping the drool from my chin."

"You silver-tongued devil. You sure know how to get a girl's heart beating faster."

"Was it the rocking chair or the drool that got to you?"

"I know what you're doing, and I love you for it."

"I don't know what you're talking about." Before

she could say anything more, he sat up straight and pointed to the right. "My God, I think we actually made it."

David waited with renewed impatience as the boat eased against the dock. The last thing he'd wanted to do with Carly was spend the day wandering through the rambling chambers of Hampton Court. He would have preferred a drive in the country, stopping at a quiet inn, and making love on a feather bed in front of a crackling fire. "You're going to love it here," he told Carly, seeing the excitement building in her eyes. "The place reeks with history."

"Do you think we can go through the maze and still get back in time to meet Andrea?"

"We'll go there first."

"If we do that, we might not see everything in the palace."

He shuddered. "You're going to turn tourist on me, aren't you?"

"This could be my only chance to ever do something like this." She took his hand. "I want it all, David."

It shamed him to realize how easily he forgot what she had given up for him. "Then you shall have it," he said standing and pulling her up beside him.

He would search his memory for every site, monument, building, or tourist trap that had caught his fancy when he'd first come to London and do whatever it took to get her there in the little time they had left. In the future, when she saw something on television or in a movie that had been filmed in London, she would smile and remember.

And he would be with her.

27

Carly *dragged her* hand in the water as she stared at Andrea and Jeffery in the boat ahead of them. No, she reminded herself, it wasn't a boat they were in, it was a punt.

Oxford had surpassed every one of Carly's expectations. As they walked through the town visiting the colleges, an actual physical ache for the years of school she'd missed came over her. She found herself longing for the freedom and excitement that came with learning and the exchange of ideas.

The plan she'd brought with her—to try to talk Andrea into coming home to go to college—died unspoken. How could she in good conscience ask her daughter to give up something she herself would have traded ten years of her life to get?

Besides, it wasn't the next three years that would take Andrea from her forever, it was the young man who was even then looking into her daughter's eyes with undisguised passion.

"A shilling for your thoughts," David said.

Carly looked up at him and smiled. "Why so much?"

"Because the look on your face told me I'd never get them for a pence."

"I was thinking how much I like Jeffery."

"Me, too."

"I didn't want to, you know."

"That doesn't surprise me. If things work out between him and Andrea, England will be her permanent home."

"Something tells me she would stay even if she wound up with someone else. This is her home now. It's where you are. I can't imagine her ever being happy living in Baxter again."

David slowed his rhythmic movements with the pole and concentrated more closely on Carly. "You don't seem as upset about that as I'd expected you would be."

"I guess I've had time to grow accustomed to the idea." She brought her hand in from the water, flicked it in the air and patted it dry on her skirt. "Or maybe it's seeing how happy she is here. And how good you are to her and for her."

"Your being with her these past few days is a big part of her happiness."

"We stayed up to talk last night. She tried in every way imaginable—other than coming right out and asking—to convince me to leave Ethan and to move over here with Shawn and Eric."

"I'm sure she thinks it's only a matter of time before Victoria and I call it quits. And she figures with you here, and available, we'd eventually get together."

She had the feeling he wasn't talking about Andrea and her needs as much as his own. Intended or not, he'd added yet another layer of guilt to those she'd laid on herself. Andrea wasn't her only child, even if she was the neediest. "And I'd like it if South Africa stopped killing its citizens," she said, the words coming out sharper than she'd intended.

"What do you suppose the chances are that either one of us is going to get what we want?"

"Hey, back off," he said, meeting her flash of anger with one of his own. "I'm just the messenger. And besides, I wasn't telling you anything you didn't already know."

Knowing the tension between them was readily explosive and that a minor confrontation could escalate into a fight as easily as a kiss could lead to making love, Carly avoided the challenging look he shot her and turned her attention to Andrea and Jeffery's punt. She watched them for several seconds and then frowned.

"What's wrong?" David asked, picking up on her concern.

"I don't know. Just a second ago, Andrea was hanging over the side like she was going to be sick. Now she's got Jeffery's handkerchief covering her face."

David twisted to look over his shoulder. "It looks like she's got a nose bleed."

"See if you can catch up to them."

When they pulled along side the other punt, Jeffery was hunkered down in front of Andrea, brushing her bangs back from her forehead. "No cause for alarm," he told them. "She's been sneezing right along. That last one must have broken a blood vessel."

Carly would have felt more reassured if Jeffery had been a little further along in his premed studies and if Andrea's crisp white blouse hadn't looked as if it were a shade darker than her complexion. She took a packet of tissues from her purse and handed them to Andrea. "I have more if you need them," she said, keeping her voice casual.

"Perhaps we'd better get her indoors," David added, his gaze sweeping the banks of flowers on either side of them. "Just in case it is the pollen that's bothering her."

"The Victoria Arms is just up the way a bit," Jeffery said to David. "We could drop Mrs. Hargrove and Andrea off there. They could have a pint and a little something to eat while we're returning the punts."

David looked at Carly. "How does that sound to you?"

"Fine. Will you meet us or should we take a cab back to the bridge?"

"Perhaps we should wait to see how Andrea's feeling when we get to the pub," Jeffery suggested. "You might want to head straight away to the hotel."

Andrea took the handkerchief from her nose. "Would the three of you please stop treating me like an invalid? It's only a nosebleed, for God's sake." As she talked, a trickle of blood escaped her left nostril. Jeffery took the handkerchief and gently wiped it away.

"Personally, I'd just as soon we go back to the hotel and wait for you there," Carly said to David. "I could use a nap before dinner."

"Cut it out, Mom," Andrea said, taking the tissues Carly had given her and pressing them against her nose. "You're no more tired than I am."

"A bit out of sorts, are we?" Jeffery said to Andrea.

She glared at him. He grinned back. Her anger was no match for his good humor. "You always do this to me," she said, a smile playing at the corner of her mouth.

"Does that mean we're going to the hotel?" Carly asked.

Andrea held up her hand. "No, it means that if David and Jeffery don't hurry back to the pub to pick us up, they just might find we've tipped a few too many." She gave Jeffery a sweet smile.

Jeffery slapped his knees and stood. "What say, David? Are you up to the challenge?"

"Last punt to touch the dock pays the bar bill."

As it turned out, Carly ordered stout and Andrea settled for a soft drink. The pub was unusually quiet and when they were settled, it was all Andrea could do to stay awake.

That night, reluctantly, and only after Jeffery promised to stay with Andrea, Carly agreed to go out to dinner with David. At Jeffery's suggestion, they went to Le Petit Blanc.

The atmosphere and solicitous service were wasted on Carly, who was only interested in something to stop the rumbling in her stomach. They might as well have gone to the Pizza Hut they'd passed on their way there.

"I'm worried about Andrea," she said, unfolding her linen napkin and laying it across her lap.

David looked at her over the top of the wine list he was reading. "She's starting to concern me, too. I knew she was pushing herself, but I had no idea she'd gone this far. She's exhausted."

"Has she been sick?"

Putting the list aside, David gave her question his full attention. "She had a couple of colds this past winter, but as far as I know, that's it."

"As far as you know? What in the hell does that mean?"

David reached across the table and took her hand. "If she's pregnant, she wouldn't come to me until she and Jeffery had decided what they want to do about it."

Carly caught her breath in surprise. "Do you honestly think that's a possibility?"

"Come on, Carly. You've spent enough time with them to be able to answer that question yourself. I told you over a year ago where I thought their relationship was headed."

She closed her hand tightly around David's seeking his strength. "Dear God, I hope that's not it."

"Let's not borrow trouble. Maybe she's just run down and needs to catch up on her sleep. You saw how intense she is about her studies. She's set up goals that are very important to her." He brought her hand up and touched his lips to her fingers. "I promise you I'll get her to a doctor the day after you leave."

"And that you'll call as soon as you find out anything?"

"Even if I know it's when Ethan is home."

The waiter arrived. David placed their order and asked that the wine be brought immediately. When they were alone again, he picked up where they had left off. "As hard as it will be for us to accept, should Andrea really be pregnant, she and Jeffery are the ones who will have to decide what they want to do about it. We're going to have to stay out of it unless they ask for our advice."

"That's easy for you to say."

"All right," David said with a sigh. "Let's assume for a minute that Andrea is pregnant. Any advice you could give her is bound to be tainted by your own experience. You can't draw a parallel between what happened to you and what's happening to her. The father of Andrea's baby would move mountains to protect and take care of her."

Carly's shoulders sagged in defeat. "I want so much for her."

"You've got to trust her and Jeffery enough to let them work things out in their own way."

The waiter returned with their wine, opened the bottle, and poured a splash into David's glass. David picked up the glass, mechanically swirled the amber liquid for several seconds, sniffed it, and then took a sip. "It's fine," he said. When the waiter had finished pouring and left, David raised his glass to Carly.

"They remind me of us at that age," she said, lightly touching her glass to his.

He sat back in his chair, his gaze locked on hers as he took a drink of wine. "How hungry are you?"

"Not very," she said. "Why?"

"How long did you tell Andrea we would be gone?"

"A couple of hours." A slow seductive smile formed. "Why?" she asked.

"Sitting here looking at you has made my appetite shift to another part of my anatomy."

"What did you have in mind?"

"There's a charming hotel just outside of town. . . ."

"We don't have any luggage."

David laughed. "This coming from the woman who made love to me in the gardener's toolshed at Hampton Court?"

Carly could feel heat rising up her neck at the memory. "That was different," she said, lowering her voice even more.

"Oh? How's that?" he asked, plainly enjoying himself.

"No one saw us go in."

"But what about the gardener who winked at us when we came out?"

Her jaw dropped. "What gardener?"

"The one who brought you your scarf."

"Oh, my God." She groaned.

"I take it you'd rather we stay here?"

She thought a minute. Suddenly serious, she said, "I wish it was me who was pregnant."

"Jesus, Carly," he said, anger heavy in his voice. "Why do you say things like that?"

"Because it's true."

He took the napkin from his lap and flung it on the table. "And it's impossible. So why bring it up?"

"Tubal ligations have been reversed."

"But not yours. Not now. Not ever. At least not for me, right?"

As if just then realizing the cruel game she'd been playing with them both, she looked down at her lap. "I'm sorry, David. I don't know what came over me."

"Let's get out of here."

She folded her napkin, put it on the table and picked up her purse. David stood, took out his wallet, and left twice what the bill would have been. When they were outside, Carly asked, "Where are we going?"

"I'm going to drop you off at the hotel and go for a walk."

"Can I come with you?"

"I don't think so. I want to be alone for a while. Besides, Andrea might need you."

"Jeffery is with her. If she does need something, he'll get it for her."

"You're cutting me up into little pieces, Carly," he said, his voice husky. "How in the hell am I ever going to put myself back together when you're gone?"

"Maybe I don't want you to," she admitted, struggling to understand what was happening between them. "Maybe I want to know for certain you're as unhappy as I am."

"How can you doubt it?"

She buried her face in his jacket. "I've made such a mess of our lives."

He took her arms and held her away from him. "All right. You've said it. You've had your thirty seconds of feeling sorry for yourself. Feel better?"

"No."

"I didn't think so."

She had never come closer to giving defeat the fertile ground it needed to grow. "I think I need something to take my mind off today."

"And what would that be?"

She slipped her arm through his and started walking toward the car. "How about if I show you?"

"Anytime, anyplace," he said, his voice heavy with wanting her.

"Tonight—at that charming little hotel you were telling me about," she told him, giving herself permission to forget everything and everyone else for the next two hours. There would be time enough for Andrea and Jeffery and the rest of the world tomorrow. Tonight was hers and David's.

28

Andrea brushed at the grass stains on her riding breeches and let out a disgusted snort. There seemed to be something almost prophetic about her keeping clean when there was any kind of party at the Armstrongs'. If she wasn't spilling punch on her skirt, she was dropping caviar on her blouse. Staying away from food was the obvious answer. Who would have thought the gentlest horse in the stable would dump her on her rear end?

When David first mentioned skipping Stratford-Upon-Avon and the drive through the Cotswolds in favor of spending a couple of days at Hawthorne, Andrea had exploded. She was convinced the change in itinerary was to accommodate her and completely unnecessary. And then Jeffery had stepped in and said he thought it was a grand idea, the perfect opportunity for her mother to meet his parents. The clincher was when he told her that he would take a couple of days off from school and come with them.

Although she'd fought the decision, she'd been glad for the unpressured time she'd had with her mother and David and grateful for the chance to be with Jeffery and to be able to sleep in every morning.

She looked up and saw Jeffery approaching from the stables. "I just got them out of the cleaners," she said, still trying to work the worst of the stains out of her breeches. "And now look at them."

"Afraid your mum might think we stopped for a bit of fun?" Jeffery teased. "Come along in. We can sneak you up the back staircase and nick some fresh clothes for you from Anne's closet. Your mum will never suspect a thing."

She fell in beside him, easily matching his stride, making up for his four-inch height advantage with her long legs. "I think I'd almost rather have her suspect we were fooling around than to find out I fell off my horse," she said, tugging off her hat.

"She does seem preoccupied with how you're getting on."

"To put it mildly. She keeps looking at me as though she expects me to keel over at any minute." She shot him with an accusing look. "And telling her I had another nosebleed didn't help."

"Sorry about that."

"We're going to have to be more careful from now on."

He bent to pick up a rock from the path and toss it into the nearby field. "How do you mean?"

"I was thinking, that if for some strange reason my nose does its thing again, you should tell everyone you hit me."

"Oh, that's a clever way around it."

She feigned a surprised look. "Don't worry, I'll tell them it was accident."

"And your mum will have you booked on the next plane home."

She laughed and playfully hit him on the arm with her hat. "She knows you could no more hit me than you could nick one of those strawberries we saw sitting alongside the road."

"You can't go about taking another man's possessions," he said. "But keeping your wife in line is another matter altogether."

"Wife?" she said, stopping to stare at him, a smile playing at the corner of her mouth. "You've yet to make a formal proposal and already you're calling me your wife?"

"Sorry," he said with exaggerated surprise. "Shall I go down on bended knee before you this very minute?"

"Don't tempt me."

He grabbed her hand and pulled her behind an oak tree. Pinning her between himself and the broad trunk, he kissed her, tenderly and then with growing passion.

"Sometimes I think I'll go out of my mind waiting for you to finish school in London," he said.

She wrapped her arms around his waist. "Two more months. I'm marking the days on a calendar I've got in my room."

"What did you tell Carly about going to the States this summer?"

"I haven't said anything yet."

He was quiet for several seconds. "It's all right, you know. I'll have you forever. She's only got you a couple more years."

It was so like him to clear the path for her. "I love you, Jeffery."

"That doesn't mean I'll be glad to see you leave, mind you."

"I do miss my brothers and Grandma and Grandpa. I'd really like you to meet them."

"And what about Ethan?" he asked gently. "You couldn't have lived with him all that time and not have feelings for him, too."

He was always careful to include Ethan any time they talked about her life before she'd come to England. Even after she'd told him the way Ethan had tried to manipulate her into not coming back, Jeffery had remained neutral. He was convinced there would be a day when the two of them worked things out.

"He won't let me miss him," she said. "Every time I try, he finds a way to remind me that I'm David's child, not his. I think he's afraid of me."

"What a clever bit of baggage you are to have finally figured that out."

She made a face at him. "Don't act superior."

"I didn't mean it that way at all," he said. "Of course he would be afraid of you. For one thing, without you here, your mum wouldn't have any reason to see David. And from what I can tell, they're quite good friends still." He'd hesitated at the "friends" part. He sat down, his back to the oak, then brought her down with him. She stretched out, her head in his lap.

"Do you think there's something going on between my mother and David?" she asked.

"I thought you didn't much like speculating about other people's private lives."

"This is different."

"Why's that?"

"Because I want my mother to be happy and I think she still loves David."

"Seems to me you're forgetting something. David already has a wife and your—"

"I know," she said, drawing her knees up and propping her hat on them. "It's just that it's so wrong for them to love each other and never get to be together."

"Are you saying you'll up and leave me if another chap catches your fancy?"

She glanced up into his eyes. The teasing look she'd anticipated wasn't there. "That's impossible," she told him. "You are the person I was put on this earth to be with. All you have to do is look at what I've gone through to find you." She pulled him down for a kiss. "And that, Mr. Armstrong, is simply the way it is and the way it will always be."

Carly moved away from the window where she'd been watching Andrea and Jeffery, picked up her champagne glass, and went over to David. "I think they'll be a while," she said. "They've been waylaid."

One of David's eyebrows rose in question. "You told Andrea we were coming a little early, didn't you?"

"At this moment, I don't think Andrea knows or cares what time we got here."

"Ahhh, I see."

"When were Jeffery's parents supposed to arrive from London?"

David looked at his watch. "A half hour from now, give or take."

"Andrea warned me they were likely to be upset at Jeffery's taking time off from school."

"Three days aren't going to hurt him."

She stopped to look more closely at the collection of Chinese porcelain vases lining a mahogany bookcase. "I thought I heard him say something about joining us at Bath on Saturday."

"I'm sure that would please Andrea. In case you haven't noticed, she's ecstatic over how well the two of you have hit it off." He walked over to the cheese tray, cut a slice of Stilton, laid it on a cracker, and handed it to her.

She wrinkled her nose at the offering. "No thanks. I have this thing about eating blue food."

"Come on, give it a try. When you get back to Baxter you can tell everyone you had some authentic English food."

Gingerly she took the cracker and took a bite. After several seconds, she said, "Okay, so every rule has its exception."

"That's one of the things I love about you. You're always willing to admit when you're wrong."

She smiled sweetly. "I can't tell you how good it makes me feel to know that you remember the times I've been wrong about something."

"It's what makes you so endearing." He sat down and motioned for her to join him. She perched on the arm of his chair. "Seems to me Andrea isn't as tired as she was last week," he said. "What do you think?"

"She looks better to me, too. But that doesn't mean—"

He held up his hands in surrender. "I'll get her to the doctor. I promise."

Carly let her gaze sweep the room. "Are the things in here as old and expensive as they look?"

"You should recognize some of the paintings, or at least the artist."

"But are they real?"

He chuckled. "Yes."

"Andrea never mentioned any of this. I had no idea Jeffery's family had a key to the mint."

"I don't think she sees it. She seems to have a blind spot when it comes to money and position. At parties, she's as likely to strike up a conversation with one of the servants as she is one of the guests."

"And how does Jeffery feel about that?"

"I believe it's one of the things he loves most about her."

Carly tipped her glass and took a long swallow of champagne. "And how do the Armstrongs feel about her?"

"Meaning?"

"By comparison, she comes from pretty ordinary stock."

"If that matters to them, they've done a good job of hiding it."

"The real test will come if it turns out she is pregnant. How do you think they'll react?"

He put his hand on her leg and gave her knee a squeeze. "If you can give me one good reason to engage in that particular guessing game, I'll play. Otherwise, I'm going to wait until I know something concrete."

Carly glanced toward the window. "I just want her to be happy." She'd known it was going to be hard to leave when the time came; she'd had no idea the pain would start this soon. She and Andrea still had five days together and already she was dreading the moment they would say good-bye. "I want you to promise me something else," she said, filled with a sudden need.

"Anything within my power."

"Do whatever you can to make sure she comes to Baxter this summer. I have this feeling it will be the last time."

"That's a bit melodramatic, don't you think?"

"Think about it, David. If she is pregnant, she and Jeffery will be starting their lives together in a matter of months."

"Has it occurred to you that they might choose not to have the baby?" he asked and reached for her hand.

"Jeffery might feel that's an option, but not Andrea."

He brought her hand to his mouth and gently tapped her knuckle against his lip. "How would you feel if I came to Baxter with Andrea?"

She knew exactly how she would feel. "Ethan isn't Victoria. He would do everything he could to make sure we were never alone together."

"You didn't answer my question."

"What do you have in mind, David, meeting on the sly whenever possible for some clandestine lovemaking? Is that the way we're to live our lives from now on?"

"Do you have a better suggestion?"

"Even if it were possible, the rest of the year would be a living hell for me. You of all people should know I'm not cut out for something like that."

"It would only be until Shawn and Eric were grown."

"And at what age do you think they'll be old enough to understand and forgive me for dumping their father to pursue my own life? When do you think they would be mature enough to understand how calculating their father is? Eighteen? Twenty? And if they ever reach the right age, will they question my sanity for staying with Ethan as long as I did? I'm damned if I do and damned if I don't."

"When does your happiness count? And, goddamn it, when does mine?"

Almost as if on cue, there was a sound at the back of the house. Andrea's voice called out, "Jeffery and I will be down as soon as we wash up."

"Take your time," David answered. He waited several seconds and then turned to Carly. "Well?"

"I thought we weren't going to get into this discussion again."

"I lied."

"We keep saying we're not going to waste what time we have left by arguing and yet we keep doing it over and over again."

David leaned forward and buried his face in his hands. Then dropping his hands between his knees, he looked up at her again. "I'll let it go for now," he said, "But that doesn't mean I'm through trying."

She believed him and wished with all her heart it would make a difference.

29

Carly lifted her suitcase overhead and shoved it onto the closet shelf, symbolically and physically putting the final touches on her trip to England. She'd been home a week and had slipped back into her routine with such comparative ease she was finding it hard to believe that seven days ago she'd been on the other side of the Atlantic Ocean.

Ethan had been in a surprisingly good mood when he'd met her at the airport, welcoming her with open arms, acting as if the trip had been his idea. And now here she was facing a Thursday morning identical to hundreds of others she'd had over the years, cleaning the kitchen, making beds, and waiting for her mother to stop by for a cup of coffee on her way to pick up groceries.

If not for the lingering feeling of loss, she could almost convince herself the trip had been a figment of her imagination.

While she luxuriated in remembering her time with Andrea, whenever thoughts of David arose, Carly did everything she could to put them to the back of her mind. Sometimes it worked, more often it didn't.

She'd never believed it was better to have loved and lost. If you didn't know what you were missing, how could it hurt you? But then she would think of David and what it would be like to lose even the memory of him and she was willing to pay any price not to have that happen.

After she'd arrived home and handed out the presents she'd bought for everyone, Ethan had noticed and commented on the fact that she'd bought nothing for herself. She'd smiled and told him that her gift was intangible, but priceless. She hadn't wanted to tell him her plans right away, but the flash of jealousy she saw in his eyes told her it wasn't the time for mystery. So instead of waiting until she'd had time to grow accustomed to the idea herself, she announced her intention to begin painting again.

Ethan had laughed.

An errant breeze fluttered the curtain across the room. Downstairs there was a knock on the door followed by her mother's cheerful voice, "It's me, honey. Are you in the kitchen?"

Carly went to the stair railing and called down. "I'm up here, Mom."

"I just finished reading David's new book. It's a humdinger. Best so far."

"Why don't you start the coffee? I'll be right down." She returned to the bedroom to close the window, not wanting to take a chance that the weatherman might be wrong about the rain.

Barbara looked up from the newspaper as Carly entered. "Did you see this?" she asked, holding up the front page. "The president's off to another summit meeting. London this time." She laid the paper back on the table. "How does it feel having seen Big Ben for yourself?"

Carly smiled. "Fantastic."

The smell of freshly brewing coffee filled the air. Carly went to the cupboard and took out a plate covered with plastic wrap. "I had to hide these last two pieces of the coffee cake I made for us last night. The boys haven't stopped eating since I got home."

"Other than the nights they had dinner with me and Wally, I think they pretty much lived on pizza and hamburgers."

"While I was filling up on smoked salmon, caviar, and Stilton cheese," she said, feeling a twinge of guilt.

"And basking in the love of your daughter."

"I can't tell you how much better I feel about her being in England now that I've been there myself. From now on when she talks about her room at Hawthorne or what the fields look like around the house, I can share it with her."

"And Jeffery?"

This was the first time Carly and her mother had had a chance to talk alone. "I like him almost as much as Andrea does. But then, it would be hard not to. He's bright and funny and dotes on her. I've never seen her as happy as when she's with him."

"What does he look like? Is he as handsome in person as he is in the pictures we've seen?"

"Even more so."

"Can you imagine what their children will look like?"

Carly forcefully controlled the smile she felt forming. There was no sense letting her mother in on David's and her suspicions prematurely. He would be calling with the results of Andrea's physical any time now.

"It's a little disconcerting to think of myself as a grandmother," Carly said, placing a piece of the coffee cake onto a plate. She added a fork and napkin and slid them across the counter. "Grandmothers are supposed to look old." She grinned in anticipation of her mother's reaction.

"Like me?" Barbara said, with a snort.

"I said old, Mom, not ancient."

Barbara laughed. "My, my, aren't we in a good mood today."

"Sit down while I get the coffee. I've got a million things to tell you."

"First I want to hear about Victoria. What's she like?"

Carly cringed. It was one thing to lie by omission, another as the result of a direct question. "I don't know any more about Victoria now than I did before I left. No, that's not true. I know she's richer and better connected than we thought and that she collects paintings of dogs."

"You never saw her all the time you were in England?" Barbara asked carefully.

"She was on the continent." Realizing how pretentious that sounded, she added, "Victoria is on some committee that's preparing a celebration of the two-hundredth anniversary of Mozart's death."

"Seems to me it would be more appropriate to celebrate his birth."

Carly started to breathe a sigh of relief that her mother was going to let Victoria's absence drop. She should have known better.

"Then you and David were alone?" she asked.

"Andrea was there."

"As I recall, you said she was in school the first week."

"Where are you heading with this?" Carly asked, already tired of dancing around the subject.

Barbara cut a corner of cake and chewed thoughtfully for several seconds before answering. "Have you changed your mind about staying with Ethan?"

"I wish it were that simple," Carly said with a sigh. She reached for coffee cups. "But that's not a real answer, is it? No, I haven't changed my mind, but it isn't Ethan I'm staying with. It's Shawn and

Eric." She was adding sugar to Barbara's cup when the telephone rang.

"Want me to get that?" Barbara asked.

Carly nodded. "If it's Ethan ask him if I can call him back later."

Barbara picked up the phone. "Hargrove residence. How may I help you?"

Carly smiled at the formality, the last visible remnant of her mother's years of working as a secretary.

"David!" Barbara exclaimed. "How nice to hear your voice. And it's so clear. Just like you were calling from across town." She paused. "She's right here. Let me get her for you." She held the phone out to Carly and mouthed, "Want me to take a hike?"

Carly shook her head. "You've heard something?" she asked, excitement mixing with fear at the prospect and consequences of Andrea being pregnant.

"We got back from the doctor's office a couple of hours ago," he said, his voice a strange monotone.

"And?" she prodded.

"It isn't what we thought."

"Well, what is it then?"

"Jesus, I don't know how to tell you this."

Her heart leapt to her throat. "Don't do this to me, David." Her mind tried to focus on the possibility of bad news and Andrea being intertwined somehow, but couldn't. "Don't make me stand here and guess what you mean. Just tell me whatever it is."

Several more seconds passed before he said, "Andrea has leukemia."

"There has to be some mistake," Carly said evenly.

"I already went through that with the doctor," he told her. "I even made him check with the lab to be sure there was no chance her file had been mixed up with someone else's, before I allowed them to do the bone marrow testing. I didn't want Andrea to have to go through hearing something like this unless we were certain."

"But she isn't sick. She was just tired."

"Remember the nose bleeds? And the bruises she said she got when she fell off the horse? And how pale she looked? And remember how you kept feeling her forehead and saying you thought she had a fever? They're all symptoms."

"Of a hundred different things," she said, her impatience rising. "The same thing happened to me when I was anemic."

"Being anemic is part of having leukemia. The mutated white blood cells are growing so fast, they're crowding out the red."

"You're acting as if you want to believe she's sick."

"That's not fair, Carly," he said, his voice heavy with fatigue. "I've been with the doctors all morning. I've read the lab results. I've seen the sores in her mouth. I'm the one who spent an hour with her yesterday morning trying to get her gums to stop bleeding after she ate a piece of toast."

He had closed the escape routes, leaving her no place to run. She put her hand over her mouth to block the cry of fear she felt rising.

"What is it?" Barbara asked anxiously.

"Carly?" David said. "Are you still there?"

"I'm here," she told him, struggling against the waves of light-headedness washing over her. She started to sway. Barbara brought her a chair.

"Put your mother on the phone," David said.

"I'm all right." She looked at her mother. A sickening feeling of déjà vu came over Carly as she flashed back to when Shawn had been in his accident. "How is Andrea taking the news?" Behind her she heard her mother's quick intake of breath.

"For God's sake," Barbara said, her voice desperate. "Would you please tell me what's going on?"

Carly held her hand up and mouthed, "In a minute."

"I don't think it's really hit her yet," David said.

"Or she's already into denial. She's giving me a hard time about starting treatment before school is over."

"And that's not an option?" The long pause that followed was as frightening as anything David had told her.

"No."

Carly bit down hard on her lip. A coppery taste filled her mouth. "Why not?" she managed to ask.

"Because she's—just because it's not. This lympho — Wait a minute, I've got it written down someplace."

Carly heard the rustle of paper in the background and locked on to the normality of the sound, trying to ground herself with inconsequential details in a world gone mad.

"Here it is," he said, picking up the phone again. "It's called lymphocytic leukemia. There's more, but until you've picked up the jargon, it won't make sense." He hesitated. "According to Dr. Reardon, she has one of the bad ones."

"Bad ones?" she repeated. "What in the hell is that supposed to mean? They have good and bad leukemias now?" She knew she was using anger to hold her own fear at bay and that it was unfair to make David her target, but she couldn't stop herself.

"It means that she has to start her chemotherapy immediately."

"Or?" she demanded, challenging him, daring him to tell her the worst.

"Or we'll lose her."

She was instantly and unreasonably furious with him for not bothering to qualify his words with a could or a maybe or a might. "Who is this Dr. Reardon anyway? I've never heard Andrea talk about him. Has she seen him before? Does he know her? Is he a specialist?" She didn't wait for answers. "I want a second opinion. And I want it from Dr. Hopkins. He's known Andrea all her life. I have complete—"

"There isn't time," he told her with infinite patience. "I have everything set up for her to go into the hospital the day after tomorrow. We can't mess around with this, Carly. We don't have the luxury."

"You had no right to decide something like that without consulting me first."

"There wasn't anything to decide. If Andrea doesn't get immediate and intensive chemotherapy, she's going to die. It's as simple as that."

She squeezed her eyes shut and pressed her palm against her forehead.

Barbara placed herself in front of Carly, demanding with her physical presence that she be paid attention to.

Before Carly could figure out a way to lessen the blow, the words tumbled out. "David says Andrea has leukemia."

Barbara looked as if Carly had hit her. She stood perfectly still for a long time and then turned and walked out of the room. Torn between going after her and maintaining even the tenuous connection to Andrea that David provided, Carly found she could not let go of the telephone. "Is Andrea there?" Carly asked. "I want to talk to her."

"She's asleep. After everything she went through this morning, she was so tired when we got home she could hardly make it to her room. Besides, I think it would be better if you took some time to absorb the news before you talked to her. She's already had to deal with one parent falling apart on her. She doesn't need another."

"How did this happen, David?"

"I don't know," he said, frustration heavy in his voice. "No one does."

"Is it my fault?"

"How in the hell could it be your fault?"

"It might be genetic."

"Goddamn it, Carly, would you listen to yourself?

Do you really think it's going to make Andrea better if you take the blame for her leukemia. For the first and last time, you had nothing to do with Andrea getting sick."

"You can't know that for sure," she said, the weight of what had happened eighteen years ago crushing her.

"We'll talk about this when you get here," he said, temporarily abandoning his attempt to reason with her. "When do you think that will be?"

"What?" She was lost in her own private hell and only half listening.

"You are coming, aren't you. Andrea's going to need you here to help her get through this."

Carly thought about the suitcase she'd put away less than and hour ago. "I'll be there as soon as I can."

"You're going to have more questions when you've had a little while to think about this. I know I did. You can call me anytime."

She didn't want to let him go. "I'm sorry I tried to take this out on you."

"It's all right, Carly. I understand."

"You'll let Andrea know I'm coming?"

"I'll have her call you as soon as she wakes up."

"She's going to be okay, isn't she, David?"

"Of course she is," he said, but not with the conviction Carly needed to hear. "And when she comes out the other side, she's going to have a lust for life that will blow us all away. None of us will be able to keep up with her. She's going to look up in the sky and see rainbows when everyone else is running around with their heads down trying to keep from getting rained on."

Nothing could have told Carly more clearly how terrified David was. He was already trying to infuse his own strength into Andrea. "I love you," she told him.

"We'll get through this."

"Have you told Jeffery?"

"Not yet," he admitted.

"When?"

"I think I should let Andrea decide that."

"She'll want to put it off until he's finished with his exams."

"That will never work. He's going to figure out something's wrong long before then."

"My God," she breathed. "How am I going to tell Shawn and Eric?"

"Why don't you let Ethan do it? He's good with them and the last thing you need—"

"My mother," Carly groaned, interrupting him. "I forgot she was here. I've got to go find her."

"Call me as soon as you know when you're coming."

"I will." She stretched the phone cord as far as it would go to see if Barbara was in the living room. She wasn't. Before hanging up, she added, "Tell Andrea I love her."

Carly found Barbara in Andrea's bedroom, sitting on the edge of the bed. "Mom?" she said, coming into the room. "Are you all right?"

"She's the innocent. Why is she being punished?" Barbara lifted her head to look at Carly. "It should be me."

"Don't do this to yourself," Carly said, recoiling at the pain she saw in her mother's eyes, at the tears running down her face.

"It isn't right. She won't even be eighteen for two more weeks. She has her whole life ahead of her."

Barbara's grief and guilt left little room for Carly's own. "She's going to beat this, Mom. They've made real strides in the treatment of leukemia in the past ten years. Especially in young people." Where had that come from?

"Her beautiful hair . . ." Barbara pulled a tissue from the pocket of her skirt and wiped her eyes. "She's going to lose it, you know."

Carly sat down on the bed beside her mother. "It'll grow back. From what I've heard, it could even return curly. Wouldn't that drive her crazy?"

"Wally had a cousin—" She shook herself. "Never mind."

"I remember, Mom. He had leukemia and he died. Wally flew there for the funeral."

"That was a stupid thing for me to bring up." She stiffened her spine. "You don't need anyone doing that to you, least of all me."

"I'm scared, too, Mom. I know there are lots of people who get leukemia and die. We're just not going to let Andrea be one of them."

Even as Barbara wiped the tears away, new ones took their place. "Tell me what you want me to do."

Carly hadn't had time to figure out what she was going to do herself, let alone give out assignments. "I don't know. I suppose I should call Ethan. David thinks he should be the one to tell the boys." Carly thought a minute. "I know what you can do for me. Call the airlines and see if I can get on a flight to London tomorrow. I was going to try to leave tonight, but that wouldn't be fair to the boys."

"It'll cost you a fortune to get a ticket on such short notice," she said, standing.

"I'll put it on the Mastercard."

"Why don't you let me pay for it?"

"Because you're going to need your money for you and Wally. As soon as Andrea feels up to it, I want you to fly over with Shawn and Eric. Ethan too, if you can get him to come."

"Are you sure Ethan would want you to charge

the tickets on—" She didn't finish. "I think all of us flying over together sounds like a grand idea."

Carly got up and put her arms around her mother. "What would I do without you?"

"I'm sorry I fell apart before. It won't happen again."

"You're allowed, Mom."

"And you're allowed, too," she said. "You've got to stop acting like you're invincible, Carly. We both know it isn't true. If ever there was a reason to have a good cry, this is it."

"I don't need the headache and stuffed-up nose. I've got too much to do."

"Better a headache than an ulcer."

Carly guided her toward the door. "Stop acting like a mother."

"I'll call you as soon as I find out something. Do you want me to come back tonight to help you pack?"

"You're going to have your hands full with Wally. I may need you to drive me to the airport tomorrow, though."

Barbara nodded and started down the stairs. She was at the front door when she turned and said, "When you talk to Andrea, tell her I love her. And don't forget her grandpa." Fresh tears glistened in her eyes at the mention of Wally. "He's going to be devastated."

"I'll give her the message."

"And tell her that—" She shrugged. "There's really nothing else to be said, is there?"

"If there is, you can tell her yourself when you get there."

"One more thing." Barbara shifted from one foot to the other, clearly uncomfortable with what she would say next. "Try not to forget Ethan was her father a long time before David came into the picture.

He's going to be remembering the little girl who used to ride on his shoulders and call him Daddy."

Barbara knew Carly better than she knew herself. Ethan was a natural target for Carly's fear. Who better to lash out at than the man who had done everything in his power to make sure Andrea never came home again?

And who else had the power to make what she had to do even more difficult?

"Thanks for reminding me," she said, her mind already beginning to map out the strategy she would employ with Ethan.

Later that evening Carly studied him as he sat across the kitchen table from her, trying to read the myriad of emotions she saw playing across his face. Her mother had been right about how upset he would be. The only thing she hadn't taken into consideration was how quickly he would recover and begin "putting things in perspective," as he had succinctly summed it up.

"I understand why you want to go over there to be with her as soon as you can, Carly," Ethan said with an obvious show of patience. "All I'm saying is that if you'd just wait a couple more weeks, you could get in on a super-saver rate and your ticket would be a third of what you're paying now." He got up from the kitchen table to pour himself another cup of coffee. "I don't know what makes you think we have any more money to spend on something like this now than we did a month ago."

"This isn't negotiable, Ethan," she told him. "I'm leaving tomorrow whether it suits you or not. I guess I was wrong to think you'd be with me on this."

"Now wait just a minute. That's unfair, and you know it. The only reason I'm not getting on that plane with you is that I'm not as ready to give up on her as you seem to be."

"What in the hell is that supposed to mean?"

"Face it, Carly. People don't go rushing to the bedside of someone they expect to live."

"Is that right? What about Shawn's accident? As I recall, I was in a pretty big hurry to get to the hospital that time, too."

"That was because you didn't know he only had a couple of broken bones."

The memory dredged up old angers. "And who's fault was that?"

"There you go again, remembering what suits you and forgetting the rest. You know how upset I was at the time. I couldn't be expected to—"

"Skip it, Ethan. I've heard it before." She swept up the sugar he'd spilled and took it to the sink.

His spoon made a loud clanking noise as it hit the sides of his porcelain mug. "I suppose you thought I was lying when I told you we didn't have the money to go to England this year?" he said, going back to their original argument.

"Why is it that when you want something, it's never a problem? If we're so tight, why did we get a new station wagon when there wasn't anything wrong with the old one? Even the mechanic said it was good for a couple more years."

"You know how I feel about trading in the cars while they still have some resale value."

She propped her hip against the counter and glared at him. "How dare you? This is a child who called you father for fifteen years and you have the nerve to tell me the trade-in value of a used car ranks higher than seeing her?"

"You can't squeeze blood from a turnip. Just because you want there to be more money, doesn't make it happen."

"Why is it you resort to clichés every time you're wrong?"

"I'm sorry I'm not as clever with words as your first lover, but then I didn't know it was a criteria for having a civil discussion with you."

She ignored the taunt. "If we don't have it in savings, then you can sell some those precious stocks of yours." The stunned look on his face would have been comical if the subject hadn't been so serious.

"That's my retirement," he said, much the same way she imagined he would have responded had she asked him to give the employees at the plant all of Christmas Eve off instead of only half a day.

"Then just sell my half."

"It doesn't work that way."

"What you're really saying is that I have nothing in this marriage I can call my own."

"And you think I do?"

"You have the control, Ethan, that's as good as having everything in your name."

"I suppose your mother gave you the money to buy your ticket this time, too?" he asked, blithely going on.

"I put it on Mastercard."

He fixed her with another stunned look. "Without asking me?"

"You might as well know it all," she said, taking perverse pleasure in what would come next. "I got an advance on the card, too. If I'm careful, it will be enough to see me through at least a month over there. As a matter of fact, I maxed the card out. I wouldn't try to use it if I were you. It could be embarrassing."

"Goddamn it, Carly. Do you know what the interest is on a charge card? We could have gotten a loan at the bank for half that."

"*Could* is the operative word." She shrugged. "Of course you still have the option of taking out that loan if you don't want to compromise your portfolio."

"What's happened to you, Carly? I feel like I don't know you anymore."

A profound sadness stole over her. "Isn't that funny? I was just thinking the same thing about you. It's been years since I had a glimpse of the compassionate person you used to be. What happened to the man who married a scared and pregnant young girl in order to give her and her baby a home? You would have sold your soul to be a part of our lives back then." Tired of the futility of their argument, she crossed the room to go upstairs and pack.

"The man you used to know grew tired of chasing a dream. I finally decided it was time to stop running and do what I could to hold on to what I had."

Carly paused at the doorway. "And I guess I finally grew tired of trying to help you off your treadmill. Look where it's left us, Ethan."

30

Carly leaned her head against the leather upholstery in the back seat of David's Bentley, the woman she'd claimed to want to meet less than three weeks ago sitting two feet away. She couldn't help but think about the old saying—be careful what you wish for. It wasn't that Victoria had been anything less than gracious, it was more that Carly had been hoping against all logic and reason that Andrea would be the one to meet her at the airport.

Carly had seen a dozen pictures of Victoria; none of them had done her justice. She had the bone structure of a high-fashion model, thick dark hair that swept her shoulders, and dark, wide-set eyes that could dismiss someone or something with a blink. It was obvious—by the way she moved, talked, and conducted herself—that she'd been born privileged. Carly had felt clumsy and tongue-tied from the moment they'd met.

"David said you would likely be exhausted," Victoria said. "He meant to come himself, but was a bit pushed for time what with making the arrangements for Andrea to go to hospital tomorrow morning."

"I've felt better," Carly admitted. "But I'm not sure whether it's fatigue or worry."

A quick, sympathetic smile pulled Victoria's full lips into a less rigid shape. "It's a dreadfully sad business that's brought you here, certainly. Not at all like last time."

Carly felt strange talking to Victoria about that trip. "I was sorry to miss meeting you then. I had hoped to thank you personally for all you've done for Andrea."

"She's really a lovely child. Not as I'd expected at all. Keeps to her own company most of the time, but manages to conduct herself quite well socially when the occasion arises."

It was the tone of Victoria's voice, not the words, that told Carly everything she had just said was intended as a compliment. "How is she today? Have you seen her?"

"Still resistant about going to hospital, I'm afraid."

"It seems like months since I've seen her."

Victoria crossed her legs and adjusted her skirt before saying anything more. "I'm afraid it's inconvenient for me to be out of the city while you're here this time," she said, with a slight crack in her confidence. "David assured me you'd understand that I felt it a bit awkward to have you staying at the house. Subject to your approval, of course, I've made other arrangements. I've a dear friend who has quite a nice flat near the hospital who's not using it at the moment and has let it to us. For the entire summer, if need be."

"How close to the hospital is it?"

"Only a block and a bit." She was obviously relieved to see that Carly wasn't upset at being turned away from the manor. "There's a woman who comes in twice a week and several quite good restaurants near by."

Carly's midwestern background demanded that

she pay the rent on the apartment herself, but it was not the kind of thing you talked about to someone like Victoria. She'd settle up with David before she returned home. "I appreciate your finding something so close to Andrea. It will make visiting her much easier for me."

"She's in for a bit of a rough go, I'm afraid."

An unreasoning surge of jealousy hit Carly. How dare Victoria know so much about what Andrea was going through when Carly knew practically nothing? "I wish she'd let us tell Jeffery," she said. "He's wonderful with her and I think she's going to need him to get through this."

The look on Victoria's face clearly indicated what a bad idea she thought contacting Jeffery was. "I'm sure the Armstrongs will appreciate Andrea's reluctance to tell Jeffery just yet. They have a high regard for him and for his studies."

Plainly nothing she could say would turn Victoria into an ally where Jeffery was concerned. Carly let the subject drop. She stared out the window, looking for landmarks that would indicate how much farther they had to go to reach the city. "I would like to stop by the house to see Andrea before we go to the flat."

"Of course," Victoria said with a polite smile.

"Andrea tells me you've been working on a special project for the upcoming Mozart bicentennial," Carly said, steering the conversation onto safer ground.

It was all the encouragement Victoria needed to launch into a subject that carried them the rest of the way into London.

Carly held her breath as she walked slowly into Andrea's room, as much out of shock at seeing how fragile and pale her daughter looked as fear of waking her. How could so few days make such a difference? Or had she been blinded when she'd been here then, only seeing what she'd wanted to see? Looking at Andrea now, it was ludicrous to think anyone could ever attribute her illness to pregnancy.

Andrea stirred and opened her eyes. "Mom?"

Carly went to the side of the bed and knelt down on the floor, afraid she would disturb Andrea by sitting next to her. "I got here as soon as I could."

Andrea frowned. "I told David not to let you come. Shawn and Eric need you at home."

"Your brothers are capable of taking care of themselves—at their age, they'd better be." Carly brushed the hair back from Andrea's forehead. "What time are you scheduled to be admitted tomorrow morning?"

Andrea rolled to her back and stared up at the ceiling. "I'm not."

"But Victoria said—"

"I don't care what she said. I'm not going."

"Why are you being so stubborn about this?"

"Because I know what they're going to do to me."

Carly flinched. "Well, I don't, so I'd appreciate your telling me," she said, recognizing Andrea's need to get something off her chest. "Or at least I don't know everything."

"There was a girl at my school who got cancer last year. After they operated on her, she had to take all this really strong chemotherapy junk. She got so sick she had to drop out of school." She turned her head and pinned Carly with a pleading look. "I've only got a few more weeks, Mom. I can't let that happen to me."

"There has to be a way you could keep up with your studies at the hospital. I'll help you. So will David." She offered what she hoped was an encouraging smile. "I promise you, one way or another, we'll get you to Oxford."

"I can't take the chance. It's only a couple of weeks."

"Sweetheart, a couple of weeks can make—" Carly stopped at the smile Andrea gave her. "What's that for?"

"You always haul out the 'sweetheart' when you intend to put the muscle on one of us."

"Am I really that transparent?"

"Sometimes. Shawn said you called him sweetheart twenty times when he was in the hospital."

Carly smiled. "Okay, so it's out with sweetheart. How does 'baby' sound instead? Better yet, how about 'sugarpie?' "

Andrea laughed out loud. "Why don't you change to something really subtle, like lambkins? We'd never catch on."

"What's all the noise in here?" David asked, filling the doorway.

Carly's heart added an extra beat when she turned to look at him. He'd still been at the hospital when she'd arrived. "Andrea was just unraveling my Super Mom cape." She settled more comfortably on her haunches. "I'm afraid I'm grounded until I can get it fixed."

David came into the room. He stopped at the foot of Andrea's bed and stared down at her. "How does Chinese sound for dinner?"

Andrea made a face. "I'm not very hungry."

"It may be one of the last things you get to hold down for quite a while."

Carly's jaw dropped. How could he talk to her like that? Didn't he know how scared she already was? "From everything I read on the plane, that's not necessarily true," she said, unable to keep the anger from her voice.

"In Andrea's case it will be." Still looking at Carly, he said to Andrea, "I take it you haven't told her about what's in store for you yet."

Carly couldn't believe what she was hearing. This was not the same man she had called before leaving home. Only hours ago, David had been so distraught about what was happening he'd been unable to talk through the tears. "I just got here," she said to David, reining in her anger. "So far all we've discussed is Andrea's refusal to start treatment until she's finished school."

Now his gaze shifted to Andrea. "I told you, that's not an option. You're going to the hospital if I have to drag you there kicking and screaming and sit on your lap the whole time they drip that god-awful stuff into you."

It wasn't until then that Carly understood what was going on. David was handling his own fear in the only way he knew how. If immediate chemotherapy was Andrea's best hope, there was nothing she could say or do that would talk him into waiting. "I think he means it," Carly said.

Andrea turned so that her back was to both of them. "Why don't I have any say in this? It's my body."

David ran his hand across the back of his neck. "Because right now, I love you more than you love yourself." His voice softened and grew strained. "I told you, there's no way I'm going to risk losing you."

Andrea curled into a fetal position, drawing her knees up tight and tucking her hands under her cheek. "I'm tired," she said. "I want to go to sleep now."

"That won't make it go away," David said.

"No more," Carly protested, reeling under the impact of all she'd heard and seen.

"All right," David told her. To Andrea he said, "I'll see you later."

David and Carly were halfway to the door when Andrea stopped them. "Chinese sounds good. But could we have it a little later?"

David closed his eyes and swallowed hard as if

physically trying to hold in his emotions. "Egg rolls and beef and broccoli sound all right?"

"I think I'd like some mu shu pork, too."

"All right."

"And some sweet-and-sour chicken."

"Anything else?" David said with amused patience.

"Fortune cookies."

He retraced his steps to her bed, bent, and kissed her. "We don't need them," he said softly. "We already know how everything is going to turn out."

31

"Been here long?" David asked, walking across the hospital foyer toward Carly, his arm loosely draped around Andrea's shoulders.

"Only a few minutes," she lied. Actually, she'd been there almost an hour, showing up early to familiarize herself with the building in an effort to take each piece of the intimidating experience and cut it down to a manageable size. When David stopped beside her, Carly put her hands on either side of Andrea's face and gave her a kiss. "How are you this morning?"

"Fantastic," Andrea shot back. "Great. On top of the world. Next question?"

"If you're not careful," Carly warned, "I'm going to lay some psychiatric crap on you and say you're striking out at me because you're scared shitless and can't find any other way to express your feelings."

"Going to?" Andrea said.

"That's just a warm-up."

Andrea's lip began to tremble. Tears glistened in her eyes. "All right, I'm scared. So what does that prove?"

"It proves we can be honest with each other and

get through this together instead of at each other's throats."

"Sounds like a good idea to me," David said.

"This is all too Partridge family for me," Andrea said, wiping her eyes.

Carly smiled. "We'll work on that," she said. "Maybe we can meet somewhere in the middle, make it a little more like the Addams family."

A nurse stepped off the elevator and came toward them. "We've Andrea's room all prepared for her, Mr. Montgomery." She smiled at Andrea. "We should be getting you up there and prepared for your surgery straight away."

"Sister Nash, I'd like you to meet Mrs. Hargrove, Andrea's mother."

"How do you do?" the sister said, extending her hand.

Andrea turned to Carly. "Are you coming up later?" she asked, her effort to seem in control of the situation taking its toll on her composure.

She reached for Andrea's hand and gave it a squeeze. "I'll be there as soon as I've talked to the doctor."

Sister Nash smiled. "We'll be off, then, since we're a bit pushed for time. Doctor has a number of broviacs scheduled for this morning."

The double-line broviac that would be inserted under the skin on Andrea's chest was the first step on her long journey. The line would provide immediate access for the chemotherapy, blood transfusions, and antibiotics, even providing nutrition if it became necessary. But it would also be a constant reminder—at least in the beginning—of how sick Andrea was. In a few days, if she reacted as strongly as predicted to the drugs that had been prescribed for her chemotherapy, none of them would need any reminder of her illness.

Carly forced her mouth into an encouraging smile.

"If we get tied up with the doctor, remember you're supposed to call your grandmother Barbara at noon. Shawn and Eric spent the night there so they could talk to you, too."

Sister Nash gently touched Andrea's arm. "We're off, then," she said cheerfully.

Carly watched them go, her heart in her throat. After they had disappeared in the elevator, she turned to David. "We might as well get this over with."

According to everyone David had talked to, Dr. Richard Reardon was the best pediatric oncologist in England. Some had even gone so far as to say the best in Europe. He looked too young to have earned such a lofty reputation, but his success rate couldn't be argued with. He was blunt and aggressive and always seemed to be in a hurry.

David had tried to prepare Carly for what she was about to hear by giving her as much information as he could remember from the discussions he and Reardon had already had. Whether or not it had done any good was another matter.

"Have a seat," Dr. Reardon said, leading Carly and David into his office. "I'll be with you momentarily—soon as I finish signing these papers." Several seconds later, when they were both in chairs opposite his desk, he looked up. "Would you prefer I answer your questions right off or give you my standard speech?"

"Why don't you start and if I have questions, I'll ask them as you go along," Carly said.

David noticed Carly's hands clasped together in her lap, the grip so tight her knuckles had turned white. It was the only outward manifestation of her nervousness. To the casual observer, she would seem the picture of calm.

Dr. Reardon leaned back in his chair. "I believe surprises should be saved for birthdays and Christmas." He hesitated, as if waiting for David or Carly to comment. When neither did, he went on. "As you know, your daughter has one of the more difficult types of leukemia. Our goal is to get her into remission and that is going to take six to eight weeks of intensive therapy. She will be very, very sick during this time."

"I've been reading some books I picked up at the library," Carly interrupted. "One of them said not everyone gets sick."

"Andrea won't be one of them. Not with the dosages we'll be giving her. She will lose her hair, require frequent blood transfusions, be highly susceptible to infection, and likely lose her appetite entirely. In which case we'll sustain her with intravenous feedings through the broviac. Still, she'll lose weight. Another thing you should be aware of, even with the antibiotics we'll be giving her, the mouth sores she's already developed will get worse. Also, she'll develop diarrhea and have severe cramping."

David chanced a look at Carly to see how she was taking the rapid fire devastation. Her body was rigid, her face a mask.

"As I previously said, our goal is to get her into remission as quickly as possible."

"And then she'll be through with the chemotherapy?" Carly asked.

"The initial treatment, but not the maintenance." Dr. Reardon frowned. "Mr. Montgomery hasn't explained the procedure for the transplant to you?"

"Carly just arrived last night," David said. "I thought she'd heard as much as she could handle from me and decided it would be better to have you explain the transplant process anyway."

"What kind of transplant?" Carly asked, clearly confused.

"Bone marrow," Dr. Reardon answered. "In Andrea's case, it's her best chance for full recovery."

"Where does the bone marrow come from?" Carly asked.

Richard Reardon rocked forward in his chair and leaned his elbows on the desk. "This is where it gets a bit tricky, I'm afraid. Mr. Montgomery has explained that Andrea and her brothers don't share the same father. Is that correct?"

Carly nodded.

"They were our best bet, but not the only one. We'll want you to be tested, of course, but we're also tapping into the donor network here in England and on the continent. Should that prove fruitless, we'll contact the one in the States. The chances are fairly good that we'll be able to come up with someone suitable."

"Fairly good?" David prodded.

"For the general populace, it runs about one in ten thousand."

Carly readjusted herself in the seat. "Which means it isn't necessary for a relative to be the donor?"

"Certainly not. However, as you would expect, the closer the relation, the higher the odds of finding a perfect match. There's been some publicity lately about mums having another child for the sole purpose of acquiring a donor. In Andrea's case that's not an option, unfortunately."

"What if there isn't a perfect match for Andrea anywhere?" Carly asked.

"Then we'll go with the best we've got, which is likely to come from someone inside her family, most probably you or Mr. Montgomery. But, considering the circumstances, it might just as well be an aunt or uncle."

Carly hugged herself, seeming to grow smaller in the chair. "How soon can I be tested?"

"This afternoon, if you like." There was a light tapping on the door. Dr. Reardon looked toward the noise and barked, "Yes?"

The door opened wide enough for a woman to poke her head through. "Sorry, Doctor. But Jamie Peterson's having some trouble and Sister was wondering if you could come up."

"Tell her I'll be there straight away." He pushed his chair back and started to stand. "I'd hoped for more time this morning, but . . ." He shrugged. "Feel free to call with questions whenever you like. Otherwise, we'll be running into each other in Andrea's room, I'm sure."

"Thank you," David said.

Carly didn't move. When the doctor was gone, David turned to her. "Are you all right?"

"What if there isn't a suitable donor, David? We could lose her."

"Stop borrowing trouble."

"I can't help it. Without any full brothers or sisters, the odds are already stacked against her."

David had never seen her so scared. "He said the chances were one in ten thousand. I did some checking and the registry in the States alone has over a hundred thousand people on it. We'll find someone."

"But what if we don't?"

He wouldn't let her maneuver him into that corner. It was unthinkable that Andrea might die. He refused even to consider the possibility. "Then you'll have to go to Andrea's father and his family and ask them to be tested."

Her head moved back and forth slowly, as if she were in shock. "I can't," she whispered.

"What?" David asked, sure he hadn't heard her correctly.

"I can't go to Andrea's father."

"Why in the hell not?"

She hung her head. "He's dead."

Not until that moment had David realized how

much he'd been counting on having that little ace in the hole. "What about his family?" He was unwilling to let it go.

"I can't go to them either."

"Can't? Or won't?" he said.

She turned to him, the look in her eyes a plea for understanding. "You want it to be simple, but it's not. Andrea and I aren't the only ones involved."

"Who are you protecting?" He didn't know how to get through to her. "And why, for God's sake?"

She reached for her purse. "I want to see Andrea now."

Frustrated beyond words, he followed her out of the office.

Carly's heels echoed in the empty hallway leading to Andrea's room. She'd left David in conversation with the doctor who had operated on Andrea that morning. There were sounds of machines and metal clanging and, incongruously, children's laughter somewhere on the floor, but no visible people. She'd stopped at the floor station to see if Andrea had been assigned a room number and was pleased to find out that it was on the park side of the hospital.

Carly had taken a walk through the park that morning. Although the daffodils were gone and the tulips waning, other flowers were coming up to take their places. Soon there would be a riot of color just outside Andrea's window, enticing her with beauty and renewed life.

It was funny the things that had given Carly pleasure since she'd arrived the night before—David sitting at Andrea's bedside reading her an article from the paper, Andrea's teasing delight over the single gray hair she'd found mixed in Carly's deep auburn, Victoria's willingness to let them have the evening alone.

And now, a private hospital room on the right side of the hall.

When Carly had naively suggested Andrea might like being in a room with someone her own age, the sister had told her it wasn't an option. Andrea was isolated to protect her from infection. Her visitors would be kept at a minimum for the same reason.

It seemed nothing would be simple or easy anymore where Andrea was concerned.

She glanced at the room number she was passing and realized Andrea's should be next. As she neared the door she heard voices inside and slowed to peek through the glass in the door before going inside. Her breath caught in happy surprise to see Jeffery sitting on the side of the bed, holding Andrea's hand. The love between them filled the room with its brilliance.

Carly stepped away from the door, not wanting to intrude on their moment. If it was possible for anyone to bring Andrea through what lay ahead with the sheer force of loving her, it would be Jeffery. She and David would be willing to trade their own lives for hers if given the opportunity, but they couldn't give Andrea the will to fight for herself the way Jeffery could.

Carly had lost track of how long she'd been standing outside Andrea's room when she saw David approaching.

"What are you doing out here?" he asked.

"Giving Andrea and Jeffery some time alone."

He gave her a smile filled with irony. "I was sitting in the lounge by myself so that the two of you could be together."

"When did you call him?"

"What makes you think it was me?"

"Who else?"

"Actually, it was Victoria who got him here. She went to Jeffery's parents last night to tell them what was going on. They drove up to Oxford and picked him up this morning."

"I don't understand. When I said something to Victoria about calling Jeffery she was horrified. What made her change her mind?"

"I don't know. She surprises even me sometimes." He leaned against the wall. "Perhaps it was seeing the pain and fear you were feeling. Or maybe it was discovering how deeply she cares about Andrea herself."

"I've decided not to wait until Dr. Reardon has checked the registry for potential bone marrow transplants before asking Ethan to have the boys tested. Even if it turns out they aren't suitable donors for Andrea," she said softly, "they might be for someone else."

"What about your mom?"

"I'm sure she'll want to be tested, too." A slow smile formed. "Something tells me no one in her family will be safe once she finds out genetics can play a role in HLA typing."

"Too bad she doesn't know who Andrea's father is." He turned and pinned her with a stare. "Or does she?"

32

Carly stood by the window in Andrea's room and stared at the garden in the park across the street. She felt something cool on her cheek and reached up to wipe it away, only then realizing she was crying.

A noise behind her drew her attention back to the bed. Even when Andrea was asleep now, she looked as if she were in pain. Day by day, hour by hour, minute by minute, Carly was watching her daughter die. The chemotherapy was killing her as surely as the leukemia, destroying the few remaining good cells in tandem with the bad. Her hair was less than half what it had been four weeks ago and strands of the little that remained stayed on her pillow every time she turned her head. She had lost more weight than Carly thought possible, reducing an already thin body to little more than skin and bone.

During the first week, each blood transfusion had brought its own special, unspoken fear. What if Andrea were to beat the leukemia only to discover a year or two down the road that she'd been given blood infected with AIDS? That worry had begun to diminish when Andrea became so sick she couldn't hold half a spoonful of her eighteenth birthday cake in her stomach or talk without her gums bleeding. It had disappeared altogether when they were told Andrea's leukemia had shifted to nonlymphocytic, which put her into a rare and particularly lethal subtype, biphenotypic. By then, Carly would have traded anything in the future for just one more guaranteed year with her daughter.

Reason told her it wasn't the hours she spent in the room willing Andrea to live that kept her daughter's heart beating and infections at bay, it was Andrea's own spirit and the massive doses of antibiotics being pumped into her along with the poison. Still, just the thought of being more than fifteen minutes away nearly paralyzed Carly with fear.

Which was why she had put off returning to Baxter. And then with the new diagnosis, it became critical that they be prepared to transplant as quickly as Andrea reached remission. The possibility of a second remission, should the disease become active again, was highly unlikely. As of that morning, none of the data banks contacted had come up with a suitable donor, giving an urgency to the search Carly couldn't ignore any longer.

She'd come to say good-bye before going home and to promise she would be back as soon as possible. Except that Andrea wouldn't wake up long enough to hear the words Carly had so carefully rehearsed.

The door opened, and David entered. "It's time to go," he said softly. "Harold's downstairs waiting."

How could she leave without saying anything to Andrea about where she was going and why she was leaving so abruptly? Finally, unwilling to wake her from the first real sleep she'd had in days, Carly touched the blanket and whispered, "I love you."

David took Carly in his arms. "I'm sorry it had to come to this," he said. "But I think you'll discover your fears, whatever they are, have been exaggerated in your mind."

She didn't even attempt to correct him. There were only two people who could understand the far-reaching consequences of what she was about to do. David would find out how wrong he was soon enough.

Fifteen hours later, Carly was in Barbara's living room. "I prayed every day it wouldn't come to this," she said, her gaze fixed on the floor. "If there were any other way . . ."

"I didn't tell you this before because I couldn't see any reason," Barbara said, "but I've already approached your father's brothers and your grandparents about being tested. Actually, it was your uncle John I talked to, and let him talk to the others."

"He must have been stunned to hear from you after all this time." Carly lifted her head and stared at her mother. "What did he say?"

"Initially, that they'd have to think about it and get back to me."

"How long ago was that?"

"Last week."

"Then they might already have gone in?"

Barbara shook her head. "Yesterday, when you told me you were coming, I called him. He said his doctor had told him the chances that any of them being a match for Andrea were no better than we could find in the general population. They had all gotten together over dinner that night and talked about it and decided it wasn't worth taking the chance of going through the test. He was supposed to call me with the news, but just hadn't gotten around to it yet."

"Didn't you tell him how easy it was? That there really isn't any risk?" Andrea asked, already knowing the answer.

"I talked till I was blue in the face. You know what your father's family is like, Carly. Once they've made up their minds about something, God himself couldn't change it. Frank was the same way."

Carly looked into her mother's eyes and saw that she knew what was coming. "We have to tell them."

"Yes, I know," she said, the weight of it taking the crispness out of her posture. "I just wish I believed it would make a difference—and that we knew for sure we aren't going to end up hurting Andrea more than we help her."

"If we don't find a donor," Carly said, "none of it will matter."

The drive to Bill and Hallie Strong's dairy farm was through what Carly had always thought was the most beautiful country in Ohio. She had vivid memories of making the trip when she'd been a child, even then being aware that the countryside would be the only pleasant part of the journey.

The farm itself had been in the family for five generations, the business growing larger, the Strong impact in the region more powerful with each passing decade. For the past thirty years it was a given that those who expected to win political office in the region made their first stop at the Strong farm.

Carly's father, Frank, had been the youngest of five sons and the only one to move away from home —much to the anger and disappointment of his parents. After the two oldest boys were killed in World War II, Bill and Hallie Strong had become compulsively protective of their youngest.

They'd needed someone to blame for Frank's restlessness and Barbara had been an easy target. After doing everything they could to keep their son from marrying her and failing, they were wise enough to realize they would lose him permanently if they didn't make accommodations. Ten months after the wedding, Carly was born and, by producing a girl, Barbara lost even the modicum of acceptance the Strongs had afforded her. Her only redemption would have been to follow the error with a string of boys, but after three miscarriages, she'd stopped trying.

For the next twenty-one years Barbara and Carly were tolerated, if not loved, in order for the Strongs to maintain contact with their son. The day he died, so did the relationship.

Although the Strong farm was less than two hours' drive from Baxter, Carly hadn't been there since the reception that followed her father's funeral. She'd wondered if she would remember the way, but needn't have bothered. A thirty-foot-high billboard advertising the farm and its products greeted her as she crossed the county line.

"I'm still surprised Hallie agreed to see us," Barbara said as they turned off the main road and onto the farm property. "That woman took a dislike to me the day your father introduced us. She blamed me for every cold he ever had—even said it was my fault he had allergies. If I'd fed him properly and kept the house cleaner, he wouldn't have been susceptible to pollen and germs."

Carly had heard the stories before, but not for years. Wally's love and understanding had helped Barbara come to terms with the hell Frank Strong had put her through. Eventually she'd managed to put that time behind her.

"Once Hallie even insisted it was because of me Frank became a policeman, completely ignoring the fact, of course, that I met him when he stopped me for running a red light."

"If she only knew," Carly said.

"There would be hell to pay," Barbara agreed.

Carly pulled in next to a white truck with the farm

logo on the side and shut off the engine. She sat behind the wheel, closed her eyes, and summoned a picture of Andrea to bring what she was doing back in focus again. A second later, she turned to Barbara. "I wouldn't put you through this if there were any other way."

"It's no use pretending this is any easier on you," Barbara said. "I know better."

They walked up to the front door side by side, not noticing the imposing figure standing behind the screen until they were on the porch.

"I told your mother you were wasting your time coming here," Hallie Strong said to Carly, ignoring Barbara.

Carly stared at the shadowy figure behind the screen and was overcome with a sinking feeling that guilt or duty would not be the way to win her grandmother's cooperation. "Maybe so, Grandmother, but when your child is dying, you do whatever has to be done."

With a show of reluctance, Hallie opened the door to them. "I don't have much time," she said. "My program comes on the television in fifteen minutes." After a quick assessing glance at her granddaughter, Hallie turned on her heel and headed down a long hallway. "No sense opening the parlor for fifteen minutes," she said, her voice raised to be sure the insult could be heard.

Barbara and Carly exchanged looks before falling in behind Hallie. She took them to a small office and indicated they were to sit in the twin straight-back chairs pushed up against the far wall. When she was settled behind the desk facing them, she took a pencil out of the drawer and tapped its eraser rhythmically against her thumb. "I'm waiting," she said.

Carly opened her purse, took out several folded sheets of paper, and placed them on the desk. "I knew you wouldn't believe what I've come here to tell you without proof."

Hallie hesitated before reaching for the papers. After several seconds she laid them back down. Without explanation, they were meaningless. "I assume this is leading to something?"

Carly swallowed against the sudden dryness in her throat. "The doctor who told John that the odds were no higher for him and Steve to be suitable donors for my daughter than the rest of the population was missing an important genetic detail—their brother just happens to be Andrea's father."

The confused frown that drew Hallie's eyebrows together slowly disappeared, replaced with a look of growing fury. "You little witch. How dare you accuse my son of such a thing?" She got up so fast the chair she'd been sitting in hit the wall behind her. She pointed toward the door and screamed, "Get out of here."

"Not until I get what I came for," Carly managed to say, still reeling from the fact that after almost eighteen years of self-enforced silence, she'd finally said out loud that her father had been the one who raped her. Where was the expected bolt of lightning? The thunderclap?

"If you don't get out of here right now, I'll have you thrown out."

Carly stood, picked up the papers she'd brought with her from England and gathered from her father's file at the doctor's office, and put them in her pocket. With methodical movements, she placed her fists on the desk and leaned forward, her face threateningly close to her grandmother's. "If I leave here without your word that John and Steve will be tested first thing tomorrow morning, I'm taking the story straight to the newspaper. Think about it, Grandmother. Do you really want the people around here to remember your son that way?"

"Imagine what they could do with a story like this, Hallie," Barbara said, breaking her silence. She rocked forward in her chair. "And deep in your heart you know it's true. You've always wondered why Frank committed suicide. Now you know."

Hallie turned her fury on Barbara. "Shut up. I don't care what kind of proof you say you have, you'll never convince me Frank killed himself."

Carly's heart skipped a beat. The Strongs had spent years trying to convince anyone who would listen that their son had not died by his own hand. Stories about their efforts still surfaced periodically at Baxter's sheriff's office, brought home by Wally and passed on to Carly by Barbara. "None of that matters now," Carly insisted, frantic to get the conversation back to safer ground. "All you have to do is convince John and Steve to be tested and get them to agree to become a donor if either one of them is a match, and I promise I'll never see or talk to any of you again as long as I live."

Conflicting emotions played across the old woman's face. "I'll call you," she finally said.

"That's not good enough," Carly told her.

"What do you want from me?"

Carly met her gaze unflinchingly. "Your cooperation."

"First give me those papers."

Carly took them out of her pocket and handed them to her. "They're only copies, easily reproduced. You can't change the facts, Grandmother."

Hallie opened a drawer and shoved the papers inside. "Frank would never have done something like that unless—" She left the thought hanging.

"Unless what?" Carly demanded, the memories of that night rushing at her, swirling past her efforts to keep them buried.

"You must have done something that made him crazy. I remember how you used to wear your pants so tight there was nothing left to the imagination. A man can't be blamed for what he does to a woman like that."

Barbara lunged forward. Hallie backed against the wall. "Your son got exactly what he deserved for what he did to my daughter," Barbara screamed. "I would do it again, in a second."

Carly grabbed her mother's arm. "Don't do this," she pleaded, frantic to stop her mother before it was too late. "Don't let her win."

Barbara shook her head as if to clear it. "Oh, my God," she said to Carly, a sudden look of understanding flashing through her eyes.

Hallie's feral eyes darted from mother to daughter and back again. "It was you that killed my boy," she said to Barbara.

"My father killed himself," Carly insisted, watching Andrea's chances diminish before her eyes. "And the minute people around here learn what he did to me, they'll understand why he did it."

"Get out," Hallie hissed.

"Grandmother, please." Carly couldn't let it go. "Uncle John and Uncle Steve are Andrea's best chance." She held out her hands in a supplicating gesture. "She's going to die if we can't find a donor."

"She's an abomination. She should never have been born."

"She's your granddaughter, your last link with your son. Don't you understand that if she dies, it's going to be as if he were dying all over again." With each sentence, bile rose higher in Carly's throat. "She looks just like him, Grandmother," she said.

"It's no good, Carly," Barbara said. "There's nothing you can say that will change her mind." She fixed Hallie with a stare. "The real reason you hated me for marrying your son was that you wanted him for yourself. He used to tell me about the times you would take him to bed with you when his father was out of town."

Hallie's eyes filled with venom. "He was a baby when I did that."

"He was ten years old."

Carly recoiled at the hatred flowing between her grandmother and mother. It had become a living, breathing presence that behaved as if it had been nurtured in the almost two decades they'd been apart instead of wasting away. Only this time there was a new victim—Andrea.

Without saying anything more, Carly stepped around her mother and headed for the door. It had been a mistake to try to reason with her grandmother. They should have gone straight to her father's brothers.

"Where do you think you're going?" Hallie said, springing after her, her speed and agility belying the fact she was less than a month away from her eighty-fifth birthday.

"To talk to Uncle John."

"He isn't here."

Carly reached the front door and whipped around to face her grandmother. "Then I'll wait."

"It won't do you any good. John does what I tell him."

"He might not be as willing for the entire county to know what his brother did as you are. He's going to be around to face the consequences a lot longer." Carly took a step toward her grandmother. "Make no mistake about it, old woman, you've met your match in me. There is nothing I won't do to save my daughter."

"Where in the hell have you been?" Wally asked, hurrying down the sidewalk to greet Carly and Barbara as they pulled into her mother's driveway. "You were supposed to be back four hours ago."

"Mom will tell you about it," Carly said, shifting the car into reverse in preparation to leave. "I want to get home before Ethan does."

"I think you'd better come inside," he told her.

Carly frowned. "Can't it wait?"

He shook his head. "I'm afraid not."

"What is it, Wally?" Barbara asked getting out of the car and walking toward him.

"Not out here," he said.

The headache that had been threatening all afternoon, finally hit Carly. She squinted against the throbbing in her left temple as she shut off the car and grabbed her purse.

"We've spent the past three hours trying to chase John and Steve down," Barbara said, standing on tiptoe to give Wally a kiss.

"You weren't looking in the right place," he said ominously. "You should have tried the sheriff's office."

Carly put her hand to her temple. "I didn't believe she'd do it."

"I think you'd better tell me exactly what happened today," he said, opening Carly's door.

Half an hour later, when Carly had finished relaying the details of Barbara's and her meeting with Hallie, and had answered all of Wally's questions, he sat back in his chair and with a heavy sigh told them, "I'm afraid the shit has hit the fan, ladies."

"What is that supposed to mean?" Barbara demanded, her nervousness manifesting itself in a short fuse.

"A couple of hours ago, I got a call from a friend of mine who works in the sheriff's office in Boehm County. He told me the Strong family was pulling in every political favor they ever handed out in order to get the investigation into Frank's death reopened."

"They don't have any proof," Carly said, hoping she sounded more convincing to them than she did herself.

"Maybe not," Wally said gently. "But they have a motive."

"Andrea," Carly breathed.

"Did you leave the lab results behind?" he asked. Carly nodded.

Wally groaned. "I wish you'd told me you intended to do that."

"It was the only way I could think to convince her."

"You weren't there, Wally," Barbara said. "You can't imagine what that woman is like."

"What's going to happen?" Carly asked.

Wally stood and went over to the sink to start a pot of coffee. He insisted that he thought better when he was doing something. "If the Strongs were anyone else, I'd say they were spinning their wheels. But when you've got half the people in the county owing you, that gives you clout."

"But he didn't die in Boehm County," Carly said.

"That will only slow things down some," Wally said. "What I can't understand is Hallie wanting everyone to find out what a son of a bitch her boy was."

"That's easy," Carly responded. "She's already made him the victim. The whole thing was my fault. I drove him to it."

"Jesus, she didn't say that."

"And more," Barbara told him.

Wally dropped the measuring spoon filled with coffee on the counter. "The woman's crazy."

"Now you have some idea what we're dealing with."

"She's not going to be talked out of this," he said,

more to himself than the two women sitting at the table.

Carly buried her face in her hands. "I'm sorry. I should have known what would happen, but I was so sure Grandmother Hallie would do anything to keep people from finding out."

"You did what you had to do," Barbara said. "And now I'm going to do what I have to do."

"Which is?" Wally asked, suspicious.

"I'm going to drive back up there tomorrow and tell them what they've undoubtedly already figured out for themselves—how and why I shot Frank. I'll tell them I was scared and decided to make it look like a suicide because I didn't want Carly to go through any more than she already had." She sent a pleading look to Wally. "It's the truth. They'll have to believe me."

Wally went over to Barbara and knelt down in front of her. "I know what you're trying to do, but there's no way you're going to keep me out of this," he told her. "A rookie could put the pieces together once he saw the name of the responding officer."

Carly felt herself being dragged back to that night. It had taken years, but in the end time had done what determination could not—given her occasional respite from the night Andrea had been conceived. Gradually she'd been able to get through each new day a little better than the last. At least that was how it had been until David showed up three years ago.

And now it was as if it were happening all over again—her father finding the birth control pills in her purse and attacking her in a drunken fury, his anger turning to lust, her mother coming home and discovering them, the flash of fire from her father's gun, the blood, her mother holding her, their tears mixing, and then the panic.

Wally had been her father's deputy and the first to arrive at the house. It hadn't taken him five minutes to see through their story about suicide and figure out for himself what had taken place. Without comment he'd changed the position of her father's body, placed the gun in his hand, and told Carly to get out of the house and not come back until the ambulance and coroner were gone.

That night had been their secret since, love binding them as tightly as fear of discovery and retribution. And now there was no way to protect each other anymore, and no way to keep Andrea from learning the truth.

Carly had come home to save her daughter. If there was a deity somewhere in charge of cruel jokes, he was undoubtedly laughing his head off at that one.

"How long do we have?" Carly asked Wally.

He turned his attention from Barbara. "It's hard to say. Gossip moves pretty fast around here. Especially when it's this good."

Reluctantly, weary almost to the point of collapse, Carly stood. "Could you watch the boys tonight while I tell Ethan?"

"Of course," Barbara said.

"Do you want us to tell them for you?" Wally added. "They might take it better coming from us."

Every instinct told Carly she should be the one to break the news, but there just wasn't time. She couldn't take the chance of waiting another day, and Ethan would be all she could handle that night. "Would you mind if they stayed with you and I came over to tell them in the morning?"

"Why do you insist on carrying the whole burden yourself?" Barbara asked. "Let us help you."

"If it weren't for me, none of this would be happening."

Barbara and Wally sat in stunned silence for several seconds. "What in the hell are you talking about?" Wally finally managed to get out.

For the first time that day, tears filled Carly's eyes. "I've gone over and over it in my mind," she said, her lip trembling with the effort to get the words out. "I must have done something that night, I must have acted in some way that gave him the idea he could . . ." A tear broke free and rolled down her cheek. "Don't you see? It's all my fault. Everything. Your lives, everything you've worked so hard to achieve is going to be taken away from you because of me."

"My God," Barbara said, stunned. "I had no idea you felt this way."

Wally raked his hand through his hair, then stood, rocking back and forth from his heels to his toes. "How could I have been so goddamned blind? I've seen it a hundred times and it still blows me away—some no-good bastard rapes a woman and she falls all over herself trying to figure out what she did to deserve it." He slowly turned his head to look at Carly. "I'm sorry I failed you, missy. I should've known you would take this on yourself."

Barbara got up and put her arms around Carly. "And all this time I've been blaming myself for staying with Frank when I knew what kind of man he was. If I had left him when you were a baby—"

"Please don't, Mom. You couldn't have known what he would do."

"He was a mean drunk, Carly. I've asked myself a hundred times if I went to that meeting just to get away from him, hoping he'd be passed out when I got home."

Carly was nearly choking on her own guilt, she couldn't handle her mother's, too. "None of it matters now, Mom. We have more important things to think about."

Barbara stared at Carly long and hard as if assessing her stability. "You're right," she finally said. "But we're not through with this."

Carly nodded and reached up to wipe the tears from her cheeks.

"Do you want me to pick the boys up from school and bring them over here?" Wally asked.

"Maybe that would be better," Carly told him. "That way I can get Ethan to come home early. I'm scared to death someone else is going to get to him first."

33

Gathering the sheer curtain in her hand, Carly pulled it aside to look out the front window. If Ethan had left immediately after talking to her, he should have been home fifteen minutes ago. It was too soon to worry that he might have gotten in an accident, but not that someone might have called him to let him in on the "news."

On the way home from her mother's Carly had tried to concentrate on how and what she would tell Ethan, but she couldn't get Andrea out of her mind long enough to form a cohesive idea. She couldn't let go of the thought that she'd failed her daughter. What had ever made her think emotional blackmail would work on Hallie Strong? Carly should have pleaded with her grandmother, and then if necessary, gone down on her knees and begged. Now Andrea's only hope was that one of the smaller donor banks somewhere would come up with something.

The ever-optimistic Wally had suggested they try to use the publicity that would come from the re-opened investigation to get people to go in for HLA typing. Carly had smiled and told him she thought it was a great idea. She didn't have the heart to point out how few people would follow through when they found out it was nearly as expensive as a night out on the town and not covered by insurance.

So far, Carly had been the one who'd come the closest to matching Andrea; only it wasn't like a game of horseshoes where close counted for something. Without a perfect match, the chances for rejection and failure rose dramatically.

Carly had released the curtain and started to turn from the window when Ethan pulled into the driveway. As if on cue, her temple started to throb again. Even after all the turmoil and hard feelings they had been through the past three years, she found her heart breaking for him. His world was about to fall apart as surely as he would help it along.

She opened the door as he stepped on the porch, searching his face for a sign that someone else had gotten to him first. All she saw was a look of irritation at being called home two and a half hours before quitting time.

He stepped inside, dropped his briefcase beside the hall table, shrugged out of his jacket, and hung it on the newel post. "God, it's hot out there," he said, loosening his tie.

"I made some iced tea."

"I'd rather have a beer, if we've got any cold."

"I'll put one in the freezer." A hysterical laugh began to build over the completely ordinary conversation they were having while their lives were falling apart around them.

"No, don't bother." He tossed his tie on top of his jacket. "The tea's okay."

She headed for the kitchen. He followed.

"Now, what's so important it couldn't wait until tonight," he said, pulling out a kitchen chair and sitting down.

Where should she begin? "I went to see my Grandmother Hallie today."

"I thought you two—" He hesitated. "Oh, I get it. You wanted to see if you could get her to go in for testing."

"Actually, it was my uncles John and Steve that Dr. Reardon thought might be Andrea's best possibilities." The day she'd asked to see the good doctor in private to explain Andrea's genetic background was the first time she'd seen a crack in his rigid facade. Carly gave Ethan his tea and sat down across from him.

"But I thought you said the family ties had to be at least a generation closer."

She swallowed. Why in the hell couldn't she just come out and say it? What was the sense of coming at it from every way but straight on? "John and Steve are Andrea's uncles."

He frowned. "You mean great-uncles."

"No," she said softly. "My father was also Andrea's father."

"That's impossible. David is—" As understanding hit Ethan, the confusion turned to revulsion. "You mean to tell me you were sleeping with David and your own father, too?"

She was too stunned to answer immediately. It had never occurred to her that he might put that particular perverted interpretation on what she would tell him. Disappointment bore deeply in her chest, the pain stealing her breath. "He raped me," she said, feeling as if it had just happened to her all over again.

There was a long pause. "Jesus Christ," Ethan said, "why didn't you tell me?" There wasn't a glimmer of apology in his look or manner for having jumped to the wrong conclusion.

"I didn't tell anyone," she said, a profound weariness coming over her. "I couldn't. If anyone found out, my mother would have been tried for murder. They would have arrested Wally, and probably me, too, on conspiracy."

"Barbara shot him? But I thought he—"

Carly could see a spark of understanding as he began to fill the details in for himself. She decided to let him work it out on his own.

"She came home, saw what had happened, and killed him," he supplied several seconds later.

"It was my idea to try to make it look like he'd committed suicide. I couldn't bear the idea that she would be put in jail for trying to help me."

"And with Wally's cooperation you pulled it off."

"Yes."

"He must have been in love with your mother even back then."

His words hit like a baseball bat. If Ethan's first thought was that Wally had acted out of self-interest, what chance did they have in a courtroom? "Why do you say that?"

"What other reason could there be?"

"Compassion?"

"Don't make me laugh. No one sticks his neck out that far without self-interest goading him."

"That's a specious thing to say, but I'm not going to argue with you about it."

Ethan eyed her. "So after all this time, why take me into your confidence now? What makes you think you can trust me any more today than you could back then?"

"The choice of who I tell or don't was taken out of my hands today. By tomorrow everyone will know." She propped her elbows on the table and pressed her fingers to her temples. "I made the mistake of trying to outmaneuver my grandmother Hallie by showing her proof that her son was Andrea's father. I thought she would do anything to keep me quiet."

" 'Anything' meaning making John and Steve get tested."

"Yes."

"But she decided going after you and Barbara would be more satisfying."

"I don't know how I could have been so wrong."

"Wait a minute," Ethan said, his eyes narrowing in thought. "Wait just a fuckin' minute. What you're really telling me is that you let Andrea go off to live with David when you knew he wasn't her father. That's what this is all about, isn't it?"

Finally, it was out in the open. "If you recall, you didn't leave me much choice. Either I let it be known who Andrea's father really was, or I let her go. I did the only thing I could."

"I don't believe this. Does David know?" He threw his hands up in the air. "What a stupid question. Of course he knows."

"Not who Andrea's real father is."

"But he sure as hell knows it's not him. Or have you had him dancing at the end of your string all this time, too?"

"He's aware Andrea isn't his," she admitted.

Ethan sat very still for what seemed like an eternity. "And he still took her home to live with him. Well, I guess I don't have to ask why."

"Don't make this worse than it is," she said.

Ethan let out a long, bitter laugh. "I just found out my wife gave her firstborn to her ex-lover to keep from telling me a secret she knew goddamn well I'd never tell, and you have the guts to say that to me?" He fixed her with a look of pure hatred. "How do you think it makes me feel knowing you trusted David more than you did me? After all we've been through together, after Shawn and Eric, this house, the bed we've shared upstairs for almost nineteen fuckin' years—and you tell me not to make it worse than it is?"

"I'm sorry you had to find out this way, Ethan."

"That's not good enough."

"Well, it's the best I can do. I don't know what else to say."

"It doesn't matter. There isn't anything you could say that would make a difference. You betrayed me, Carly. You gave David the trust and loyalty that should have been mine. I earned it, goddamn it. There's no way in hell I'll ever get over that."

"David had nothing to do with it. I was protecting Andrea. I would have done anything to keep her from finding out who her real father was."

"I want you out of this house. Tonight. If I never see you again, it will be too soon."

"You don't mean that."

"The hell I don't. As far as I'm concerned, David is welcome to you. The two of you deserve each other."

"All right," she said, too tired to fight him any longer. "The boys and I will be with my mother until I can find a place of our own."

"Shawn and Eric stay with me."

She caught her breath in surprise. "I'll fight you on this, Ethan," she warned, her fear giving her renewed strength.

"And you'll lose," he said with a sickening sweetness. "What court would turn two impressionable boys over to a mother who was an accessory to murder?"

34

Carly swung her feet over the side of the bed, glanced at the clock on the nightstand, and let out a groan of frustration. It was eight-fifteen and she'd promised herself she'd get up early to phone David before the rates changed. She'd thought about calling before she went to bed, but knew it would be impossible to keep what she was feeling out of her voice. David's job was to be in a positive mood for Andrea —hard enough, considering the circumstances. The last thing he needed was Carly making it harder.

She dug through her purse, took out the phone number at the hospital, and punched the buttons. After several minutes she was connected with the sister in charge of Andrea's care.

"How is she today?" Carly asked, her eyes closed, her body tense in preparation of the answer.

"Pretty much same as yesterday, Mrs. Hargrove. We've upped her lipids a bit to try to get some weight back on her and she seems to be tolerating the change just fine."

"Is someone with her now?"

"I believe Mr. Armstrong is still there. He's been quite good about staying most of the afternoon until

Mr. Montgomery comes in to take over again. Between the two of them, our girl is hardly ever alone. And then Mrs. Montgomery has been popping in several times a day, too. She doesn't stay long, but always brings a cheery bit of something with her."

"From the looks of it, I won't be getting back there as quickly as I'd hoped." The words felt as if they'd been torn from her.

"I'm sure that won't be the most welcome news, but Andrea's not one to begrudge her mum a couple more days' holiday after all you've been through."

"Would you tell her I called? And Mr. Montgomery?"

"I will. And I'll tell our girl you've sent her a big kiss and hug, too."

"Thank you," Carly said.

"Well, I'd best ring off now and see to my job."

Carly slowly replaced the receiver in its cradle. After another minute she stood and put on her robe. She felt weighted down, as if she'd put on thirty pounds during the four hours she'd been asleep.

While Carly had been home talking to Ethan, her mother and Wally had been giving Shawn and Eric the details of what had happened earlier that day, explaining how it tied into a night nineteen years ago, and trying to prepare them for what would likely be taking place with the people they loved in the near future.

At fifteen and sixteen, they were old enough to be repelled by the news that their mother and sister had the same father, but not yet mature enough to look beyond the effect it would have on their own lives. Carly was confident that in time they would realize they weren't the ones who'd been hurt the most and that they would be able to reach out to the people who needed them. But for now all they could see or feel was their own pain.

There was a light tapping on the door, followed by a soft, "Carly? Are you awake?"

"Come in, Mom."

Barbara appeared, carrying a cup of coffee. "I thought I heard you moving around in here." She handed the coffee to Carly. "How did you sleep?"

Carly put the cup on the nightstand and finished tying her robe. "I think I've figured out why you've kept this bed all these years—to make sure company doesn't stay too long."

"I'll have Wally go over to Sears on his lunch hour and buy a new one."

"I was kidding, Mom. The bed's fine."

"Who were you talking to on the phone?"

"Andrea's nurse. I meant to call earlier, but forgot to set the alarm. I'll pay you back—"

"Since you're going to be staying here for a while, I think we need to get some ground rules set down right now. I'll not hear another word of what you think you owe me or when you'll pay me back. Is that understood?"

Carly should have known better than to bring it up. There was little enough her mother could control at the moment, it was certain she would take charge where she could and do it with a vengeance. Somehow, someday Carly would find a way to pay her mother back. Until then, she wouldn't mention money again. "Did Wally go to work?" she asked, moving on to a safer subject.

"An hour ago. Now tell me how Andrea's doing."

"The same."

"Shouldn't she be getting better pretty soon?"

"It's only been four weeks."

"But I thought you said the doctor expected her to be in remission in six. Don't you think—" Barbara swallowed the last. "I'm sorry. With everything else you've got on your mind this morning you don't need me quizzing you." She reached over to adjust the collar on Carly's robe. "Now, what can I fix you for breakfast?"

Carly knew better than to tell her mother she wasn't hungry. "Oatmeal sounds good."

Barbara considered Carly's request. "It's amazing when you think about it. Wally asked for the same thing this morning. I'm surprised somebody hasn't written a book about the foods that make you feel better when you're down."

Carly took a sip of her coffee. "They're probably connected to happy childhood memories."

Barbara put her arm through Carly's. "It's nice to know you still have a few of those," she said, a catch in her voice.

"We promised we wouldn't do that to each other, Mom. No more looking back, no more regrets, and not one single, solitary 'if only.' "

"How did I raise such a smart daughter?"

Carly slipped her hand into her mother's. "I learned by example."

A half hour later, Carly was loading the dishwasher when the telephone rang. "I'll get it," Barbara said, wiping her hands on a towel.

Barbara's clipped, "Hello," was followed by a warmer, "We're doing just fine," letting Carly know it was Wally on the other end. Carly folded her antenna and went back to work, reaching for the cereal bowls and rinsing them under the faucet. Not until she heard her mother ask in a hushed tone, "Are you sure?" did she look up again.

A stricken expression crossed Barbara's face. "I'll tell her," she said. "That won't be necessary, I still have some money left that I can give her." Several seconds passed. "I told you that you don't need to do that, Wally. I have plenty." Again she paused. "All right," she said with a sigh of capitulation. "I'll meet you at the bank in an hour."

"What's going on?" Carly asked when her mother had hung up the phone.

"A friend of Wally's up in Boehm County called him this morning. He said it looks like Hallie's going to get her way on this thing. We have some time before the ball gets rolling too fast, but Wally thinks you should get out of here and back to Andrea as soon as we can make the arrangements." She hesitated. "He said not to let you tell anyone that you're leaving, not even Shawn and Eric, and that I should drive you over to Pittsburgh to catch the plane."

Wally would not have suggested anything so melodramatic without being convinced there was a real possibility that if she didn't leave now, she might not be able to leave at all. "My suitcase is at the house," she said, thinking out loud. "I'll go over there and pick it up while you're at the bank."

"What are you going to do if Ethan is there?"

"He said he wanted me out. As far as he's concerned, I'm just doing what I'm told."

The next day, Carly was in a phone booth at Heathrow listening to the telephone ring at David's house.

Victoria answered. "Carly," she said with surprising warmth, "David has been near frantic trying to reach you."

"Has something happened?" she demanded, at the same time fighting an urge to hang up before Victoria could answer.

"Sorry. I didn't mean to scare you. Andrea's the same. Hanging in there like the trooper she is. Actually, it's you David has been concerned about."

Carly almost choked on her relief. "I'm here—at Heathrow. I know I should have called before I left, but there wasn't time."

"Shall I send Harold round to pick you up?"

Carly was taken aback by Victoria's seeming change in attitude. It was as if in the short time she'd been gone, they'd become close friends. "That would take too long. I'll grab a cab."

"Will you be calling David at the hospital to tell him you've arrived, or would you like me to do that for you?"

The thought flashed through Carly's mind that Victoria was one of those women who excelled in times of crisis, but the explanation seemed too simplistic. "If you wouldn't mind—"

"Not at all. Glad to do it."

"Tell him I'll be there as soon as I can."

"He'll be pleased to hear it, I'm sure," she said.

After she'd hung up the phone, Carly stayed in the booth for several seconds trying to gather her strength. She'd been doing okay until faced with Victoria's obviously genuine show of concern. It was as if Carly had been using the hostility of those around her for fuel and without it she was lost.

A man waiting to use the phone smiled at her. "Don't you dare be nice to me," she murmured under her breath as she opened the door. "I'll break down and bawl all over your handsome blue jacket."

"Pardon, madam?" he said, stepping to one side to let her pass. "Is there something you wanted?"

"I was just talking to myself," she told him, and from somewhere, found a smile.

Carly was at the sink in the visitors' room scrubbing her hands for the prescribed three minutes to cut down on the chance of exposing Andrea to outside germs when she looked up and saw Jeffery coming toward her. "You look tired," she said by way of greeting, slipping back into the intense microcosm of Andrea's world as if she'd never been away.

He reached up and untied the hospital gown he

was wearing. "Some fresh air is all I need to set me to rights again. Thought I'd find a sweetshop and pick up some toffee. Might be good to have it around when Andrea starts thinking about food again."

"Has she said something about being hungry?"

He shook his head. "I don't expect she will until she's through with the stuff they've got her on now. I just want to be prepared."

Carly reached for a towel to dry her hands. Jeffery picked up her gown and helped her put it on. "Have you seen David today?" she asked.

"He left to get something to eat a while back. I should think he'd be back any time now."

"If you pass him on your way out, would you tell him I'm here?"

"He wasn't expecting you?"

"Not this soon."

"Then I'll be sure to keep an eye out for him. Hearing you're back will do him good."

They walked out into the hallway together and then said good-bye. As she started toward Andrea's room, she thought how different this floor was from the one where Shawn had been. There, the doors to the rooms had stood open except when the doctors were examining patients. Here, they were closed to keep out ambient germs. Shawn had been inundated with visitors, Andrea was restricted to immediate family, with Jeffery the lone exception.

Because of the bizarre transformation of Andrea's leukemia, Dr. Reardon told them he intended to continue her chemotherapy even in remission. He'd warned them that even though the drugs would be different and the dosage less, she could still be very sick.

Her only chance was a transplant.

Her best chance at a match had been her uncles.

The thought was eating a hole in Carly's stomach. How could she have been so sure and so wrong at the same time? Were there words she could have used to convince her grandmother? Was there something she could have done?

She had risked everything.

And it wasn't just that she'd come away empty-handed, she'd opened floodgates and released a torrent that could destroy the lives of the very people she'd been protecting with her silence.

35

The blinds were drawn in Andrea's room, blocking out the afternoon sun and changing the cream walls to a soft yellow. Carly quietly slipped inside and went to the bed to get a closer look at her daughter.

Andrea was wearing a brightly colored scarf wrapped around her head with the ends twisted and tied, making it look like a close-fitting hat. It could only mean that while Carly was gone, Andrea had lost most of what little hair she'd had left. The portable CD player David had given her for her birthday was sitting on her lap; the headphones covered her ears.

Carly leaned close to listen to Andrea's breathing, trying to decide whether she was asleep or just lost in the music. As if sensing her mother's presence, Andrea opened her eyes.

"Mom!" she said, and smiled. "When did you get here?" She tried to sit up, but the effort was too much for her.

Carly leaned over and pressed a kiss to Andrea's forehead, automatically checking for a temperature.

She seemed warmer than she should have been, but maybe it was the scarf. "I just walked in the door."

Andrea's smile turned into a sheepish grin. "Wait a minute." She pulled the headphones off. "Now I can hear you."

"I just walked in the door," Carly repeated.

"You missed Jeffery."

"No, I didn't. We passed each other in the hall."

"How did he look to you?"

Carly pulled a chair over to the bed and sat down. "Fine. Shouldn't he?"

"He looks so tired to me."

"To me, too," she acknowledged. "But then, that's to be expected, don't you think? He's worried about you and with all the time he's spent here in the hospital, he's probably not getting as much sleep as he's used to."

Andrea groaned. "I never thought I'd ever say this, but I'm tired of being the center of attention. I wish everyone would go back to doing what they were doing before I got sick."

Carly had to work to keep the lightness in her voice. Despite what David and the doctor had told her, Andrea didn't seem the same as when she'd left. Even the slightest movement took effort. When she blinked, it took her eyelids a fraction of a second longer to open and close. "I'll make you a deal. The minute you get well, we'll go right back to ignoring you. How does that sound?"

"Wonderful. Now why don't you tell me what everybody back home is doing."

"They're concerned about you, of course. And they all send their love. Grandma Barbara wanted to bake some cookies for me to bring, but I told her that you would appreciate them a lot more in a couple of weeks."

"David and Jeffery will shoot you if they find out."

Carly searched her mind for tidbits of information that would give her trip home an air of normality when all she could think about was Hallie. "Shawn and Patty broke up," Carly went on, "but are back together again."

"I'll bet Eric wasn't too happy about that."

"Actually, I think he's beginning to bend a little where Patty is concerned. He even went to a party at her house a couple of weeks ago."

The corner of Andrea's mouth drew up in a grin. She put her hand up to cover the grimace of pain the movement had caused. Plainly she was still having trouble with the lesions in her mouth. "Patty doesn't have anything to do with it, Mom," she said after the pain had eased, moving her mouth only as much as necessary to form the words. "Eric's been hot for Patty's little sister for months now."

"How do you know that?"

"Remember when he called to talk to you that time in Bath? You and David had gone out to dinner," she prompted.

Carly nodded.

"We were on the phone over an hour." She reached up to adjust her scarf where it had begun to slip down her forehead. "He kept talking about the dumbest things until finally I figured out what he was after—he wanted to know what a girl expected out of a guy on the first date."

A chill swept through Carly as she saw how much the effort at conversation was tiring Andrea. "Eric misses having you around. So does Shawn."

"I miss them, too." She was quiet for several seconds, as she slowly twisting the cord from the headphones around her finger. "I've been meaning to ask you something."

"Why don't you save it for later? You look like you could use some rest."

Andrea ignored her. "Do you remember the night

you told me it wasn't biology that made someone a father, it was the time they put in on the job?"

"I seem to recall saying something like that." She doubted she would ever forget that night even though after all that had happened since, she couldn't imagine herself saying those words about Ethan.

"How much time do you think it takes?"

"What are you really asking me, Andrea?"

"Is David my real father yet?"

A lump formed in Carly's throat. It was only a matter of time before Andrea learned the truth— days, weeks, maybe a month or two at the outside. "Yes," she said softly. "In every way that matters." She laid her hand on the bed and hooked her little finger with Andrea's. "In the only way that counts."

Andrea closed her eyes and was quiet so long Carly thought she'd gone to sleep.

"I've been listening to the disks Jeffery brought me the day before yesterday. They're wonderful, Mom. A guy named Yanni. Have you ever heard of him?"

"No, but that doesn't mean anything. I think the last record I bought was by the Moody Blues."

"I want you to have them. . . ."

Carly didn't like what she was hearing. "By the time you're through with them, I'll be so old—"

Andrea turned pleading eyes to Carly. "We can't do this anymore," she said, her voice no more than a whisper. "We have to stop pretending. Don't make me die without being able to say good-bye."

"You're not going to die," Carly insisted, an irrational fear that saying the words aloud would make them happen. "I won't listen to you talk that way."

"I'm so sick, Mom. And I'm so tired. I don't feel like fighting anymore."

"You can't give up, Andrea. Think of all things you have to live for." Jesus, she had to come up with something better than that. Eighteen was too young to comprehend loss of the future. How could Andrea be expected to understand what she would be missing—the maturing love between her and Jeffery, the indescribable joy that would come from holding her own child, from watching that child grow?

"I've been thinking about all the places I'm never going to see and the things I'll never do," she said, as if reading Carly's mind.

She searched her mind for the magic words that would resurrect Andrea's will to live. "Then I don't understand how you could be willing to let go." Dear God, she would never convince her like that.

"I'm not *letting* go. It's not my fault. It's just something that's happening to me."

"I'm sorry. I didn't mean that the way it sounded."

"I want to talk to you, Mom."

It was so little to ask; how could she say no? "Tell me about the music," she said, at last.

"It's not like anything I've ever heard before. There's one song that makes me cry because it reminds me of you. I think about how much I love you and how much I'm going to miss you."

"The greatest sorrow I can imagine is losing you," Carly said simply.

"Mostly the music makes me think about how lucky I've been. I've already been more places and seen more things than most people do in a lifetime." She turned her head to look at Carly, the movement slow and exhausting. "And the people I love and who love me—I've had the best, Mom. I can't be too mad that it isn't going to go on forever."

Sometimes when Carly was in the kitchen doing one of the mindless things that confined her there every day, she would think of the recipes she would one day share with Andrea, the traditions, and the little discoveries. They were the inconsequential threads that bound the fabric of mother and daughter together. "I'm afraid I'm not so unselfish," Carly said, tears burning her throat. "Or tolerant. My heart will scream to the heavens every day of my life if I lose you."

"I don't want you to be mad that I died," Andrea said. "I want you to be happy that I lived."

"They go hand in hand."

"Not if you live for me when I'm gone."

Carly was choking on her tears. But she would not cry. She could give Andrea so little. "I don't understand what you mean."

"I feel like I finally understand why you didn't go to David to tell him you were pregnant. My dreams will die because I do. But you let your dreams die so David could have his. I didn't know what it was to love someone that much until I met Jeffery. It makes me so sad to think of how empty you must feel inside."

"You filled that emptiness, Andrea."

"What will you do when I'm gone?"

"I don't know," Carly answered truthfully.

"That's why I want you to live for me. I want you to paint again. I want you to dream again. Let me give you back something for everything you've given me." A trickle of blood escaped the corner of Andrea's mouth.

Carly reached in the cabinet for a sterile gauze pad and handed it to Andrea. "Would you please rest now?"

Andrea nodded, too tired to argue.

"I'll stay until Jeffery comes back and then I'm going to take my suitcase to the flat and look for David."

"I love you, Mom."

From somewhere, Carly found a smile. "I love you, too," she said. Before she moved her chair away from the bed, she gently returned the headphones to Andrea's ears. "Sleep tight," she whispered.

"And don't let the bedbugs bite," Andrea murmured, completing the age-old childhood ritual.

36

The streetlight cast long shadows across the living room of Carly's flat. David moved past the window to the sideboard to pour himself a drink. After several seconds, he turned, glass in hand, and looked at Carly. "I used to put myself to sleep at night trying to figure out who had raped you and why you were so intent on protecting him. Not once did it occur to me that it might have been your father."

"Why should it have?" Carly said, sinking into the chair beside the window. She was exhausted to the point of numbness, her mind on the verge of shutting down out of self-protection.

"Because it was so goddamn obvious. It was all there. I was just too blind to see it." He finished his drink in one long swallow and put the glass back on the silver tray. "Your father's death, Barbara's cool reception of my condolences that day I saw her in the grocery store, that strange day at the mill when you questioned me about my feelings for Andrea." He folded his arms and hunched forward, as if in pain. "I should have known."

"It wouldn't have made any difference," Carly told him.

"You needed me and I wasn't there for you."

"Because I pushed you away."

"And I let you." He came across the room and knelt beside her, laying his arms along the outsides of her legs, his head in her lap. "I'm sorry."

"I can't help thinking about all those years I thought I was buying protection for Andrea and Wally and my mother with my silence. And now, in one afternoon, everything I've done became pointless."

"Meaning you think you shouldn't have gone to your grandmother's?"

"It was such a terrible risk. And look at the consequences. I've irrevocably damaged—if not actually destroyed—the lives of the people who trusted me." Her hands closed around the strands of hair between her fingers. "Not to mention what will this do to Andrea when she finds out."

David lifted his head to look at her. "She's stronger than you think," he said.

"She'll never feel the same about herself. How could she?"

"In time she'll understand that she's the same person she's always been. Not even something this ugly could change who she is inside."

"How do you think Jeffery will react?"

David thought a minute. "The way I would have if I had known. He loves her. Nothing is going to change that. His entire life is planned around her."

A pain sliced through Carly's chest. "Did you know she believes she's going to die?"

David sat back on his haunches. "When did she tell you that?"

"This afternoon."

"Did something happen I don't know about? Have you talked to Reardon about this?"

"She's worn out, David. Her will to fight is gone."

Some of the panic left his eyes. "That's to be expected," he reasoned. "She'll feel different once they pull her off this course of treatment and she starts to get her strength back."

"God, I hope you're right. She really scared me this afternoon. So much so, I tried to call my mom to tell her to pack everyone up and get over here on the next flight out. Thank God I'd had time to settle down before I finally reached her."

"What did you say to Andrea?"

"I tried arguing, but she begged me not to, so I just let her talk."

"You should have—"

"Don't, David," she said gently, putting her hand on his arm. "I can't bear to hear any more about the things I should and shouldn't have done in my life. Andrea was desperate for someone to listen to her. I couldn't refuse."

David turned away. The streetlight fell across his face. She saw tears trailing down his cheek. "I don't know what I'd do if I lost her," he said.

"Loving Jeffery has helped Andrea understand why I let you go instead of telling you I was pregnant." Carly put her hand to her throat, trying to ease the tightness caused from holding back tears. "She's ready to die, David. And there's nothing I can do to make her live."

He got up and moved away. "I don't want to hear that," he said roughly.

She went to him. "Don't close her off. She needs to talk to all of us about what's happening."

"How can you be so goddamned calm about this?" he yelled, his face distorted with pain.

His question brought her up short. "Because I don't believe it," she admitted. "My mind knows Andrea could die, but my heart refuses to accept that possibility."

The phone rang. David answered. "What is it?" he snapped. "Jeffery—I'm sorry about yelling at you. Carly and I were—" He paused to listen. "How high?" And then, "We'll be right there."

"What is it?" Carly asked.

"Andrea's fever spiked," he said.

For the length of a heartbeat, Carly thought about running away and finding a hole she could crawl into where nothing, where no one could find her to tell her things she didn't want to hear.

But then her heart beat again and she gathered her purse and coat and was on her way to the hospital.

37

It was raining the day they buried Andrea.

David looked skyward and thought it was as if even the heavens mourned her loss.

The service had been held in London to facilitate the number of people who'd called and asked to pay last respects. The interment was near Hawthorne on a hillside beside an abandoned church. Andrea had chosen the ancient cemetery herself because of the tombstone of a young girl she and Jeffery had found one day when they were out riding. Now the two shared more than birth dates; they had both died at eighteen, three hundred years apart.

The minister had left more than a half hour earlier. The gravedigger stood discreetly down the hill waiting and still. David, Carly, Victoria, and Jeffery remained, the umbrellas they had brought with them by their sides unopened. Silent tears had not stopped flowing from Victoria since early that morning. David felt a special sorrow for her because she had been so slow to recognize how deeply she would feel Andrea's loss.

Jeffery was inconsolable at the finality of Andrea's leaving, an alien thing for someone so young to try to understand. He couldn't imagine the next day without her, let alone a lifetime. His life, who he was, had been irrevocably changed. The loss, the sorrow, would set him apart from his friends. There would be no more carefree youth for him.

Carly had pulled into herself, speaking only to answer a question, facing the funeral and now the graveside service without tears or any outward show of emotion. She had been with Andrea when she took her last breath. Later, she'd insisted on calling home herself, not wanting Shawn and Eric or her mother and Wally to hear the news from anyone else. Even then she hadn't cried.

The rain changed, growing from a heavy mist to drops. Victoria turned to David. "I'm going to take Jeffery home now. I think you and Carly should come soon, too."

He nodded. "In a while."

She went to Jeffery and took his hand. "There're some friends of yours from school waiting for you at the house," she told him. "It's time we saw to them, don't you think?"

He looked at her with vacant eyes. "Yes, of course. You go along to the car. I'll be there in a minute."

Victoria started down the hill, touching Carly's arm gently as she passed.

Jeffery moved over to where David and Carly were standing. "I've decided to leave off my studies for a year," he told them. "Go to Greece for a bit and then maybe South America." He turned his attention to Carly. "Then, I thought I might come by for a visit. I'd think I'd like to see some of where Andrea grew up."

"She would like that," Carly said, putting her arms around him. "I would, too."

He let her go and said, "Till then."

"Until then, Jeffery," she said softly to his retreating back.

"I've been meaning to ask you something," David said when Jeffery was gone. "Before Andrea died, she called me Dad. Did you . . ."

Carly met his gaze. "No," she said. "I didn't tell her to do it. You were a wonderful father to her, David. She never doubted you. You never let her down."

"I want to go with you when you go back home."

"No—I can't take the chance."

"Damn it, we belong together. When are you going to get that through your head?"

"I have to get Shawn and Eric back, David. And I have to do whatever I can to help Wally and my mother. I can't do either if you're with me."

"And afterwards?"

She looked away, hiding her face from him. "I don't know."

He thought about telling her that Victoria had come to him the night before and told him she was going to give him a divorce so that he and Carly could be together. But it wasn't the time or place. "If you need me—"

"I'll call." She walked over to the grave and picked up a lilac the wind had blown from the casket. "Promise me you'll always bring her lilacs in the spring," she said.

It was such a small request, but it told him everything.

She would never call.

Carly slipped her key into the lock and opened the front door. She stood in the foyer for several seconds, listening to the quiet, seeking a sense of homecoming. Nothing happened. The emptiness inside her would not be satisfied so easily.

She hadn't called her mother to tell her which flight she would be on, wanting her arrival to be as quiet as possible. There was so much to do. First, and most pressing, was arranging the memorial service. Shawn and Eric hadn't even seen Andrea sick; they would need a way to say good-bye if they were ever going to accept what had happened.

Too bad that wouldn't work for her. She had said good-bye, over and over again—at the hospital, at the funeral, at the graveside. The words did nothing to ease the ache or the longing. Nor did it stop her from thinking of just one more thing she wanted to tell Andrea.

The trick would be to keep busy. She would fill each day to overflowing. There would be no time for thinking or remembering or hurting.

Carly shrugged the strap of her purse off her shoulder and set it on the hall table. She had one last promise to fulfill, one last thing to do for her daughter.

"Muffin," she said, listening for the telltale thump as he hit the floor jumping off Andrea's bed. Her call was met with silence. She went into the kitchen, glancing at his food and water dishes. They were untouched. And then she saw him in the corner, curled up on Andrea's sweatshirt.

"Muffin?" she called again, going to him. When he didn't respond, she knelt down and put her hand on his chest. There was no heartbeat. "Oh, Muffin," she said, catching her breath. "How could you take the coward's way out? Andrea will never forgive you."

Carly sat on the floor and gathered Muffin in her arms, carefully wrapping Andrea's sweatshirt around him. She held him close, the way she had longed to hold Andrea but couldn't because of all the tubes running into her body, sustaining the fragile hope for a miracle.

Finally, the tears came.

38

Three Years Later

Carly stood back from the painting she'd just hung on the wall of the artists' co-op, stared at it for several seconds, and then rehung it a few inches higher. The artist, a young man who'd transferred to the University of Colorado from San Jose State University in California, was a new member and anxious to see his work on display. It hadn't been that long since she'd been in the same position. Now her work was being shown in one of the premier galleries in Denver and although sales seemed to happen in clusters, they were enough to keep her from having to use the money Ethan sent every month.

It felt good to be supporting herself, even if it meant she ate more salad than steak. Salad was better for her, anyway.

Finally satisfied with the painting, she went over to the desk to sort through the mail. Buried deep in the stack was a letter from her mother. After discovering Carly only went to her own post office box once a week, Barbara had started sending everything to the gallery. Carly put the rest of the mail aside and opened the bright yellow envelope.

May 15,
Dear Carly,

I wanted to get this off before Wally and I leave for Florida. Can you believe it? I finally got him to agree to go after ten years of trying. Of course I'm not sure I could have pulled it off without promising we would make it a triangle flight and stop by to visit you and the boys on our way home.

Anyway, the big rush was to tell you I saw your uncle Steve yesterday. He said Hallie was in the hospital. She had a stroke last week and from the looks of it, won't be coming home for a long time, if ever. He said her speech was affected and likely wouldn't come back. I keep telling myself it's my Christian duty to feel sorry for her, but the devil gets his due on this one. The only sympathy I can summon is for the nurses who will have to take care of her.

Carly turned to the next page, a warm feeling coming over her at the mention of her uncle Steve. The quiet, unassuming man she'd spent most of her life believing an enemy had turned out to be a surprising ally. Not only had he gone in for the HLA testing the day he found out about his brother being Andrea's father, he'd been the star witness for Barbara at her trial, testifying that Frank's brutality had reached back to his childhood.

It was readily acknowledged by both the prosecutor and defense attorneys that the verdict would have been different had the trial taken place twenty years earlier. But the mood of the nation had filtered down to Baxter in the ensuing years and the scales of justice had tipped in Barbara's favor. Wally had quietly tried to resign his position as sheriff, thinking to save the town and his family the embarrassment of being fired. When the word got out, the townspeople signed petitions demanding that he be reinstated, and brought them to city hall. His retirement party that past summer had coincided with the town's annual Fourth of July celebration and had been a party no one was likely to forget.

Ethan came by to give us some things to bring to the boys. I can't get over how much he's changed. From the looks of it, he's stopped drinking and is finally managing to get his life together again. Gossip has it he's seeing a woman over in Linndale. Wouldn't it be nice if something came of it? I'd like an excuse to stop worrying about him.

Gotta run, sweetheart—still haven't gone shopping for my bikini. Ha ha. Couldn't you just see that? Say hello to the boys and tell them that Wally hasn't stopped talking about the fishing the three of them are going to do when we get to Colorado.
I love you,
Mom

Carly still couldn't think about Ethan without the good years they'd had together being overshadowed by the bad. The custody battle had never taken place. Shawn and Eric were old enough to decide where they wanted to live, and to Ethan's amazement, they chose to stay with her.

The next year Shawn had gone away to college— the University of Colorado in Boulder—to be with Patty. Carly and Eric had visited him there several months later and had fallen in love with the stark majesty of the Rocky Mountains. That summer, when Eric graduated from high school, they'd rented a

U-Haul trailer, packed everything they owned in it, and headed west.

Carly folded the letter and put it in her purse to share with Shawn and Eric when she saw them later that night. She was stepping around the counter when a flash of red caught her eye. It was Shawn driving his grandmother's Mustang into the parking lot. He stopped in front of the co-op, noticed her watching him, waved, and hopped out of the convertible without opening the door.

"What are you doing here?" she asked as he came inside, inordinately pleased to see him. "I thought you had a class this afternoon."

"It was canceled."

"And Patty was busy."

He grinned. "Yep."

"So having nothing else to occupy your time, you thought you'd come see me?"

"I have more to do than I want to think about. Actually, I'm here on a mission," he said mysteriously.

"Something that couldn't wait until tonight?"

He blinked.

"Don't tell me you forgot you were coming to dinner?"

"Oh, my God, was that tonight?"

"I made enough lasagna to feed an army."

He put his arm around her. "Then you wouldn't mind feeding an army, would you?"

She laughed. "How many should I expect?"

"Martha's sister and her boyfriend are here for the weekend."

"Martha, the friend of Patty's who has the sister who works for the governor?"

"Uh-huh."

"Oh, good, I've wanted to meet her for a long time now."

Shawn groaned. "I told you, she doesn't have anything to do with funding for the arts, Mom." He walked over to the counter and began picking through a bowl of wrapped candy. "You're turning into a real nut case about this project." He put a piece of candy in his mouth and cocked his head to one side, listening. "Don't you ever get tired of that music?"

"Never. It reminds me of—"

"Andrea," he finished for her.

"Of course Andrea," she said softly. "But what I was going to say is that it reminds me life should be celebrated—every day. I'll never waste another moment or tolerate another regret."

"Boy, did you just give me the perfect segue." He reached in his pocket and took out a folded piece of paper. "I picked this up at the student bookstore today."

She took the paper from his outstretched hand, curious and suspicious at the same time. She caught her breath when she saw the photograph. It was David.

"He's going to be in Denver tonight, autographing his new book," Shawn supplied.

After several seconds Carly carefully folded the flyer and handed it back to him. "I understand it's doing really well."

"Have you read it?"

Carly shook her head.

"There were some copies at the bookstore. I picked one up and looked at it."

"And?" she asked, curious despite herself.

"It's about a girl who has leukemia and then goes on to become a famous actress."

A lump formed in Carly's throat.

"The title is *The Way It Should Have Been*."

Carly had read an article about David in *People* magazine over a year ago that said he was finally working again after losing his daughter. It also mentioned his divorce, something Carly undoubtedly would have known earlier if she hadn't sent his letters back unopened and refused to return his phone calls. For more than a year after she'd come home, she was unable to think about seeing David again without having the memory of Andrea's death almost overwhelm her.

When she thought about that first year without Andrea, it was always in the context of traveling through a long dark tunnel. Everyone she loved had needed a piece of her to help them get over their own grief. Shawn and Eric most of all.

There had been nothing left to give David.

And then, just as she was beginning to recover, Jeffery had arrived for his promised visit and had stolen the keystone to the new life she'd started to put together. For months afterward it was a struggle to get through each day.

Again, there had been nothing left for David.

"David couldn't have loved your sister more if she had been his own child," she told Shawn.

"Did Andrea ever find out about what your dad did to you?"

"No," Carly said softly.

"I'm glad. I never had the guts to ask you before, but I always wondered."

"Why did you bring me the flyer, Shawn?"

"At first I wasn't going to because I know when you think about him it brings everything back, but then I was flipping through the book and saw the dedication. He still loves you, Mom. I think you outta check it out." He grinned. "You're not getting any younger, you know. Single guys your age are pretty hard to find."

The chime over the door sounded. They both turned to see Eric come striding in waving a piece of paper. "Hey, Mom, you'll never guess who's going to be in Denver tonight."

Shawn turned back to his mother. "Looks like that

makes it two out of two who think you should go," he said.

"Two out of three," she corrected him.

"What the hell, it's still a majority."

Carly eased her way around the people waiting in line to have their books signed by David. She'd never been to an autographing before and was bemused by the number of fans.

The closer she got to the table, the more convinced she was that she'd made a mistake in coming. For the first time in three years she was at peace with herself. Seeing David would only bring the pain back again.

The two women standing next to Carly moved closer together, guarding their position in line. The taller one dipped her head and said to her friend, "Did you read the dedication? Does anyone know who this Carly woman is?"

Curiosity tugged at Carly. She spotted a large display of *The Way It Should Have Been*, went over and picked up a copy, not realizing until the book was actually in her hand how afraid of it she was. She didn't want to know what wondrous things Andrea had missed, even if only in David's imagination.

A band tightened around her chest as she turned the pages. And then there it was.

Carly—the lilacs are in bloom. Whisper my name and I will find you.

She stared at the words until tears stole them away.

"Carly?"

She turned and saw David get up from his chair and start toward her.

Her doubts vanished. After a lifetime of wandering, she was home again.

AVAILABLE NOW

SILVER SHADOWS by Marianne Willman

In this dramatic western of love and betrayal, Marianne Willman, author of *Yesterday's Shadows*, continues the saga of the Howards. Intent on revenge for wrongs done to his family, half-Cheyenne Grayson Howard unexpectedly finds love with a beautiful widow.

THE WAY IT SHOULD HAVE BEEN by Georgia Bockoven

From the author of *A Marriage of Convenience* comes a story of drama, courage, and tenderness. Carly is reasonably happy with a stable marriage and three wonderful children. Then David comes back to town. Now a famous author, David had left twenty years before when Carly married his best friend. He'd never stopped loving Carly, nor forgiven her for leaving him. Yet, Carly did what she had to do. It was the only way to keep the secret she must hide—at all costs.

THE HEART'S LEGACY by Barbara Keller

When Céline Morand married the man she'd dreamed of for years, she thought the demands of love and duty were the same. But an unexpected trip to the lush plantation of her husband's cousin in Louisiana ends Céline's naiveté and opens her heart to a man she can't have.

LADY OF LOCHABAR by Jeanette Ramirez

In this beautiful, heartbreaking love story, Maggie Macdonald is but seven years old when Simon Campbell saves her life after his father's army has massacred her entire family. As fate would have it, they meet ten years later and enter into a forbidden love.

OUT OF THE PAST by Shirl Jensen

When Debbie Dillion moves to Texas to pick up the pieces of her life, she finds her dream house waiting for her. But soon Debbie wonders if she has walked into a living nightmare, where someone is willing to do anything to hide the past—even commit murder.

WHEN DESTINY CALLS by Suzanne Elizabeth

A delightful time-travel romance about a modern-day police officer, Kristen Ford, who would go to any distance—even to the rugged mountains of Nevada in the 1890s—to find her soul mate.

Harper Monogram   **The Mark of Distinctive Women's Fiction**

COMING NEXT MONTH

TAPESTRY by Maura Seger
A spellbinding tale of love and intrigue in the Middle Ages. Renard is her enemy, but beautiful Aveline knows that beneath the exterior of this foe beats the heart of a caring man. As panic and fear engulf London, the passion between Renard and Aveline explodes. "Sweeping in concept, fascinating in scope, triumphant in its final achievement."—Kathryn Lynn Davis, author of *Too Deep For Tears*.

UNFORGETTABLE by Leigh Riker
Recently divorced, Jessica Pearce Simon returns to her childhood home. Nick Granby, the love of her youth, has come home too. Now a successful architect and still single, Nick is just as intriguing as she remembers him to be. But can she trust him this time?

THE HIGHWAYMAN by Doreen Owens Malek
Love and adventure in 17th century England. When Lady Alexandra Cummings stows away on a ship bound for Ireland, she doesn't consider the consequences of her actions. Once in Ireland, Alexandra is kidnapped by Kevin Burke, the Irish rebel her uncle considers his archenemy.

WILD ROSE by Sharon Ihle
A lively historical romance set in San Diego's rancho period. Maxine McCain thinks she's been through it all—until her father loses her in a bet. As a result, she becomes indentured to Dane del Cordobes, a handsome aristocrat betrothed to his brother's widow.

SOMETHING'S COOKING by Joanne Pence
When a bomb is delivered to her door, Angelina Amalfi can't imagine why anyone would want to hurt her, an innocent food columnist. But to tall, dark, and handsome police inspector Paavo Smith, Angelina is not so innocent.

BILLY BOB WALKER GOT MARRIED by Lisa G. Brown
A spicy contemporary romance. Shiloh Pennington knows that Billy Bob Walker is no good. But how can she ignore the fire that courses in her veins at the thought of Billy's kisses?

*M*Harper Monogram   **The Mark of Distinctive Women's Fiction**